I0771281

ECONOMY OF FORCE

PHIL WARD

Published by Military Publishers, LLC
Distributed by Military Publishers, LLC
Austin, Texas

www.philwardauthor.com

ISBN: 978-0-9895922-6-0

Cover design by Stewart A. Williams
Map illustrations by Tom Houlihan

For ordering information or special discounts for bulk purchases, contact

MILITARY PUBLISHERS LLC
3616 FAR WEST BLVD., SUITE 117, BOX 215 AUSTIN, TX 78731

DEDICATION

Senior Master Sergeant Grady W. Williams, USAF
1915-1980

Economy of Force is dedicated to Grady Woodrow Williams in recognition of his lifelong commitment to our military and our country. Born in 1915 in Milam County, Texas, he was the youngest of 16 children. As a young man growing up on his family farm, little did he know he was part of a generation of sixteen million who would serve our country in World War II... The Greatest Generation.

Farming was not for Grady. He wanted more. At the age of 18 he left his small, familiar world and joined the U.S. Army Air Force. He took off on his life adventure. Among other places, his service took him to Hawaii where he witnessed and lived through the Japanese attack on Pearl Harbor. Then to Australia as part of General Douglas McArthur's Pacific Army and eventually he participated in the invasion of New Guinea where he fought in the jungles to defeat the Japanese.

In 1947 he transitioned to the Air Force when it was formed as a separate branch of the military. He retired in 1964 after 30 years of active duty. Like many in his generation, Grady was characterized by his patriotism, commitment to work and family, desire to help others, and motivation to work hard to succeed. This is the legacy he left to his children.

The Greatest Generation, indeed.

Randal's Rules for Raiding

RULE 1:   The first rule is there ain't no rules.

RULE 2:   Keep it short and simple.

RULE 3:   It never hurts to cheat.

RULE 4:   Right man, right job.

RULE 5:   Plan missions backward (know how
to get home).

RULE 6:   It's good to have a Plan B.

RULE 7:   Expect the unexpected.

RANKS, DECORATIONS AND NICKNAMES

RANK PROTOCOL:
The first time a person is named in a chapter or after a chapter break their full rank and name is given. Addressing military personnel by their rank is a mark of respect. At all levels rank is earned and those who have it from a corporal to a four star general are proud of it.

DECORATIONS:
In the British military officers are authorized to put the initials of their decorations after their name. In the Raiding Forces Series the protocol is the first time an officer is introduced in a book the initials of his decorations are listed following his name. After that for the rest of the book they are not.

In the U.S. military officers do not have the same privilege.

NICKNAMES:
In the British military nicknames are endemic. Radio operators are called Sparks, red heads are called Ginger, tall people are called Lofty but sometimes short people are called that too etc.

In the U.S. military there are a lot of nicknames but nothing like the British.

ECONOMY OF FORCE
LIST OF OPERATIONS

OPERATION CREEK

A raid on the *Ehrenfels* in the harbor of Mormugao, Goa, in India, to prevent it from providing information about British shipping to German U-Boats.

OPERATION FIRE EATER

The actual raiding of the islands in the eastern Aegean.

PROJECT HABAKKUK

A plan to build aircraft carriers out of an ice-based substance called pykrete, a mixture of frozen seawater and sawdust.

OPERATION LONG NECK

Secret operation to intercept diamonds being smuggled from the Congo to the Nazis and to eliminate the diamond smugglers.

Command and Control team—code name **CARD GAME**

Col. Randal, Major the Lady Jane Seaborn, Lt. Gen. "Geronimo" Joe McKoy, Captain Billy Jack Jaxx, Waldo Treywick, Captain Pamala Plum-Martin, Mandy Paige, Beverly Blackwell, King, Captain Roy Kidd, Captain Preston Butterfield, MSgt. Mack Beckwith.

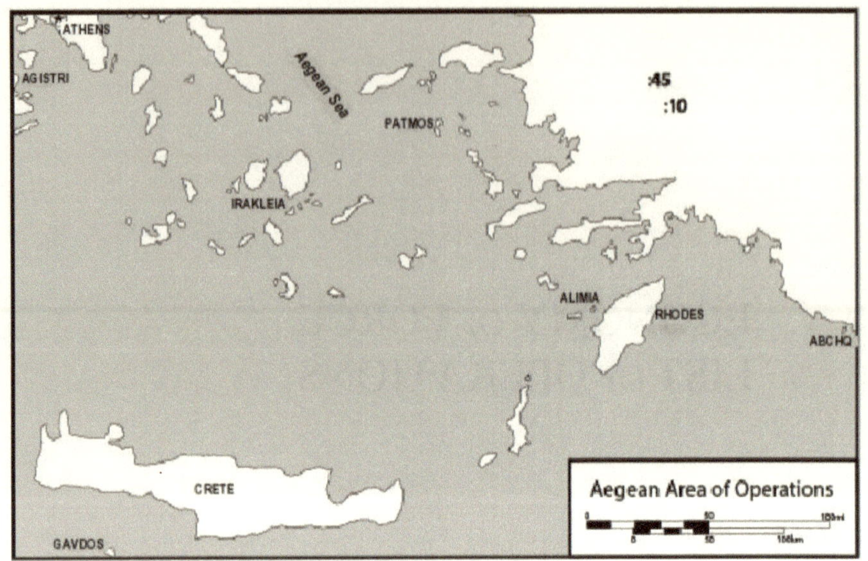

ATHENS
AGISTRI
Aegean Sea
PATMOS
IRAKLEIA
ALIMIA
RHODES
ABC HQ
:45
:10
CRETE
GAVDOS
Aegean Area of Operations
0
50
100mi
0
50
100km

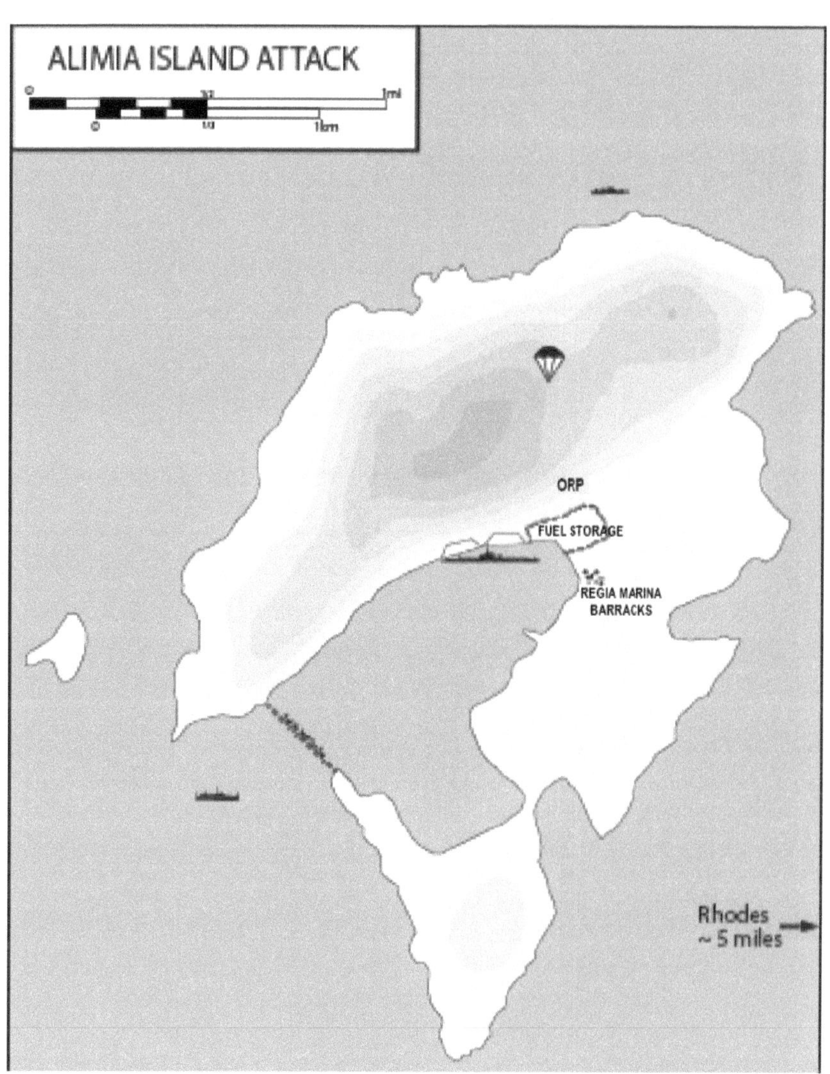

ALIMIA ISLAND ATTACK
1mi
1km
ORP
FUEL STORAGE
REGIA MARINA
BARRACKS
Rhodes
~ 5 miles

1

DUDS

COLONEL JOHN RANDAL WAS PAYING A CALL ON Lieutenant Randy "Hornblower" Seaborn's U.S. Electric Launch Corporation, Elco Naval Division-manufactured Patrol Torpedo boat (PT). It was on picket duty stationed at the narrow dog-legged entrance to the deep-water harbor located at Patmos while the evacuation of the Special Boat Squadron and Long Range Desert Group from Leros was under way. The PT boat, the smallest class warship in the Royal Navy to sail as a fighting unit, did not have a number because it had never been accepted into service, but Elco had unofficially dubbed it PT 10.

Originally built as a concept PT boat, the craft did not perform well during its U.S. Navy sea trials and was transferred to the Royal Navy under Lend Lease. After additional British evaluation, PT 10 was not considered capable of operating in either the North Sea or English Channel because it was not deemed able to handle weather over Force 5.

The boat was shipped as deck cargo to Malta. From there and with a skeleton crew, it made passage to Alexandria under its own power. Despite PT 10's shortcomings, Vice Admiral Sir Randolph "Razor" Ransom, VC, KCB, DSO, OBE, DSC, RN, Director of Operations Division (Irregular) and Commander of Small Raids Inc., was glad to have it. The Aegean Theatre had the lowest priority of any in the Allied nations' worldwide sphere, so he made do with what he could get.

The Razor had immediately set about modifying the PT's armament.

U.S. Navy Purchasing Department specifications called for four torpedo launchers firing 21-inch Mark VIII torpedoes—two forward, two aft. Each torpedo had a 466-pound TNT warhead on its tip. On paper the Mark VIIIs had a wildly optimistic range of 16,000 yards—1,000 yards maximum *effective* range or less was more like it.

Torpedoes fired from a speeding PT boat with its rudimentary Model 31 sighting system were notoriously inaccurate. Successful PT skippers got in close. They needed nerves of steel.

VAdm. Ransom removed the two stern tubes to reduce weight in an attempt to wring out a few more knots of sea speed. It was said he was considering replacing them with a fast-firing Bofors 40mm automatic cannon aft.

Brigadier General William "Wild Bill" Donovan, Director of the Office of Strategic Services, had provided Elco Mark XV Thunderbolt gun mounts for the two Italian MAS boats in service with Raiding Forces as part of VAdm. Ransom's ragtag Special Operations Navy. The mount was a beast. Recently its firepower had been upgraded based on the U.S. Navy's experience shooting up Japanese barges in the South Pacific. Now it sported four 20mm Oerlikon fast-firing cannon and six .50 M2 Browning Heavy Machine Guns operated by a single gunnery rating.

Acting on VAdm. Ransom's orders, the dockyard at Alexandria fabricated a field expedient Thunderbolt mount for PT 10. The addition of a 40mm on the stern in tandem with the Thunderbolt gun package forward might negate in part the increase in speed gained by eliminating the two torpedo tubes, but it would turn the little warship into a deadly dual-purpose torpedo/gunboat.

Lieutenant Randy "Hornblower" Seaborn, DSO, OBE, DSC, RN, was hoping his grandfather would authorize the cannon, but there had been no decision yet.

The bow watch sang out, "Enemy destroyer green one-eight-five—range 100 yards!"

Worst-case scenario coming at them at point-blank range.

Ghosting into sight out of the night was an Italian 1,500-ton *Sella*-class destroyer, slowly cruising close inshore off the entrance to Patmos' deep water harbor. The enemy vessel was one of the ships commandeered by the Kriegsmarine from the Regia Marina when Italy signed the armistice with the Allies.

Seeing the German warship was like staring at death.

Talking to himself, Hornblower recited, "Four 4.7-inch guns, four 20mm automatic cannons *and* a pair of .51 caliber machine guns . . ."

Massive firepower against a wooden PT boat.

Col. Randal knew the only weapon PT 10 had onboard that could do more than scratch the paint on a destroyer were the two Mark VIII torpedoes. And they had a spotty track record. Lt. Seaborn had provided him with a detailed rundown of the weapon's lengthy list of deficiencies.

The Mark VIII was developed and manufactured during the last war. It was an obsolete design prior to the Japanese bombing of Pearl Harbor. The U.S. Navy had replaced all of them in their inventory after sending six hundred of the torpedoes to Great Britain under Lend Lease to get rid of them.

The gyro that steered the torpedo to the target was delicate. It needed to be launched from an even keel to avoid being jarred as it left the tube. That is difficult to accomplish when pounding across the waves in a "mosquito boat" making a high-speed attack run under fire.

To launch the fish, a black powder charge in the chamber of the launcher has to be detonated to propel it out of the tube. Water or humidity—there is a lot of both at sea—can cause a misfire resulting in what is known in PT boat circles as "hot running," meaning the torpedo failed to exit the tube while the motor that propels it is still running.

The warhead was not at risk of detonating, or so the manual stated. However, eventually the torpedo tube would overheat. When it eventually got hot enough, the runaway motor would cause the tube to explode like a twenty-one-foot-long hand grenade. While not as catastrophic as the torpedo itself blowing up, the motor exploding the tube on the deck of a small boat is definitely not a good thing.

Because of the sensitivity of the gyros and threat of hot running, the tubes were heavily lubricated before and during patrols. From time to time when the black powder charge detonated it would cause the lubricants to ignite. Attempting to sneak up on an enemy warship in the dark of night with a fire blazing on deck is not recommended procedure.

Nor does it do much for sailor morale.

According to the US Navy the 466-pound TNT warhead on the torpedo was not a large enough explosive charge to guarantee a kill on ships of destroyer or larger class. The last thing any PT sailor wanted was a wounded enemy warship able to bring its complement of guns to bear on their little mahogany speedboat.

However, those were the minor problems.

What kept PT skippers and crew up at night was knowing a high percentage of Mark VIII torpedoes that ran true and struck the target precisely where aimed . . . were duds.

As in a *very* high percentage.

Col. Randal was studying the German destroyer through his Zeiss binoculars. It was dark; still, at this range he could see the Kriegsmarine sailors at their battle stations as clearly as if they were an arm's length away—which was almost the case. PT 10 was moored against the sheer side of the cliff at the mouth of the harbor. Although the boat was not under camouflage, there was still very little chance the Germans would spot it.

Under normal circumstances—"discretion being the better part of valor" and "living to fight again another day" being important concepts that came into play, Lt. Seaborn might have let the enemy ship sail on past. The problem was if the enemy destroyer got by and entered the narrow dog-legged passage to pay a call on what the Kriegsmarine's charts indicated to be a German-occupied island, it would sink the *King Duck* and destroy the *Black Cat*. Then the Nazis would be able to summon up seagoing infantry reinforcements to land ashore to attack the stranded Raiding Forces, Special Boat Section (SBS) and Long Range Desert Group (LRDG) personnel waiting to be evacuated to Advanced Base Castelrozzo (ABC).

Lt. Seaborn ordered, "Ready torpedoes."

Col. Randal thought even for a naval officer with the well-deserved nickname "Hornblower," he sounded remarkably cool considering the circumstances, which in Raiding Forces parlance would be described as, "not good."

"Stand by to fire."

PT boats launch their torpedoes in the direction the boat is traveling. The line the enemy is sailing on is called the "target ship track." Since PT 10 was stationary, Lt. Seaborn was going to fire straight ahead when the destroyer came to bear—usually the exact opposite of the way a torpedo run works. All that was necessary tonight was to make a rudimentary judgment of the target's speed, distance not being much of a factor, to determine the "initial point"—naval jargon for the position of the enemy ship when torpedoes are launched. In non-naval terms, this was known as "Kentucky Windage."

Hornblower had to fire when the destroyer, moving left to right, came to bear—or he thought it did.

In addition, he had to do the math. Distance/torpedo speed to target equals time of travel. That provides a rough idea of when the fish will strike the enemy ship. The calculations seemed like a lot of arithmetic for a PT skipper working through the stress incidental to a full-on naval engagement while massively outgunned at point-blank range. It was probably a good thing Col. Randal did not know this would be the first time Lt. Seaborn ever had launched a torpedo at an enemy warship.

"Fire One."

The black powder charge inside the tube made a muffled *WHOOMPH*. The torpedo leapt out, making a small splash when it struck the water. The fish could be seen running straight with no porpoising.

"Fire Two."

Another *WHOOMPH* and the second torpedo was away.

Lt. Seaborn was mentally ticking off the seconds to determine time to target.

"Any moment now."

CLAAANG!

The perfect shot. PT 10's torpedo slammed into the bow of the destroyer, and it was a dud.

It was arguably the worst sound Col. Randal had ever heard.

Lt. Seaborn ordered, "Commence fire!"

The Thunderbolt gunnery rating, the sailors manning the six additional .50 Browning M2 HMGs and every man not standing a watch position below deck opened on the destroyer with Browning Automatic

Rifles (BARs) and Thompson submachine guns (SMGs) in a desperate effort to sweep the ship's deck with automatic weapons fire. The intent was to prevent the enemy gunners from standing to their weapons. A solid wall of fire vectored in on the Nazi destroyer. Tracers glanced off the armored gun shields and ricocheted up in the air.

The result was an impressive light show. Unfortunately, the barrage was causing little actual damage to the destroyer. It was putting a lot of enemy sailors out of action, however.

KABOOOOOM!

The second torpedo struck home resulting in a "Pyro" Percy caliber end-of-the-world-type flash explosion. One second: nothing. The next: a brilliant light like the world's biggest flashbulb had popped and covered the entire horizon. A geyser of water shot up at least 100 feet in the air, followed by a strange onion-shaped white cloud that engulfed the destroyer, making it disappear temporarily.

Then the mist blasted apart in a shattering explosion. The warhead must have penetrated to the ship's fuel tanks or ammunition locker—possibly both. The cloud metamorphosed into a gigantic fireball. A tidal wave of sound from the detonation struck PT 10 so hard it rocked the boat—or it seemed like it did. That was followed by a wall of heat so intense that Col. Randal wondered if his eyebrows were singed.

Not only was he deafened, but his night vision was destroyed.

Four hundred sixty-six pounds of TNT had done the job despite U.S. Naval Board reservations it might not be enough.

Col. Randal stared at the monstrous fireball where an enemy destroyer had been seconds before. There was no longer a ship to be seen. The *Sella*-class destroyer had literally come apart at the seams.

It had vanished—Hey, Presto!

Col. Randal said, "Probably not such a good idea to park this close to the next enemy destroyer you blow up, Randy."

Lt. Seaborn said, "Italian naval designers have a reputation for being dreadfully incompetent. Our ships have "all-or-nothing armor" which protects the vital areas and seals them off to prevent a cataclysmic explosion like this. Would you say tonight is as bad as when Captain Stirling blew up the lighthouse at the end of OPERATION TOMCAT, sir?"

Col. Randal said, "Pretty close."

"My impression as well, Colonel."

MAJOR THE LADY JANE SEABORN, LG, OBE, RM SAID, "LET you out of my sight for one minute and see what happens."

Colonel John Randal said, "Well, I could say the same thing about you."

With no torpedoes left, PT 10 had returned to the anchorage. Lieutenant Randy "Hornblower" Seaborn was ashore making a report to his grandfather, Vice Admiral Sir Randolph "Razor" Ransom.

Everyone was shaken by the turn of events.

The Kriegsmarine *Sella*-class destroyer had been less than a quarter mile from the wharf when it exploded. Because of the pair of steep hills at the entrance, the dock area was shielded from the blast. However, the sound of the explosion was magnified due to the close quarters in the harbor. The flash had lit up the sky wall to wall, and then the fireball had risen over the top of the hills.

The blast had taken everyone on Patmos by surprise. Alarmed townspeople cautiously congregated on the beach to ascertain what new evil had befallen them. The war had instilled a victim mentality in the islanders.

Beverly Blackwell said, "I thought a volcano erupted."

Captain Pamala Plum-Martin, DSO, OBE, DFC, RM, said, "Agreed."

Captain "Pyro" Percy Stirling, DSO, MC, said, "On the bright side, I shall not be blamed for this one."

VAdm. Ransom walked over. "In my estimation, if they are aware of anything amiss the Kriegsmarine shall likely believe the explosion was caused by a ship that struck a mine—could be a British vessel for all anyone knows. The Kriegsmarine has its hands full with the invasion. Most likely no one gets around to investigating for a day or two, if then."

Col. Randal said, "Won't find much."

VAdm. Ransom said, "Colonel, I want you to take your key people and fly out immediately."

Col. Randal said, "Sir . . ."

VAdm. Ransom said, "Your work is finished here. It is imperative we move our most important personnel back to ABC to regroup and rebuild. Nothing is gained by remaining. The risk of being captured is not worth it. I shall be setting sail as well with the LCT and the MAS boats the moment the two of them arrive."

"Yes, sir." Col. Randal glanced at Beverly and Capt. Plum-Martin, pointed his finger in the air and made a circling motion. "Crank it up ladies."

Lieutenant General "Geronimo" Joe McKoy strolled over. "What's going on, John?"

Col. Randal said, "Have everyone who jumped in load back on the *Black Cat*. I want you, Lady Jane, Butch, Dr. Winthrop and Major Jellicoe aboard as well. Oh, yeah, Jackson Taylor's on the *King Duck*. Pull him off and put him on the plane. We're flying out—now."

Lt. Gen. McKoy said, "We've got Mack, Mike Mikkalis and Horndog still on Leros. We can't—"

VAdm. Ransom said, "Colonel Randal is complying with my orders, General. We need you people to be the nucleus for our counteroffensive. Raiding Forces and attachments are all that's left as building blocks for future operations in the Aegean."

"Wilco—can do, Admiral. You men on the dock saddle up. We're pulling out."

Lady Jane said, "Why would you want to fly Jackson's body back on the *Black Cat* when you could give the space on the plane to someone else?"

Col. Randal said, "Lieutenant Taylor's not exactly dead, Jane."

Lady Jane said, "Are you having me on?"

"Negative—I'm never going to live it down."

The Hudson arrived out of the night, glided in and splashed into the harbor. No one was expecting the plane. The converted amphibian taxied to the dock.

Wing Commander Paddy Wilcox, DSO, OBE, MC, DFC, climbed out. The former Canadian bush pilot had his trademark black eyepatch flipped up.

"Heard you could use a hand, Colonel. Pulling people out of places they don't need to be any longer is my stock in trade—borrowed your airplane."

Col. Randal said, "Get ready for a quick turnaround, Wing Commander. Any crew onboard?"

"I'm flying solo."

"Fourteen PAX then?"

"Affirmative—works for me."

Col. Randal made eye contact with Captain Billy Jack Jaxx. He was talking to Lady Jane and King but immediately excused himself and walked over.

Col. Randal said, "Locate Major Jellicoe. He's probably with General McKoy at the *Black Cat*. Have him report to me here immediately. Send Lieutenant Hamilton with him."

"Yes, sir."

VAdm. Ransom came over, "I intend to remain here until Brandy and Penelope return. My plan is to load all the people they bring out onto the *King Duck*. Then sail for ABC the instant the troops are on board.

"Beginning Morning Nautical Twilight (BMNT) is 0645 so Skipper Finley shall likely not be able to travel much more than twenty miles before having to put in at some convenient island and go under camouflage. Can I count on you to have The Great Teddy be aboard the LCT to supervise?"

Col. Randal said, "I've already sent for him, sir."

"Outstanding," VAdm. Ransom said. "I am banking on the Germans being so occupied with invading Leros they shall not be doing much else in the way of naval and air operations elsewhere for the time being. Still, why take a chance?"

VAdm. Ransom had picked up that phrase from being around Raiding Forces for so long. Although not a rule, it was one of the unit's fundamental concepts that came with the implied warning—ignore this missive at your peril.

Col. Randal said, "What are your plans for Veronica, sir?"

"Mrs. Paige can continue to extract evaders utilizing the caiques for as long as she feels it feasible. I shall suggest she find an alternate island to use as MI-9's staging base. There are several nearby to choose from."

"I'd like you to keep your eye on her, Admiral," Col. Randal said. "She is not a woman to stand down no matter how hopeless the situation—unless ordered."

VAdm. Ransom said, "Never fear, Colonel. I shall be monitoring MI-9."

Major the Earl Lord George Jellicoe, 2nd Earl, DSO, MC, arrived on the dock. He had been aboard the *King Duck* supervising the loading of his troops. They had come out with their arms. Maj. Jellicoe was a commander who paid a considerable amount of attention to what was referred to in the British Army as "man management."

Col. Randal said, "Change of plans, Major. Select thirteen key SBS and/or LRDG people plus yourself. Priority to officers and NCOs. Then report to Wing Commander Wilcox aboard the Hudson that just came in. You'll be flying out. Raiding Forces starts rebuilding immediately upon arrival back at ABC. I want to hit the ground running."

"Yes, sir."

"I'll be flying out right behind you aboard the Catalina. Be prepared to give me a rundown on the status of the SBS when it lands. Have your recommendations ready for what you think a reorganization should look like."

Maj. Lord Jellicoe said, "With pleasure, Colonel. My people shall not soon forget you came to retrieve us in person without the benefit of official authorization."

Col. Randal said, "I'll be expecting your briefing, Major."

"Wilco."

Lady Jane was waiting at the *Black Cat* when Col. Randal and King arrived. Everyone else was already aboard. They climbed in and took their place on the last seats on the canvas benches that ran along the bulkheads.

As soon as the Catalina made its takeoff run across the harbor and lifted into the air, Beverly made her way back and traded places with King. The Merc went forward and sat in the co-pilot's chair to ride with Capt. Plum-Martin.

The group in the tail of the plane consisted of Lt. Gen. McKoy, Major General James "Baldie" Taylor, Col. Randal, Lieutenant Jackson Taylor, Doctor Layton Winthrop, Capt. Jaxx, Lady Jane and Beverly.

Unlike civilian airlines where first-class passengers are seated in the front of the plane, in the paratroops the "studs" ride in the tail.

Beverly said, "Aren't you going to say, 'Let's get the hell out of Dodge,' Johnny—we're all waiting to hear it."

"Negative. I'm on this aircraft against my will."

Lady Jane said, "Ever since the Gunfight at the Blue Duck, I have wondered where you came up with that line."

Lt. Gen. McKoy said, "Originally Wyatt Earp said it to Curly Bill Trampus on Tuesday, June 6, 1876."

Beverly laughed, "What time of day was it General?"

Capt. Jaxx said, "Yeah, could you be a little more specific, sir."

Lady Jane said, "How could you possibly know the exact date?"

Lt. Gen. McKoy said, "The U.S. Marshal's main office in Topeka, Kansas, has a copy of the *Dodge City Times* newspaper from back in the day reportin' the story. It's framed under glass in the lobby of their buildin'. Those deputy marshals quote Wyatt Earp ever' chance they get. It's a law enforcement thing."

Capt. Jaxx said, "As much as you like women, Jackson, being cooped up in a nunnery must have been cruel and unusual . . ."

Col. Randal was wondering, "How did it come to this? Hard to keep these people down."

THE SUN WAS SWIMMING OUT OF THE TURQUOISE-BLUE Aegean Sea as the *Black Cat* came in to land at Advanced Base Castelrozzo (ABC). Lieutenant Colonel Sir Terry "Zorro" Stone, KBE, DSO, MC, and Mandy Paige were waiting on the dock with Happy to welcome them back. Off to the right a line of infantry was advancing up the steep escarpment where Captain Roy Kidd was leading counter-Brandenburger operations.

The dog went wild with joy when he saw Lady Jane deplane.

Lt. Col. Stone said, "Welcome back. GG has a meal waiting in the main dining room. Jellicoe and his people are already there."

Mandy said, "Ian Fleming has arrived from Naval Intelligence Division, London. Other than hoping to make a date with Beverly he is here to see you, John. Tightlipped as to why."

Colonel John Randal said, "Right after breakfast I'll be having a short meeting in Jane's suite. Schedule the Commander to come in once it's concluded."

"Wilco."

"Lord Jellicoe is going to lay out his initial thoughts on rebuilding the SBS—you and Terry sit in."

Mandy said, "Love to."

As they were walking to Advanced Base Castelrozzo Headquarters (ABCHQ), Lt. Col. Stone said, "We took out another Sea Raider yesterday."

Col. Randal said, "What's that make now?"

Mandy said, "If we are to believe the two Nazis Brandy interrogated, we are down to only four Brandenburgers unaccounted for."

"Good."

Major the Lady Jane Seaborn said, "ABC is not safe until we kill them all."

Col. Randal said, "Not much compassion out of you, Lady Jane."

"Not a drop."

The war in the Aegean had turned paradise into a very bad place.

Lt. Col. Stone said, "Stephanie has arranged for temporary quarters for the LRDG—theirs were destroyed during our air raid, as I am sure you recall."

Col. Randal said, "Their commanding officer Jake Easonsmith was killed on Leros."

Lt. Col. Stone said, "In that case I shall have his personal belongings packed up and moved out of his room at ABCHQ. Stephanie can arrange to have everything shipped to his next of kin. Any idea who his replacement might be?"

Col. Randal said, "A Major Owen. He's on a caique somewhere off the coast of Turkey. I don't know much about him or why he wasn't on Leros with his troops.

"Locate the Major and have him report to me here, Terry."

"Understood, I suspect we should anticipate difficulty amalgamating the LRDG into Raiding Forces. They have always been an independent command and cannot refrain from basking in the glory of days past."

Lieutenant General "Geronimo" Joe McKoy said, "The Long Range Desert Group's been snakebit ever since the Desert Fox got hisself run out of the desert."

Col. Randal said, "That is a fact."

Lt. Gen. McKoy had a rule of thumb developed from years of experience. It was left unsaid but both men knew the other was thinking it: "Once a thing gets snakebit it stays snakebit."

Lady Jane said, "We shall make improving the LRDG's morale a top priority."

The Ranger Task Force troops filed into ABCHQ and stacked arms along one wall in the hallway. Gear belonging to the SBS and LRDG was stacked along the opposite wall.

Inside the Other Ranks' dining room, Major the Earl Lord George Jellicoe's people were wrapping up their meal. It was the first hot food the men had tasted in weeks. SBS spirits were already picking up.

Col. Randal stopped by the table where Maj. Jellicoe was sitting, "Briefing in Lady Jane's suite in one hour—you're up."

"Yes, sir."

Col. Randal and Lady Jane placed an order with GG then proceeded to her suite. Flanigan was already at the desk outside the door. After providing him with the names of the people he should admit for the briefing, the two went inside to shower and change clothes.

One of the mess orderlies delivered their meal while they were in the bedroom getting dressed. He set a table in the living room since the dining area was being used for a map room and to hold briefings.

Then he made himself scarce.

Lady Jane said, "This is fun."

Col. Randal began to unwind—a little. "Yes it is."

Dining in a room all alone was one of their great pleasures.

Lady Jane said, "We are not giving up my island to the Nazis—clear?"

"Crystal."

THE BRIEFING IN MAJOR THE LADY JANE SEABORN'S SUITE was about to get underway. Present were Lieutenant General "Geronimo" Joe McKoy, Major General James "Baldie" Taylor, Colonel John Randal, Lieutenant Colonel Sir Terry "Zorro" Stone, Major the Lady Jane Seaborn, Dr. Layton Winthrop, Captain Billy Jack Jaxx, Captain Butch "Headhunter" Hoolihan DSO, MC, MM, RM, Lieutenant Jackson Taylor, Waldo Treywick and Mandy Paige.

Major the Earl Lord George Jellicoe was standing and chatting with people in the front-row chairs. He had a casual, laid-back way about him and was clearly comfortable in front of an audience. However, when Beverly Blackwell slipped in at the last minute fresh from a shower with her damp hair slicked straight back, looking like a Greek goddess with a good tan, the SBS commander became momentarily distracted. It was understandable.

Maj. Jellicoe was curious about the eclectic composition of the crowd. He had met the silver-haired cowboy general but wondered about the man sitting next to him in a beautifully cut tailor-made suit with a faint bulge under his left shoulder. Were those custom-rolled cigars he was handing out? Why was there an anthropologist in the room? And why were two good-looking girls included in a classified session about his secretive small-scale amphibious raiding unit?

Seemed unorthodox.

This was not the first time Maj. Jellicoe had attended a Raiding Forces briefing. Even so, he was only now beginning to appreciate how unconventional the unit might actually be. He was comfortable with unconventional.

Col. Randal said, "We're good, Major."

Maj. Jellicoe began immediately. "The Special Boat Section was formed by Roger Courtney in 1940—a big game hunter who believed that you could sneak up on the enemy by floating down a river in a canoe because he liked to hunt that way in Africa. No one was much interested in his proposal.

"The Royal Navy pooh-poohed it. However, Admiral Keyes, the chief of Combined Operations at that time, allowed Roger to proceed with a demonstration to determine the effectiveness of canoes as men-of-war. The target was the Commando Training ship, *Glengyle*.

"One morning the ship's crew woke up to find crosses chalked along the waterline to simulate limpet mines; two breech-blocks and three Oerlikon coverings had mysteriously vanished. To drive home his point, Courtney, wearing a swimming suit and dripping wet, arrived at a high-level navy conference—the officers of the *Glengyle* were having breakfast in a local hotel—and threw down the ship's after pom-pom cover.

"Combined Operations promptly instructed him to raise the first Special Boat Section of twelve volunteers. The SBS eventually reported to the Mediterranean and operated out of Alexandria with the First Submarine Flotilla. Following a year of hair-raising missions raiding coastal targets, knifing and garroting enemy sentries, Roger was ordered back to the UK to form No. 2 SBS.

"With Roger gone, through a series of misadventures—primarily senior commanders in the Plans Division of Middle East Headquarters not understanding how to utilize their specialist skills, the SBS became attached to the SAS. For the record that development happened after I was called back to England and ordered to expand the unit to a 230-man squadron—thus a name change was in order . . . SBS now being called the Special Boat Squadron. Order, counter-order, and disorder ensued. Upon returning to Egypt, we began jeep raiding and over time, due to not being used, our skills as amphibious raiders/beach reconnaissance operators/small boat specialists began to atrophy.

"There was a culture clash between SAS and SBS that was never satisfactorily reconciled. The SAS liked to arrive at a target with all guns blazing while the SBS preferred to work in pairs, sneak around back, slip inside, slit the Nazi's throats, place our explosives and then be gone with no one the wiser until the bang.

"After David Stirling was captured the SAS was broken up. We in the SBS became independent once again. Unfortunately, Plans Division decided to use us as line infantry on Leros. It was a role we had no training, equipment or the mindset to perform.

"When we arrived on the island I had 180 men under command. My best estimate is less than half of them made it out fit enough to remain in service, possibly less. We shall not know until they can be assembled here on Castelrozzo.

"Prior to being sent to Leros and following much trial and error, our organization settled on patrols consisting of one officer, one NCO and five men. The basic SBS building block. Typically we combine patrols if the mission profile calls for a larger footprint on a given operation.

"Col. Randal instructed me to lay out what I thought a reorganization should consist of now that we are a part of Raiding Forces. Well, that's it. We need to return to our small-scale amphibious raiding roots and operate in the seven-man patrol configuration. Five patrols, each led by an officer form a section. Three sections constitute the Special Boat Squadron.

"We prefer to rely on stealth, striking out of the sea at night and living by our wits."

Captain Stephanie Fawcett-Tatum, RM, entered the room, came around and handed Col. Randal a piece of paper.

Col. Randal said, "We get the idea, Major. Structure your outfit as you see fit. Coordinate with Colonel Stone—make it happen."

Maj. Jellicoe said, "With pleasure, sir. SBS has not . . ."

Col. Randal said, "Captain Fawcett-Tatum has just handed me a late-breaking report. Italian troops belonging to the 33rd "Acqui" Division on Cephalonia initially resisted a landing on the island by the German 1st Mountain Division with elements of the 999th Light attached. The Italians eventually surrendered at which point the Nazis executed over 5,000 officers and men in cold blood. That is all."

BEVERLY BLACKWELL SAID, "JOHNNY, YOU HAVE TO COME watch our yoga class."

Colonel John Randal said, "Jack says Rocky's banned men from the in-house phase of her daily training program."

Beverly laughed, "She banned Billy Jack but I'm pretty sure she'll make an exception for you just this once. Class starts in ten minutes."

"OK."

After Beverly left to go change into her yoga gear, Major the Lady Jane Seaborn came out of the bedroom in her black leotards with Happy. The dog was dancing around.

Lady Jane said, "Follow me."

As they left the suite, Col. Randal told Flanigan to phone down to the Tactical Operations Center (TOC) to have the duty officer—Captain Stephanie Fawcett-Tatum was going to be in the yoga class—inform Commander Ian Fleming he had been delayed. He and Lady Jane went up the stairs to the third floor. Royal Marines, Wrens and FANYs were streaming into the room Rikke "Rocky" Runborg used for her daily one-hour exercise program prior to their run and swim.

Rolls of floor mats were stacked by the door, and each of the girls picked up one on her way in. Lady Jane took two. She and Happy went in and took up side-by-side positions with a rolled-up mat lying in front of each of them.

Col. Randal stayed off to one side of the room feeling out of place. He had no idea what to expect. Other than to say "Hi John" as they came by, the women ignored him. This was serious business. Rocky was a fanatic for physical fitness.

The former Norwegian ballet dancer took up her position at the front of the class and unrolled her mat. That was the signal to get started. As Lady Jane started to unroll hers, Happy put his nose down and unrolled the mat in front of him, keeping perfect pace with Lady Jane. Then they lay down on their mats side by side.

Col. Randal did a doubletake.

Rocky started doing pushups.

Lady Jane started doing pushups.

Happy started doing pushups.

Then Rocky went to her hands and knees and arched her back raising her head toward the ceiling in a stretch. Lady Jane followed suit. And Happy did too, pointing his nose straight up.

Rocky lay down on her stomach. Lady Jane and Happy went to theirs.

Rocky laid her forearms on the mat and arched her hips in the air. Lady Jane and Happy did the same, the dog leaning on his front paws and raising up on his hind legs in perfect synchronization. It was like the workout was choreographed—which it probably was.

Back on her hands and knees, Rocky stuck first one then the other leg straight behind her in a hard stretch. Lady Jane did as well. Happy never missed a beat, sticking out one hind leg then the other—left then right.

Col. Randal thought he might be hallucinating.

Rolling over on her back Rocky brought her legs straight up, reached out and touched her toes. Lady Jane did too. Col. Randal was pretty sure this was the end of it for Happy, but he did exactly the same thing—front paws touching rear paws straight up in the air.

The dog was clearly enjoying himself and he knew all the moves.

Lady Jane kept her head turned watching Happy as she was going through her routine. The German shepherd kept his turned too, never taking his eyes off her for a second mimicking every move she made. The two were clearly communicating with each other on some telepathic level–Happy had no idea he was a dog.

Lady Jane glanced over and gave Col. Randal a big wink followed by one of her heart attack smiles—it lit off like a flash bulb.

Were Beverly and Lady Jane trying to cheer him up after the fiasco on Leros?

If so, it worked.

2
MOLE HUNT

COMMANDER IAN FLEMING, RNVR, AND COLONEL JOHN Randal were sitting in the office he rarely used in the TOC aka Operations Room. Major Peter Fleming, his older brother—the famous adventurer, journalist, travel writer and husband of British movie star Celia Johnson, was with him. The two Flemings and Lieutenant Colonel Sir Terry "Zorro" Stone had attended Eton together.

Cdr. Fleming said, "Peter is doing a spot of understudying Dudley at A-Force then he is off to the CBI to take charge of D-Division."

Knowing who Peter was working with, Col. Randal thought it did not take much imagination to guess the D stood for Deception. Sometimes when playing at spies, the spooks did things that made it hard not to laugh.

Cdr. Fleming said, "I have three reasons for flying to Castelrozzo to see you, Colonel.

Col. Randal said, "Let's hear 'em."

"I need Captain Hoolihan to be on loan to Naval Intelligence Division to train my 30 Assault Unit," Cdr. Fleming said. "They failed to get ashore at Dieppe, were hopeless in Sicily and did not perform particularly well at Salerno. I am afraid the standards of the Royal Marines Troop 33 who compose the unit have fallen on hard times due to the rapid buildup that has taken place to meet wartime demands."

Col. Randal said, "I sent the Headhunter to train your people. He was away for nearly a month."

Cdr. Fleming said, "Actually we used the captain for another more pressing project."

"And what might that have been?"

"Need to Know, old boy, sorry. Classified and all that."

"Tell me again what it is 30 Assault Unit is supposed to do."

"Everything I am about to say to you is Top Secret, strictly Need to Know. Not to be shared with anyone. I shall not be telling the entire story, you understand."

"Fair enough."

Col. Randal had been working with intelligence organizations long enough to have become disenchanted with their obsession with secrets—most of which were not all that secret. "Need to Know" was almost never adhered to. Those in the know sharing the information with select friends after first advising them never to tell anyone, who then . . . The supposed secret was often already known to the enemy, who was not particularly interested in it. In the intelligence world, possessing the "Need to Know" was often more about being a member of an exclusive club than protecting operational security. Only select insiders were authorized to have the "Need to Know"—and not all of them.

There was a conceit about it: I have the need. You don't.

Lieutenant General "Geronimo" Joe McKoy was known to say, "If you have a secret don't tell it to anybody."

That was the oldest trick in the book. But the thing about old tricks is they work. Something else Geronimo Joe liked to point out.

Cdr. Fleming said, "My 30 Assault Unit is intended to be a crack intelligence team composed of Royal Marines who go in with the first wave of an invasion to seize by whatever means necessary enemy code books, cipher machines, and classified documents. Only the Marines Troop 33 assigned to NID have not turned out to be quite so crack.

"It has been rather more difficult than anticipated to organize what I call my Red Indians. The best solution would be for you to assign Captain Hoolihan to NID permanently to command 30 AU for me. Knowing that is not likely I shall settle for him putting my lads through an intensive retraining program."

Col. Randal said, "You could not have picked a worse time to ask me to loan out my most experienced amphibious raiding officer."

Cdr. Fleming said, "You would be well advised to allow the captain to establish a personal relationship with NID and my 30 AU. One never knows what the future portends. Certain people in high places have designs on you Colonel, but then that is strictly Need to Know and at this point in time you do not possess it."

Col. Randal clicked on.

"What does that mean, exactly?"

Cdr. Fleming said, "When the Allies open the Second Front a combined US/UK intelligence operation classified *above* Top Secret is laid on to swing into action that will require an unorthodox Special Operations commander with your particular skill set. That is all I am at liberty to disclose at this time. Other than to inform you the mission is one that shall have far-reaching implications for the Allied world long after the present conflict has concluded.

"My primary purpose for being here today is to alert you to the likelihood of a most important assignment in your future. As Peter would say—being a journalist such as he is—I buried the lede by making my pitch for the Headhunter first."

Col. Randal said, "I see."

"My final reason for being here is to tell you it has been brought to the attention of NID that you have been offered the command of a parachute regiment in the 82nd Airborne Division. Admittedly a most attractive offer. One it is understood you initially rejected but promised to consider. That would prove to be a pity because it would take you away from Special Operations to play a conventional parachute infantry role any number of other officers are qualified to perform.

"Doing so would remove you from contention for the task I made reference to which I want to reaffirm has national strategic implications for both our countries."

Col. Randal realized Cdr. Fleming did not possess a Need to Know for so much as the code name of OPERATION LONG NECK—much less the details. The diamond interdiction operation prevented accepting any assignment that took him out of Raiding Forces. The Parachute Infantry Regiment command was off the table. But Cdr. Fleming, not having the Need to Know about LONG NECK, would have no way of knowing that.

At times the obsession for secrecy kept the left hand from knowing what the right hand was doing even when it would be helpful—the world of intelligence was complicated.

Cdr. Fleming did not mention Col. Randal's new assignment as Paratroop Advisor to Major General Sam Houston Blackwell's Troop Transport Command (TTC). Not because he was not aware of it, he was. Why not say something then? The short answer was the relationship between Raiding Forces and TTC had possibilities that might prove beneficial to NID. And it posed no threat to the future assignment he was alluding to.

But then that was Need to Know.

Col. Randal said, "Let me get this straight, Commander. You want to borrow Captain Hoolihan—again. I'm not to transfer to the 82nd Airborne and need to keep myself on call for an unspecified assignment that may or may not come up sometime at a later date?"

Cdr. Fleming said, "You always were a quick study."

Col. Randal said, "And I thought this conversation was only leading up to you wanting me to fix you up with Beverly."

Cdr. Fleming said, "There is that."

OUT IN THE TOC COLONEL JOHN RANDAL PULLED CAPTAIN Stephanie Fawcett-Tatum aside. "Find Butch and have him meet me in Lady Jane's suite."

"When do you want him there, John?"

"Now."

"Brigadier Clarke has flown in. He is having tea with Lady Jane and Beverly in the senior officer's private dining room. Waiting to meet with you."

"Can you hold him off for a while? I need to talk to the Headhunter in private first."

"Absolutely, John."

On the way out he encountered Major the Earl Lord George Jellicoe.

Col. Randal said, "Recruiting replacements is a problem for SBS. With the war having moved on to Italy the pool of candidates in this theatre has been drawn down. Link up with Lieutenant Taylor. He has an OSS outfit called the Maritime Unit en route from the States. Don't know much about them but I intend to assign the MU to work with you when they arrive."

Maj. Jellicoe said, "Maritime Unit—sounds like it has possibilities."

Col. Randal said, "What are your thoughts on recruiting?"

Maj. Jellicoe said, "The 10th and 11th Parachute Battalions were raised for who knows what. Currently they are sitting idle. Plans Division has not the faintest notion of how to employ them. I know several of the officers quite well. Service in SBS with the promise of action may hold some allure. Possibly they can recommend a few of their best troops to pirate."

Col. Randal said, "We have a contingent of the King's Own Royal Regiment arriving when the *King Duck* comes in. They'll need parachute and small boat training but all of them were a part of a provisional unit called Strike Force I commanded during the siege of Habbaniya. If any show interest they're yours, George—good men."

Maj. Jellicoe said, "When the LCT steams in, I shall be waiting on the dock to greet them, Colonel."

Col. Randal said, "Your Special Boat Section has been bounced around from place to place. Never given a chance to utilize your primary skills. We'll try to treat you better than that. In return I'm going to expect improved organization and you need to tighten up on discipline—I've been reading your after-action reports."

Maj. Jellicoe said, "Understood, sir."

Col. Randal said, "Your SBS operators' tactics are entirely too casual. Working against Italians you could get away with it. That's not going to fly with the Germans."

"I quite agree, Colonel."

Captain Butch "Headhunter" Hoolihan was waiting at Flanigan's desk outside the door to Major the Lady Jane Seaborn's suite when he arrived. They went inside. No one else was to be allowed in.

Col. Randal said, "You have a story to tell me, Butch."

"Sir?"

"Commander Fleming is downstairs. He has requested you train his 30 Assault Unit. But you were already supposed to have trained them—took a month to do it. So, what is it you're not telling me, Captain?"

Capt. Hoolihan said, "Sir, that is classified."

Col. Randal stuck one of Waldo's long, thin, custom-rolled cigars between his teeth. He did not offer one to the Headhunter. And he did not look pleased.

"Butch, if you don't give it up you're about one click off of being assigned to NID permanently—a request for your transfer has been made."

"OPERATION CREEK, sir."

"What might that be?"

"A raid on the harbor of Mormugao, Goa, in India, similar to our cutting out operation at Rio Bonita."

"Tell me."

"Three German freighters, the *Ehrenfels,* the *Braunfels* and the *Drachenfels,* took refuge in the Portuguese territory of Goa at the beginning of the war, overstayed the seventy-two-hour limit and were interned. Later the Italian ship *Anfora* arrived. The Royal Navy knew about the ships but did not perceive them as any threat.

"Then SOE's India Mission at Meerut began intercepting coded messages to German U-boats revealing the positions of Allied ships sailing from Bombay—forty-six were sunk in a ninety-day period as a result of the transmissions. Next it was learned a Nazi spy known as "Trumpet" and his wife were in Panaji—the capital of Goa. Baldie, calling himself 'Colonel Stewart,' went to Goa with Lieutenant Colonel Lewis Pugh, the Director of SOE India's country section of Force 136.

"They kidnapped the couple.

"Under interrogation the Nazis revealed a secret transmitter was hidden aboard the *Ehrenfels.* Invading Goa to take it out was not possible due to Portuguese neutrality. There were no good options for dealing with the problem and the shipping losses were not sustainable.

"Eventually sir, what SOE decided on can only be described as a covert operation so desperate any rational person would call it insane. Whoever suggested the idea had to have been drunk."

Col. Randal said, "That bad?"

Capt. Hoolihan said, "Worse, the plan was to use volunteers from the expatriate community in India to carry out a raid on the *Ehrenfels*. Sergeant Major Mikkalis and I flew out to Calcutta with Commander Fleming to recruit and train volunteers from two of the local auxiliary regiments for the mission, sir. It turned out 'auxiliary regiment' was a polite term for uniformed weekend drinking club."

Col. Randal said, "I thought the Sergeant Major was working up his caique—the *Santa Claus*?"

"Indented for leave at Commander Fleming's request, sir."

"I see."

Capt. Hoolihan said, "SOE's plan—refined as best it could be by General Taylor masquerading as Colonel Stewart—was to load out on a barge and sail to Mormugao, enter the harbor, board the *Ehrenfels*, sink or capture the ship and sail it to Indian waters. We recruited fourteen volunteers from the Calcutta Light Horse and four from the Calcutta Scottish—bankers, solicitors and businessmen. All middle-aged British patriots past prime military age and not in the best physical condition but eager to do their bit, sir."

Col. Randal said, "Lovely."

"One volunteer only had a single good eye but that was enough for Admiral Nelson—we signed him on."

"You're kidding."

Capt. Hoolihan said, "In the event of capture our story would be that the boarding party was a bunch of drunk civilians who stole a barge and invaded Goa in an alcoholic blackout—I am not making this up, sir.

"The men were not to be in uniform. And they were armed only with sporting shotguns with the barrels sawed off—no Stens or Thompson submachine guns. Anyone who had a pistol brought it. I thought the mission was more likely to turn out like the Charge of the Light Brigade than a surgical cutting-out operation carried out by the brave hearties of the Calcutta Light Horse. Actually sir, it was worse than it sounds."

Col. Randal said, "I can see how it might have been."

Capt. Hoolihan said, "After a loosely termed Commando crash course the troops loaded out on a barely seaworthy barge, the *Phoebe*, and set sail. Sergeant Major Mikkalis and I traveled with them under strict orders from Colonel Pugh that we were only there in an advisory capacity and were to remain on the barge when the *Ehrenfels* was boarded. The lighthouse and luminous buoy marking the harbor were not working the night we arrived off Goa which proved fortuitous."

Col. Randal said, "Bet it was."

"General Taylor—I mean Colonel Stewart—Red, Mandy, Beverly and Pamala had flown in and were standing by with Commander Fleming in Vasco da Gama, the town where Mormugao harbor is located, to create a series of diversions. The idea was to employ the same basic model to cover the attack on the *Ehrenfels* as the one we used at Rio Bonita, sir.

"General Taylor—aka Colonel Stewart—bribed local port authorities. The women hosted a reception for the senior military, political and social elite. Commander Fleming arranged with the local bordello to provide free hookers to entertain the crews of the interned ships.

"Did I mention Lady Seaborn was there as well, sir? She was the guest of honor at the reception. The social elite in Vasco da Gama all wanted to meet her."

Col. Randal said, "No, you left that out, Butch."

Capt. Hoolihan said, "Prior to sailing, Colonel Pugh issued last-minute orders to the boarding party to avoid shooting anyone if at all possible. But no plan survives the first contact with the enemy. When the assault went in on the *Ehrenfels* the no-shoot order fell apart, sir. The ship's captain was killed along with five members of the crew. Those reservists really took it to the Nazis.

"After the *Ehrenfels* was believed to be secured and as preparations were being made to get her underway, German sailors who had stayed hidden during the attack managed to go below and open the seacocks. Realizing the ship was sinking, explosives were hastily placed on the radio transmitter.

"The demolitions team must have bought into the block of instruction on the "P for Plenty" formula. The demo men used every stick of plastique in the boarding party, sir. When the charge in the radio room exploded, the entire freighter went up in flames—not part of the plan.

"Seeing the *Ehrenfels* on fire, the captains of the other three merchantmen panicked and scuttled their ships. Mission accomplished—just not the one you thought, sir. I never trained Commander Fleming's Red Indians.""

Col. Randal said, "Some tale."

Capt. Hoolihan said, "Sorry to keep it from you, Colonel, but I was under strict orders. OPERATION CREEK—Need to Know Only."

Col. Randal said, "So, I'm to believe you and Sergeant Major Mikkalis flew out to India, recruited a party of hard-drinking expats, invaded a neutral Portuguese protectorate and then stood by and watched out of shape, over-the-hill insurance brokers, bankers and lawyers, armed with shotguns carry out a complex raid requiring split-second timing and precision execution and did nothing except supply moral support?"

Capt. Hoolihan said, "That's my story, sir, and I am sticking to it."

MANDY PAIGE WAS WAITING OUTSIDE THE SUITE TALKING to Flanigan when Colonel John Randal walked out.

"I have a report, John."

"No one else comes in, Flanigan."

She was one person he always made time for. Brigadier Dudley Clarke would have to wait.

Mandy said, "Billy Jack has been tireless in his efforts to hunt down the Brandenburger Sea Raiders but he has not been able to round up all of them. The problem is we have information that at least one of the Nazis is being sheltered in the home of a local Greek woman. This could be a sensitive situation politically since Captain Merryweather is always voicing concern about the importance of winning the hearts and minds of the locals. How would you like me to proceed?"

Col. Randal said, "What do you want to do?"

Mandy said, "Go to the woman's house, drag her out by the hair and shoot her in front of her neighbors. Bentley deserved better than to be murdered by those Sea Raiders."

Col. Randal said, "OK."

Mandy laughed, "We both know that's not going to happen. I feel better for you having said I could. If I wanted to. Thanks for that."

Col. Randal said, "I know you have a plan."

Mandy said, "We should bring in Major Zargo to handle the situation. If he is not available, Major Adair needs to meet with the mayor and turn over our intelligence on the collaborator. Let the island administration deal with her. We do not offend the locals that way."

Col. Randal said, "Make it happen."

Mandy said, "On the other thing you asked me to look . . ."

Col. Randal said, "How's that going?"

Mandy said, "The obvious people to have informed General Donovan about General McKoy's displeasure with his new role in LONG NECK would be: you, me, Lady Jane, Jack, Beverly, Red, Rocky, King, Pam, Waldo, General McKoy or possibly Jim Taylor provided he knew—it is not clear he does or why he would if he did."

Col. Randal said, "How did you arrive at that list of suspects?"

Mandy said, "Except for Jim, Red and Rocky, all of them are CARD GAME—the only people we know for sure who are aware of General McKoy's feelings. Three of us on the list have applied to be granted U.S. citizenship. Donovan's law firm is handling the paperwork. Which means we three are in frequent contact with OSS or attorneys who report to Wild Bill.

"Rocky has also applied for citizenship, and Red trained flight attendants for OSS to do what she does for MI-6. They both have the opportunity and means to provide back-channel information to General Donovan."

Col. Randal said, "Who do you like for it?"

"Neither of us or you would have sent someone else besides me down this rabbit hole. Possibly Lady Jane mentioned something to Wild Bill but I doubt it. She went through virtually every intelligence school MI-6 and SOE have. She would never reveal information about CARD GAME players even under torture. Besides, due to Lady Jane's station in life she never tells anyone anything because she does not want to risk being quoted. We can safely scratch her off the list."

Col. Randal said, "Good to know."

Mandy said, "We can forget Waldo as well. He sees Raiding Forces as the family he never had. If that were not enough, he would never do anything to jeopardize his share of the diamonds LONG NECK recovers. Besides . . . that old ivory poacher be a snitch for OSS? Not likely. That stipulated, he might have mentioned something harmless to Rocky and we both know she's a triple—or maybe a quadruple—agent."

Col. Randal said, "Yes we do."

Mandy said, "Jack would never discuss CARD GAME with anyone, for any reason even with a gun to his head.

"King and Pam . . . their loyalty is to you, not OSS. It's not them.

"It is unlikely Red would know General McKoy's feelings since she is not read into LONG NECK . . . much less CARD GAME.

"General McKoy could find a way to communicate with Donovan if he wished. But why would he want to? The General is not one to voice a complaint to anyone other than you. He has motive, means and opportunity. Be a mole for OSS? Not in a million years.

"Beverly . . . she has known Donovan all her life. Report information concerning Raiding Forces much less CARD GAME to him—zero probability. But she might have mentioned something to Bronc. Wild Bill is General Blackwell's attorney and hunting companion . . ."

Col. Randal said, "Bronc has no direct knowledge of LONG NECK other than he has heard the codename. Beverly knows that. It's not her."

Mandy said, "Agreed. And you can never under any circumstances on penalty of death ever let Beverly know we had this conversation. She would be crushed. Worse than I was when you kept me in the dark about the diamond interdiction program before inviting me into CARD GAME."

Col. Randal said, "National security . . ."

"It's all right, John. I completely understand. Nevertheless, it hurt my feelings."

Col. Randal said, "I know it did."

Mandy said, "Beverly loves you. She would never get over knowing we had a conversation about the possibility of her doing anything not in your best interest."

"So, how did Donovan find out?"

Mandy said, "Not the faintest idea."

Col. Randal said, "Jane tells me you're my muse."

Mandy's eyes flashed pleasure, "Lady Jane said that?"

"I'm not sure what a muse is exactly," Col. Randal said, "but if I had one, I would never intentionally hurt her feelings."

Mandy said, "Nice of you to say. I may have underestimated you, Johnny. In truth, Lady Jane is your muse."

Col. Randal said, "Keep looking for our mole."

THE SOUND OF RUNNING COULD BE HEARD OUT IN THE hall. Captain Billy Jack Jaxx shouted, "Is the Colonel in, Flanigan?"

"He is not to be . . ."

Colonel John Randal opened the door, "What's up, Jack?"

"One of our patrols made contact with a Sea Raider, sir. He's making a run for it. Want to go check it out?"

"Let me grab my weapon."

Col. Randal secured his 9mm Beretta MAB-38 submachine gun. It was freshly lubricated. In Raiding Forces, weapons were cleaned immediately following an operation. Unexpected events like this one had a way of cropping up.

Col. Randal said, "Mandy, check with Terry to confirm if he's reached out for the commander of the LRDG, Major Owen. Tell him to have one of the duty pilots pick him up. If the Major protests make it clear it's not a request."

"On the way, John."

"I don't want Pam or Beverly flying."

"Understood."

As they were thundering down the stairs Col. Randal said, "What's the story, Captain?"

"Not sure, sir. Lieutenant Starrett returned from Italy while we were away—missed his DZ by over a hundred miles and still beat most of our people back. He took out his own patrol when the morning sweep failed to make any additional contact and flushed a Brandenburger. Chase is lucky like that. He sent a runner requesting support."

When they reached the bottom of the stairs King was there talking to Private David Hale, formerly of the 575th PIR, a member of Capt. Jaxx's Small Operations Group (SOG) and the runner Lt. Starrett had dispatched for assistance. The Lovat Scouts were standing there with them.

King said, "Hale says they spotted an armed man. Fire was exchanged and they gave pursuit. Lieutenant Starrett is asking for reinforcements because he only has three men with him, Chief."

Col. Randal said, "Lead off, Hale. Let's roll."

Lieutenant General "Geronimo" Joe McKoy caught up with them as they headed out the door. Up the escarpment to the left, in an area swept two days previous, a red smoke grenade popped. Lt. Starrett was marking his position.

Col. Randal said, "Jack, when we link up let the Lieutenant keep running the show."

"Wilco."

Capt. Jaxx knew Col. Randal intended to use this as an opportunity to personally evaluate one of his junior officers. Only he would think of being a lane grader in an actual combat situation where shots were likely to be exchanged. OCS at Fort Benning was never like this.

They raced up the path leading toward the billowing red smoke. Lieutenant Chase Starrett's patrol had chased the Brandenburger out of the built-up area but not quite over the top of the escarpment. The terrain on Castelrozzo beyond the last houses was rugged with large jutting rock features everywhere, and a plateau farther back in the middle of the island. The rocks were the reason virtually all the residences were built on the gradient to the sea and along the shoreline almost to the water's edge.

In between the giant rocks, overgrown mountain laurel bushes formed intermittent patches of scrub brush. Some of it was almost impenetrable. The German had escaped into one of them making pinpointing his exact location difficult.

Digging the Nazi out was going to be a deadly cat-and-mouse game. The German was sure to fire on the patrol from concealment. This was different than clearing a point-type target like one of the houses. If a Brandenburger was in a structure, blowing it down with the Nazi trapped inside was a viable option.

Not so with a Sea Raider concealed in thick brush. The only choice was to go in and get him.

Lt. Starrett and his men were in the prone position at the edge of a large patch of dense green scrub brush when Col. Randal and his reinforcements arrived. They dropped down to the ground next to them. From here on, movement would be by inches.

The fact that the Sea Raider was now badly outnumbered mattered little. Only the point man worming along the ground through the dense foliage would be able to bring his weapon to bear. This was small unit patrolling reduced to its most basic form.

The kind Col. Randal tried to avoid.

Raiding Forces preferred to arrive out of the night taking advantage of the element of surprise, achieve superior firepower in a tightly concentrated place, overwhelm the opposition, and be gone.

That did not mean Col. Randal was not good at patrolling in restricted terrain. He was. Two years detached from the U.S. 26th Cavalry Regiment to the Philippine Scouts going after insurgents deep in the jungle pretty much made him an expert.

He knew one little mistake is all you got.

Capt. Jaxx said, "It's your patrol, Lieutenant. We're here to back you up. What's your next move?"

Lt. Starrett did not have the benefit of having been a jungle fighter. However, he was an avid deer hunter and his preferred method of fair chase was to "still hunt." Sitting in a stand did not hold much appeal.

Still hunting does not mean being still. The hunter moves through the woods painstakingly slowly, always keeping the wind blowing in his face so the deer are not able to catch his scent. The trick is to spot the deer before the deer spots you. Movement gives away either the hunter or the deer—still hunting is exacting work. That experience would be helpful for the situation at hand, but deer do not shoot back.

Lt. Starrett whispered, "We've been tracking a blood trail but it's starting to run out, sir."

Col. Randal realized that changed the equation. Following up a blood trail meant at the end of it there was a very dead or very hacked-off Sea Raider with an automatic weapon. Only one of those two possibilities being the desired result.

Lying on the ground within a few feet of an unseen enemy who wants to kill you as much as you want to kill him is a strangely tranquil experience. Anyone who has never done it would likely not believe that could be true. Those who have usually never get around to mentioning the tranquil part—if they ever tell the story.

Col. Randal knew the Brandenburger had one advantage—if he knew how to use it. Modern weapons use smokeless powder. If he fired a single shot and then stayed in place not moving an inch, no one would be able to spot him in the thick growth.

But firing off several rounds or making any movement—that would give him away.

The problem for Lt. Starrett was the Nazi did not have to move—but his people did. And if the Nazi shot one of his men, then the medical evacuation effort would become a major tactical nightmare. More of his men would have to move into the killing zone to extricate the casualty providing additional targets for a shooter they could not see.

Unless, that is, some way to suppress the Brandenburger's fire could be implemented.

These are the things a small unit commander has to understand and work through prior to issuing his orders. This was not calling in an airstrike, adjusting artillery or even establishing local fire superiority. It was, "What tactics do I employ to kill the enemy without him killing any of my people or me?"

There is nothing wrong with a patrol leader factoring in trying to stay alive . . . in fact it was a good thing. It made him take extra care in working out his moves. And while it might sound self-serving, he was no good to his troops if he were dead.

Working through the short list of highly dangerous tactical options with an armed opponent in close proximity is mentally exhausting—as in extremely. The patrol leader must be able to visualize the contested ground in three dimensions and work out a plan of action. The final decision on what to do being arrived at under duress made more difficult because there is usually no one to consult with about what to do next. And no approved school solution for every situation.

Not everyone is cut out to lead combat patrols.

Beverly had once told Col. Randal he was "as laid back as a snake" or maybe that was Lady Jane quoting her. Either way it was a good description of how Lt. Starrett was going about the business of deciding on the best way to winkle the Nazi out without taking friendly casualties. He was neither rattled nor excited and he did not get in a hurry.

Important aspects of leadership.

The fact that Lt. Starrett was demonstrating an air of calm in the face of a tactical situation involving an armed and dangerous enemy and was not backing down—clearly his intent was to go in and kill the Nazi— gave his SOG operators and Col. Randal's reinforcements confidence in his ability to bring the contact to a successful resolution.

Besides, there *was* that 100-mile misdrop at Benevento. And the epic fight back to friendly lines. The SOG operators in the patrol today had been in his stick.

They trusted him implicitly.

One last option occurred to Lt. Starrett and that was to set fire to the brush and burn the Brandenburger out. The problem was the bushes were green. No joy.

"All right, boys, we have to go in and dig him out."

This sent a ripple of apprehension through a tightly focused group of special operators.

"We're going to break down into four two-man teams. Hale, you're on me. Captain Jaxx, you're on Sergeant Schmidt, sir. Lovat Scouts, you're on each other. General McKoy, sir, it's you and King. Colonel Randal—rear security."

Col. Randal said, "Negative . . ."

Lt. Starrett said, "Yes sir, rear security, you're not getting killed on my watch, Colonel."

Col. Randal wondered how many times in the past he had said those exact words to someone else. It did not feel so great when the role was reversed. But Lt. Starrett was the on-scene commander, and he was making the right call. As Raiding Forces Commanding Officer, he was the most difficult individual to replace if killed or incapacitated. Being thought valuable by your troops has its pluses—there were minuses.

He had just been sidelined for his own protection which was a new experience for him.

Lt. Starrett said, "We'll spread out with ten-yard spacing between teams and assume the low crawl position. When you hear three slaps on the stock of my carbine that's the signal to move out on line. Keep working your way forward until we make contact. Direct fire only. Don't try to use grenades in this thick stuff. Chances are they would probably just hit something and bounce back."

Col. Randal handed Capt. Jaxx his 9mm Beretta MAB-38 in exchange for his .30 Baby BAR. The shorter lighter submachine gun would handle better in the tight quarters. He could not believe he was being ordered to be a spectator by the most junior lieutenant in SOG.

The Lovat Scouts had their scoped 7X57 Westley Richards rifles slung over their shoulders, barrel down, in the event the opportunity for sniping presented itself. Both of them had brought M1 carbines for close work. They silently passed the red stag hunting rifles to Col. Randal. He stacked them against a rock where they would be safe.

Lt. Starrett said, "Everybody good to go—yes? Stand by to move out on my command."

Col. Randal was observing developments closely. Lt. Starrett had the advantage of arguably the best group of men in Raiding Forces assembled for his patrol. However, for any leader not 100 percent confident in his ability, this would be an intimidating team to give orders to. The young SOG officer was making it look easy.

As he and King came by, Lt. Gen. McKoy said, "Now you know how I've felt with you tryin' to keep me outta the action every chance you got all these many years, John."

Col. Randal said, "I'll take that under advisement in future."

The four two-man teams spread out in accordance to orders. Then they assumed the prone position. This was deadly serious business. Danger lay ahead.

Col. Randal did not enjoy watching events unfold.

WHAAAP! WHAAAP! WHAAAP!

On hearing Lt. Starrett's signal, the men disappeared into the underbrush. There was no sound. One second they were there and the next everyone was gone.

Like one of the Great Teddy's magic tricks—Hey, Presto!

Col. Randal had taken up a relaxed semi-prone position leaning back against one of the scrub brushes. He was marking time, not happy to be left out. Waiting was boring, even with an armed Nazi only yards away.

Anyone who had never done anything like this would probably never believe that could be true either.

In fact, Col. Randal was not even facing the direction where the Nazi was thought to be hiding. He was lying back looking down the slope of the escarpment toward the harbor. There was a loud ringing *CRAAAAACK* like the sound of a bullwhip popping one inch or less from his left ear and a small piece of bark flew off the trunk of the laurel he was leaning against.

A single round fired by the Brandenburger had somehow made its way through the dense entanglement and struck the trunk of the bush about an inch from where his head had been resting. It was as close a call as it was possible to have.

When being shot at, two sounds are heard: the *thump* and the *crack*.

The *crack* is the bullet breaking the sound barrier. The sonic shockwave makes a distinctive ringing snap when it goes past. You hear the sound behind you. People tend to duck when they hear the crack but the danger, at least for that round, is already over.

When you hear the *crack,* it means the bullet missed so it should be a reassuring sound. But it's not. Since the *crack* is heard *behind* you it is often confusing which direction the round was fired from. Throw in surprise, fear, shock, etc., and being under fire does not have much to recommend it.

No less a light than Prime Minister Winston Churchill had once written, "Nothing in life is so exhilarating as to be shot at without result." But Col. Randal had never found bullets cracking past to be all that thrilling.

The *thump* is the sound of the cartridge as it ignites in the chamber of a weapon when the firing pin hits the primer. However, at really close range or in thick cover you never hear it. Or possibly you hear it but don't notice it in all the excitement incidental to being shot at point-blank.

Strange the things that come to mind at times like this. Col. Randal had not thought about the *thump* since one of the first classes in the Cavalry Officers Basic Course where the student officers were seated in a defile and unseen rifles were fired over their heads from different directions and ranges. When the *crack* was heard, the student was supposed to start counting until the *thump* was heard, then mentally work through a math formula that would tell how far away the shooter was. Whoever dreamed up that lesson plan had clearly never been shot at with serious intent.

Col. Randal had never heard a *thump* in combat. Not even once. And he could not remember the formula.

He rolled over to study the situation. Was it aimed? A warning shot? A stray? It was impossible to see more than a few feet, if that, through the intertwined trunks of the laurels.

There was no way to observe what was going on with the patrol or the Nazi.

No return gunshots from any of the four teams. The only explanation was they were unable to see anything either, so everyone held their fire—which demonstrated restraint and perfect fire control discipline. The natural impulse upon being engaged by an unseen assailant is to fire up everything to your front—spray and pray. Moving up on an armed adversary you cannot put eyes on is exacting work requiring patience, skill and cool nerves. Movement is by inches with long pauses to study what lies ahead in between each small advance. There is no way to rush things.

Intense concentration and fire control discipline are a must— superior eyesight is a plus.

Col. Randal checked around his position. Nearby were three massive rocks jutting out of the ground, typical of the terrain found in parts of Castelrozzo. The tallest was a fifteen-foot pillar that was leaning at a slight angle uphill.

It offered possibilities.

The smaller of the two rocks might give him a leg up to make it to the top of the tall one. His orders were to pull rear security. Lt. Starrett had not specified where to place himself in order to conform to those instructions.

He decided to attempt to scale the tall pillar.

Col. Randal had taken climbing classes when attending the Commando Basic Training Center (CBTC) at Achnacarry, Scotland. Mountaineering was religion at the school. As a result of that experience, he pretty much hated rock climbing.

That did not mean Col. Randal was not reasonably good at it—he was.

Scaling the rock turned out to not be all that difficult. When he got to the top, sat down and dangled his legs off the end of the pillar, he had an excellent view of—nothing. Even with his Zeiss binoculars the laurels were so thick it was like trying to spot something through a shag carpet.

One of the things the instructors at Achnacarry tended to say at every opportunity was, "You lads are Commando soldiers, not bloody Supermen. There's no 'S' on your chest." Maybe not, but right now Col. Randal could have used X-ray vision.

The patch of scrub brush was about a hundred yards wide by three hundred yards deep. If the Brandenburger tried to sneak out either side, it would give him a shot. At the top of the escarpment there was an open belt for fifty yards before the plateau began.

Since he was armed with Capt. Jaxx's .30 Baby BAR, if the Nazi showed himself he would be within easy range. This was more like it. Col. Randal stuck one of Waldo's cigars between his front teeth and waited. Maybe Lt. Starrett's teams would flush the Brandenburger and give him a chance to snipe the Nazi.

After what seemed like a long time, a single gunshot popped. Col. Randal identified it as coming from a .30 M1 carbine. In the rush to stay on the trail of the wounded Nazi he had failed to ask Lt. Starrett what type of weapon the Sea Raider was carrying.

Since they were impersonating Americans, all the Nazis they had found so far had been armed with U.S. Army-issue of one type or another. Some had been .30 M1 carbines. Half the men in Lt. Starrett's patrol were carrying them. There was no way to know who fired the shot.

"CLEAR!"

In a few minutes King came out the right side of the brush two hundred yards up the slope with his 9mm SIG MKPO submachine gun slung. He was dragging a body. Lt. Gen. McKoy was right behind him carrying an extra M1 carbine.

Col. Randal stood up and waved. King spotted him, waved back and dropped the Nazi. No sense lugging a dead man all the way down the escarpment. Troops from the security battalion could come police him up.

Lt. Gen. McKoy and King walked to where Col. Randal was waiting, having climbed down off his perch. Before the rest of the patrol could arrive the three had a quiet word.

King said, "Nazi bled out before we got to him. It may have been a wound from an earlier engagement, Chief—there was a bandage. We removed it."

"What was the gunshot a second ago about?"

Lt. Gen. McKoy said, "I let one off. Chase deserves credit for runnin' down this evildoer. Demonstrated a lotta individual initiative takin' his boys out after the mornin' sweep had gone end of mission."

Col. Randal said, "Yes, he did."

"It's your call, John. I just set the deal up."

There is a little known rarely exhibited concept of leadership called "loyalty down." Loyalty is expected to travel up the chain of command. In the best military units, it flows back *down*.

Lt. Starrett arrived.

Col. Randal said, "Nice job, stud."

3
GODFATHER

BRIGADIER DUDLEY CLARKE MET WITH COLONEL JOHN Randal and Major the Lady Jane Seaborn in their suite. King was on the door with strict orders not to allow anyone inside. No exceptions. Brig. Clarke's arrival on Castelrozzo had not been expected. The Brigadier inviting Lady Jane to sit in was not typical behavior. The commander of A-Force never included women in important meetings even though his headquarters had what were called "Dudley's Duchesses", modeled on Raiding Forces Royal Marines.

Col. Randal clicked on.

He had no idea why.

Brig. Clarke said, "Where to start . . . in the past, Colonel, I have attempted to convince you, without providing much in the way of substantive details as to the why of it, that the Aegean Campaign is of immense strategic importance. In light of the recent setbacks I felt it was necessary for us to sit down together at our earliest convenience to give me an opportunity to reemphasize that what I have been trying to convince you of is still in full force and effect.

"Nothing has changed.

"Without getting into highly classified minutiae you are not now and will never be cleared for—what is important to know is the relationship between A-Force and Raiding Forces is about to become even closer. And more vital to the war effort than ever before."

Col. Randal was not aware he had a relationship with A-Force but the statement did not come as any surprise. Brig. Clarke was the preeminent puppet master staying in the shadows pulling strings. Probably a lot of people were working for him who had no idea they were.

Brig. Clarke said, "Naturally the recent debacle in the Aegean shall have an enormous impact on *how* you go about conducting future operations. The losses in no way hamper the *why* certain missions must be undertaken. Regrettably the motive behind them is to remain sealed until the end of the war plus seventy-five years. I shall never be able to explain the details of the reason I ask you to perform certain tasks. No one now living shall ever know what took place behind the scenes except for a handful of the principal players of which you are not one—sorry Colonel, State Secrets, Need to Know and all that."

Col. Randal said, "I see." Which meant he did not . . . or did not want to.

Brig. Clarke said, "Recently it was brought to my attention you were offered a rather lucrative position in the U.S. 82nd Airborne Division. Commander Fleming informed me he discussed with you his reasons for not being keen on your accepting the posting. On that I am in lockstep agreement with him.

"However, let me be perfectly clear. My motive for desiring you to remain in command of Raiding Forces is separate and apart from anything the Commander is involved in. Fleming has no direct knowledge of A-Force's long-range strategic plans though he may be read in at some later date. Since it is not possible for me to explain them to you, I certainly shall not be briefing him at this point.

"Is any of this making sense?"

Col. Randal maintained a perfectly straight face. Brig. Clarke had inadvertently revealed that he too was unaware of the details of OPERATION LONG NECK—good to know.

Lady Jane glanced at Col. Randal clearly amused by the doublespeak.

Col. Randal said, "Not exactly."

Brig. Clarke said, "Let me try to be more precise then. In the future A-Force—and apparently NID as well—intend to call on Raiding Forces to carry out certain strategic missions. The assignments, at least the ones my office originates, may appear innocuous or even nonsensical at times. Know that this is an illusion. In fact the missions you shall be tasked to carry out for A-Force are extraordinarily vital to the big picture."

Col. Randal had no idea what he was talking about.

Brig. Clarke said, "I do not know the details of what Fleming is working on and he does not have any clear idea of my operations even though the commander may believe he does. What I do know is it is imperative for you to remain in command of Raiding Forces at least through the opening of the Second Front. I require someone I can depend on to assist me in facilitating the progression of A-Force's long-range plans between now and that time, while not asking questions I am not at liberty to answer."

Col. Randal said, "Got it—maybe."

Brig. Clarke said, "Can I count on you not to make any career moves without discussing them with me first?"

What Brig. Clarke neglected to say was he had the ability to make the offer to command a parachute infantry regiment or any other assignment go away. No one, not even senior U.S. generals or British field marshals, was to be allowed to interfere with his interests intentionally or unintentionally. Should some ranking officer attempt to thwart A-Force, a confluence of seemingly unrelated events would conveniently converge to deflect the effort. The offending party would never suspect he had been checkmated by a silent hand. In the event the motive behind the interference was a petty power play, malicious or personal in nature—as happened from time to time in the higher echelons of the military—the offender would find himself transferred to command some remote outpost where he would play no further role of any significance in the war.

All very subtle—no fingerprints.

Brig. Clarke wielded God-like power. He had no hesitation about using it. And no one knew.

Col. Randal said, "If it weren't for you, Brigadier, we wouldn't be having this conversation. I'll discuss any possible change of my status prior to. You have my word."

He was not going anywhere. Something the A-Force commander would be aware of if he had detailed knowledge about the diamond interdiction program. He clearly did not—which was worth knowing.

Brig. Clarke said, "We have always worked well together from back in the early dark days. Went on the first Commando raid together. It is time to build on that relationship and take it to the next level.

"Now what I am about to tell you is classified above Top Secret..."

For the second time that day, Col. Randal was hearing the same caution almost word for word.

" . . . even codenames, acronyms etc. are not to be shared with anyone not presently in this room.

"Lady Jane, you were asked to sit in because you exert enormous influence on the Colonel. Keep him on the straight and narrow for King, Country, and me. I need to hear the both of you say you understand and will comply."

Lady Jane said, "I understand and will comply, Brigadier."

Col. Randal said, "Wilco."

Brig. Clarke said, "There is an organization called the London Controlling Section—LCS. It does in Europe what A-Force does in this part of the world—deceive the enemy. A certain Colonel John Bevins, whom I believe is known to you Lady Jane, has recently been appointed to be its Controlling Officer."

Lady Jane said, "My godfather."

Brig. Clarke failed to mention that he handpicked Col. Bevins for the assignment for exactly that reason.

Col. Randal said, "Thought you said he was your uncle."

Lady Jane said, "I shall explain later, John."

Brig. Clarke said, "I understand Raiding Forces maintains an element at Seaborn House for the express purpose of carrying out clandestine cross-channel operations in support of MI-6, SOE and quite possibly NID."

Col. Randal said, "Affirmative."

Brig. Clarke said, "The two of you shall be traveling to London in the next few weeks in order for Colonel Randal to have an interview with Colonel Bevins. If everything works out, as I am confident it shall, Raiding Forces Europe needs to start making preliminary plans to conduct additional highly classified small-scale operations from Seaborn House for the LCS. Those missions are to be accorded priority over all other commitments. The tasks must be performed to the letter. Simply go and do per instructions—your best men on each assignment."

Col. Randal said, "I'm going to need a few more details."

The "priority over your other commitments" might be a problem since he was not cleared to know the details of one operation being run from Seaborn House because it was so secret.

Brig. Clarke said, "All in due course, Colonel. Simultaneously with the work out of Seaborn House here in this part of the world Raiding Forces shall be carrying out the same type of activities for A-Force. The old firm back together again."

Col. Randal said, "Let's try not to get your ear shot off this time around."

KING SAID, "MRS. SEABORN AND CAPTAIN HONEYCUTT-Parker's boats are about to arrive at the dock, Chief."

Colonel John Randal and Major the Lady Jane Seaborn went downstairs to greet the two MAS boats.

Lady Jane said, "Did you fully understand what Dudley was talking about?"

Col. Randal said, "You're the one with all the intelligence training. I was counting on you to explain it to me."

Lady Jane laughed, "Secrets on top of secrets. Everyone has secrets, though some are not really secret."

Col. Randal said, "Learn anything?"

Lady Jane said, "Typical agency versus agency spy games with us triangulated in the middle. While Dudley may be aware an operation called LONG NECK exists, he does not know the details. And he has no idea about CARD GAME. We shall keep it that way. Other than that, it all seemed rather vague."

Col. Randal said, "Good report."

"Thank you, John."

"We need to talk."

"Dinner for two . . . our suite tonight?"

"Works for me."

Lieutenant Randy "Hornblower" Seaborn was waiting on the dock when Col. Randal and Lady Jane arrived. His PT Boat 10 had reached ABC earlier, having proceeded independently when the two MAS boats broke off to link up with the *King Duck* to drop off their passengers.

The two MAS boats moored alongside the pier. First to step off Brandy Seaborn's boat were Vice Admiral Sir Randolph "Razor" Ransom and Master Sergeant Mack Beckwith.

The only other passenger was Veronica Paige. She was aboard on orders from VAdm. Ransom. He had ordered her to return to Castelrozzo to resume managing MI-9's theatre-wide commitments—at least that is what the Razor told her. Sergeant Major Mike "March or Die" Mikkalis, was taking her place as the on-scene Escape commander, continuing to bring evaders off Leros by caique. The Allies had soldiers on the run on any number of islands: sailors from ships that had been sunk who had made it to an island and downed aircrew on islands around the Aegean who needed rescue.

In addition, MI-9 had the ongoing mission to train Royal Air Force (RAF) and United States Army Air Force (USAAF) aircrew stationed in the theatre on escape and evasion techniques in the event they found themselves shot down over enemy territory. And the Secret Intelligence Service (MI-6) and Special Operations Executive (SOE) continued to make requests for Escape caiques to insert or extract certain of their agents when the boats went to make a rescue.

The scope of Veronica's MI-9 (Escape) operation had exploded in recent days.

The *King Duck,* Lieutenant "Warthog" Finley's Landing Craft Tank, would be steaming in later tonight.

MSgt. Beckwith reported to Col. Randal, "Sir, it is my duty to report Private First Class Norvel Hansen MIA."

Col. Randal said, "What's the story, Sergeant Major?"

MSgt. Beckwith said, "Horn Dog went up the trail to bring down one last group of SBS personnel to be evacuated and never returned, sir. He didn't have to make the trip. I told him so. We ran out of time. The decision was made to depart Leros without him. We had a tight turnaround to return to Patmos so Skipper Finley could get the *King Duck* away before daylight—Hansen knew that. I'll be putting him in for a decoration . . . above and beyond, Colonel."

"Good."

A crowd of people from ABCHQ was gathering to welcome the boats back. As usual the group stood by observing silently. They were there to pay tribute to those home from a dangerous mission—not celebrate. Raiding Forces personnel were accorded celebrity status on returning from a mission. Then it was back to business. Glory is fleeting and the next operation was always out there over the horizon . . . waiting.

The war never stopped.

Col. Randal pulled VAdm. Ransom aside, "Dudley Clarke and Ian Fleming are on the island, sir."

VAdm. Ransom said, "I have no time for visiting firemen, Colonel; get rid of them."

Col. Randal said, "Unknown to the other, each of them has privately advised me they have changes to our mission profile in the works. We need NID and A-Force to understand Raiding Forces is in *your* chain of command, Admiral—at least in the Aegean."

VAdm. Ransom said, "I hear you loud and clear, Colonel. Thanks for informing me. This calls for a preemptive strike."

"We did not have this conversation, sir."

"What conversation?"

MAJOR ZARGO ARRIVED AT ABC. COLONEL JOHN RANDAL and Mandy were waiting for him at the dock when the Walrus dispatched to fly him to the island landed. The tough scar-faced commander of the Greek Sacred Squadron (GSS) was delighted to see them. The three had first met at RAF Habbaniya during the siege.

Col. Randal said, "Mandy has a situation that requires your personal attention, Major. Things are a little crazy around here at the moment, so I'll leave you in her capable hands. If you need anything, Captain Fawcett-Tatum has instructions to track me down."

Maj. Zargo said, "Given the choice, Colonel, who in their right mind would choose to deal with you when they could work with Mandy?"

Col. Randal said, "No one I can think of."

Mandy said, "Sorry to pull you away from your command on such short notice, Major. But we need to resolve the issue of a Greek national collaborating with a German Brandenburger here on Castelrozzo."

Maj. Zargo said, "Sorry to hear it. Collaboration with the Nazis is not unknown. Some of the things people do are difficult to explain."

As they made their way to the TOC, Col. Randal said, "When you're ready to fly out I have something for you to take back."

"What would that be, Colonel?"

Col. Randal said, "One hundred .30 M1 carbines in the cosmoline and twenty-three armory reconditioned .30 M1941 Johnson Light Machine Guns."

He knew the Greeks loved M1 carbines. They called them "Winchesters" even though they were made by a number of companies. Captain Billy Jack Jaxx carried one manufactured by Rock-Ola—the jukebox company. Now occasionally when he went on an operation his last command to his troops before moving out was "Let's rock" or "Time to boogie."

The .30 M1 carbine could deliver semi-automatic rapid fire out to 100 yards. The carbines were fast handling in close quarters, had slightly more range than 9mm or .45 caliber submachine guns, virtually no recoil and it was possible to carry a large amount of ammunition. Important considerations when making the selection of an individual weapon for raiding.

The shoulder-fired, magazine-fed .30 M1941 Johnson Light Machine Gun was the GSS LMG of choice.

Maj. Zargo said, "The arms will be much appreciated."

MAJOR DAVID LLOYD OWEN, THE SENIOR SURVIVING officer of the Long Range Desert Group, flew in next. The LRDG had demonstrated a fierce independent streak in the past. Their officers had a reputation for being prima donnas, which stemmed from their exalted status as the world's most elite desert-capable long-range reconnaissance specialists. For that reason Colonel John Randal elected to meet with Maj. Owen in his office to create a more professional atmosphere.

When taking command of a new subordinate unit, the new commander—in this case Col. Randal—has one chance to get it right. If things do not go well initially, no matter what happens later he will almost never be able to completely recover from the bad start. As Major General Sam Houston Blackwell liked to say, "First impressions are important."

Not all commanding officers understand that rank alone is not enough to carry them through. Col. Randal was not taking chances about first impressions. Standing on one side behind his desk was Lieutenant General "Geronimo" Joe McKoy. King was on the other side.

They were armed to the teeth.

Maj. Owen walked into the office and saluted. He had met Col. Randal briefly when the LRDG was based out of Siwa Oasis between the Qattara Depression and the Great Sand Sea. Today was his first visit to Advanced Base Castelrozzo. Compared to the primitive living conditions the LRDG was used to at Siwa, where they quartered under canvas in their glory days, the luxury of Mussolini's former palace came as a shock.

The ambience in Col. Randal's office was somewhat intimidating because of the two men standing behind the Colonel staring holes in him. One appeared to be a U.S. Army lieutenant general . . . if that was even possible. And the other a stone-cold killer.

Col. Randal returned the salute but did not bother to make introductions. He was prepared to relieve Maj. Owen on the spot if the conversation did not go the way he wanted. Pleasantries at this stage were irrelevant.

The twenty-six-year-old LRDG commanding officer did not realize Col. Randal was about to pass the traditional responsibility to set the tone of the initial interview with a new subordinate unit's commanding officer back to him—a neat trick.

Now it was Maj. Owen who only had one chance to get it right.

Col. Randal said, "Give me a report."

Maj. Owen said, "The LRDG has been decimated, sir. An ill-conceived raid on Levitra Island that may have been ordered as punishment because some of our patrolmen on a work detail on Leros failed to salute the commanding general when he drove past. We were not allowed to recon the island in advance, which proved disastrous. That failed mission, where the Group took more casualties in one night than it had in four years in the desert, followed by Leros being conquered by the Nazis has rendered the unit combat ineffective for the present.

"Approximately 50 LRDG patrolmen have been or are in the process of being brought off Leros with their arms. Over 125 of our people are missing or dead. The New Zealand government is pulling their personnel out of the LRDG after years of superlative service. The Kiwis are furious at GHQ Cairo for misusing their troops as line infantry. Altogether it's a crushing blow that shall be difficult to recover from, sir.

"The experience level of our losses cannot be replicated by simply transferring in new men. After standing down from desert patrolling the LRDG spent three months conducting intensive training in mountaineering, small boat handling, long-distance signaling . . ."

Col. Randal said, "What's your plan, Major?"

Maj. Owen said, "I have no plan, sir. Attempt to rebuild the LRDG? Disband it? Be absorbed into Raiding Forces? I am open to suggestions. The Levitra and Leros fiascos—wasted by bloody fools."

Col. Randal said, "How long have you been with the Group, Major?"

"Two years, sir."

"All right then here's what you're going to do," Col. Randal said. "Some of your Leros people will be arriving here later tonight. The LRDG barracks building on Castelrozzo was destroyed in an air raid while you were away. Link up with Lady Jane after we finish here for a tour of your new quarters.

"Take the rest of the afternoon off, then tomorrow morning start reorganizing. My intention is to utilize the LRDG in a pure reconnaissance role similar to your old Road Watch days on the Via Balbia. Only instead of your gun trucks you'll travel by caique and pull duty on distant islands deep behind the lines in German territory serving as Beach Watchers observing and reporting enemy sea traffic.

"That work for you?"

Maj. Owen said, "Yes, sir!"

Col. Randal said, "General McKoy has contacts in the Southern Rhodesian Reconnaissance Regiment. His guerrilla Force N mule cavalry battalion supported the Regiment in Abyssinia. The Rhodesians have agreed to allow us to recruit up to a platoon's strength of their people—they're yours.

"Admiral Ransom, commander of Small Raids Inc., who you'll meet later, is not giving up on trying to convince the New Zealand government to reconsider their decision to pull their people—or at least allow us to retain a few of your most experienced patrolmen—we'll see.

"So, what's my new LRDG going to look like, Major?"

Maj. Owen said, "Our basic reconnaissance element is the four-man party, sir. Two parties compose a patrol—one officer, two NCOs and eight other ranks per patrol. What I propose is a Group of two squadrons of eight patrols each. It shall take a while to recruit and train to full strength but if needed we are prepared to send out up to ten patrols almost immediately, sir."

Col. Randal said, "Been giving your next move some thought."

Maj. Owen said, "Quite right, sir. Only I never actually believed anyone would allow me the opportunity to present my plans much less implement them. You shall not regret your decision to allow me to reorganize like this, Colonel."

Col. Randal said, "Make sure I don't."

COLONEL JOHN RANDAL NOTICED LIEUTENANT COLONEL Sir Terry "Zorro" Stone, Major Zargo, Mandy and Captain Billy Jack Jaxx huddling in a corner of the TOC. He walked over to listen in.

Mandy said, "You cannot simply kick down the door, charge in and shoot everyone inside, Jack. I know you want to. Going in with guns blazing is not on this time."

Capt. Jaxx said, "Why not?"

Lt. Col. Stone said, "We have a Greek national, Chloe Hasapis, sheltering one of the Nazis. She is likely to be inside the residence at the time we make entry. This is an entirely different set of circumstances than Brandenburgers hiding in abandoned houses we can blow up."

Maj. Zargo said, "No reason to treat collaborators with silk gloves on my part simply because they happen to be Greek. While we should proceed with all due care to avoid offending the locals, I advise you to draw the line at putting your own people at risk for the sake of public relations."

Lt. Col. Stone said, "Quite right, you make a good point Major—still . . ."

Mandy said, "Just use your discretion, Jack."

Maj. Zargo said, "Chloe Hasapis is a dead woman if that helps with your planning."

Mandy said, "We shall turn her over to you to deal with, Major. Whatever you decide after that is fine with Raiding Forces. With your permission I would like the opportunity to question her prior to. It is likely she and the Brandenburger have discussed at least some aspects of the Sea Raider attack. She may be able to provide intelligence useful in rounding up the remainder of the Nazis at large."

Maj. Zargo, said, "If a plan can be formulated that does not increase the risks to the raid team, then by all means steps should be implemented to ensure the woman is taken alive. Personally, I like the idea of going through the door with Captain Jaxx—as you say—guns blazing. My country cannot tolerate the existence of collaborators without severe repercussions."

Lt. Col. Stone said, "Suggestions?"

Capt. Jaxx said, "Lure the Hasapis woman out of the house. Take her into custody. Then Major Z and I can go in and shoot the son of ..."

Mandy said, "Excellent!"

Maj. Zargo said, "Where were you when we needed you at Habbaniya, young Captain?"

"On trial at Fort Benning for shooting a prisoner I was escorting, sir."

"Found innocent?"

"Negative."

Maj. Zargo said, "Should you ever feel a need for a change of scenery I can always find a spot for a bloody-minded officer like you in the GSS."

Col. Randal said, "You can't have him."

Vice Admiral Sir Randolph "Razor" Ransom came into the TOC. Col. Randal walked over to confer with him.

VAdm. Ransom said, "I spoke with both Fleming and Clarke independently of each other. Neither of them made mention of new projects for Raiding Forces. I provided them adequate opportunity to do so. What does that tell you, Colonel?"

Col. Randal said, "We're going to need a plan, sir."

VAdm. Ransom said, "Already in the works."

Back in the meeting on the other side of the TOC, Capt. Jaxx was designated mission commander for the apprehension of Chloe Hasapis and takedown of the Brandenburger Sea Raider.

Under the Geneva Accords giving aid and comfort to an enemy combatant made a person a collaborator and/or traitor. If a Brandenburger was found in Chloe Hasapis' house and she was not being held against her will, Major Zargo was going to execute her. That was a given.

The consequences of collaboration were well known.

The first thing Capt. Jaxx did was send for the Lovat Scouts. He wanted them to put eyes on the target while the plan to raid it was being developed. They were assigned a radio operator each, then dispatched to take up hide positions covering the front and rear of the Hasapis house. The Scouts were instructed to call in situation reports (SITREPS) every thirty minutes. In the event a male was spotted inside the premises they were green-lit to take the shot if one presented itself.

That would be the best of all possible outcomes.

How to entice the woman to voluntarily leave the property of her own accord was proving to be more challenging than it originally sounded. Every option suggested was rejected for one reason or another. Major Clive Adair arrived, having been sent for by Capt. Jaxx.

It was hoped the "Mayor of Castelrozzo" might have a workable suggestion—no joy.

Maj. Adair did offer up a couple of cautions. "If the locals learn Hasapis is harboring a Nazi, word spreads fast on ABC and a mob might try to storm her house. An enraged crowd of women attacking your objective at the same time you are would pose problems."

Capt. Jaxx said, "That's a definite Rodge."

Maj. Adair said, "In the event the Hasapis woman is taken into custody and then released because it has been established the Brandenburger held her against her will, the local Greeks will never believe the story. Chances are they will murder her at the first opportunity unless we ship her off the island. Most likely there is no happy ending to this situation."

Maj. Zargo said, "I agree with Clive's assessment."

The two had worked together at Oasis X and were on a first-name basis — except no one knew Major Z's first name.

Captain Lionel Chatterhorn, Vulnerable Points Wing, came into the TOC, also having been summoned by Capt. Jaxx. A detective in civilian life, he offered a completely different take on the development.

"How did you obtain the information the Hasapis woman is harboring a fugitive?"

Mandy said, "A tip phoned in by one of the neighbors."

Capt. Chatterhorn said, "A woman, no doubt, there being few local men left on the island."

"Correct."

"How do you know your informant is telling the truth?"

There sometimes comes a point in mission planning when everything you thought you knew is suddenly called into question. It is like hitting a wall at full speed. Leaders at all levels in the military are taught never to use the word "assume."

But everyone does.

Capt. Chatterhorn said, "In this case the two women could be involved in a long-standing feud. There might have been a past love triangle. Maybe Ms. Hasapis cut down some of the informer's shrubbery. Neighbors can hate each other for a multitude of reasons or for no reason at all."

Until Capt. Chatterhorn questioned the validity of the intelligence, everyone had taken the phone tip at face value.

Capt. Jaxx said, "Whoa, maybe we might need to dial back a little."

Lieutenant General "Geronimo" Joe McKoy strolled over to join the conversation. Col. Randal was right behind him. Mandy brought them up to speed on Capt. Chatterhorn's take on the situation.

Lt. Gen. McKoy said, "Lionel's dead right. You never can tell. Stool pigeons have been known to work their own angle. Always best to confirm what your informants are tellin' you before chargin' in.

"You know snitches, Jack, your law enforcement background and all."

Capt. Jaxx said, "You'd think—want to run surveillance, General?"

Lt. Gen. McKoy said, "Fenwick and Ferguson are up there now in overwatch positions puttin' eyes on. They're in radio contact with the TOC?"

Capt. Jaxx said, "Affirmative."

Lt. Gen. McKoy said, "I'd say let's let Captain Chatterhorn handle the stakeout from here on out. He's Scotland Yard—gotta lotta practice at surveillin' evil-doers. OK by you Lionel?"

"Thought you would never ask, General."

Lt. Gen. McKoy said, "Jack, you plannin' on honchoin' the operation?"

"I'm thinking about letting Lieutenant Mascuch take it," Capt. Jaxx said. "We haven't had a chance to see him issue a full-fledged Op Order yet. I'll be in overall command. What's your thought, General?"

Lt. Gen. McKoy said, "Good idea. Let's see what he's got. Gives you and me time to start workin' out a way to persuade the Hasapis woman to exit the house before the balloon goes up. Might be a tricky proposition—her likely to be unpredictable and all. Could be some serious emotions runnin' hot when we hit that door."

Capt. Jaxx said, "We need background intel."

Mandy said, "Working on it, Jack."

Maj. Zargo said, "I would like to be involved when you extract the woman, Captain."

Capt. Jaxx said, "Can do, Major Z, sir."

"We need to interview the informant," Mandy said. "She should be able to draw a floor plan of the target. That would give us the perfect opportunity to evaluate her story."

Maj. Adair said, "Provide me the woman's full name or address and I shall have her brought to you here."

Raiding Forces officers might not be able to leap tall buildings in a single bound. They did not have superpowers. But when a roadblock presented itself, everyone pitched in and worked the problem. No recriminations, no finger-pointing—teamwork, teamwork, teamwork.

Col. Randal watched and listened, well-pleased.

MAJOR THE LADY JANE SEABORN, HAPPY AND BEVERLY Blackwell came into the TOC. They were there to link up with Major David Lloyd Owen. Captain Stephanie Fawcett-Tatum joined them.

Lady Jane said, "The moment we received word the LRDG had been attached to Raiding Forces, David, the three of us started making arrangements for your troops to have new quarters on Castelrozzo. The temporary barracks your lads stayed in before deploying to Leros was bombed by the Luftwaffe.

"Total loss, the building burned to the ground."

Maj. Owen said, "LRDG has experienced an unfortunate run of luck of late."

Lady Jane said, "We intend to change that, Major. You have a home in Raiding Forces. We shall be taking care of your needs. Captain Fawcett-Tatum is going to meet with you later to go over the details of how our team of female Royal Marines will provide you with support. Also we contract with locals for laundry service and to clean your billets. Your men will not be pulling work details.

"All you have to concern yourself with is rebuilding the LRDG back to the fabled unit it once was."

Beverly laughed, "Knowing Johnny, he'll probably have you sending out Coast Watch parties before sundown. Don't be surprised when he does."

Maj. Owen said, "Thanks for the warning."

Capt. Fawcett-Tatum said, "*King Duck* radioed thirty-four of your patrolmen are aboard. We have procured a new set of battle dress for each man. Not knowing their sizes there is a mix of everything. Your people shall have to trade around until we are able to compile an accurate clothing catalog for them. Once we have it, three sets of battle dress per patrolman shall be issued except for boots. Two pair each . . . you shall like our lightweight canvas-topped raiding boots.

"As soon as we have foot sizes we shall have them made for you in Cairo."

Beverly said, "Following a hot meal, a bunk with clean sheets is waiting for your boys when they arrive."

Maj. Owen said, "They shall appreciate the luxury after sleeping on the ground for the last three months."

Lady Jane said, "Let's go tour your new quarters. We cannot wait to show them to you. Follow me."

Having been precipitously ordered to report to Castelrozzo, Maj. Owen had not known what reception to expect. This was not it. Maybe for the first time since leaving the desert the Long Range Desert Group actually had found a home.

Based on what he was hearing so far, the LRDG never had it so good.

CAPTAIN BILLY JACK JAXX SAID, "ARE YOU PREPARED TO accept a mission?"

This was the standard question put to troop leaders about to be given a combat assignment. It sounded like a question but that was deceptive. No one in Raiding Forces ever said anything but "Yes, sir."

Lieutenant Ricky Mascuch said, "Yes, sir."

And he went on full-blown Red Alert.

This being as much a leader evaluation exercise as a combat operation, Capt. Jaxx went through the formal Warning Order protocol. The idea was to give the patrol leader, Lieutenant Mascuch, a Mission Statement for him to use as the basis to prepare his Warning Order and then his Operations Orders for the troops he would be leading.

During his preparation, he would have full access to the Raiding Forces Operations staff to answer his questions or address any needs.

"Situation: Friendly Forces: We are on Castelrozzo Island located in the Dodecanese Chain of the Aegean Sea.

"Enemy Forces: Brandenburger Sea Raiders in platoon(-) strength conducted a failed raid on Castelrozzo. The Germans have gone into hiding on the island. Following a series of counter-Brandenburger operations most of the Nazis are accounted for. One is reported to be in hiding in the residence of a local Greek woman—Chloe Hasapis, who is alleged to be providing him sustenance and comfort for reasons not understood at this time.

"The location of the house is known. A pair of two-man teams led by Lovat Scout snipers currently have it under observation at this time.

They are green-lighted to take out the Brandenburger in the event the opportunity presents itself.

"Mission: Take the female Greek homeowner into custody outside her house if at all possible. Following the apprehension of the woman a six-man assault team is to make entry, kill or capture the Nazi hiding inside—priority to taking him prisoner . . ."

MAJOR TRAVIS MCCLOUD, MAJOR DUKE SLATER AND Major Jack Dance walked into the TOC responding to a summons from Colonel John Randal. The three had been in Italy to greet the 575 Ranger Task Force men from their commands trickling in from the scattered drop on Benevento. Major General Sam Houston Blackwell had flown fifty-three Rangers back with them. Those men were at Raiding Forces Headquarters outside of Cairo getting ready for a week of leave prior to reporting to Castelrozzo for duty. By now over half the Rangers who had made the jump had returned to friendly lines.

Col. Randal met with the officers individually in his office—which was getting a lot more use lately.

Maj. McCloud was first. He had joined Raiding Forces as a member of the American Volunteer Group (AVG) before the U.S. entered the war. An airborne infantry officer at Fort Benning, he had been recruited by the Counterintelligence Corps (CIC) to be embedded in the AVG forming to serve in Egypt. His assignment was to monitor Raiding Forces. He liked what he saw and became a full-fledged member, choosing to remain after the AVG was disbanded following Pearl Harbor.

Not the original intent of the CIC.

Col. Randal said, "General Ridgway of the 82nd Airborne Division and General Lee of the 101st both need battle-experienced battalion commanders. They asked me if I had anyone to recommend—promotion goes with the assignment.

"You interested, Travis?"

"Trying to deep-six me at long last, sir?"

"Negative! I hope you turn down the offer. That said, you're a West Point graduate, a highly skilled veteran special operations officer with a serious amount of time in combat and one of the most capable troop commanders I have ever served with. Take the assignment and my guess is you find yourself in command of a regiment before long. The army needs experienced officers commanding its troops—you're one of the best."

Maj. McCloud said, "This is quite a shock. Mind if I think about it, sir?"

Col. Randal said, "You just did. Congratulations, Colonel. It's your call but I suggest the 101st. They'll be the next airborne division to deploy to the ETO. Go to the States, train your new battalion, take some time to enjoy yourself. You have a bright future, Travis."

"Thank you, Colonel. I appreciate you looking out for my best interests. It has been an honor and a privilege to serve under you—I mean that, sir."

Col. Randal said, "Don't mention to the others what we've talked about. I'd like to get their initial reaction the same way I got yours. See Stephanie, she'll make your travel arrangements. Here's one of Waldo's cigars to celebrate your promotion."

"I've learned a lot from you, Colonel . . ."

There was not much more to be said. People come and go in the military. But leaving a unit can be hard—on everyone.

The two of them had seen a lot together.

Maj. Duke Slater was in next.

Col. Randal said, "Duke, General Ridgway of the 82nd Airborne Division needs battalion commanders. Promotion goes with the job."

Maj. Slater said, "Are you transferring me, sir?"

"Negative. I am merely a messenger proffering the offer."

"I like it here, Colonel."

"Understood. However, American mothers deserve to have their sons led by the best."

"What do you recommend I do, sir?"

"Take the assignment, Duke. If it doesn't work out to your satisfaction, contact me. You'll always have a place in Raiding Forces. I'll transfer you back in forty-eight hours or less—just say the word."

Maj. Slater said, "Don't feel great about it but I'll accept the assignment. I'm holding you to your promise. As I said, I like it in Raiding Forces, sir."

Col. Randal said, "Congratulations, Colonel. Take one of Waldo's cigars to celebrate. Talk to Stephanie—she'll coordinate your transportation."

Maj. Jack Dance was last. "Travis and Duke left here with cigars. Someone having a baby or did they finally make you a general, sir?"

Col. Randal said, "The COs of both the 82nd and 101st Airborne Divisions have asked me to recommend qualified officers to take over battalions. You're the most experienced candidate I have since you've been commanding the 10th Ranger Battalion for over a year—interested?"

"Not a chance, Colonel. I'm where I need to be. Besides, if I left Raiding Forces I wouldn't be around to see what's going to happen next. Situation we're facing now . . . got to be interesting."

Col. Randal said, "You're passing up an automatic promotion to Lieutenant Colonel."

Maj. Dance said, "No big deal, sir. I'm National Guard. I won't be staying in after the war. My plan is to go back home to Florida, develop beachfront real estate and be a weekend warrior."

Col. Randal said, "Not turning down the opportunity because of Stephanie, are you?"

"Sir, I respectfully refuse to answer that question..."

COLONEL JOHN RANDAL AND MAJOR THE LADY JANE Seaborn were sitting at a small candlelit table in their second-floor suite. White tablecloth. Fine china. Crystal goblets. Egyptian cotton napkins. GG had personally come to ensure the food had been delivered and all the details of the intimate setting had been made to his satisfaction.

King was at the desk outside the door. Captain Pamala Plum-Martin was sitting with him, as she had begun doing lately when not flying.

No one had seen that relationship coming.

Brandy Seaborn was hosting a dinner for the VIPs who had descended on Castelrozzo. All Raiding Forces officers who were on the island were in attendance. Col. Randal and Lady Jane would join them later.

It had been a busy day. Tomorrow promised to be more of the same. Col. Randal needed to spend time with each of the senior visitors. Long-range plans that would serve as the outline of operations for the foreseeable future needed to be made.

It was in Raiding Forces' best interest to get it right. The Germans had all the advantages—at least on paper.

Colonel Randal saw possibilities.

Lady Jane said, "How are the plans to capture the Brandenburger working out?"

Col. Randal said, "Jack and General McKoy are hitting the house where the Nazi is hiding at first light. Jack's letting Lieutenant Mascuch be the raid team commander. He's turned the operation into a training exercise."

Lady Jane laughed. "Exactly the way you taught him."

Changing the subject, Col. Randal said, "OK, I'm confused. Explain this godfather relationship with Colonel Bevins."

Lady Jane said, "In England agreeing to be a godfather is an important commitment not to be undertaken lightly. Godparents are selected with care. There are responsibilities. At the time when I told you Colonel Bevins was my uncle I was not quite sure you would understand the significance of my having a godfather in my life, especially after my family was killed in a plane crash."

Col. Randal said, "Some people have them in the U.S. but they're usually only honorary."

Lady Jane said, "In England, godfathers serve as role models, mentors, confidants, someone to go to for guidance. It is understood in the event of the death of the parents the child is raised by the godparents. They are addressed as 'uncle' or 'aunt'—I was not misleading you."

"So, you're close?"

"Very."

"What can you tell me about the London Controlling Section?"

"Other than the LCS having a highly classified function that seems to combine elements of intelligence, psychological warfare and deception, I know virtually nothing about it. Presumably it is modeled on A-Force.

"Uncle John asked me to be the committee's secretary."

Col. Randal said, "When did that happen?"

Lady Jane said, "Right after he was appointed 'London Control.'"

"And you turned down the offer?"

Lady Jane laughed. "You may have transferred out two of our best officers today, John Randal, but you are not getting rid of me that easy."

"So why didn't you mention it?"

"It was a non-issue. You know I always tell you everything. We never keep secrets from each other, babe."

Col. Randal said, "OPERATION CREEK."

Lady Jane's green eyes flashed momentary panic. "You were away. With all the drama since, I failed to say anything. Mandy, Pamala, Beverly and I flew in to Mormugao, Goa, with Red, hosted a party for the social set, then slipped out of the colony across the border to India. An SOE team recruited primarily from a territorial unit called the Calcutta Light Horse came in by sea and blew up a German freighter interned in the harbor known to be transmitting Allied shipping data.

"A girl's trip is all there was to it."

Col. Randal knew from talking to Jim Taylor that their E&E back to India had consisted of riding horseback for over a hundred miles through partially jungle terrain. "We need to be straight with each other, Jane. No secrets. No holding back."

"Agreed, John."

"Honesty is the best policy—100 percent."

Lady Jane said, "Beverly said she overheard you and Bronc talking. What does "outkicked your coverage" mean as it relates to me?"

Col. Randal lied, "I have no idea."

4

TOO MUCH CLOAK
NOT ENOUGH DAGGER

LIEUTENANT RICKY MASCUCH CONDUCTED HIS LEADER'S recon before last light. The former 551st Parachute Infantry Battalion, "GOYA" (Get Off Your Ass), had experienced a long war but until the drop on Patmos it had all been spent in training. The battalion had gone through Jump School in the Frying Pan at Fort Benning, Georgia, served in Panama, and then been shipped back to Camp Mackall in North Carolina where Colonel John Randal had recruited him.

The 551st PIB was one of the most overtrained parachute infantry units in the U.S. Army.

Lt. Mascuch suspected his assignment was a setup. Captain Billy Jack Jaxx had a reputation as the No. 1 lead-from-the-front hard charger in an outfit full of hard chargers. He was not the type to delegate the raid team takedown of a Nazi in hiding to someone else without an ulterior motive.

What might that be? His best guess—Capt. Jaxx wanted to observe him issue an order, task organize his team and execute his assignment. No problem. He knew how to conduct a patrol, although there had never been a live enemy armed and ready to fight on the objective when he had done it before.

It is said in the Army, "You fight how you train."

Which gave Lt. Mascuch something to think about. Not everything they tell you in the Army is true.

Capt. Jaxx had instructed him to pick six men. First thing, Lt. Mascuch went in search of Master Sergeant Mack Beckwith. He wanted the best people and needed his advice on who that might be.

"Sergeant Major, we have a report of a Brandenburger Commando hiding in a house. I've been ordered to take out a patrol to neutralize him. I need an assistant PTL—you interested?"

MSgt. Beckwith studied the young officer carefully. It took a lot of guts for a brand-new-to-the-unit lieutenant to request the senior NCO to act as his assistant patrol leader.

And it was smart.

In his opinion, the fact Lt. Mascuch would ask instead of order spoke well for him. The role of a Sergeant Major is to be the conduit between the enlisted troops and the commander, meaning Col. Randal. From time to time, Sergeants Majors have also been known to counsel lieutenants and captains they felt could use the benefit of their wisdom. This was usually an experience no recipient of said wise counsel ever wished to repeat. Company grade officers—especially lieutenants—are well advised to tread lightly around Sergeants Majors and not ask them to be their assistant anything.

On the other hand, while they do not advertise the fact, there is nothing a senior NCO likes better than mentoring a talented young officer who seeks out his help. Especially one who treats him with the same degree of military courtesy normally accorded field grade officers or above. It does not happen as often as might be imagined.

MSgt. Beckwith said, "What do you know about the mission, sir?"

Lt. Mascuch said, "A local Greek woman is reported to be sheltering a Nazi in her home not far from here, Sergeant Major. With daylight fading fast we'll probably have to wait and hit the place at first light tomorrow. General McKoy and Captain Jaxx are working on a plan of action to lure the woman out of the house so she doesn't get killed in the crossfire.

"As soon as they have her in custody the plan is to make a dynamic entry and light the Nazi up—Captain Jaxx and Major Zargo will be the point element on the entry team."

MSgt. Beckwith said, "In that case, Lieutenant, we'd best move out and put eyes on while we still can."

"Roger that."

COLONEL JOHN RANDAL AND MAJOR THE LADY JANE Seaborn made their way downstairs to the dinner Brandy Seaborn was hosting. They invited King and Captain Pamala Plum-Martin to accompany them. In addition to the senior officers who had arrived on the island earlier, Major Baltimore "Mongo" Farquhar, MC, CO of the Lancelot Lancers, and Captain "Dynamite" Dick Coogan were also present—the latter having been tapped to be Major Duke Slater's replacement.

Captain Roy Kidd was senior with longer service in Raiding Forces, making him the obvious candidate for promotion, but his role in CARD GAME prohibited him from being away from RFHQ for extended periods of time.

In addition to the senior personnel and squadron commanders, every Raiding Forces officer on ABC at the time was in the room, as were all of Lady Jane's Royal Marines, FANYs and Wrens who staffed the TOC. It was the perfect opportunity to have what the military called a "dining in." For Raiding Forces officers it was a rare chance to visit with each other face to face. Most of their contact with each other came over the radio.

There was an uncharacteristic air of doom and gloom in the room even though GG had outdone himself for the event. His life ambition was to relocate to Hollywood and open a restaurant to cater to movie stars. Unknown to him, Lady Jane had decided to make it happen. She had a history of rewarding people who had taken care of Col. Randal at some point in the past.

As they made their way to the head table, Col. Randal spotted a surprise guest he had not known was on the island—Brigadier General William "Wild Bill" Donovan. When the general learned of the British surrender on Leros he had flown in to evaluate what effect it would have on Col. Randal's operations going forward. With the exception of

Detachment 101 working behind Japanese lines in Burma, Raiding Forces was the only large-scale mission OSS had operational worldwide.

Brig. Gen. Donovan needed Raiding Forces to maintain its island base. He had long-range plans for Castelrozzo to be used as a stepping stone for inserting OSS Operational Group (OG) personnel into the Balkans. That made Wild Bill the third officer from three separate intelligence agencies with high hopes of using Raiding Forces to facilitate future operations of their own design.

By any measure, it was an unusual amount of interest in such a small—even with the SBS and LRDG attached—special operations unit.

When Col. Randal and Lady Jane made their way to the main table at the front of the room, Lieutenant Colonel Sir Terry "Zorro" Stone tapped a crystal glass with a butter knife. Everyone in the room stopped what they were doing and looked up.

Col. Randal held out a chair for Lady Jane but remained standing. "Before we move on to dessert I'll keep this short and simple. The war in our AO has been a disaster. The Germans have captured all the major islands. Their navy rules the waves and the Luftwaffe has achieved air superiority over the ATO. Castelrozzo is the last base in the Aegean still in Allied hands.

"Lady Jane informed me earlier tonight we're not giving up her island."

Everyone laughed but it was an uneasy laugh.

Col. Randal said, "The Nazis believe they hold all the cards. That's fine. All it means is now we've got 'em right where we want 'em."

The room went dead silent.

"The impending campaign in the Aegean is a lot like what Captain Hoolihan and I found when we parachuted into Abyssinia. The Italians had established outposts at regular intervals along their high-speed roads to guard them. They were sitting targets.

"We attacked. The Italians reinforced. Then we moved on to the next weak outpost and attacked it.

"The Aegean has at least 1,200 islands . . . possibly as many as 6,000 according to Doctor Winthrop. No one knows for sure. When the Germans garrison the inhabited islands, as they'll be forced to do if for no other reason than to make a demonstration of force to the Greeks, we can raid them at our leisure—the way the Headhunter, General McKoy, Mr. Treywick and I did those Italian outposts. With so many targets, the Nazis will never know where we'll strike next or when. And there's not one thing they can do about it.

"Raiding Forces is going back to basics. Guerrilla war from the sea and plenty of it. Hit and run, then do it again somewhere else at a time and place of our own choosing—constant pressure."

Lieutenant General "Geronimo" Joe McKoy was sitting at the head table. He stood and began clapping. Captain Billy Jack Jaxx jumped up from his table across the room, cheering. Soon everyone in the audience was on their feet. If those in attendance had been anticipating a Churchillian last-ditch "we will fight them on the beaches . . ." type pep talk, what they got was a simple Mission Statement—no doom and gloom.

It was on.

CAPTAIN BILLY JACK JAXX, CAPTAIN ROY KIDD AND Mandy were in Beverly's suite. The former UT beauty queen had a collection of 78 rpm records and a turntable. They were having a great time dancing. Jack Cool and Capt. Kidd may have been the two worst dancers in the history of music but they made up for lack of talent with enthusiasm.

Down the hall, Waldo Treywick and Rikke "Rocky" Runborg were in her room enjoying a nightcap. Waldo had flown in from Cairo where he had been meeting with The Three. It was something he did periodically to let the mobsters know he was keeping his eyes on them. The gangsters were expected to keep Mr. Big, meaning him, current on every illicit diamond transaction in the Middle East and needed to be reminded from time to time what would happen in the event they failed in their mission.

At every opportunity Waldo mentioned the "second mouse gets the cheese"—a reminder the original Big Five, the first mouse, had flown off into the wild blue yonder in a pilotless plane.

Rocky was not cleared to be read into LONG NECK. She thought he had been on a business trip. Which was true. Waldo bought and sold ivory as a cover for his involvement in the diamond interdiction program.

While not getting rich, the ex-ivory poacher was turning a respectable profit as an ivory trader.

Down the hall Alex "Cat" Gataki was scratching her nails on Captain Butch "Headhunter" Hoolihan's door.

Lieutenant Colonel Sir Terry "Zorro" Stone and Major the Earl Lord George Jellicoe were on the roof with Red and one of her Flying Clipper girlfriends swimming nude in the Royal Marines' private pool. The two officers had known each other all their lives and shared a common interest—women.

Major Jack Dance and Captain Stephanie Fawcett-Tatum were taking a walk along the beach.

Brigadier General William "Wild Bill" Donovan, James "Baldie" Taylor, Commander Ian Fleming—who was disappointed Beverly had disappeared after the dining in—and Major Peter Fleming were having a drink in the small bar on the ground floor of RFHQ. This was a golden opportunity for the intelligence officers to compare notes on current and future operations of mutual interest.

And to practice their tradecraft by withholding secrets while trying to learn those of the others—the first liar never had a chance.

Major the Lady Jane Seaborn and her favorite cousin, Brandy, were in the master bedroom of her second-floor suite stretched out across the super king-sized bed laughing, talking and smoking cigarettes like teenage girls. Happy was on the floor and not so happy because he was not allowed to be on the bed with them.

King and Captain Pamala Plum-Martin were on the couch in the living room.

Outside by the suite's private pool, Colonel John Randal and Lieutenant General "Geronimo" Joe McKoy were having a drink, watching the twinkling lights on the Turkish mainland and enjoying a couple of Waldo's cigars.

Col. Randal said, "Have any idea why Churchill is so determined to conduct this campaign in the Aegean?"

Lt. Gen. McKoy said, "Yeah, I do, John."

"Would you care to share?"

"I don't know anything anyone else doesn't, but I can read a map," Lt. Gen. McKoy said. "You've got to back out and take a look at the big picture. I'm talkin' all 'a Europe."

"So what does your map study tell you, General?"

"The quickest way to win this war is to go straight across the English Channel, drive on Berlin and kill Hitler—both 'a us know that. Problem is we don't have the manpower or equipment to do it right now. Just not feasible even though Marshall and Eisenhower lobbied for it six months ago—what you get when you've got greenhorns at the helm.

"Throw in the complication of the British and Americans both wantin' the same result but havin' entirely different ideas on how to go about achievin' it and you got yourself the makin's of a genuine inter-Allied coalition problem."

Col. Randal said, "I see."

Which meant he had no idea what Lt. Gen. McKoy was talking about, how it applied to the current military situation in the Aegean or related to Raiding Forces.

Lt. Gen. McKoy said, "Marshal and Eisenhower want to quit pussy footin' around and go straight at Nazi Germany, and who's to blame 'em . . . not me. Churchill, well, he saw what happened in the last war with both sides stalemated in the trenches over in France killin' each other for four years to no gain and he ain't real eager to do that again."

"Can't blame him," Col. Randal said.

"The Prime Minister's idea is to bleed the Third Reich usin' indirect means before goin' in for the kill."

"What does that mean?"

"Nazis tied down in the Aegean, in Italy and the Balkans are Nazis who won't be sittin' behind the Atlantic Wall on the beaches 'a France armed and ready when we do come stormin' ashore to open up the Second Front," Lt. Gen. McKoy said. "Churchill ain't exactly wrong but not doin' much of 'a job sellin' it in Washington."

Col. Randal said, "So Raiding Forces' mission is to draw off Germans from the main point of attack."

"There you go—only nobody's going to tell us that till after the war's over," Lt. Gen. McKoy said. "Classified. Need to Know."

"I like it."

"Yeah, it's a good mission. Every Nazi sittin' on an island out here in the middle 'a nowhere twiddlin' his thumbs is one who ain't gonna be pullin' a trigger when our boys finally do hit those beaches in France."

Col. Randal said, "I know you're not thrilled about having to take over LONG NECK . . ."

Lt. Gen. McKoy said, "Ain't unhappy about it either, John. Just didn't want to get tied down on the sidelines in the Congo is all. I was afraid you might be benchin' me."

"I quit trying to do that a long time ago, General."

"Yeah, well, that's what I was thinkin' when you assigned me the job."

Col. Randal said, "My thought was to put my best officer in command of Raiding Forces' most strategic operation. Not that I have any idea what LONG NECK's about."

Lt. Gen. McKoy said, "I've studied the Congo backward and forward till I thought I'd go blind in the face. The only natural resource the colony produces that I don't know all the uses for is uranium. And it doesn't seem all that important.

"Makes wristwatches and compasses glow in the dark is about all."

Col. Randal said, "We're not interdicting uranium—we're going after diamonds. Or to be more precise . . . diamond *smugglers.*"

Lt. Gen. McKoy said, "Well there you go. I've been thinkin' Lady Jane might've nailed it a while back. Diamonds could be smoke and mirrors. Sorta like one 'a Teddy's tricks—him distractin' the audience with one hand while he makes the magic happen with the other. LONG NECK may be nothin' more than 'a way to connect the dots from diamonds to smugglers to Nazis."

Col. Randal said, "Run that by me again."

Lt. Gen. McKoy said, "Traffickers have the means and opportunity to smuggle *uranium* as well as sparklers. Take out the smugglers and it don't get smuggled. End of story."

"Could be right."

"The whys and wherefores don't matter much—except for the part where we get to keep the sparklers," Lt. Gen. McKoy said. "Everyone from the President on down wants those smugglers to disappear without sayin' so. We're makin' it happen big time under the guise 'a interceptin' diamond shipments—could be the stones are just the distractor.

"Now you see smugglers, now you don't, Hey, Presto—mission accomplished."

Col. Randal said, "You just answered your own question as to why I made you the officer-in-charge of LONG NECK—figuring out things like that."

THE *KING DUCK* STEAMED IN AT 2330 HOURS. MAJOR THE Lady Jane Seaborn and Happy were already on the dock with Captain Stephanie Fawcett-Tatum, Beverly and Mandy when Colonel John Randal and Master Sergeant Mack Beckwith arrived. Captain Billy Jack Jaxx showed up a few minutes later. He had no real reason to be there but typically could be counted on to be available in the event his services became needed—the art of being a good officer is to be in the right place at the right time.

Major the Earl Lord George Jellicoe and Major David Lloyd Owen were on hand as well to greet their troops returning from Leros.

Disembarking from the Landing Craft Tank in the dark was not optimal. Castelrozzo was under strict blackout restrictions. No lights were showing—except in the Beaten Zone. The Luftwaffe had air superiority. Their nearest landing ground was on Rhodes—only a thirty-minute flight away.

Why take a chance?

As the troops filed off the LCT they were met by MSgt. Beckwith who directed them to their individual assembly areas. There was one for the Special Boat Squadron, the Long Range Desert Group and for the former Habbaniya Strike Force personnel from the 1st Battalion, King's Own Royal Regiment. Though relieved to have been evacuated, the men were bitter and sullen.

Troop morale was at rock bottom.

Major Valentine Fabian, former commander of Strike Force, reported to Col. Randal.

"Have your people form up, Major."

"Yes, sir."

Lady Jane said, "Nice to see you again Major Fabian. You remember Mandy Paige from Habbaniya. She's about to escort your people to our open mess for a hot meal. Then she will show them to the temporary barracks they'll occupy until your men's duty assignments can be determined—a shower and new uniforms are waiting. Welcome to Castelrozzo."

Lady Jane had met the Strike Force commander briefly after parachuting into Habbaniya with Rita Hayworth and Lana Turner, Col. Randal's slave girls, before the counterattack against the Rebels of the Golden Square had taken the King's Own to Baghdad and other desert battles.

Maj. Fabian said, "On behalf of my troops, thank you Lady Seaborn. The lads shall appreciate the first-class treatment. Not an experience they have enjoyed in quite a while."

Col. Randal said, "This is Major Jellicoe. He is here to extend an invitation for your men to volunteer for service in the SBS. You two get together to discuss the details. I've promised the Major first shot at recruiting. Those of your people who do not opt for the Special Boat Section will be given the opportunity to join one of our Raiding Forces squadrons—both units will essentially be carrying out the same type of missions. Or they can apply for the Long Range Desert Group to perform strategic reconnaissance. I want your people to serve in the unit of their choice. Those who do not volunteer for special service will be transferred to a battalion in your regiment."

"What are my prospects, sir?"

"We'll talk later, Major. We try to put round pegs in round holes in Raiding Forces. Understand . . . you and any of your Strike Force people who decide to stay on with us will have to complete parachute training, small boat handling, mountaineering, etc. before being assigned as individual replacements to their chosen units within Raiding Forces. Won't be an easy transition—but I'll have a job for you if you want it."

"Understood, sir."

Mandy walked up and hugged Maj. Fabian, she was glad to see him. The siege of RAF Habbaniya tended to have that effect on veterans of the battle when they met up—minus the hugging. Then Mandy left to guide the King's Own Strike Force personnel to ABCHQ for their hot meal.

Beverly escorted the SBS while Lady Jane took charge of the LRDG which, from all appearances, she was taking on as a personal project.

Capt. Jaxx said, "Lucky Long Range Desert Group."

Col. Randal said, "Now if they'd only lose the word Desert . . ."

"You think the LRDG realize people are laughing at their name, sir?"

"Not as hung up on their past as those people are."

"We're going to need to give the LRDG an attitude adjustment, Colonel."

"That is a fact."

COLONEL JOHN RANDAL AND CAPTAIN BILLY JACK JAXX walked into the TOC together. Commander Ian Fleming was there chatting up one of the FANYs. Jack Cool broke off for his room because he had a late date.

Col. Randal said, "Commander, do you have a minute?"

As they were walking to Col. Randal's office, Cdr. Fleming said, "What can I do for you, sir?"

"I'd like clarification concerning the mission planned to coincide with the Allies landing in France."

Cdr. Fleming said, "Never mentioned France, Colonel. Quite sure I said the Second Front. One in my line of work must be discerning."

Col. Randal said, "If you want to continue to work with me on your projects, Fleming, quit playing secret agent. I don't need classified details. But give me the overview or find someone else."

"The trait I have always found most admirable in you, Colonel—other than your exquisite taste in women—is your willingness to take on projects for the Naval Intelligence Division without the melodrama others put us through," Cdr. Fleming said. "At least until now. What is different this time, might I ask, sir?"

Col. Randal said, "Too many commitments. Not enough people. I need information to allocate my resources. You want to drop in unannounced, dangle the prospect of another mission for Raiding Forces sometime in the future and then spring the details on me at a time to be announced when it suits you—not going to happen, Commander."

Cmdr. Fleming said, "Enough time to plan. Is that what is troubling you, sir?"

Col. Randal said, "The obsession with Need to Know is keeping those who actually do need to know certain things from being able to. I'm not even cleared for what one of my own teams is doing out of Seaborn House. I can't brief all of my people on every mission we're running out of ABCHQ."

Cdr. Fleming said, "You are quite serious about rejecting NID's offer I presume?"

"If you want Raiding Forces for your operation, give me a briefing," Col. Randal said. "I need to know who, what, when and where. I don't require the why—which should conceal any legitimate secret."

"Sounds like you have developed a problem with the way we in the cloak and dagger crowd do business, Colonel."

"Roger that," Col. Randal said. "Too much cloak not enough dagger."

Cdr. Fleming said, "Quite! What if I were to provide you with a brief sketch of one of the targets of the highly classified operation I spoke to you about? It should adequately serve as an example of the kind of thing NID and possibly OSS shall be wanting Raiding Forces to carry out starting the day the Second Front is opened."

"Let's hear it."

"This is above Top Secret. I should not be sharing it with you at this point . . ."

"Get to it, Fleming."

"There is a small group in Germany called the Vril Society. It is headed up by one Marina Orsic—a lady reputed to be the most beautiful woman in the world. She is what is described as a spiritualist. However, instead of communicating with the dead, she is in contact with what she claims are 'super beings'—extraterrestrials who created us or upgraded us genetically, organized our ancient civilization and lived among us for a time as gods and goddesses."

Col. Randal said, "This is not the time . . ."

Cdr. Fleming said, "Oh, it gets better. The super beings telepathically provided Miss Orsic with the blueprints for a saucer-shaped craft capable of flying two thousand miles per hour plus, make ninety-degree turns at speed, travel to the stars—carry bombs. The woman has no engineering or architectural technical training. It is not possible she could have designed the plans on her own or that anyone now living could have done it for her.

"We have a copy of them and that *is* classified Top Secret Need to Know and no one has the need—not even you, Colonel."

Col. Randal said, "I'm done here."

"The Nazis are building it."

"You're kidding."

"Not after the dressing-down you gave me," Cdr. Fleming said. "I am being candid, Colonel. We cannot allow that mystery craft to be completed. It would be the ultimate Wonder Weapon. By the time the Second Front opens I am expected to have expanded my Red Indians—30 Assault Unit will be the cover for a beefed-up Raiding Forces Europe. Elements under your command will airland or go ashore with the first wave to carry out specific national level tasks.

"I repeat, the purpose of the exercise shall be for Raiding Forces to go in with the invading troops either by sea, glider or parachute to capture high-value individuals who possess certain knowledge that will give the U.S. and Great Britain a technological advantage post-war. We need to get our hands on the best rocket scientists, naval engineers, technicians, aircraft designers, etc. And we need to do so before the Russians do. Your mission, should you choose to accept it, will be to capture the most beautiful woman in the world."

Col. Randal said, "Now that sounds like a plan."

Cdr. Fleming said, "What I have provided you is for starters—only disclosed because you blackmailed me. The Red Indian program likely shall still be ongoing even after we defeat the Nazis. We have a lot of work ahead of us. I need you fully onboard, Colonel. Raiding Forces has a rule 'Right Man, Right Job.' You have been selected."

"Why didn't you just say so in the first place?"

"It is classified, old boy—Need to Know."

ONE OF THE VULNERABLE POINTS WING SECURITY MEN was on duty outside Major the Lady Jane Seaborn's suite when Col. Randal arrived on the second floor.

"Has Lady Jane made it back yet?"

"Yes, sir. She arrived a few minutes ago."

"Thanks."

Col. Randal continued down the hall. All the rooms on the second floor were suites. Three at the far end were reserved for visiting VIPs. He found the one he was looking for. It was not that difficult. A new brass plate on the door had been installed with WILD BILL engraved on it. Lady Jane ordered it as soon as she learned he was in residence.

Chances were she would keep the suite reserved for him exclusively from now on. Lady Jane had Brigadier General William Donovan sized up. He liked his perks.

She knew her way around VIPs.

The Chief of OSS came to the door in a robe. "Come in, Colonel."

Col. Randal said, "I won't take up much of your time, General. Quick question—what do you know about a plan to capture high-value Germans with certain skills who will help give the U.S. and U.K. a technological advantage after the war?"

Brig. Gen. Donovan said, "How did you hear about this?"

"Fleming wants Raiding Forces involved with NID's 30 Assault Unit."

"What you are inquiring about is a highly sensitive national-level black program. It is still in the preliminary planning stage," Brig. Gen. Donovan said. "Certain parts of the operation must be kept secret from some of our Allies—meaning virtually all of them. The operation does not have a codename at this point because it does not now and never will officially exist, and if it had a name, well . . ."

Col. Randal said, "Understood, sir."

Brig. Gen. Donovan said, "Here's what you need to know. Make sure to be in the driver's seat on this one, Colonel. When Commander Fleming firms up a request for Raiding Forces to work with 30 Assault Unit, do everything in your power short of canceling LONG NECK to command the ground element.

"Contact me the instant the ask formalizes."

"Yes, sir."

"Communicate directly with me about this project," Brig. Gen. Donovan said. "No one else. I'll clear you to bring certain of your people in at the appropriate time."

"Wilco."

Brig. Gen. Donovan said, "Good talk."

As Col. Randal turned to leave, Brig. Gen. Donovan said, "Quite an inspiring speech tonight. You serious or merely a charismatic speaker?"

"I meant every single word, sir—we're going to war."

"That's what I came to hear."

Col. Randal slid into the silk sheets next to Lady Jane. She was curled up on one side. Her mahogany hair splayed across the pillows.

Lady Jane said, "I saw you speaking to Ian. What could he possibly want at this time of night?"

"I'd tell you, babe, but then I'd have to . . . it's Need to Know, Eyes Only."

"You *really* want me to know, babe."

"The Commander is tasking me to capture the most beautiful woman in the world."

Lady Jane said, "How nice for you."

She rolled over and threw one tawny leg across his chest, putting him in a scissor lock. Col. Randal could not help noticing all the working out with Rocky had not been wasted. Lady Jane was toned.

"We shall see who kills who, John Randal. Besides, I have higher clearance than you."

"I told Fleming I'd already captured the most beautiful woman in the world."

Seeing he was the one pinned, maybe it was not the best choice of words.

Lady Jane said, "Good answer."

LIEUTENANT RICKY MASCUCH ISSUED HIS OPERATIONS order at 0500 hours—or as the troops like to call any time before sunrise "zero-dark-thirty." Operations Order, Mission Order, Patrol Order . . . all are essentially the same thing. This was a team-sized mission so it could have been called a Team Order.

"*Situation . . .*"

Lt. Mascuch had a couple of things going for him. He and Master Sergeant Mack Beckwith had managed to perform a leader's recon before last light. MSgt. Beckwith had done a take down before. He knew the best way to go about it.

Captain Billy Jack Jaxx, who was observing, liked to say, "If you ain't cheating, you ain't trying." He immediately recognized that Lt. Mascuch was adhering to Raiding Forces Rule Number 3: "It never hurts to cheat." Instead of feeling like he had busted the Lieutenant, Jack Cool gave him bonus points.

Nice job, Mascuch.

"*Mission . . .*"

The former GOYA bird was already gaining a certain notoriety in Raiding Forces. The troops loved the acronym. And anyone who jumped out of a glider backwards had to be badass.

"*Execution . . .*"

Actually, Lt. Mascuch had more than his notoriety going for him. MSgt. Beckwith helped him pick his team. They were all SOG operators who had been under Lt. Mascuch's command during the assault on the 999th's bar on Patmos. He was known to them—which is important. And this would not be the first house on Castelrozzo that SOG had taken down with a Brandenburger inside, so the men had an idea of what to expect.

Capt. Jaxx gave him additional points for personnel selection, though he was beginning to feel like Lt. Mascuch could be overdoing it on the cheating part. He might as well just call the Brandenburger on the phone and say, "Hands up, Nazi."

"*Command & Signal . . .*"

Capt. Jaxx noted Lt. Mascuch had failed to mention weather. He did not ding him for that one. Colonel Randal had skipped it prior to the drop on Benevento. It was not a problem. The takedown was going to happen no matter what the meteorological conditions might be.

"Administration and Logistics . . ."

Except for the weather, Lt. Mascuch never missed a beat. He did it by the book—step by step. The Colonel would have been pleased. So Capt. Jaxx was pleased.

When an order is being issued, protocol stipulated all questions be held until the end. The reason for this iron-clad proviso is because interrupting the briefer might cause him to lose his train of thought and leave out something important. The traditional closing statement of an order is, "This concludes my briefing. What are your questions?"

The measure of a good order is how many are asked. Each question meant the briefer had missed or failed to explain some point adequately. You get a perfect score if no one asks anything.

Lt. Mascuch said, "This concludes my briefing. What are your questions?"

No one asked any.

The SOG operators did not care about the weather.

The *Concept of the Operation* which fell under the *Execution* paragraph was basically the same as the one SOG had used for all the other houses they had taken down. The difference was a Greek national was believed to be inside so they could not simply blow the place up with explosives, have the *King Duck* blast it with its two Tiger tank's 88mm guns or one of the Walruses drop a bomb on it.

The plan, developed by Lieutenant General "Geronimo" Joe McKoy and Capt. Jaxx, was to have Police Officer Diakos knock on the door at first light asking if anyone had seen a missing child. Major Zargo and Capt. Jaxx would be crouching on either side of the entry having previously moved into position under cover of darkness. The instant it opened they would grab the woman—or the Nazi should he be stupid enough to answer the door.

While Officer Diakos secured the woman outside and Mandy searched her, Maj. Zargo and Capt. Jaxx would each throw a No. 69 stun grenade through the windows. Then they would effect entry, guns blazing, which would be the signal for Lt. Mascuch to initiate his follow-on assault. The SOG team would trail them in, flow through and proceed up the stairs to clear the second floor.

It was a good plan . . . and simple.

Which earned Lt. Mascuch additional bonus points for following Raiding Forces Rule Number 2.

COLONEL JOHN RANDAL SLID IN NEXT TO LOVAT SCOUT Munro Ferguson in his overwatch position on a rooftop directly across the street from the Hasapis house. It was still dark, prior to sunrise. There was just enough light to see the target but nothing was going on.

Scout Ferguson was not surprised when Col. Randal showed up on the roof. In fact, he wondered what had taken him so long to get there. The Colonel was not the type of commander to sleep in with an operation in progress.

"Any sign of the Nazi?"

"Negative."

"How about the woman?"

"Inside, sir."

Neither of the Lovat Scouts was much of a conversationalist. Not that it mattered. Scouts Ferguson and Fenwick had served with Col. Randal for so long that drawn-out verbal communication between the three of them was not necessary.

CAPTAIN BILLY JACK JAXX, HAVING BEEN SELECTED TO BE the Raid Team commander, was the perfect example of Raiding Forces Rule Number 4—Right Man, Right Job. Lieutenant Ricky Mascuch, the Assault Team Leader, had developed the Concept of the Operation and the Scheme of Maneuver and issued the OP Order, but Jack Cool was responsible for the success or failure of the mission. That meant it was going to be done by the numbers.

No cutting corners, no shortcuts—possibly overaggressive execution was in the cards.

The fact that this operation was small in scale or of a type SOG had carried out on multiple occasions in no way diminished the complexity or danger. Great care had to be taken in the execution. It is said in military circles "no plan survives the first contact with the enemy." While not always the case, it *is* true nine times out of ten—at least that's the way it seems to those who have commanded in combat.

This was no time for complacency.

When the operation commenced, the situation developed fast. Before Officer Diakos could arrive, Captain Jaxx noticed the door was ajar. Major Zargo made eye contact and nodded. They both immediately threw in their No. 69 concussion grenades—which was not the plan.

This action fell under "improvise and adapt."

BOOOOOM! BOOOOOM!

Maj. Zargo and Capt. Jaxx rushed in through a cloud of smoke and stopped in their tracks—causing the SOG operators led by Lieutenant Ricky Mascuch charging the door behind them to stack up. The team was looking at a scene they would never forget.

A naked woman was hanging by her heels from the railing on the second story with her throat cut—a shock for even the veteran SOG operators.

Capt. Jaxx signaled Lt. Mascuch to pass through, continue on up the stairs, resuming the assault plan.

"Clear. Clear. Clear."

The Brandenburger was not in the house.

Colonel John Randal realized things had gone wrong. He leapt off the roof and attempted a parachute landing fall on the cobblestone path and made a poor job of it. That hurt. Not what he had intended for this morning.

Capt. Jaxx met him at the door when he hobbled across. "Sir, you need to see this."

Inside he saw the naked woman, presumably Ms. Hasapis, dangling from the second-story balcony over a large pool of partially congealed blood.

Capt. Jaxx said, "The Sea Raider's not here, sir."

Col. Randal said, "Send for General McKoy."

From the door, Lieutenant General "Geronimo" Joe McKoy said, "You didn't think I was goin' to sit this one out did you, John?"

Col. Randal said, "What do you think happened here, General?"

Lt. Gen. McKoy said, "Looks like our informant had herself a change 'a heart. Probably got to feelin' guilty about bein' a rat. Tipped off the Hasapis woman we were comin.' Happens sometimes. When Chloe told the Nazi, he butchered her like a hog. Stripping and hanging her like this is for pure-dee show—wanted to shock us.

"He's a mad dog, needs to be put down—that part's clear as day."

Capt. Jaxx ordered, "Stay outside, Mandy. Don't come in here."

It was too late.

Mandy said, "Oh my . . ."

Col. Randal took her back out into the street.

Maj. Zargo ordered, "Officer Diakos, locate the town mayor and bring him here immediately."

The policeman took off at a trot.

Mandy said, "If we had immediately launched the raid instead of worrying about civil affairs, she might still be alive."

Col. Randal said, "Maybe, maybe not. I thought it was the right call at the time. This one's on me, Mandy, don't beat yourself up."

Maj. Zargo said, "Mandy, take two men with you. Go to the informant's house. Bring the woman here by force if necessary. I want her to see what she has done."

Capt. Jaxx ordered, "Collins, you and Anderson are on Mandy."

Col. Randal said, "Captain, get a dog team up here. The Brandenburger must have slipped out before Fenwick and Ferguson arrived yesterday. Maybe we can still pick up the trail."

Maj. Zargo said, "Colonel, with your permission let me take over the Hasapis affair. When the mayor arrives, I intend to order him to have every resident on the island assemble and file past this door to get a firsthand look at what happens to those who collaborate with the enemy.

"Leave the woman hanging where she is until everyone has an opportunity to see her."

Col. Randal said, "Handle it any way you want, Major."

Maj. Zargo said, "Nice to see you have not changed, Colonel. Still an easy man to work with."

A Vulnerable Points Wing dog handler and his dog arrived on the run.

Mandy came back with the informant. She owned the house directly across the street. The one Col. Randal had jumped from.

The Lovat Scouts joined the group in the house.

With all the activity Col. Randal ordered, "Lieutenant Mascuch, get everybody outside and set up a perimeter."

This was a Greek issue Raiding Forces needed to stay out of.

Maj. Zargo grabbed the informant by the hair and dragged her inside. She screamed like a panther when she saw her neighbor. And kept screaming. Standing out in the street it was painful to hear. Even for SOG, who were not what could be described as touchy-feely types. The operators looked at the ground or the sky, over the horizon, anywhere to avoid making eye contact with each other.

The Vulnerable Points Wing dog began working but could not pick up a scent.

Now there was a Nazi on the loose.

MANDY SAID, "MAY I SPEAK TO YOU IN PRIVATE?"

Colonel John Randal clicked on.

"Sure. Let's go to my office."

Mandy shut the door, "I wanted to say thank you."

"For what?"

"For all you did at Habbaniya. Chloe Hasapis naked hanging by the heels with her throat cut is exactly what I pictured was going to happen to me when the Golden Square Rebels overran the base. Then you arrived . . ."

Col. Randal said, "Fooled me, Mandy, you were way cool."

Mandy said, "I still have nightmares."

Col. Randal said, "Why don't the two of us go have a cup of coffee? Maybe we can talk this through."

"Coffee?"

"You have tea. I'll have coffee."

"Love to."

Col. Randal had no idea what to say to her. It came as a surprise to learn Mandy was troubled by Habbaniya, which was in the distant past as far as he was concerned. Pam, Brandy, Red—she had been held captive for a brief period until rescued, Penelope and Veronica had all been there too. Did they feel the same?

A conversation with Lady Jane was high priority. He needed her advice on what course of action to take now that this unexpected problem had come to light. The women were important people in his life—he had to get this right. The implications of what was in store for them if the Iraqis captured the base were clearly different than they had been for him—which were bad enough.

War leaves scars no one can see.

5
WORST VACATION EVER

A CROWD GATHERED ON THE DOCK. LIEUTENANT TED "THE Great Teddy" Hamilton, OBE, was about to conduct a demonstration of his Royal Navy Submarine Deception Device (RNSDD) Mark 2. This was a new and improved version of the RNSDD Mark 1 he had previously shown to Vice Admiral Sir Randolph "Razor" Ransom. One hundred yards offshore, Lieutenant Randy "Hornblower" Seaborn was standing by aboard PT 10 to deploy the device on command from the Great Teddy.

Colonel John Randal was talking to Captain Billy Jack Jaxx while they waited. "I'm promoting Cord Granger and Clint Hays."

Capt. Jaxx said, "My two best SOG officers, sir?"

Col. Randal said, "I need captains more than you need lieutenants. You trained 'em, Jack. Do it again with new people."

"Can I have who I want, sir?"

"Any lieutenant."

"Jake the Snake for one, Colonel."

"I'm promoting Jake too."

"You're not making this easy, sir."

"I've got confidence in you, stud."

Lieutenant Ricky Mascuch was telling Major Baltimore "Mongo" Farquhar, "The thing about jumping a glider is there's no prop blast to instantaneously make the chute deploy. You fall straight down like a rock."

Maj. Farquhar, said, "Quite! Bloody gliders, etc., whoever invented the bloody contraptions should be bloody well shot etc., etc." The major was a veteran of the glider training done when the Lancelot Lancers were studying the feasibility of utilizing them to land Raiding Forces gun jeeps.

VAdm. Ransom said to Commander Ian Fleming, "If Naval Intelligence Division wishes to maintain a continuing relationship with Small Raids Inc., then NID needs to supply me with a qualified liaison officer."

Brigadier General William "Wild Bill" Donovan was telling James "Baldie" Taylor and Major the Lady Jane Seaborn about Vice Admiral Louis "Dickie" Mountbatten, DSO, RN, almost accidentally killing Air Chief Marshal Charles Portal, Chief of the British Air Staff at the Quebec Conference.

"The Admiral was putting on a private demonstration of a revolutionary new material for aircraft carrier construction to a few of the senior attendees, to include the President of the United States and the British Prime Minister—I was in the room.

"Before the Admiral went out to the CBI while still in command of Combined Operations, the renowned scientist and inventor Geoffrey Pike brought him Project Habakkuk—a plan to build aircraft carriers out of ice. Actually, it was a substance he invented called pykrete—frozen seawater and sawdust.

"The idea is not as crazy as it sounds. To prove it could work, Mountbatten shot a block of ice with his revolver and it shattered. Then he fired at a block of pykrete. The bullet ricocheted off and nearly hit Air Chief Marshal Portal between the eyes.

"At that point the Secret Service rushed into the room, pistols drawn, thinking a gunfight had broken out between the two heads of state."

Lady Jane laughed. "One would expect more from our world leaders. Firing a pistol at a hard target in a closed room. What did Dickie think was going to happen?"

Veronica said to Beverly, "I am hoping you shall be available to devote more time to working with me in your capacity as the OSS MIS-X officer . . ."

Brig. Gen. Donovan overheard the two women and stepped closer. "Mrs. Paige, I have been looking forward to the opportunity of meeting with you. One of the purposes of my trip was to explore the possibility of OSS becoming a more active partner in your Escape activities."

Eavesdropping from nearby, Brigadier Dudley Clarke smiled a small little secret smile.

Lieutenant General "Geronimo" Joe McKoy and Waldo Treywick arrived with Major General Sam Houston Blackwell. Troop Transport Command had flown additional 575th Ranger Task Force personnel who had recently returned from behind the lines at Benevento back to RFHQ in Egypt. Bronc was taking advantage of the need to ferry the Rangers as a long-distance navigation training exercise for his aircrews. From RFHQ, it was easy to hitch a ride on to Castelrozzo where he could visit his daughter Beverly.

Col. Randal had not been aware he was on the island until the three walked up.

Maj. Gen. Blackwell was more than a little disappointed to discover Brandy Seaborn was away. While most of the LRDG was on Leros, two reconnaissance teams had been stationed on uninhabited islands conducting beach watching duty. They were still there. The two MAS boats were enroute to extract them so Major David Lloyd Owen would have all his people present when he began his reorganization.

Col. Randal said to Lady Jane, "We need to talk."

Lady Jane laughed, "Another enchanting round of 'honesty is the best policy'?"

Col. Randal said, "On second thought maybe that's not the way to go in every case—this is about something else. I need wise counsel from my senior female officer."

"Aye, aye, sir."

"Cut that out, Jane."

"You started it."

Maj. Gen. Blackwell was saying to Capt. Jaxx, "So y'all just stood out in the open wing shooting Nazi paratroopers?"

Capt. Jaxx said, "Pretty much sir."

VAdm. Ransom ordered, "Fire when ready, Lieutenant."

Lt. Hamilton raised his megaphone. "Execute. Execute. Execute."

One of the ratings on the stern of the PT boat tossed the RNSDD Mark 2 overboard. The Mark 2 consisted of a weighted broom handle painted black with a sardine can fastened to the tip to make it resemble the head of a periscope. When the device righted itself in the water, that is exactly what it looked like—a submerged submarine with its periscope raised.

VAdm. Ransom said, "Nicely done, Lieutenant Hamilton."

Col. Randal said, "Affirmative."

Lt. Gen. McKoy said, "Yeah, Ted—man of the hour."

Maj. Gen. Blackwell said, "No German pilot in his right mind will be able to resist bombing that broomstick—outstanding, son!"

Brig. Clarke was wondering how he might go about enticing Lt. Hamilton to transfer to A-Force.

Col. Randal pulled Lieutenant Colonel Sir Terry "Zorro" Stone aside. "With all the brass on the island, maybe you better lay on a briefing for later this afternoon to make everyone feel like they're getting their money's worth for their trip."

"One dog and pony show coming up, old stick—Hey, presto!"

COLONEL JOHN RANDAL AND MAJOR THE LADY JANE Seaborn stepped in his office and shut the door.

Col. Randal said, "Not sure what's going on, Jane. Habbaniya keeps coming up in conversation. That's a new development—any idea why?"

Lady Jane said, "Possibly it has something to do with our being isolated on the last island in the Dodecanese the Nazis have not occupied. At Habbaniya you were surrounded by Iraqi rebels. There is a similarity."

Col. Randal said, "You might be right."

Lady Jane said, "By the time Rita, Lana and I parachuted in the attack was essentially over. Still, knowing we were encircled by men who would rape us and then sell us at auction to a slave trader from some hideous medieval country was less than comforting."

Col. Randal said, "Yeah, I can see how that might be. Mandy said she still dreams about the siege. You believe Pam and the others do too?"

Lady Jane said, "Why not ask them? They would appreciate the concern. Not many commanders with all the challenges you have would take the time to be interested about a girl's bad dreams. A most attractive quality in you that people never get to see. One of the reasons I love you so much."

"Mandy's . . ."

"Are you having bad dreams, John?"

"Only when my eyes are open."

WHEN COLONEL JOHN RANDAL AND MAJOR THE LADY JANE Seaborn walked back out into the TOC, Captain Stephanie Fawcett-Tatum said, "General Blackwell requests the pleasure of your presence in his suite, John."

Before breaking off to go upstairs Col. Randal said, "Thanks for the advice, Jane—I'll make it happen."

King was sitting at the desk in front of Lady Jane's suite on the second floor when he arrived at the top of the spiral staircase. The Merc pointed down the hallway. "Generals McKoy and Blackwell are in the Wild Bill suite. Captain Jaxx recently joined them, Chief."

Col. Randal knocked on the door.

Brig. Gen. Donovan said, "It's open."

Inside Col. Randal found the officers gathered around a dinner table. They were inspecting three submachine guns. Everyone present was a soldier and a hunter. Two were also law enforcement. One was all of the above *and* an exhibition class shootist.

These men knew their weapons.

Brig. Gen. Donovan said, "I brought a collection of toys for big boys, Colonel."

"So I see, sir."

On a blanket spread over the table were an M1928 .45 Thompson submachine gun, a 9mm Sten submachine gun and a strange-looking submachine gun of a type Col. Randal had never seen before. It looked like it belonged in an auto garage. Each of the weapons had a silencer mounted on the barrel. (A purist would likely describe the mount as a suppressor—it not actually being possible to make a firearm completely silent. For all practical purposes the terms were interchangeable because Hollywood always described suppressors as silencers in the movies, which is where the average person picks up what little they know about firearms.)

Col. Randal had not been aware silencers *or* suppressors could be mounted on submachine guns. Possibilities came to mind.

He was interested.

Lt. Gen. McKoy said, "Wild Bill wants us to do a deep dive on these SMGs, John. Field test 'em under realistic conditions. Meaning living, breathing, bad guy targets."

Brig. Gen. Donovan said, "OSS has a requirement for quiet fully automatic weapons for clandestine work. What we want is suppressed submachine guns that provide more firepower than High Standard and Colt Woodsman .22 pistols offer us. These three examples are what we have to choose from.

"Due to the limitations of wartime manufacturing it is entirely possible we will be asked to accept consignments of all three models. I want you to rate them and be a hard grader. OSS needs to have facts in hand to push for the best weapon to supply our agents in the field."

Col. Randal said, "We can do that. Wait one, sir."

He went to the door, opened it and signaled down the hall for King.

When the Merc arrived Col. Randal said, "General McKoy's our resident firearms expert. Captain Kidd runs a close second. King's our best clandestine operator. The General, Captain Kidd and King can conduct a field test here on Castelrozzo—Jack, you assist as duty permits.

"We'll deploy the SMGs with our raiding teams to obtain an opinion from troops in the field."

Brig. Gen. Donovan said, "Outstanding!"

Col. Randal said, "General, you're in charge. Pick a good one—I'm going to want all we can get."

Lt. Gen. McKoy said, "Sounds like a plan to me, John . . . we'll wring 'em out. About time we had ourselves an interestin' project for a change."

Capt. Jaxx said, "That's a definite Rodge."

Soldiers do like their toys.

Major General Sam Houston Blackwell said, "What's the chances me and Wild Bill fly in sometime to tag along on one of your raids? See how these bad boys work down range."

Col. Randal said, "Less than zero, General."

Maj. Gen. Blackwell said, "Beverly says you have a tendency to be a spoilsport."

Brig. Gen. Donovan said, "Nevertheless Colonel, I fully intend to observe one of your small-scale Commando operations up close and personal. You piqued my interest with your Constant Pressure Concept. I need to see it in action."

Col. Randal said, "Not this trip, sir. The situation is too fluid at this time. Once it stabilizes and our operational rhythm is established, we can talk."

Brig. Gen. Donovan said, "While your concern for my welfare is much appreciated, I intend to hold you to that pledge."

Hoping to change the subject, Col. Randal said, "What can you tell me about the SMG that looks like it was bolted together in a junior high school auto mechanics class, General?"

Brig. Gen. Donovan said, "What you are looking at, gentlemen, is a United States Submachine Gun, Caliber .45, M3 with integral silencer manufactured by General Motors Guide Lamp Division. The nonstandard nomenclature for it actually is 'Grease Gun'—that's what everybody calls it. Won't win any beauty contests but it performed well in our trials at the Farm in Virginia."

Lt. Gen. McKoy said, "Gun's so pug ugly a man could almost take a likin' to it."

Brig. Gen. Donovan said, "The M3 has an add-on booby trap device called the Bushmaster . . ."

COLONEL JOHN RANDAL, MAJOR GENERAL SAM HOUSTON Blackwell and Beverly were having coffee in the open mess.

Maj. Gen. Blackwell said, "I'm glad to finally have an opportunity to visit your private Mediterranean hideaway, Colonel. Been looking forward to taking a look at your operation for a long time. Beverly's told me a lot about it. Hope you don't mind me poking around and kicking the tires."

Col. Randal said, "Feel free, General. Nothing we're doing out of ABC is particularly secret even though all our missions are classified. Beverly can show you anything you want to see."

Maj. Gen. Blackwell said, "You know Donovan's my attorney and he comes down to the ranch for a week every year to hunt quail."

Col. Randal said, "Yes sir, I do."

"He tells me he knew Joe McKoy back in the day during the Punitive Expedition down in Mexico. Says he was a living legend. Civilian Chief of Scouts with the honorary rank of lieutenant colonel."

"So I've heard, sir, but not from the General. He doesn't say much about it."

"Maj. Gen. Blackwell said, "Small world all our paths intersecting the way they have—Beverly, she knew Jack at UT. Now here we all are sitting on this little island in a theatre of war nobody back home has ever even heard of."

Beverly said, "When you think about it like . . ."

Maj. Gen. Blackwell said, "You understand Donovan's not going to give up on the idea of going on one of your raids. You're aware he landed on Sicily with the 'The Big Red One' and went ashore at Salerno as well."

Beverly said, "And that was a good idea—why?"

Maj. Gen. Blackwell said, "I didn't say it was a good idea, baby. They don't call him Wild Bill for nothing. Just giving Johnny advance warning about a problem he's going to run into sooner or later."

"I'll keep it in mind, sir."

"When the time comes, you're going to need a plan."

"I can see that, General."

Beverly said, "Johnny has too much going right now without the distraction of all you visiting brass hats, Daddy."

Maj. Gen. Blackwell said, "I wanted to check in on my Paratroop Advisor. He's family now. We have to look out for him—can't blame me for that."

Beverly said, "Shouldn't you be someplace commanding Troop Transport Command?"

Maj. Gen. Blackwell said, "Draft age is forty-five—that's for registering. The President of Enterprise Airways, better known as Trans Texas Airline, barely made the cut. He registered in Houston but probably wasn't going to get called up. So I had the Draft Board drop a dime on him, talked the USAAF into a direct commission to full colonel and made him my Deputy Commander for Operations—runs the show."

Beverly laughed, "You always have been a good delegator."

Maj. Gen. Blackwell said, "My job as commander of Troop Transport Command is to follow Raiding Forces Rule Number 4—'Right Man, Right Job.' Besides, I wanted to be free to do things like drop in to see my daughter in her work environment when I wanted to."

Beverly said, "This is a really inconvenient time for a parental visit."

Maj. Gen. Blackwell said, "Point taken. I'll stay out of the way. Low profile."

Beverly said, "That'll be a first."

Col. Randal said, "Mandy had something happen this morning that stirred up old memories from the Habbaniya siege. She could use a friend. Can I get you to talk to her, Beverly—without letting her know I asked?"

"Absolutely."

Maj. Gen. Blackwell said, "Habbaniya—what's that?"

Col. Randal said, "A small RAF flight school fifty miles outside of Baghdad. The Iraqi Army revolted and surrounded it with an estimated ten thousand Golden Square rebels. The bad guys held the high ground immediately outside the wire. Their artillery fired straight down into the cantonment at us—point-blank range, around the clock."

Maj. Gen. Blackwell said, "Sounds like the Alamo."

Col. Randal said, "The base commander deserted his post and hijacked a plane. Stuck a Thompson submachine gun to the pilot's head and flew out to India. The wives and daughters of the garrison's families were convinced they would meet a fate worse than death—raped and sold into white slavery. It was not a question of 'if'—only when."

Maj. Gen. Blackwell said, "What were you doing there?"

"I was on R&R to hunt desert big horned sheep."

Beverly said, "Worst vacation ever!"

"Guess you didn't get in much hunting," Maj. Gen. Blackwell said.

"Only animal I shot was Mandy's horse Blackie."

Maj. Gen. Blackwell said, "Ouch!"

"Red was there," Beverly said. "Johnny rescued her from the rebels—ask her to tell you the story."

Maj. Gen. Blackwell said, "Explains why she's so high on you, Colonel. Wasn't real sure where that was coming from. Glad we got that cleared up."

Col. Randal said, "Beverly, your conversation with Mandy is strictly confidential between the two of you. You don't have to report back to me. All I want to know is if she's all right."

Beverly said, "I'll go right now."

Col. Randal said, "Before I forget . . . first chance we need to talk about your future with MIS-X Escape."

Maj. Gen. Blackwell said, "Is that code for 'when I'm not looking over your shoulder'?"

"Yes it is, Daddy."

VICE ADMIRAL SIR RANDOLPH "RAZOR" RANSOM CAME TO the door of the canteen and spotted Major General Sam Houston Blackwell and Colonel John Randal sitting at the table.

"Mind if I join you?"

"Not at all, sir," Col. Randal said.

"Randy's orders promoting him to lieutenant commander came through. How do you want to handle it, Colonel?"

"He know about this?"

"Negative."

"You do the honors, sir."

Maj. Gen. Blackwell said, "Wouldn't Brandy be the appropriate person to pin on his new brass when she gets back?"

VAdm. Ransom said, "In both the British and American military systems it's traditional for a mother or wife to pin on a new officer's first rank insignia. After that there is no fanfare for promotions up to flag rank. In Raiding Forces the Colonel simply advises an officer or NCO they have been advanced in grade, usually at some time or place they do not expect.

By doing it that way the power to exercise higher command flows directly from Colonel Randal to the individual being promoted.

"It's a very personal rite of passage similar to being knighted—one I wholly endorse."

Maj. Gen. Blackwell said, "Yeah, that's a good system. I may have to steal it from you for Troop Transport Command."
Col. Randal said, "In Randy's case I'll be deferring the privilege to you, Admiral."

VAdm. Ransom said, "I shall have young Hornblower in my office in thirty minutes."

Col. Randal said, "All right then, sir. I'll be there to witness. Let's make this happen."

COLONEL JOHN RANDAL SAID, "GENERAL, I'D LIKE YOU TO meet Waldo Treywick."

Major General Sam Houston Blackwell said, "Pleasure's all mine, Mr. Treywick. Friends call me Bronc."

Col. Randal said, "Since Beverly's taking care of that other thing for me, I've asked Mr. Treywick to step in and show you around—full access. We met the day I jumped into Abyssinia, and he was in my gun jeep patrol running operations out of Oasis X. Try to get him to tell you about his ivory hunting days."

Waldo said, "What'd you like to take a look at first, Bronc?"

Maj. Gen. Blackwell said, "I hear the locals on the island are being required to view the recent Nazi atrocity—let's go check that out."

Col. Randal watched as the two headed toward the door, fairly confident he had put a round peg in a round hole with his choice of tour guides.

Waldo was saying, "Got my start in the Army durin' the last one scoutin' the square heads with P.J. Pretorius up the Rufiji River after the German cruiser . . .

COLONEL JOHN RANDAL HAD MADE ARRANGEMENTS FOR Brigadier General William "Wild Bill" Donovan to be briefed by Major the Earl Lord George Jellicoe and Major David Lloyd Owen individually on the status of the Special Boat Squadron and the Long Range Desert Group. That was taking place now. He wanted to allow Wild Bill to have the opportunity to make his own estimate of the situation.

The two of them would meet later in private to discuss their thoughts on the amalgamation of the units into Raiding Forces. Col. Randal also planned for Brig. Gen. Donovan to visit with Major Zargo. He was aware OSS intended to insert OG teams into mainland Greece eventually. Major Z, as he was being called by Raiding Forces personnel, was the perfect contact to help facilitate the project.

In the past Brig. Gen. Donovan had promised to send Raiding Forces an Operational Group of Greek speakers. It never happened. Not a problem because Col. Randal had not been impressed with the idea. But now he needed them. The small-scale raiding campaign Raiding Forces was gearing up to launch would require at least one Greek interpreter to be organic to every team. He was hoping getting Brig. Gen. Donovan together with Maj. Zargo would motivate him to send the OG.

Col. Randal had one more item on his agenda for Brig. Gen. Donovan. He wanted OSS to rearm Raiding Forces and attached units with all U.S. weapons except for submachine guns and sidearms. In the past, when operating out of gun jeeps, the mixture of U.S. and British arms had not posed a significant problem. In the desert, logistics were straightforward. The patrols stored enough ammunition aboard their jeeps to sustain their operations and were resupplied in the field by airdrops of prepared packages. Clandestine dumps of supplies and ammunition were secreted around the desert. Or the patrol could return to Oasis X when their supply was depleted.

The airdrop practice was not going to work for amphibious operations against distant islands. Raiding parties would have to depend on the amount of ammunition each individual could physically carry when he went ashore. Having compatible ammo and being able to redistribute it among team members in the midst of a firefight was a must for small-scale Commando raiding.

Col. Randal knew the changeover was not going to be popular with everyone. Trading in their old familiar weapons was likely to meet with resistance of the British troops. Particularly those being required to give up their beloved .303 Bren guns, which had achieved almost cult status among automatic riflemen. So as a consolation he decided to allow the troops to continue the practice of carrying the sidearm of their choice no matter of manufacture or caliber.

COLONEL JOHN RANDAL AND JAMES "BALDIE" TAYLOR were sitting in Major the Lady Jane Seaborn's suite.

Jim said, "How long did it take Veronica to inform you she was working for me after I gave her the word?"

"Same day."

"Told Dudley the idea was a fool's ploy. Veronica's loyalty is to Raiding Forces. He wants to use Escape for some of his A-Force Deception activities—whatever those may be. Asked me to inform her the Secret Intelligence Service was taking over so she would be more compliant with requests he would front as coming from MI-6. I only went along with the scheme so the Brigadier would owe me later."

Col. Randal said, "Dudley loves his smoke and mirrors—so do you."

Jim said, "No harm can come from it, Colonel. Escape is a satellite organization of SIS. Broadway wants to use MI-9, not run it—neither does Dudley. Knowing Veronica, I am confident she will be delighted to assist A-Force in any way she can even without all the intrigue."

King knocked on the door and then stuck his head in, "You are wanted in the TOC, Chief."

When Col. Randal and Jim arrived in the TOC there was a small crowd gathered in front of the gigantic, oversized wall map of the Aegean AO that covered one entire wall. The map had been intended for use to brief Il Duce Benito Mussolini about the goings on in the Italian-controlled islands. Although the former dictator had never spent a night in his palace on Castelrozzo, the map was perfect for Raiding Forces to use as a plotting board since it was behind glass and they could mark on it in grease pencil.

Lieutenant Colonel Sir Terry "Zorro" Stone handed Col. Randal an 8x10 photo of a periscope sticking out of the water. At first he thought it was a shot of the Great Teddy's RNSDD Mark 2. Then he noticed the white feather trailing in the water behind the periscope.

This was a picture of a submerged sub underway.

Vice Admiral Sir Randolph Ransom said, "What you are looking at is a Regia Marina Argonauta-class submarine. This photo was snapped earlier today by a Beaufighter radar operator on a plane returning from a dawn anti-shipping patrol north of Alimia. The Italians maintained a small submarine refueling station on the island prior to the armistice—two sub pens."

Brigadier General William "Wild Bill" Donovan said, "You can identify the class of submarine from a grainy photo showing only part of a periscope?"

VAdm. Ransom said, "I am after all, a sailor."

Brig. Gen. Donovan said, "Very impressive, Admiral."

Captain Billy Jack Jaxx, who had an uncanny knack for being in the right place at the right time, said, "So what does the photo tell you, sir?"

VAdm. Ransom said, "Hard to say, Captain. We know at least three Italian Fascist submarine crews elected to continue fighting in the Nazi's service. I am going out on a limb and speculate this is one of them. The refueling station on Alimia is likely still in operation.

"I believe the sub in this photo is en route to take on fuel."

Capt. Jaxx said, "What's the word on Alimia?"

Doctor Layton Winthrop, who had been pointing out locations on the map before Col. Randall arrived, said, "It's a three-square-mile island located about five miles off Rhodes. Alimia is known for its large, protected deep-water harbor. The few Greek residents living there prior to the war were relocated by the Italians once hostilities broke out. Except for goats, donkeys and a few Regia Marina sailors, the island is uninhabited.

"One of my agents on Rhodes visited Alimia fairly recently, masquerading as a sponge fisherman. He reported the Italians have a 250,000-gallon fuel depot under camouflage netting to conceal it from aerial observation. Only a handful of sailors—meaning fewer than a dozen men, were observed. Their barracks are to be found on the east side of the harbor."

Col. Randal looked at Alimia on the map. VAdm. Ransom had climbed up on a four-foot ladder and circled the island with a red grease pencil. It looked something like an extracted molar lying on its side at a forty-five-degree angle with the tip of the southern root snapped off, creating its own tiny, pyramid-shaped islet. The harbor, protected by the tooth's roots, looked almost as large as the land mass.

Major General Sam Houston Blackwell and Waldo returned from their tour of the Brandenburger's handiwork at the house on the escarpment and joined the group at the map.

Lieutenant General "Geronimo" Joe McKoy said, "Any possibility you can send in one of your subs to torpedo that baby while she's refuelin,' Admiral.

Professor Winthrop said, "I failed to mention the anti-submarine nets at the entrance to the harbor."

Maj. Gen. Blackwell said, "Bombing concrete submarine pens dug in the side of a cliff face is almost never successful."

Col. Randal said, "Typically what would a refueling event look like, sir?"

VAdm. Ransom said, "The sub would arrive off the island and remain submerged until nightfall then under cover of darkness enter the harbor and seek shelter in the concrete pens while it took on fuel."

Lt. Gen. McKoy said, "How far is Alimia from here?"

Lieutenant Commander Randy "Hornblower" Seaborn said, "One hundred six nautical miles, sir."

Brig. Gen. Donovan said, "In your estimation, on a scale of one to ten, how valuable a target is an enemy sub, Admiral?"

VAdm. Ransom said, "Ten without doubt."

Lt. Col. Stone said, "How long does it take to refuel, sir?"

VAdm. Ransom said, "With the relatively basic setup one would expect on an island as small as Alimia—eight hours maybe . . ."

Mandy rushed into the TOC. "Lady Jane found our missing Nazi. She is in trouble, John, come quick!"

Col. Randal said, "Keep working the problem, gentlemen."

Then he dashed out of the building at a dead run with Mandy leading the way toward the Hasapis residence.

No one kept working the problem.

As they were running up the path, Mandy said, "Beverly was assisting me observe the women as they filed by to view the atrocity. We were hoping to discover an indication that any of the other local ladies might be in sympathy with the Nazi.

"Lady Jane and Happy came up to check on us. Suddenly the dog ran off and she chased after him. He went two houses down and darted inside through an open window with Lady Jane right behind.

"Gunfire erupted immediately. Now Jane is pinned down inside. Beverly is out front engaging the German.

"No one else was nearby, including Officer Diakos, so I came for help."

As they approached the Hasapis residence, they could hear women screaming and gunshots coming from inside and outside the house where Lady Jane was trapped. Col. Randal easily identified the sounds. Her—formerly his—9mm Browning P-35, Beverly's Colt .38 Super and the Nazi's .45 Thompson submachine gun. For the initiated, sounds can tell the story of a battle in progress almost as well as, if not better than, visual observation.

What Col. Randal was hearing was a savage close-range firefight. He knew Lady Jane started with thirteen rounds in her Browning and two spare magazines in a canvas pouch on her pistol belt. In her purse she would have the 32 ACP aka 7.65 Walther PPK he had also given her. Beverly had ten rounds in her Colt .38 Super with two spare magazines on her pistol belt. For backup she carried an eight-shot .32 ACP Remington M51 in her boot.

The handguns were no match for a .45 Thompson submachine gun.

At a dead run, Col. Randal and Mandy rounded the corner onto the cobblestone walkway leading to the scene of the battle. The sharp bark of the PPK was heard for the first time. Lady Jane was down to her last eight rounds.

Up ahead Beverly came into view firing through one of the ground-floor windows.

Col. Randal ordered, "Stand fast, Mandy."

He ran to the house, did a roll past Beverly under the window, and came up on the far side. "You OK?"

"Jane's nearly out of bullets."

"How about you?"

"My last mag of .38 Supers."

Col. Randal tossed her one of his spares. "Top it off. I'm going in on three. Cover me."

Col. Randal slid along the wall to the front door. It was cracked open. A quick head check revealed the opening was not wide enough for him to observe much inside — he did not want to alert the Nazi to his presence just yet. The .45 Thompson submachine gun continued to roar from an elevated position on the second floor.

Col. Randal made eye contact with Beverly. He held up three fingers and then silently counted them down. On signal, she stood up and commenced rapid fire through the window as he kicked the door all the way open and stepped inside—Colt .38 Super at the ready.

At this point, events were taking place in slow motion but a lot was happening fast.

Out of his peripheral vision Col. Randal could see Beverly's pistol blazing away through the window and Lady Jane firing her Walther PPK over the top of a couch at a man in bloody khakis at the head of the stairs who had a .45 Thompson submachine gun balanced on his left hip. He was shooting one-handed, holding the weapon under his right arm because the other was dangling down useless—shattered by a bullet.

When the door crashed open the startled Nazi attempted to shift his fire.

Col. Randal put five rounds in his chest.

Over his shoulder Capt. Jaxx said, "Think you got him, sir."

Jack Cool.

FIFTEEN MINUTES LATER THE GROUP REASSEMBLED IN front of the gigantic wall map.

Colonel John Randal said, "Commander Seaborn, are you prepared to accept a Warning Order . . ."

6
RAIDING FORCES'
DIRTY LITTLE WAR

COLONEL JOHN RANDAL ASKED MAJOR GENERAL SAM Houston Blackwell and Brigadier General William "Wild Bill" Donovan to step into his office. They closed the door.

Col. Randal said, "We're not having this conversation for reasons that will be clear."

The two generals glanced at each other wondering where this might be going. They were both experiencing the full-blown aftereffects of a major adrenaline rush from the life and death engagement they had witnessed after chasing Col. Randal and Mandy to the house where the Brandenburger was shooting it out with Major the Lady Jane Seaborn and Beverly. Their visit to Raiding Forces was proving more adventurous than either officer anticipated.

It's not every day a father gets to see his daughter standing her ground in a full-on gunfight.

Col. Randal said, "We've lost air superiority over the Aegean. That means our method of operations has to be modified. For some time now I have been letting Captain Plum-Martin and Beverly fly combat missions neither the RAF or USAAF authorize for female pilots. With the recent turn of events in our AO I'll be ordering a no-fly zone north of Castelrozzo for both of them.

"I'll handle Pam but if Beverly refuses to comply I want you to take her home."

Maj. Gen. Blackwell said, "Beverly is of the belief her flying skills bring value to the unit—feels pretty strongly about."

Col. Randal said, "That's not the point, General."

Brig. Gen. Donovan said, "Are you under the impression females under your command have been unnecessarily put at risk?"

Col. Randal said, "That argument could be made, sir."

Maj. Gen. Blackwell said, "You do understand the distinction between air superiority and air supremacy?"

"Not entirely, General."

Maj. Gen. Blackwell said, "Air superiority is when one side or the other establishes control of certain airspace—it can be long term, short term or patchy in places. Air supremacy on the other hand is when one side or the other owns the skies—the opposition can't fly.

"The Luftwaffe's gained air *superiority* out here in the Aegean Theatre of Operation because the airfields on the islands they've captured give them the clear advantage. That stipulated, Allied air can still fly missions into German air space utilizing the elements of stealth and surprise. Our airmen can even establish short-term air superiority of their own at certain times and places if they play their cards right.

"I know this because my Air Intelligence Officer briefs me on developments in the Aegean even though we don't operate here—yet. Don't think for one minute I'm an unconcerned father not keeping up with his daughter—I am."

Brig. Gen. Donovan said, "Bronc's staff hounds my office daily for fresh intel on the ATO because he's cracking the whip on them to keep him informed."

Maj. Gen. Blackwell said, "All that needs to happen is Allied air planners have to modify their tactics to deal with the new reality. Low-level intruder flights to avoid radar. Quick ins and outs. No loitering over a target. Beverly's capable of flying those mission profiles. I know for a fact you've been ordering her to do exactly that for some time now.

"You managed to figure it out on your own."

Brig. Gen. Donovan said, "OSS is 13,000 strong. Women make up over thirty-five percent of our strength. They serve as agents, organize guerrilla bands, conduct sabotage, work as clandestine radio operators and couriers, carry out assassinations, set up escape lines for downed fliers—

they do it all. There's nothing you're allowing the women of Raiding Forces to do I'm not sending female operatives out to perform on a daily basis worldwide. OSS women are being killed, captured, tortured and thrown in concentration camps. We just don't advertise the fact."

Maj. Gen. Blackwell said, "That's no lie."

Brig. Donovan said, "As far as the general public knows all women are allowed to do in the war is organize a dance at the local USO, plant a Victory Garden, join one of the services and be a driver, secretary, nurse etc. Or work in industry as a "Rosie the Riveter" on an assembly line to take a man's place to free him up for military service.

"Transferring Beverly back to my HQ is your prerogative, Colonel. That's on you. But I won't be the one ordering it, and if you do, it may not keep her from volunteering for a field assignment in some other theatre."

Maj. Gen. Blackwell said, "Don't look at me. I'm not telling that cowgirl she has to go back to the ranch. *Hell* no."

Col. Randal said, "You're not much help, gentlemen."

Maj. Gen. Blackwell said, "Yeah, well, we may be a big disappointment but you've turned out to be a hand, Johnny—the real deal. Girlfriend's trapped in a house by a homicidal Nazi maniac. No calling backup. Don't ask for help.

"You just go John Wayne the front door and shoot the son of a bitch."

Brig. Gen. Donovan said, "Marched straight back here as if nothing out of the ordinary happened and laid out a concise plan of action to sink the submarine arriving off Alimia later tonight. That was impressive."

Maj. Gen. Blackwell said, "Yeah, when did you develop your scheme of maneuver—during the shootout?"

COLONEL JOHN RANDAL INTRODUCED MAJOR GENERAL SAM Houston Blackwell and Brigadier General William "Wild Bill" Donovan to Major Zargo. The three hit it off right from the start due in part to their being in a position to help each other. James "Baldie" Taylor came to sit in on the meeting.

Brig. Gen. Donovan said, "Colonel Randal tells me he wants to equip the Greek Sacred Squadron with U.S. arms."

Maj. Zargo said, "So he has informed me as well. The upgrade would increase my men's firepower. Particularly your M1 Garand rifles."

Brig. Gen. Donovan said, "Provide me a list of what you require, Major. I shall have my staff make the arrangements immediately upon my return to the States. You won't object to OSS describing the consignment as being provided to partisan guerrilla forces?"

Maj. Zargo said, "Since it is how we imagine ourselves, that would be perfectly satisfactory, General."

Maj. Gen. Blackwell said, "I'll make sure the arms and munitions are flown in to you ASAP. General Donovan and I know you GSS boys will put 'em to good use. You've come highly recommended by Colonel Randal."

Maj. Zargo said, "While small-scale island raiding is the model for GSS for the foreseeable future, should OSS have an interest in supplying partisan groups on the mainland at a later date it would be my pleasure to offer assistance coordinating those activities for you."

Brig. Gen. Donovan said, "Precisely the subject I was hoping to have a conversation with you about, Major. OSS is extremely interested in securing your services in that regard. How would you see something like that work?"

Maj. Zargo said, "My preference would be to funnel as much of the military stores as possible through Raiding Forces. Colonel Randal and I have a long-established working relationship. The best way to go about this is for me to introduce OSS officers under his command to the most active partisan leaders. You provide advisors to him here at ABCHQ and deliver the weapons and equipment to Castelrozzo. Colonel Randal and Admiral Ransom can shuttle the OSS advisors in with the delivery of the weapons to the resistance units along the coast on the mainland with the assistance of the Levant Schooner Flotilla. Possibly General Blackwell has thoughts on how to go about supplying the partisan bands in the interior."

Maj. Gen. Blackwell said, "Actually I do, Major. General Donovan and I have been discussing the idea of forming a USAAF Special Operations Squadron. There's possibilities in this part of the world if we put our minds to it. Not a lot of assets available so we'll need to be selective."

Jim made eye contact with Col. Randal but refrained from saying anything. Deciding who to arm and who not to was going to be more complicated than it sounded—politically. Maj. Zargo was setting himself up as the Distribution Officer who decided on the allocation of military aid to Greek guerrillas.

The problem was that there was a toxic undercurrent of national politics brewing in the Balkans. Communist versus Nationalist civil wars in both Greece and Yugoslavia were likely to erupt at the end of the current conflict. The Russians were known to have their eyes on the region postwar in support of the Communists. The British as well as the U.S. favored the Nationalists. Weapons supplied to Greek guerrilla units now to fight the German occupiers could be used against each other later. There was the very real possibility military equipment supplied at great effort would be hoarded and not used against the Axis powers at all.

While Col. Randal was dimly aware of the situation, he did not understand nor have any interest in politics. His concern was killing Nazis. What happened in someone else's country after the war was not his business.

Col. Randal said, "Gentlemen, I have pressing matters that require my attention. Going forward it might be advisable to bring Admiral Ransom into the conversation. He'll be the driving force in organizing the seagoing supply lines. For my part you can count on Raiding Forces to support your plans in any way we can subject to his approval. Arming and equipping the Greek Sacred Squadron is my primary priority—supplying guerrilla units on the mainland is secondary until that's accomplished."

As he was leaving, Maj. Zargo was saying, "I understand OSS wants to insert teams of advisors and possibly larger Operational Groups..."

Back out in the TOC, Col. Randal saw Vice Admiral Sir Randolph "Razor" Ransom talking to Brigadier Dudley Clarke and Commander Ian Fleming. The Admiral waved him over.

"I have informed Commander Fleming he needs to provide Small Raids Inc. with a qualified NID liaison officer acceptable to me to facilitate our continued assistance with his special projects."

Acting as he was hearing this for the first time, Col. Randal said, "Good idea, Admiral."

VAdm. Ransom said, "Fleming, understand you cannot simply pop in unannounced with all manner of projects for Small Raids Inc. as you have with Raiding Forces in the past. While we wish to be an active NID partner, if you desire our continued cooperation you shall have to honor the chain of command. To be clear, that would be—you to Randal to me."

Cdr. Fleming said, "Aye, aye, sir."

VAdm. Ransom said, "Understand Raiding Forces is a standalone organization. The Colonel can accept or reject a proposed mission without kicking it up to Small Raids Inc. In the event he decides to pass on a given project do not waste your time trying to go over his head. Sell him on your plan, come up with a new one he signs off on or return home empty handed."

Col. Randal knew the Razor was talking to Brig. Clarke as much as he was Cdr. Fleming. The Admiral was staking out his command authority in the ATO in no uncertain terms. While there were the remnants of several broken-up Commando and Special Forces-type units still in theatre the hard reality was if Raiding Forces/Small Raids Inc. did not take on a mission it was not likely to be carried out.

Cdr. Fleming said, "Quite right, Admiral. NID unequivocally wishes to continue our close relationship with you and the Colonel. He and I have a long track record of working together going back to the first days of the war."

Brig. Dudley Clarke did not make any comment but he was fully cognizant of what had just transpired.

Col. Randal said, "Admiral, can I have a moment?"

They walked to the side of the room.

"Sir, you need to drop in on the meeting taking place in my office— I'd like you there."

VAdm. Ransom glanced across the TOC and saw who was in Col. Randal's office through the large plate glass window. "Thanks, I shall."

There was a lot of jockeying for position taking place among the high-ranking visitors to Advanced Base Castelrozzo. Everyone had their own agenda. Col. Randal saw nothing wrong with that. They all had a mission to perform. Nevertheless, VAdm. Ransom needed a seat at the table for any discussions concerning seagoing operations in his AO, particularly when they involved long-term commitments.

Col. Randal spotted Captain Billy Jack Jaxx talking to Doctor Layton Winthrop. Likely trying to find out as much information as he could about Alimia. He made eye contact.

Capt. Jaxx excused himself and came over.

"Jack, inform King, the Lovats and Sergeant Major Beckwith to be in attendance at the Op Order at 1500 hours."

"Yes, sir."

"Either Captain Coogan or Captain Stirling needs to be present as well."

"Roger."

After Capt. Jaxx departed, before he went to stake out his position in upcoming Greek operations requiring sea support, VAdm. Ransom said, "If Naval Intelligence Division does decide to send a liaison officer to Small Raids Inc. I intend to put him to work full-time for SRI. Instead of having a spy in our midst the NID officer shall become one of us. We can use a competent naval intelligence specialist on staff."

"You do go straight to it, Admiral."

VAdm. Ransom said, "As you rightly pointed out, we were in need of a plan. No time like the present to start implementation of one. Now all I have to do is get Jim Taylor onboard with what I have in mind."

Col. Randal said, "You can count on Jim, sir."

VAdm. Ransom said, "We shall see—there is this other angle I am working . . ."

WHEN COLONEL JOHN RANDAL ARRIVED AT THE TOP OF THE stairs on the second floor, King was at the desk. "Tread lightly, Chief!"

"What does that mean?"

"Beverly is in there with Lady Jane. She made a reference to your sex life, mothers and dogs on the way past. Language I never expected to hear from one of Texas' Ten Most."

The almost imperceptible touch of amusement flickering around one corner of King's mouth was about as close as the Merc ever got to a smile. The look could be intimidating under different circumstances. Right now it failed to provide much in the way of useful information.

Col. Randal said, "Lovely."

Inside the suite, Major the Lady Jane Seaborn and Beverly were sitting on the couch in the living area. Neither woman was smiling. That was not a good sign. Normally when the two were together they never stopped laughing.

Beverly looked up at Col. Randall and launched a preemptive strike. "I thought we were friends?"

"We are."

"How could you order me home?"

Col. Randal glanced at Lady Jane—no help there.

"I haven't ordered you home."

"You asked my father and General Donovan to take me back to the States if I protested being grounded—why would you do that?"

"Well, I was hoping . . ."

"If that's how you feel, I'll go start packing."

Beverly stood up and stormed out of the room.

Lady Jane said, "That went extraordinarily well."

Col. Randal said, "I was only trying . . ."

"So, you are grounding Pam and Beverly?"

"Negative, just from flying north of Castelrozzo. I don't want the girls put at risk. Women don't fly direct combat missions in the RAF or USAAF and I've been letting them."

"What changed?"

"Besides the balance of airpower shifting, my conscience got to me."

Lady Jane laughed, "Try to do the right thing and it blows up in your face—oh, John."

There was nothing she enjoyed more than watching him trying to get out of trouble of his own making.

Col. Randal said, "This isn't funny, Jane."

Lady Jane said, "Maybe we should start over and take it from the top, babe."

LIEUTENANT GENERAL "GERONIMO" JOE MCKOY SAID, "Doesn't sound like you have me penciled in for this one, do you, John?"

"Negative, only six people are going to be on the ground—we're putting the 'small' back in small-scale."

Lt. Gen. McKoy said, "This mission's too good to miss out on. Blowing up a 250,000-gallon fuel dump. Got to be a pretty good show."

Colonel John Randal said, "Bronc's flying the drop tonight with Wild Bill along as an observer. Randy will be stationed off Alimia in PT 10 prior to. He'll be sailing immediately following the Operations Order.

"You can be aboard the Hudson observing or the PT boat—your choice, General."

Lt. Gen. McKoy said, "Think I'll travel with Hornblower. Put me in the catbird's seat to see the whole shooting match up close and personal. OK with you if Waldo tags along? He doesn't like to miss out on much."

Col. Randal said, "Sure, take him with you. As many of his cigars as we smoke, we wouldn't want Mr. Treywick feeling slighted. I'm in enough trouble with hurt feelings around here as it is."

Lt. Gen. McKoy said, "So I've heard. Sounds like you've stepped off in it, John."

News spreads fast in Raiding Forces.

Major the Earl Lord George Jellicoe walked over from where he had been studying the wall map.

"Lieutenant Taylor briefed me on his cockleshell raid. Classic SBS mission. Sank a tanker and put a destroyer out of action with limpet mines. Wish we had been in a position to carry it out, sir."

Col. Randal said, "SBS was busy at the time."

Maj. Jellicoe said, "You failed to mention being aboard the folboat with Taylor. That's some oversight, Colonel."

Col. Randal said, "I was just along for the ride Jackson did all the work."

Maj. Jellicoe said, "In the future, sir, I would like first crack at small boat missions. Lieutenant Taylor confirmed you are attaching his MU team to SBS. Admiral Ransom and I have been discussing making enemy shipping a high-priority target. The Nazis have enough deep-water harbors in their possession for us to call on multiple places unexpected without establishing a pattern. It is time to return to our original mission of surreptitious nocturnal limpet mine attacks."

Col. Randal said, "Sounds like you're making drop ahead plans, Major."

Maj. Jellicoe said, "All things considered, sir, I would say the SBS reorganization is progressing quite nicely. Better than anticipated. Much better actually."

Col. Randal said, "Let's get the new OSS people integrated, then you and I can sit down with the Admiral and start working out the details of how to turn your ideas into actions."

Maj. Jellicoe said, "Very good of you, sir. SBS has never had a long-range plan since I have been in command. It will be a novel experience."

"You'll still be conducting raids with the rest of Raiding Forces," Col. Randal said, "but we want you to get back to sneaking into harbors and blowing up ships."

Maj. Jellicoe said, "Lieutenant Taylor claims he has a new idea for a covert technique we can use to slip in and out with our demolitions utilizing something called paddleboards.

"Whatever those might be, sir?"

Col. Randal said, "Think standing up on a surfboard with a paddle."

"Ingenious. Jackson—he is a wild one."

Col. Randal said, "Likes the ladies."

"Sir Terry and I shall make a point to include him on our next debauch to Beirut."

Mandy rushed up. "Is it true Beverly is returning to the States?"

Col. Randal said, "That's what she says."

"You have to stop her."

"So how am I supposed to do that?"

"Think of something!"

Col. Randal spotted Captain Roy Kidd across the room and walked over. "I've asked OSS to re-equip Raiding Forces and all attached elements with U.S. weapons. General Donovan has agreed to supply the arms and General Blackwell offered to fly them in."

Capt. Kidd said, "That's terrific, sir. I'll get with Captain Jaxx. We'll need to start kicking around ideas on how to structure the TO&E

for our teams with the new weapons." Except for the Long Range Desert Group, which continued to call their personnel "patrolmen," the term "patrol" was beginning to be replaced in Raiding Forces' lexicon with "team."

Col. Randal said, "Mad Dog's still at Camp Mackall training paratroops. By the time he completes the assignment I want you to have a Raiding Forces Battle School organized. All British and Commonwealth troops to go through it first on a priority basis. You supervise their transition to the new U.S. weapons. Then we'll run everyone else through."

Capt. Kidd said, "Yes, sir."

Col. Randal said, "Once that's done I want Battle School to transition into a Close Quarters Combat shooting and small unit tactics refresher course—to be ongoing. On his return Captain Reupart will assume command and you can go back to operating. During stand-downs you continue to be a part-time instructor. I want intensive focus on individual marksmanship against multiple targets at the ranges and under the conditions we can expect to engage enemy personnel at night—I do mean intensive, Roy."

"Understood, sir."

"General McKoy will be available to you, time permitting. He's the best instructor we have so utilize him. The two of you get together and design the marksmanship syllabus. Limit bullseye shooting to the zeroing of weapons. Mr. Treywick's our most experienced reconnaissance man. Use him when he's available—we'll see what kind of instructor he makes."

Capt. Kidd said, "Sergeant Volkmann would be a perfect fit for this type of assignment, sir."

Col. Randal said, "You've got him—the Lovats too."

"I like the sound of this project, Colonel."

Col. Randal said, "Our teams will be downsizing boots on the ground while at the same time increasing the tempo of raiding. The best force multiplier to compensate for lack of troop strength is superior small unit tactics combined with Olympic-class CQC practical shooting skills. Your mission is to design a program to increase our people's lethality, Roy."

Capt. Kidd said, "Any chance I can have Captain Jaxx help develop the block of instruction on tactics? He'd be a great instructor."

Col. Randal said, "Affirmative, you can put me down to teach as well when I'm here. I'll get with Jack. We'll work up the small unit tactics lesson plans."

"That will be a big help, sir."

"Initially all troops complete the full CQC. Then following their stand down, every three weeks each team will go through a rigorous refresher evolution prior to being put back in their squadron's mission rotation. From this point forward shooting skill is not optional in Raiding Forces," Col. Randal said.

"Yes, sir!"

"RTU underperformers."

Capt. Kidd said, "This is the type of training most commanders talk about but never get around to implementing because it's too much trouble, sir. If done right what you're planning will dramatically increase the team's combat power."

Col. Randal said, "Get it right then."

CAPTAIN BILLY JACK JAXX SAID, "ARE YOU PLANNING TO pull the plug on Brandy and Legs Parker too, sir? And what about Veronica?"

Colonel John Randal said, "That's enough out of you, Jack."

"I'm just asking, Colonel."

Col. Randal said, "In the course of my trying to keep Beverly and Pam safe, things sort of spiraled out of control, crashed and burned, then blew up."

"How's it going to play out, sir? We can't let Beverly go back to Texas."

"I have no idea."

Jim came over and pulled Col. Randal aside. Speaking quietly so no one else could hear, he said, "I shall make this short and to the point. We can talk in greater detail later. No matter who comes to you or what is proffered, under *no* circumstances allow Raiding Forces to be drawn into fighting on mainland Greece, Yugoslavia or Albania. Stay out of the

Balkans other than to coordinate shipments of arms and OSS advisors to partisans.

"Do I make myself clear?"

"Crystal."

The two men stared hard in each other's eyes, then Jim turned and walked away. They had served together for too many years in too many bad places for Col. Randal not to understand what was left unsaid. The MI-6 officer was looking out for Raiding Forces' best interests but needed plausible deniability about doing it.

This was no drill.

Brigadier General William "Wild Bill" Donovan approached. "The jaunt to Castelrozzo has proven highly productive, Colonel. Truthfully I was not expecting much more than a pleasant visit to a beautiful island. The trip was an excuse for General Blackwell and myself to get away. Spend some time together since we won't be able to work in our annual bird hunt this year."

Col. Randal said, "Good to hear, sir."

Brig. Gen. Donovan said, "Bronc had the opportunity to witness his daughter in a gunfight—not a daily occurrence even in Texas. And you—well, you've provided me an opportunity to get a foothold in European underground activities exclusive of MI-6.—who don't want OSS encroaching on what they see as their private preserve. Never anticipated that as a possibility. The Brits have been freezing us out. Major Zargo seems like he's going to be the goose that laid a golden egg."

Col. Randal said, "We were together . . ."

Brig. Gen. Donovan said, "I know. He told us the moment you left the room. The two of you were at the Siege of Habbaniya. A little-known engagement that makes those of us who weren't involved feel like we missed the seminal event of the war. Even Lady Jane flew out from England to parachute onto the base to be there with you.

"Must have been some battle. I understand President Roosevelt's son Jimmy was there as an observer towards the end."

Col. Randal said, "Had its moments, sir."

Brig. Gen. Donovan said, "Sounds like you're having one of your own right now with Miss Beverly. What's your thinking, Colonel? You have a reputation for a lightning-quick ability to devise a plan on the move under duress. I for one would like to hear your next move?"

"Wish I had one, General."

"Better shake it up. OSS needs Troop Transport Command supporting the ATO since no one else in the U.S. Armed Forces is going to. If Beverly returns home who's to say if Bronc might not lose interest in a military backwater? I would not want that to happen."

After Brig. Gen. Donovan strolled away, Captain Butch "Headhunter" Hoolihan came over. "I sat in on your Warning Order this morning, sir. Sounded like you might need me tonight?"

"No, Butch I don't, but let's step into my office for a minute."

Col. Randal rummaged through a drawer. He pulled out his old epaulets with the single crown that denoted a British Army major and tossed them on the desk. The insignia had seen hard service. Most of it with the Headhunter close by at the time.

Col. Randal said, "Put 'em on, Major. I hope they bring you as much good fortune as they have me."

"Sir, are you serious?"

"Reorganize your troop to squadron strength. Three troops commanded by captains with three teams of eight Marines, each led by a lieutenant. You'll need more junior officers. Your choice on the officers but I approve and promote. Choose your deputy commander wisely because you'll be away on other assignments for extended periods of time."

"Where do I find the additional Royal Marines, sir?"

"You'll figure it out, stud."

"Yes, sir."

"On another subject—and this is important, Butch— sometime in the next fifteen minutes I want you to 'accidently' run into Commander Fleming. He's requested you be loaned to NID again to train his 30 Assault Unit Commando.

"Make it happen—and right now."

"Sir?"

"Your mission, known only to the two of us, is to make yourself invaluable to Fleming. Train his Red Indians. Accept assignments he may offer you from time to time to lead 30 AU intel ops. Only clear 'em with me prior to. At some point the Commander's going to try to steal you away from Raiding Forces—don't let him do it."

Maj. Hoolihan said, "Sir, are we infiltrating the Naval Intelligence Division?"

Col. Randal said, "We would never do *that . . .*"

KING WALKED INTO THE TOC, SPIED COLONEL JOHN RANDAL and came straight over. One glance at the Merc and Col. Randal clicked on. He had no idea why.

"Lady Seaborn sent me to inform you she has reserved a table for you in the officer's mess and is there now waiting for your arrival, Chief."

ABC Headquarters maintained three mess halls. The officer's mess, the NCO's mess and the Other Ranks' mess. The same food was served in all three.

In the British Army, Sergeants Majors are accorded many of the rights and privileges officers enjoy. They have the option to eat in either the officer's or NCO's mess. The U.S. Army does not have the same policy for Sergeants Major, as it was a title, not a rank. So Col. Randal granted the privilege of dining in the officer's mess to Master Sergeant Mack Beckwith—who usually preferred to eat with the NCOs.

The officer's and NCO mess halls were only open at mealtime. The Other Ranks was an open mess that was kept running all day. Anyone could use it during the hours the other two were closed. Since a great deal of military business was conducted by personnel of various grades over coffee or tea at all hours, the mess halls played an important role in helping to maintain the smooth functioning of Raiding Forces' day-to-day operations.

That Major the Lady Jane Seaborn would have reserved a table was not a normal occurrence. She could have any table she wanted any time she wanted.

As they walked down the hall into the Other Ranks' mess, King said, "Watch your six, Chief."

Then he peeled off and went to sit with Captain Billy Jack Jaxx, Waldo Treywick and Mandy—the Merc and the former ivory poacher having been accorded the rights and privileges of captains.

Col. Randal spotted Lady Jane sitting at a table prominently located in the center of the dining room. Captain Pamala Plum-Martin was seated to her left. Beverly Blackwell was on her right. Typically when those women were together they were having fun.

Clearly not the case today.

The room became markedly quieter as Col. Randal walked over to the table.

"Mind if I join you ladies?"

Lady Jane said, "Please do."

No hint of the legendary heart attack smile.

Across the room at their table Lieutenant General "Geronimo" Joe McKoy remarked to Major General Sam Houston Blackwell, Brigadier General William "Wild Bill" Donovan and Brigadier Dudley Clarke, "Trouble in paradise incoming fast boys—HE on the deck."

At another table, Vice Admiral Sir Randolph "Razor" Ransom turned to his grandson Lieutenant Commander Randy "Hornblower" Seaborn. "This might go badly. What could Jane have possibly been thinking to engineer this confrontation so publicly?"

At their table on the other side of the room, Commander Ian Fleming said to Major Butch "Headhunter" Hoolihan, "Glad its Randal who has to face the music—not I."

Lieutenant Colonel Sir Terry "Zorro" Stone, Major the Earl Lord George Jellicoe and Lieutenant Jackson Taylor walked in behind Col. Randal, saw what was happening and immediately sought out a table with an unobstructed view.

Lady Jane said, "I thought the four of us could give you an opportunity over lunch to explain the rationale behind your decision to restrict Pam's and Beverly's flying, John."

Col. Randal felt the old familiar icicle-stabbed-through-the-heart sensation normally associated with dangerous encounters he was not likely to walk away from unscathed. "First off, I want to make clear there was never any intention to ground either of you as has been reported."

A good try but zero response. Clearly the women were not going to make this easy. Col. Randal felt like he was tiptoeing through a minefield. And not harboring kind feelings about a certain drop-dead gorgeous Royal Marine major for putting him in this position.

"My thought was and still is, with the air power advantage having shifted to the Luftwaffe, flying missions north of Castelrozzo will have to be modified to conform to the current situation whether we like it or not."

Still no reaction.

Col. Randal said, "Bronc explained the difference between air superiority and air supremacy, which was not entirely clear to me at the time I was making the decision to set up a no-fly zone."

Capt. Plum-Martin, who had been studying him with the poise of a cobra calculating the best opportunity to strike, said, "This no-fly zone— would it apply equally to the male Special Duties pilots as well?"

"Ahhh . . ."

Lady Jane said, "John, why not explain the catalyst that motivated you to restrict the girls' flying?"

Col. Randal said, "It was *The Saturday Evening Post*."

Beverly said, "*The Saturday Evening Post*?"

Col. Randal said, "An article by E. Fowler Draper, the magazine's first female war correspondent. Her bio said she was from Austin, Texas. Caught my eye because you went to UT, Beverly."

Capt. Plum-Martin said, "Is this supposed to be some kind of a joke, John?"

"Negative, the story was titled "Women in Uniform." Ms. Draper covered the various jobs women in the U.S. and the U.K. perform in order to free men for front-line duty. And she specifically pointed out that even though women were serving in every branch of the military, in various assignments, neither country allowed them to participate in direct combat operations," Col. Randal said. "So I got worried. Continuing to allow you to fly the missions you have been was putting you in harm's way in direct contravention of both countries' national policies.

"I did not feel good about that."

Beverly said, "Pam and I get grounded because of an *article* you read in a magazine—are you crazy?"

Col. Randal said, "When you put it like that . . ."

Capt. Plum-Martin said, "Nothing has changed for Raiding Forces' air operations, John. We almost never flew north of Castelrozzo anyway except on specific intruder missions that took into consideration the Luftwaffe air bases on Rhodes, Crete and the other islands with airfields. If we only go out under cover of darkness, at low altitude to avoid radar, with a flight plan designed for whatever it is we are tasked to carry out and immediately return to ABC—the risk is exactly the same as it's always been."

Col. Randal said, "That's what Bronc told me."

Beverly said, "Then why didn't you say something, Johnny?"

"Because you weren't speaking to me."

That went better.

At his table Brig. Gen. Donovan said, "What just happened? They have started laughing."

Lt. Gen. McKoy said, "Looks like John musta pulled a rabbit outta his hat—'Hey, Presto.'"

Maj. Gen. Blackwell said, "Can't imagine what Beverly could possibly think's so funny but it's always been hard to keep that little girl's spirits down."

Lady Jane said, "Are you lifting the no-fly zone, John?"

Col. Randal said, "It never went into place."

Beverly said, "Excellent."

Capt. Plum-Martin said, "Very good, John. You have always been reasonable. One of the qualities I have always admired about you."

"While we're together there's something else I'd like to talk to you about," Col. Randal said. "We have seven island chains with something over 250 inhabited islands in our AO. It's possible Nazi sympathizers reside on every single one. Mandy's MI-5 Counterintelligence, Beverly you're our OSS X-2 Counterintelligence officer at least on paper. I want the two of you to team up and organize a joint CI Task Force. Identify collaborators and we'll go snatch them. I'll loan Jack to the project on a mission-specific basis—SOG top priority.

"Pam, you and King may find it necessary to spend additional time on LONG NECK business in Morocco. Do what has to be done. However, as time permits, I'd like you to work with Mandy and Beverly."

Capt. Plum-Martin said, "I should very much like to be involved, John."

Neither of them mentioned she was MI-6.

Col. Randal said, "Amassing the intelligence on so many islands and then planning direct-action missions to take the collaborators into custody is going to be a major undertaking. It may prove useful to have one of you accompany Jack's SOG teams to aid in identifying the individuals targeted once the snatch missions get cranked up."

Beverly said, "I'm in."

Lady Jane said, "Not without me."

Col. Randal said, "All right then, ladies—let's do this."

Now he got the heart attack smile.

At his table, Capt. Jaxx said, "No idea what's happening over there. I was expecting blood on the ground."

Mandy said, "Definitely."

King said, "GG's bringing another chair . . . Lady Jane wants you to join them, Mandy."

Across the room, VAdm. Ransom said, "What could Randal possibly have said to pacify those women?"

Lt. Cdr. Seaborn said, "No idea, sir. The Colonel is usually not much of a people pleaser."

Later as they were walking up the stairs to their suite, Lady Jane said, "I have been standing by on pins and needles waiting for my dressing down for chasing after Happy and all the trouble it caused. What is taking so long for the ax to fall, John?"

Col. Randal said, "Haven't had time to get around to making my decision about what to do."

Lady Jane said, "You are not seriously considering having me returned to my unit?"

Col. Randal said, "Raiding Forces *is* your unit."

COLONEL JOHN RANDAL ISSUED HIS OPERATIONS ORDER at 1500 hours. The men alerted to go on the mission were sitting in chairs arranged in front of the giant wall map in the TOC. Behind them were the visiting officers with Lieutenant General "Geronimo" Joe McKoy, Lieutenant Colonel Sir Terry "Zorro" Stone, Major the Lady Jane Seaborn and Waldo Treywick. Everyone else on duty, passing through the TOC, or who had come to watch Col. Randal issue his briefing was standing in a semicircle in the back.

It was a large crowd.

An order for an imminent mission was what passed for high drama in Raiding Forces—better than any Hollywood production. In fact, the sensation those going on the raid felt was not unlike that they were living a war movie. Mission prep never seemed quite real no matter how many ops they had been on.

Only it was.

The officers and men being briefed were stone-cold professionals. They had worked together for years. Three of them, Lieutenant Commander Randy "Hornblower" Seaborn and the two Lovat Scouts, went back to the very first days of Raiding Forces.

While this was to be a tiny operation, its scheme of maneuver was complex with a lot of moving parts. The difficulty factor was exacerbated by the nature of raids in the ATO. Actionable intelligence was rarely available—what little they had was often long out of date. No one agreed on how many islands there were in the Aegean or even what constituted an island.

In a perfect world a reconnaissance team would infiltrate the targeted island prior to the raid. The recon operators would assess the best place to land, the route to the objective and put eyes on the target. Then prepare a SALUTE report.

SALUTE is one of those acronyms the military loves—Size, Action, Location, Unit, Time, Equipment.

One of the most important responsibilities a recon team leader has, after performing the reconnaissance and while still in enemy territory, is to assemble his men in a tight perimeter so he can disseminate the information gathered for the SALUTE report. The team may have broken down into smaller elements to investigate different locations—so everyone on the team might not have seen the same thing.

Disseminating the SALUTE report in the field ensures every team member knows what is in it. Should only one man make it back—mission accomplished.

When the Long Range Desert Group was eventually reconstituted, Raiding Forces would have the capability of sending in dedicated reconnaissance specialists to put eyes on the target prior to a raid—at least when time and the terrain allowed. Many of the islands were so tiny, recon going in advance of the raid would be impossible because the LRDG patrolmen would be spotted no matter how stealthy they might be.

Tonight's mission was not ideal for a military planner. Col. Randal was working from a grainy photo of a periscope belonging to a Regia Marina submarine believed to be headed toward Alimia to refuel, and a months-old intelligence report produced by a former archeologist's assistant who had never served a day in the military acting as an SOE agent. According to that report there were a pair of concrete submarine pens, an estimated 250,000-gallon fuel dump, and at least ten Italian Fascist sailors on the island.

For tonight's raid there was not enough time to do things by the book which asked for Who, What, When, Where, Why. All Col. Randal could do was try to guess at the answers to those questions. "Guess" was not a banned word in Raiding Forces but it should have been—its use was limited when possible.

The raid on Alimia was what was known in military terms as a "Quick Reaction." That meant responding to a late breaking report of enemy activity, going in fast with unconfirmable intelligence and the raid team commander relying on the skill, training and mental acuity of his troops to rapidly adapt to the situation once they had boots on the ground.

Quick Reaction translates into high risk—it can also be described as "flying by the seat of your pants".

Col. Randal said, "Concept of the Operation: Commander Seaborn will depart Castelrozzo for Alimia at 1800 hours. Time to target is approximately four hours. When the PT boat is thirty minutes out, the Commander will radio ABCHQ his position. At that time a six-man team consisting of Captain Jaxx, Sergeant Major Beckwith, Mr. King, Lovat Scouts Fenwick and Ferguson and I will board the Hudson for the flight to Alimia. General Blackwell is the pilot. General Donovan will be onboard to observe the parachute insertion.

"The team will drop on the saddle located between these two hills in the center of the island," Col. Randal tapped the location on the map with a wooden pointer.

"While the team is airborne en route to the drop zone, Commander Seaborn, standing by offshore Alimia in PT 10, will close on the mouth of the harbor. His boat will set up a block to prevent the Italian Argonauta-class submarine believed to be refueling in pens located there from being able to depart.

"Captain Honeycutt-Parker, already at sea on an MI-9 mission, has been diverted to this beach." Col. Randal tapped the location with the pointer on the north side of the island.

"The Captain will notify ABCHQ immediately upon her arrival. Colonel Stone will then radio the Hudson confirmation she is in position. The MAS boat will stand by to extract the raid team subsequent to the withdrawal phase.

"Immediately following the drop, the Strike Team will assemble and advance to a location approximately here," the pointer tapped the map, " . . . to establish their Objective Rally Point. Order of march to the ORP is King, me, the Sergeant Major, then Captain Jaxx followed by the Lovat Scouts." Col. Randal pointed to a spot on the map two hundred yards from the harbor.

"Upon arriving in the ORP the team will break into two elements. Captain Jaxx and the Lovat Scouts will immediately advance to the west side of the harbor to establish his Final Objective Rally Point located approximately here." The pointer tapped the location. "Once in the FORP with the target—the fuel dump—in sight, his element will pause.

"My team consisting of the Sergeant Major, King and myself will pause for ten minutes and then follow Capt. Jaxx's team out of the ORP and move to the right side of the harbor to our FORP located in sight of the small Regia Marina barracks located here."

The pointer indicated the position.

"Our mission will be to create a diversion designed to pin down the enemy troops in the vicinity of the barracks and draw off sentries from the fuel storage area, allowing Captain Jaxx's team freedom of movement throughout his target. The sound of our firing is Captain Jaxx's signal to infiltrate the POL dump, place the prepared charges and withdraw.

"Once his people clear the area, Captain Jaxx will put up a red flare. That will be the signal for my party to break contact. Both teams will then travel independently to the Extraction Point where they will link up with Captain Honeycutt-Parker . . ."

The pointer tapped the beach previously indicated on the north side of Alimia.

" . . . for the return to Castelrozzo.

"The purpose of the exercise is: 1: To announce to the Nazis that Raiding Forces is still in business. 2: To destroy a valuable enemy fuel facility. 3: Force the Italian sub being refueled to put to sea in the belief the submarine pens are about to be overrun by a ground attack only to run head-long into Commander Seaborn's PT 10, which will engage with all organic weapons.

"Command and Signal . . ."

After Col. Randal said, "This concludes my briefing," Vice Admiral Sir "Razor" Randolph Ransom stood up. "I would like to revisit something the Colonel glossed over—the 'Why we are doing this?' This operation was designed from inception as a submarine ambush. I am not aware of anything like it having been attempted previously—ever. If tonight goes as planned, Raiding Forces shall be making naval warfare history. To all involved I say, 'fair winds and following seas—Godspeed.'"

As close to emotional as anyone had ever heard the Razor.

7

SILENCED OR SUPPRESSED

IMMEDIATELY FOLLOWING THE OPERATIONS ORDER FOR the Alimia mission, people lined up to speak to Colonel John Randal. Captain Billy Jack Jaxx was first. "Good opportunity to test the silenced submachine guns General Donovan brought us, sir."

Col. Randal said, "Issue them to your people. Mine will be making noise. Let me know when you plan to test fire. I'll try to be there to observe."

"Wilco."

Next was Lieutenant Ted Hamilton.

"Sir, you need to include me in your diversion element. I can be your Brixia gunner. Those 45mm mortar rounds will definitely make the sound signature of a ground attack more realistic."

"Not happening, Lieutenant."

Captain "Pyro" Percy Stirling was waiting behind The Great Teddy.

"Colonel, you mentioned your intention is for me to be made a squadron leader at some point in the future. This might be my last chance at a pure demolitions job. Any possibility you have room for one more?"

Col. Randal said, "Much as I'd like to see you blow that fuel storage facility sky-high for old times' sake Percy, that would be a negative. What you can do is go get with Colonel Stone. He has something he'd like to give you."

"Sir?"

"His old epaulets—consider yourself promoted stud."

"Never occurred to me you meant so soon, Colonel."

Col. Randal said, "You're going to take over Duke Slater's old squadron. I've got plans for you, Major. But as soon as you and Colonel Stone are finished, I need you to supervise preparing the explosive charges for Captain Jaxx's people."

"With pleasure, sir."

"Talk to Jack about how he wants you to time the fuses."

Lieutenant General "Geronimo" Joe McKoy was next. "Pretty slick, John. You're turnin' into a first-class military politician."

Col. Randal said, "General, please anything but that."

Lt. Gen. McKoy said, "It's true. Bronc gets to fly a combat drop authorizin' him to paint another one of those little white parachutes on the nose of his fancy designer airplane. Wild Bill gets to go on an actual mission he can brag about to the President when he gets back to Washington. And you get 'em both to depart your immediate area happy as clams.

"Always good policy, politically speakin', to have the big brass sayin' adios with smiles on their faces."

Col. Randal said, "Jack intends to take General Donovan's suppressed SMGs tonight. He's going to test fire prior to. You might want to be there."

Lt. Gen. McKoy said, "Get a jump start on our evaluation for Wild Bill, that's good. Appreciate the heads up, John. I'll be there."

Mandy was next. "I contacted R. J. and informed him of our counterintelligence plans. He is flying in from Cairo to discuss ways for us to structure the program. R. J. says targeting collaborators is the perfect use of our small-scale raiding teams. Did you come up with the plan as a way to pacify Beverly and Pam or was it something you had in mind for a while?"

Col. Randal said, "Chloe Hasapis sheltering the Brandenburger gave me the idea. I never saw that coming."

Mandy said, "Me either. I cannot wait to get started. We shall make you proud, John."

"Always do."

Col. Randal walked over to where Brigadier General William "Wild Bill" Donovan was talking to Major the Lady Jane Seaborn.

Brig. Gen. Donovan said, "I was just saying how enthusiastic I am about the campaign to hunt down Nazi sympathizers throughout the islands. I have a couple of girls in my office we sent through the X-2 Counterintelligence Course to give them a feel for OSS work. I have telexed orders for them to be transferred to Castelrozzo by next available air to assist Lady Jane. Both women have excellent secretarial skills."

Col. Randal said, "Keep in mind Lady Jane has a rule everyone on her staff has to be parachute qualified, General."

Brig. Gen. Donovan said, "No problem on that count. Once word filtered back to OSS quoting Mandy on the orgasmic side effects incidental to jumping out of an aircraft in flight, every girl in the Outfit immediately signed up for airborne training."

Lady Jane laughed, "As well they might."

Brig. Gen. Donovan said, "My aide tape-recorded your briefing, Colonel. Textbook example of how it's supposed to be done. I intend to make the tape mandatory listening for all OG candidates. If you ever feel the need for a break, you two come to Washington. We could use you as a guest instructor at the Farm, as we call the old Congressional Country Club commandeered by OSS for the duration to train our agents."

Lady Jane said, "I would love to, General. Getting John to take…"

Col. Randal said, "Probably not anytime soon, sir. Our operational tempo is getting ready to step it up."

Brig. Gen. Donovan said, "Keep it in mind. The offer's on the table. Work on him, Lady Jane."

Captain Stephanie Fawcett-Tatum came by. "Penelope called in a SITREP. She is ten miles out from Alimia standing by under camouflage at an uninhabited islet awaiting nightfall to move to the pick up point."

The MAS boat standing by to move into position after dark was the next-to-last piece of the small but complex plan that contained sea, air and land components. It was classic Rule Number 5: "Plan missions backward (know how to get home)". Now that the raiding party had an exit strategy in place, the mission was green-lit.

Col. Randal said, "Inform Jack."

Across the room Master Sergeant Mack Beckwith was in a conversation with Vice Admiral Sir Randolph "Razor" Ransom and

Major General Sam Houston Blackwell. Col. Randal made eye contact. The Sergeant Major excused himself and came over.

Col. Randal said, "We're good to go, Sergeant Major. Get with King. Our element will be armed with the 9mm SMG of choice tonight. We'll need thirty magazines per loaded all tracers—make it happen."

"I'm on it, Colonel. How about stun grenades? They create a lot of noise."

"As many as we can carry—pick a number."

"Yes, sir."

"Touch base with Captain Jaxx about test firing. We'll do ours when he does."

"Wilco."

"Set up a time for us to draw parachutes."

"King already took care of that, sir. Our chutes are stored in your office."

"Don't you let me forget anything, Sergeant Major."

"I won't, Colonel—no problem sir."

At this point, mission prep started to pick up speed. There is a maxim in the military, "Hurry up and wait." It is 100 percent true 100 percent of the time. This was the start of the hurry-up phase. It was almost as if the clock suddenly fast-forwarded.

Beverly blazed into the TOC with her faded blue jeans tucked into alligator peewee cowgirl boots, her perfect white teeth flashing beneath piles of feathered blond hair—she was in search of Col. Randal.

"I want to make it absolutely clear I wasn't ever really mad at you, Johnny—not personally."

Col. Randal said, "Fooled me."

"You were only being protective. Love that, actually, but don't tell anybody I said so. By the way, you revealed something about yourself today I didn't know."

"What might that be?"

"You have a conscience."

"That's classified."

Overt public displays of affection are not condoned for active-duty armed forces personnel. However, for that rule of soldierly etiquette to apply, an individual must be governed by military authority. Beverly had never been able to actually visualize herself as being in the service. She gave Col. Randal a big hug and kissed him on the cheek in front of everyone in the TOC.

Across the room, Lady Jane winked at him.

Lt. Gen. McKoy strolled over after Beverly left to help her father conduct his preflight inspection of the Hudson. He handed Col. Randal a handkerchief to wipe the lipstick off his cheek. "Way to go, John. Not only did you lift the never-implemented no-fly restriction on the girls, but now you're lettin' 'em go on counterintelligence raids to snatch up collaborators. And somehow Lady Jane managed to get herself in on the rotation. Sounds to me like you went backwards, son. It ain't easy being king."

"Roger that."

TYPICALLY THE GENERAL INSTRUCTIONS PARAGRAPH OF A Warning Order would have covered uniforms, weapons, equipment, etc. and the various times certain pre-mission tasks were to be carried out— like drawing parachutes, test firing weapons, conducting rehearsals and performing other tasks incidental to carrying out a raid deep in enemy territory. However, the Alimia operation did not fit neatly into a standard type of box. In fact, almost no mission ever did, no matter how much effort was expended to standardize the process of preparation for them.

Only the bare basics had been briefed, as per Raiding Forces Rule Number 2—keep it short and simple—a mark of professionalism. It is never a good idea to overload troops with too much information. A commander wants his people focused on the mission, not trying to remember unnecessary details.

Everyone on Strike Team was a long-time special operations veteran. They worked together with a cohesion never achieved by traditional line infantry or paratroopers and only rarely by British Commando or American Ranger units.

Strike Team personnel knew what they were doing. And they knew from the briefing and past experience what the other team members were doing as well. They performed at a level of execution bordering on military extra-sensory perception.

Other than to designate the location of the drop zone and decide on a general time window for takeoff contingent on when Lieutenant Randy "Hornblower" Seaborn's PT boat was in position, there was not much more for Col. Randal to do at this point. Except make himself readily available to answer any questions that might come up.

Strike Team did not require much hand-holding during the preparation phase. The men knew the drill. They had "Go" bags packed with everything needed to launch on a moment's notice, though there was mission-specific gear that needed to be brought along tonight. Captain Billy Jack Jaxx's team would be taking suppressed SMGs and prepared demolitions, and a flare pistol with red flares.

Mission prep does not get much simpler, but then that was the idea.

Even so, Colonel John Randal was a stickler for planning—the issuance of Warning and Operations Orders and pre-mission preparation had to be done by the book. He scheduled a rehearsal for 1700 hours. That would allow time to get in a quick test fire of their weapons.

Capt. Jaxx came into the TOC with Lieutenant Chase Starrett. They had been carrying out an inspection of the Hudson to make sure everything was in readiness for the drop. Lt. Starrett would be the static jumpmaster tonight—meaning he would not be exiting the aircraft. Not normal procedure in Raiding Forces.

In most cases Col. Randal jump-mastered combat drops on the planes he was aboard and led the stick out the door—always first to jump. The safety check for a towed parachutist and retrieval of the static lines was left to the loadmaster. Tonight, that would be Corporal Tom Murphy aka Murph the Surf—Beverly's navigator and jack-of-all-trades on the Hudson. Lt. Starrett would assist him with the task of pulling in the static lines.

For this drop the protocol was going to be modified slightly to free up Col. Randal to focus exclusively on the mission, not the getting there, until the last second. Lt. Starrett would jumpmaster up until the command "Stand in The Door." The stick, consisting of Col. Randal followed by King, Master Sergeant Mack Beckwith, Capt. Jaxx and the Lovat Scouts—in that order—would close on the door. At that point, Lt. Starrett would relinquish his jumpmaster responsibilities to Col. Randal, give the command, "It's your door, sir," and move away to the tail of the aircraft.

Major General Sam Houston Blackwell would activate the green light when the plane reached the Final Point—the location for the jumpers to exit the aircraft. The Final Point was an imaginary line Maj. Gen. Blackwell selected from a map study prior to departure marked by some easily recognizable terrain feature or features he would be able to see at night. Crossing that line would be his indicator to turn on the green light.

Regardless of the electronic signal, Col. Randal— at this point acting as the jumpmaster—would give the command "GO" and lead the stick out the door after he personally made a head-check to visually confirm the aircraft was over the DZ. Strike Team would be jumping a short three-second drop zone—the rule of thumb on timing is one second per jumper not counting the first man in the door. Strike Team had four jumpers not counting Col. Randal. They would have to stack the door and exit fast, having less than a second each to exit the aircraft.

There was no margin for error on this jump.

Maj. Gen. Blackwell's flight plan called for the Hudson to travel past Alimia far out to sea, loop around and come back across the island to make the drop. He would be flying just above the waves and then climb up to 500 feet to achieve minimum jump altitude then drop back down for his egress.

As Bronc cheerfully pointed out, the beauty of the plan was, "Following the drop I'll be headed back toward Castelrozzo at wave-top level going like a bat out of hell." The idea being to minimize the response time enemy night fighters on Rhodes had to scramble if they picked the Hudson up on radar when it popped up to jump altitude.

Considering Rhodes was only five miles distant and had three Luftwaffe airfields, it was a good plan.

With the direction of flight, the limitations of the terrain and Alimia being such a tiny island, it was imperative for Strike Team to hit the DZ dead on or the stick might parachute directly into the enemy camp or even worse, the harbor. When to exit the aircraft was not a decision Col. Randal was about to delegate.

Lt. Starrett reported, "Hudson's good to go for the jump, sir."

Capt. Jaxx said, "Roger that."

Col. Randal ordered, "Have your team bring their suppressed .22s tonight as backup, Jack. We have no idea how long those silenced SMGs will run under field conditions. Even after we test fire."

Capt. Jaxx said, "Yes, sir."

He did not mention having already issued those exact instructions to his people.

VICE ADMIRAL SIR RANDOLPH "RAZOR" RANSOM LED A contingent of the ABCHQ staff, other Raiding Forces personnel and visitors in the building down to the dock to see Lieutenant Commander Randy "Hornblower" Seaborn's departure. It was a long-standing tradition to see off or greet those returning from a mission. This afternoon's was a particularly stirring event.

The Allies had been driven out of the Aegean. The Nazis had conquered, occupied or—at a minimum—controlled every island in the AO except Castelrozzo. Nevertheless, Lt. Cdr. Seaborn was setting out in his tiny wooden PT boat to give battle.

This was not a patrol. There was a fight ahead.

Waiting on the dock for the boat to get underway, Major General Sam Houston Blackwell said, "Whose picture you carryin' on your pistol today, Jack?"

Captain Billy Jack Jaxx removed his 1911 Colt .38 Super from his chest holster and handed it over butt first. There was an exotic blond wearing a lot of jewelry and not much else in the photo under the right Plexiglas panel of his pistol grip.

"Round in the chamber, sir."

Maj. Gen. Blackwell admired the photograph, "Woah, who is she and when do I get an introduction?"

Capt. Jaxx said, "One of General McKoy's dancer 'friends,' sir, a Slovenian refugee. Her name is Zsa Zsa."

Maj. Gen. Blackwell said, "Any chance she has a sister, Jack?"

Colonel John Randal, Major the Lady Jane Seaborn and Happy arrived at the dock. "Permission to come aboard?"

Lt. Cdr. Seaborn said, "Permission granted, sir."

Col. Randal saluted the Red Ensign on the stern before going aboard. VAdm. Ransom was already there with Lieutenant General "Geronimo" Joe McKoy, who was standing by listening to the last-minute instructions. This was a high-risk, high-reward operation. It was imperative Lt. Cdr. Seaborn understood his orders and had everything he needed to successfully carry them out with no questions left unanswered before putting to sea.

Brigadier General William "Wild Bill" Donovan and Major General Sam Houston Blackwell appeared. Unable to constrain himself on the dock, Wild Bill called out, "Permission to come aboard?"

"Permission granted, sir."

When Brig. Gen. Donovan joined the group there were three officers in the huddle who were the recipients of their nation's highest medal for valor. VAdm. Ransom was saying, "Give ABCHQ a SITREP when you reach your checkpoint thirty minutes out from Alimia. That triggers clearing General Blackwell for take-off.

"Upon arriving at the island, stand by a mile offshore until the Hudson flies over following the drop on its return leg to Castelrozzo. Then immediately close on the mouth of the harbor cleared for action.

"When the diversionary fireworks begin and the submarine attempts to flee the harbor, first sweep its deck with your direct fire ordnance. Have the Thunderbolt concentrate its initial bursts on the sub's conning tower to neutralize the Italian's command element and take out the crew of the deck gun. Then engage with your torpedoes—settings set for minimum depth.

"The instant your fish leave the tube have your gunners shift their fires to spray the length of the submarine. The .50 calibers and 20 millimeters will penetrate the pressure hull at such close range. There might possibly be a secondary explosion—the result we desire.

"You have a pair of depth charges along tonight. Set them for minimum depth as well. Make a run on the sub. The reverberations from their explosions should prove deadly in the shallows of the restricted harbor. Just be careful not to blow yourself out of the water.

"No matter what, Commander, do not cease firing until the target is destroyed or you have expended every last round of ammunition—including those in your sidearm."

Lt. Cdr. Seaborn said, "We shall board if necessary, Admiral."

Col. Randal was thinking a boarding party might be taking things a little far.

Wild Bill said, "That's the spirit!"

AFTER SEEING OFF PT 10, COLONEL JOHN RANDAL LINKED up with Strike Team to test-fire weapons. Test firing was always a great stress reliever prior to a mission. Everyone liked doing it. As usual, there was a group of Greek boys waiting outside of ABCHQ hoping Captain Billy Jack Jaxx would appear—"Jack's Pack." They followed him around the island everywhere he went.

Capt. Jaxx ignored them today.

Test firing is vital prior to a mission. Weapons have been disassembled, cleaned and reassembled. When going in harm's way it is a good idea to know for absolutely certain your small arms have been reassembled properly and are in good working order. It's not always the case. Mistakes get made. The test firing process is informal. Targets are seldom if ever used. In a pinch Raiding Forces personnel had been known to move off to the side of an airstrip prior to a mission to fire a few rounds into the ground. The standard is pass/fail. The weapons function or not.

If there was going to be a problem it is best found beforehand. Why take a chance? Experienced operators never do. Today the difficulty was finding a safe place to conduct the exercise. There was not much level ground and civilian houses ran up the escarpment. From where ABCHQ was located, firing into the sea meant shooting straight at Turkey—a no-go.

The team, with Jack's Pack trailing along behind, marched along the shoreline until they came to a place where a small point of land jutted out. It provided a spot that angled into the Aegean straight out to sea.

All they needed.

Col. Randal's three-man element went first. Tonight they would be carrying 30-round magazines. To increase the psychological effect of the fire, the magazines were loaded all tracer. His personal Beretta M-38 would have a 20-round magazine inserted for the jump because of it being shorter and more compact, which made the SMG easier to handle onboard the tight quarters of the aircraft.

The practice of jumping with weapons exposed and magazines inserted would make the safety-minded cringe. But then a safety-minded person would probably not load aboard an airplane en route to a distant place in order to jump out in the dark of night to do bad things to bad people. As a concession to safety, Raiding Forces SOP called for not having a round in the chamber of their submachine guns, carbines or rifles.

Not so for sidearms. A pistol not ready for action was of no more use than a paperweight.

Choosing an individual weapon was a subjective decision and one that Raiding Forces did not take lightly. Unit policy was to allow operators to carry the submachine gun and handgun they liked best provided the ammunition was compatible with .22, 9mm, .38 Super, or .45 ACP. All rifles, automatic rifles and light machine guns were in the process of being converted to U.S. Army-issue to increase firepower and standardize ammunition.

The 9mm Beretta MAB 38 was Col. Randal's SMG of choice. Built like a carbine, it handled beautifully and was very controllable on full automatic. The weapon had a few quirky features. The rear sight was adjustable for up to 500 yards which was a trifle optimistic considering the pistol round. Another was its ejection port being mounted on the left side of the receiver resulting in the brass being ejected *across* a right-handed shooter right to left. Not that anyone noticed during a dangerous encounter.

When the procession arrived, it was no surprise for Col. Randal to find Captain Roy Kidd tagging along at the rear of the column. He wanted to observe the suppressed SMGs being tested. Exotic weapons were his passion.

Capt. Jaxx was carrying the suppressed .45 Thompson submachine gun. It got a review even before they reached their impromptu firing range, "This lunker weighs thirteen pounds. Not only is it heavier than my Baby BAR, it's about as long."

By comparison, the suppressed 9mm Sten gun was nine pounds, and the suppressed .45 M3 Grease Gun came in at ten pounds.

Col. Randal's team stepped up to the water's edge and emptied their weapons into the water. Col. Randal's 9mm Beretta MAB 38, Master Sergeant Mack Beckwith's .45 Thompson and King's 9mm SIG MKPO followed by their sidearms. Col. Randal and the Sergeant Major were armed with 1911 Colt .38 Super pistols. King had his prized 9mm Lahti L-35 brought back from the Winter War—it looked like a Luger but was in all probability, designed as it had been for harsh winter conditions, as reliable as a Colt Government Model 1911. There was a story there but the Merc had never told it.

Capt. Jaxx's people were next. He shouldered the .45 M-1928 Thompson and loosed off a burst. The weapon's normally loud blast was dramatically reduced. But it was not silent. He noted the SMG was significantly more controllable with the suppressor mounted than without it.

Col. Randal said, "What do you think?"

Capt. Jaxx said, "It's heavy and unwieldy but it does have merit for clandestine work as a substitute standard, sir."

Translated, his assessment amounted to, "Use only when no other option is available."

Next up was Lovat Scout Lionel Fenwick with the United States Submachine gun, Cal. .45 M3 aka Grease Gun. It was a stubby compact weapon with a sliding wire stock. He pointed it out to sea and let rip a crisp burst. While not silent, it was quiet. The operating handle slamming home made about as much noise as the weapon firing. The suppressed .45 M3 was controllable and easy to operate.

The immediate response from the seasoned observers was a chorus of "Yeahs." The suppressed Grease Gun was a night-fighting weapon the veteran operators could appreciate. And they were a critical audience who took their personal arms seriously.

Lovat Scout Munro Ferguson went last with the 9mm Sten submachine gun. It cost $11 to manufacture but looked overpriced. The ungainly weapon was not a firearm to instill confidence. That was a misconception. In tests prior to adoption the 9mm Sten had proven as reliable as the much more expensive .45 M-1928 Thompson.

However, the suppressed Sten came with a built-in drawback. Designed to eliminate sentries or guard dogs, it could only be fired in semi-auto or short two- or three-round bursts due to its tendency to overheat. A canvas jacket was laced to the barrel as a handgrip heat shield but it was not overly effective. Raiding Forces' typical contact was short and intense at close range. Killing, incapacitating, or at a minimum gaining fire superiority over the opposition in order to maneuver on and close with being the standard required.

Any limitation on volume of fire at any point while carrying that out was a deal killer as a primary weapon. That was unfortunate because the 9mm Sten was the quietest of all three SMGs—at least 20 percent less sound signature than the M3. The *bolt* slamming into the British weapon's battery was louder than the report of the rounds.

It sounded not unlike a snake hissing.

Capt. Kidd said, "Mind if I give it a try, Ferguson?"

He brought the Sten to his shoulder and loosed off a fairly long burst, which did cause it to heat up.

"Shoots like squirting a water hose. Don't care for the balance because of the side-mounted magazine—might get used to it with practice."

Col. Randal said, "First impressions of all three based on your observations, Roy?"

"I'm liking the Grease Gun, sir."

Col. Randal said, "Any chance you can get your buddies at the 27th Ordnance to build a suppressor for my MAB 38?"

"Read my mind, Colonel."

Capt. Jaxx's team emptied their carry pistols into the water rapid fire. Then the men changed magazines and holstered their handguns. All weapons were good to go.

Test fire concluded—check.

OUTSIDE ABCHQ THERE WAS ENOUGH LEVEL SPACE ON the lawn to conduct the Strike Team's rehearsal. Whenever possible it was SOP to conduct rehearsals of everything from boarding the aircraft to the withdrawal phase—in this case that would be embarkment on the MAS boat during the egress which was not possible today because both were at sea. While conducting rehearsals is taught to all leaders at all levels in their training, not many units actually go to the trouble on the grounds that their troops have done it all before.

Not Raiding Forces. Colonel John Randal demanded his officers conduct rehearsals. Even if they limited to simply walking through the progressions of the mission. In worst case, when there was no way to conduct even a modified walk-through rehearsal, talking the troops through the mission step by step had to suffice—but it was done.

Rehearsals can be simple or elaborate given time and detailed advance intelligence. For some raids it was possible to build a mock-up replicating the target down to the last detail and days, weeks or even months could be spent rehearsing the actions on the objective. In that case, the troops had the luxury to first walk through the scheme of maneuver, gradually work up to speed and finally go full-speed live fire.

For a raid, rehearsals are important.

Tonight the plan called for Strike Team to attack Alimia's fuel depot, which would force the enemy submarine refueling in the sub pens to flee. The only problem being there was no intel on where the fuel dump was located—only a general description.

With all the unknowns, by necessity, the rehearsal was bare bones. Basically the sequence of events.

For a raid of this complexity, with little intelligence and no time to send in a recon team, it would be best if a reconnaissance aircraft could be dispatched to the island to take aerial photographs of the objective. That was not going to happen. The three enemy airfields on Rhodes precluded any daylight flyover and the sub would most likely be gone if the raid was postponed until after a photo reconnaissance flight could be made during the hours of darkness.

All Col. Randal had to go on was outdated, incomplete intelligence—except for the current sighting of the submarine. The rehearsal started on the lawn. It drew a crowd. All the visiting officers in residence were observing. Col. Randal was not unaware Major the Lord George Jellicoe (SBS) and Major David Lloyd Owen (LRDG) were present. He wanted to take the opportunity to impress on them how he expected mission preparation to be done in their commands in the future. All Raiding Forces personnel who could break away from their duties were also on hand observing with highly professional—and critical—interest.

To those uninitiated in small unit tactics the rehearsal probably looked like a waste of time—boys playing army.

That would be a mistake.

Lieutenant Chase Starrett simulating his role as static jumpmaster said, "It's your door, Colonel."

Then he backed away.

Col. Randal, standing at the head of a file consisting of King, Master Sergeant Mack Beckwith, Captain Billy Jack Jaxx, Lovat Scout Munro Ferguson and Lovat Scout Lionel Fenwick—the exact sequence of the stick of jumpers—shouted "GO."

Then Col. Randal hopped forward in a tight tuck position head down with his chin on his chest as if exiting from an aircraft. He began counting "One thousand, two thousand . . ." Each jumper in the stick followed suit until all six were standing knees bent mimicking having their hands on the sides of their reserve parachutes, elbows in tight, counting loudly.

Even to the unversed eye, the drill quit looking ridiculous. Strike Team personnel, all legends in their own right, were taking the exercise deadly serious. They were not the caliber of men to play at being soldiers. Or to take their preparation for an upcoming mission lightly.

Silly-looking or not.

As soon as Scout Fenwick, the last man in the stick, ceased counting at four thousand, Col. Randal took a knee. He purposely did not simulate making a parachute landing fall (PLF). Experience had shown more injuries came from practicing PLFs at ground level—even when doing them in a sand pit, prior to a jump, than were incurred on the actual drop.

King and MSgt. Beckwith moved up on either side of him and took a knee, making a tiny half-circle. Capt. Jaxx and the two Lovat Scouts knelt down facing out in the opposite direction completing the perimeter.

At this point the rehearsal on the lawn of ABCHQ was completed. Col. Randal tapped King on the shoulder. The Merc stood up and moved out to the path leading up the escarpment. Col. Randal fell in behind him with the rest of the stick following suit in the correct patrol order. They patrolled all the way to the top of the cobblestone walkway, every other man facing out in the opposite direction, with Scout Fenwick walking backward providing rear security.

The observers, to include Jack's Pack, followed along at a discreet distance.

Upon reaching level ground at the beginning of the plateau, King took a knee. Strike Team went into a defensive perimeter again. This was the simulated Objective Rally Point.

After a brief pause, Col. Randal reached out and tapped Capt. Jaxx on the shoulder. He stood up and, followed by the Lovat Scouts, stepped out at a 45-degree angle simulating moving toward the fuel dump.

Col. Randal looked at his Rolex. He waited a full ten minutes as called for in the Operations Order, Concept of the Operations paragraph, to allow Capt. Jaxx to get into position. Then he stood up and led his element out in a file from the other side of the ORP, to simulate his advance to the troop barracks. After a short distance, he went back down on one knee simulating being in the team's Final Objective Rally Point (FORP).

Col. Randal gave the command of "Now" and they all started shouting, "BANG, BANG, BANG. . ." The diversion.

Capt. Jaxx immediately stood up from his team's FORP and moved forward with his element, simulating entering the fuel storage area and pantomiming placing their explosives. With the charges in place, the men pulled back to their FORP.

Capt. Jaxx shouted, "RED FLARE."

That was the signal for Col. Randal's element to cease the diversion and break contact. What sets raids apart from other offensive military operations is that they are designed with a *planned* withdrawal. Get in, do the job and go home. Moving independently of each other, both elements began to exfil back. Eventually the two elements linked up, to simulate arriving at the extraction point on the beach where the MAS boat would be waiting.

It may not have seemed like much and might have even appeared pointless to some. But now everyone on Strike Team had not only heard the verbal instructions from Col. Randal when he issued the OP Order, they had walked through the mission step by step in the exact sequence it would be carried out on Alimia later that night. At this point not only did each man know his job, he knew every other man's job because he had watched them perform it.

Col. Randal assembled Strike Team for a brief critique of the exercise.

Rehearsals concluded—check.

NOW THE WAIT PHASE KICKED IN. THAT WAS WHEN THE clock stopped. There was a ball room down the hall from the TOC that was empty of furniture. It was used by Raiding Forces' teams as a Ready Room. All personnel going on the mission had their gear, to include parachutes and primary weapons, stowed there. Strike Team was sprawled on the floor leaning back against their chutes lost in their own thoughts.

Since Raiding Forces was always on Standby Alert, this afternoon's Strike Team transitioned to Standby Ready Alert which meant they were armed and equipped waiting for the word to go. Later, at a time to be determined, the team would transition to Red Alert. The men would then begin the movement to the dock, preparatory to chuting up and loading on the Hudson.

The waiting is the worst part. That's what everyone always says right up until the moment when the bad guys start shooting. Of course, flying to the drop zone in an AO where the enemy has established air superiority is not without its vicissitudes. Everyone was going to have to sit and wonder if a Luftwaffe night fighter was about to blast the Hudson out of the sky at any second.

Raiding Forces was not for the faint of heart—an active imagination being a drawback.

Captain Billy Jack Jaxx was holding court for those paying attention. "Back home in my county we had a well-oiled legal machine going for us. The criminal justice system in West Texas has a unique ability to improvise and adapt as needed to meet the constantly changing demands of protecting and serving. My grandfather—the sheriff, the county judge, the district attorney, and I held a weekly card game at the jail on Wednesday nights. Stakes weren't high but it was cutthroat poker.

"Any wrangling over an upcoming hearing or trial and any other legal maneuvering to include oral arguments was worked out in advance during our games. There was always plenty of fireworks in the courtroom but not a lot of surprises—unless somebody forgot their lines.

"A confidence man from Chicago rolled into town and attempted to swindle a couple of maiden sisters. Promised to marry both of 'em. On the sly the crook was trying to talk each of 'em into signing powers of attorney authorizing him to handle her finances.

"The swindle was going to plan until he retained the only lawyer in the county to draw up matching sets of documents for both women. Unfortunately for the conman his attorney was a regular at our poker game. Attorney-client privilege was not in effect when we had cards on the table.

"The next Wednesday night when he heard the story, the county judge said, 'Sheriff why don't you arrest that malfeasant?'

"'On what grounds, Judge?'

"The DA said, 'No crime's been committed yet, your Honor.'

"So the judge says, 'Let's get him for attempted bigamy.'"

Colonel John Randal pushed his cut-down bush hat over his eyes and dozed off. Major the Lady Jane Seaborn arrived, stretched out on the floor next to him and leaned back against his X-type parachute.

Happy slunk in and lay down on the other side with his head on his paws. The dog was trying to make amends. He had been staying out of sight after chasing the Nazi without permission.

Col. Randal reached over and scratched him between the ears.

Capt. Jaxx was saying, "We had this degenerate chicken thief named Rat Faced Ricky . . ."

Time was standing still.

2315 HOURS. COLONEL JOHN RANDAL ORDERED, "RED ALERT —Saddle Up!"

That meant Lieutenant Commander Randy Seaborn's PT boat 10 had radioed it reached a checkpoint thirty minutes out from the island. For

Strike Team it was the signal to move down to the dock and board the Hudson incidental to their drop on Alimia.

There would be one other crucial radio message from Captain Penelope Honeycutt-Parker OBE, GM, RM, to inform RFHQ when she arrived at the extraction point on the north side of Alimia. With Lt. Cmdr. Seaborn in place she would be beginning her movement now.

The men shook out their individual load-bearing gear and put it on unbuckled, slung their parachutes over their shoulders, picked up their primary weapons and swaggered toward the door. The operators moved with the casual ease of troops who had done this before. It was business as usual.

Outside in the hall the walls were lined with observers seeing them off. Non-mission personnel would not be allowed to accompany Strike Team to the dock to avoid confusion during loading aboard the Hudson. There were, however, exceptions to every rule.

Major the Lady Jane Seaborn, Captain Pamala Plum-Martin, Beverly and Mandy did not recognize that the restriction applied to them—it never crossed their mind. They escorted the team as it made its way down the cobblestone path to the dock. There was a three-quarter moon out. It was a beautiful night. Upon reaching the dock the jumpers wasted no time chuting up. Everyone paired off. Col. Randal and King worked together.

King went first. He buckled his load-bearing gear, slung his parachute pack on his back, stuck his arms through the shoulder straps, adjusted them for feel—meaning they were pulled tight—then jumped up and down to settle it on his back. Col. Randal helped ensure the chute was squarely centered then starting at the shoulders, ran his hands under the straps to confirm they were flat and not twisted.

"Bend."

The Merc leaned forward bending at the waist. Still in back Col. Randal squatted down and secured the two straps dangling down. He made sure they were flat in his hand as he passed them to King.

"Right leg strap."

King said, "Right leg strap."

He reached down and took the metaled end of the canvas strap, brought it up to his chest and clicked it into the quick release on his chest.

"Left leg strap."

There were two things that made the British X-type parachute rig far superior to the U.S. T-5. One was the soft opening shock and the other was the Quick Release System (QRS). An Army review board tested the QRS but rejected it. That decision cost American lives during combat jumps of both the 509th Parachute Infantry Battalion and the 82nd Airborne Division. And still there was no move to obtain the QRS.

U.S. Army paratroopers were expected to unbuckle their canvas shoulder straps when they landed. Not easy to do when the canvas strap was pulled in tight by the buckle due to the force of the notoriously sharp opening crack of the T-5's canopy, which caused the dreaded "riser burn". When the strap was wet, it was basically impossible to unbuckle. U.S. jumpers were issued M-2 switchblade jump knives to zip into a special pocket in the collars of their M-42 Jump Jackets to use to cut their way out of their harness in such an emergency.

The idea was more ridiculous than it sounded. If you were dangling from a tree or drowning in a swamp, the instructions were, "Reach up, fingers extended and joined, arm held at a 45-degree angle, unzip your M-42 Jump Jacket collar, take out your one each switchblade M-2 . . ."

The M-2 switchblades were popular with Raiding Forces personnel going on leave in Cairo.

Next Col. Randal went around in front and held the reserve parachute while King threaded the belly band strap through the loops on the back—the bands were tight and the process took effort to slide the thick canvas strap through. Then he moved to the right side and while the Merc braced himself, he pulled the strap with all his might to the point it was hard for King to breathe. While this was uncomfortable it was not going to cause a problem later getting out of the harness after he landed. When the safety clip was jerked off and the Merc hammered the quick release on his chest with his fist, all of the parachute straps would fall free taking the reserve with them—Hey, Presto!

The QRS made getting out of a parachute fast and easy.

Raiding Forces jumped a "Frankenstein" rig—British X-type parachute with QRS and U.S. harness for the reserve. It was the best combination worldwide for military parachuting with no second place.

Once King was chuted up, it was Col. Randal's turn.

When everyone was strapped into their parachute Lieutenant Chase Starrett had Strike Team line up on the dock. He started at the front of the stick, went down the file and performed a jumpmaster inspection on each man. He took his time. Col. Randal demanded strict accordance to procedure—no shortcuts.

Shortly after the jumpmaster inspection was complete, Lieutenant Ted Hamilton arrived at the dock carrying Col. Randal's Brixia 45mm shoulder-fired mortar, a pack full of mortar rounds, a large duffel bag and a parachute.

Col. Randal said, "You can't show up, Lieutenant, and expect to go on an operation."

Lt. Hamilton shouted, "Execute, execute, execute!"

Further down the shore, Vice Admiral Sir Randolph "Razor" Ransom lit the fuse to a device the Great Teddy had provided him and sought cover. It was good he did because the whole of Castelrozzo seemed to explode with streams of what appeared to be large caliber tracer rounds crisscrossing the sky. The booms kept coming accompanied by blinding white flashes. They went on for a long time.

Col. Randal said, "What is that?"

Lt. Hamilton said, "I call it my M1E1 World War III Deception Device, sir."

"What's the 'E' stand for?"

"Experimental, sir."

"You have more?"

"Yes, sir. In the duffel bag."

"Chute up, stud. I'll jump the Brixia and the mortar rounds. You stay right in my hip pocket—clear?"

"Yes, sir!"

Lt. Col. Randal said, "The Turks probably imagine WWIII has started."

Capt. Jaxx said, "Yeah, Ted, you need to work on your international diplomacy skills."

As Strike Team began filing aboard the Hudson, Lady Jane walked over.

"I do not want you setting off tonight still angry with me."

Col. Randal said, "For shooting it out with the Nazi? Actually Jane I thought you looked pretty good in there. You'd have taken him."

Lady Jane laughed, "Seeing you come through the door was a relief."

As the last of Strike Team was emplaning, the "no public display of affection" policy was violated . . . again.

Col. Randal made his way onboard and moved up to the cockpit where Major General Sam Houston Blackwell and Brigadier General William "Wild Bill" Donovan were waiting.

"Let's do this."

8
MILITARY POETRY

THE HUDSON MARK IV HAD A TOP SPEED OF 245 MPH. Tonight flight time to target was estimated at forty-five minutes based on the flight path for this mission. Major General Sam Houston Blackwell was flying so low that mist from the waves sprayed the windscreen. The RAF officers and crewmen who flew the Hudson class of bombers had given them the nickname of "Old Boomerang" for the model's ability to soak up enemy fire and return to base. It was a reassuring moniker for an aircraft embarking on a nighttime incursion over enemy territory. The three Luftwaffe airfields on Rhodes were a concern.

The Germans were known to have radar.

The big risk was the station being able to pick up the Hudson in time to scramble night-fighting capable interceptors. According to James "Baldie" Taylor it was not clear if there were any night fighters stationed on Rhodes. Maj. Gen. Blackwell was not taking any chances. He had the plane down flying what seemed like inches above the water, under the radar. While 245 mph may not sound very fast, for the two generals in the cockpit the effect of skimming the waves at such a low level gave the impression of screaming through the night at insane speed.

Tonight's mission required precision navigation. Alimia was a tiny three-square-mile island—actually less according to some sources. Maj. Gen. Blackwell was not only piloting the Hudson, he was also acting as his own navigator. For reasons not shared with anyone, Bronc had turned down Beverly's offer for Corporal Tom Murphy to perform the navigation. While the flight plan was fairly simple it was imperative Bronc hit it on the first pass. If he missed, he did not have the luxury of being able to circle around searching for what was a mere speck in the Aegean Sea.

Finding Alimia in broad daylight would be difficult enough under normal conditions. But avoiding enemy radar meant Maj. Gen. Blackwell had to sacrifice the altitude that would enable him to spot the island from a distance. Fortunately, Bronc was one of the most skilled pilots in the U.S. Army Air Force—a veteran of two wars and a crop duster who performed aerobatics for his own entertainment in his spare time.

In the copilot's seat Brigadier General William "Wild Bill" Donovan was trying not to look at the waves. He was wondering why his longtime hunting partner had refused the services of an experienced navigator? Except with women Bronc was not impulsive; everything he did had a reason.

Captain Billy Jack Jaxx shuffled up to the cockpit to talk football. One glance out the windscreen and he regretted having left his seat. It looked like one large breaker could reach up and slap the plane out of the sky.

He did not hang around for long.

Back in the troop compartment across from Colonel John Randal on the canvas bench seat, Capt. Jaxx said, "You have any idea how low we're flying, sir?"

Col. Randal said, "I don't want to know."

Flight time was estimated at forty-five minutes. It seemed to be taking longer but then that was always the case with a combat jump. Strike Team wanted out of the airplane in a bad way but none of them were making a big deal out of it. With no advance warning the Hudson began a hard 180-degree turn to the right.

Everyone knew what that meant.

They were on the run into the DZ. The Hudson's flight path had taken it past Alimia and now the aircraft was looping around to approach the island from the north so it would have a head start on the egress home following the drop. Tension ratcheted down and was replaced with impatience which would seem to be the opposite of what most people would expect with the jump imminent. But for seasoned veteran paratroopers, the wait was almost over. Strike Team was ready to get the mission started.

Waiting . . . was the hard part.

The red light came on over the exit in the tail of the Hudson. Lieutenant Chase Starrett was standing by the door. He muscled the locking lever to the rear. Then the lieutenant and Murph the Surf slammed the door open and secured it to the bulkhead.

Wind started howling in the open exit.

In the cockpit Maj. Gen. Blackwell was cutting back on his airspeed. He wanted to get it down to 110 mph at green light. Exiting from an aircraft flying too fast could, and probably would, result in any number of different major parachute malfunctions and end the mission before it began.

Lt. Starrett stuck out both hands with his fingers splayed and stamped his boot on the deck, "TEN MINUTES!"

Col. Randal was thinking, *Bronc must be pretty sure of himself to go with a ten-minute warning. He can't see Alimia. Not this far out at this low altitude.*

All the command did was cause Strike Team to sit up straight and start running their hands over their gear for the hundredth time. Paratroopers constantly check and recheck—everything. Over and over, feeling momentary clutches of panic when they think they had forgotten something only to find it.

The next few minutes seemed to take longer than the flight out. Had they missed the island? It was possible. Col. Randal kept his eyes on Lt. Starrett. The jumpmaster was wearing a headset staying in constant communication with the cockpit.

Lt. Starrett shouted, "SIX MINUTES!"

Actually, the operators did not have six minutes before the series of jump commands commenced. Lt. Starrett meant until the drop. Jump commands for tonight's mission were heavily condensed.

"STAND UP AND HOOK UP!"

Strike Team struggled into the upright position. It was close in the Hudson. As skilled and proficient as the operators were, standing up and hooking up their snap links to the static line was easy. Sticking the safety wire through the tiny hole on the snap link in the dim red light of the interior of the compartment—that was another story. Especially while trying to maintain balance from the buffeting of the aircraft and knowing time was running out to get it done. The jumpers stood with their knees slightly flexed to absorb the constant up and down and crabbing sideways and back motion—rolling with it, going in, doing it, this was the modern-day equivalent of a cavalry charge.

Now the adrenaline was starting to kick in.

"CHECK STATIC LINE!"

This was followed by the rasping of metal on metal—snap link on cable.

Tonight the "check your equipment" and "sound off for equipment check" commands were being left off—everyone was jumping.

Lt. Starrett was spread eagle in the exit leaning out trying to spot the island up ahead. There was no need to perform the standard jumpmaster's safety check, this being a single plane drop. As soon as he saw Alimia he swung back inside, grabbed a handful of Col. Randal's M-42 jump jacket, pulled him forward and shouted, "STAND IN THE DOOR." The rest of the stick followed, shuffling up tight and stacking the exit. The jumpers were aware of the short three-second drop zone and what the ramifications of missing it were.

Col. Randal adding an extra jumper to the stick only increased the need for a fast exit.

Suddenly the Hudson swooped up in a radical power climb, nearly throwing everyone to the deck. Knowing it was coming Strike Team had been bracing themselves. Still, it was not easy to stay on their feet. Maj. Gen Blackwell was gaining altitude to achieve minimum jump altitude.

The climb was also the signal the drop was only seconds away.

Lt. Starrett shouted, "It's your door, sir!"

Then he stepped out of the way.

Col. Randal moved into the exit. He reached up, gripped the rim that ran around it with his fingertips, then stamped his canvas-topped raiding boots against both sides to wedge them. He arched outside the aircraft looking up ahead. The wind whipped his clothes, distorted his face, and blurred his vision.

There being no checkpoints tonight he was searching for two specific terrain features. A pair of prominent hilltops. The stick would drop in the saddle between them. Spotting the drop zone dead ahead and coming up fast, Col. Randal leaned back inside and commanded, "CLOSE ON THE DOOR!"

An unnecessary order since the stick was already crushed up against each other. But on command, everyone pushed in tighter. Out of habit Col. Randal made a second head check back outside. The DZ was already on them—right there. He had lost control of the situation.

There was no time to acquire a proper body position in the door for his exit or give the command "GO" other than to shout it over his shoulder as he went out. Col. Randal exited the aircraft headfirst in a modified Superman "leaping from a tall building" body position that even Clark Kent would not have endorsed—not the approved school solution. The wind grabbed him and the sensation was of coming to a sudden halt in midair standing straight up. Then the prop blast rotated his body until he was facing the tail of the Hudson as it flew by in slow motion. He could see the rivets on the side of the plane as it went past inches from his face. It was not the first time this had happened to him. The stick came stampeding out almost running over each other. He got to watch them make their jump—that part was a new experience.

Strike Team cleared the Hudson in less than the allotted three seconds.

This was a low-level drop. Still, Col. Randal had been hoping to get a look at the objective approximately a mile in the distance on the ride down. That was not going to happen. One second he had been frozen in time and space. The next he was going a hundred miles per hour or at least it seemed that way. His body position had been so poor making the exit that the lines twisted badly when the canopy deployed, forcing his chin down on his chest. Clear indication of jumper error.

There was no way to see anything other than the tips of his scuffed-up nearly white raiding boots that had never been polished because the shine might reflect in the moonlight—at least that's what the Commando instructors claimed at Achnacarry.

The approved recovery technique for a paratrooper finding himself in this situation was to stick both arms straight out to the sides, remain perfectly still, and let the lines untwist causing him to spin like a puppet. It usually worked fine. However, virtually all training and most combat drops were from an altitude higher than this one tonight.

There was no time to attempt the maneuver. Besides, on a low-level jump coming in for a PLF with arms outstretched is an invitation for a broken arm or shattered elbow. A lot of things can go wrong jumping from an aircraft in flight. No two drops are ever exactly alike.

Who was ever going to believe he had actually stood there in the night sky and watched Strike Team exit—nobody he knew?

Because of the twists in the lines, Col. Randal was executing the "head down chin firmly on your chest" part of his "prepare to land" sequence of mental commands all jumpers run through preparatory to making their PLF. Nothing else about his parachute landing fall even remotely resembled proper form. Poor exit, questionable body position, heavy equipment in the form of a pack full of .45mm mortar rounds he had not been able to drop on its lowering line. On top of all that, Alimia consisted of rugged terrain, so the drop zone, while relatively flat, was littered with small rocks—some of which were not so small—and a breeze off the sea that might have been gusting close to excessive winds.

WHAAAAAM!

One of the most painful landings he had ever made.

Stunned by what was essentially a full-body crash, Col. Randal was not able to reach over and hammer the quick release on his chest with his fist. His failure to do so resulted in the still fully inflated canopy of his X-type parachute swinging over parallel to the ground dragging him across the rocks toward a ravine on the far side of the DZ.

Jumping right behind him in the stick, Lieutenant Ted Hamilton made a textbook-perfect PLF. The teenage officer leapt to his feet in the best tradition of the airborne—armed and equipped, ready to fight. When he saw the predicament Col. Randal was in, he raced after his X-type chute and pulled the canopy down.

King jogged over, took the Brixia and handed it to Master Sergeant Mack Beckwith who was right behind him, then swung the pack of mortar rounds over his shoulder.

"You all right, Chief?"

Col. Randal said, "There's a reason they teach you to exit in a tight tuck position."

Strike Team was assembled and prepared to move out in less than two minutes.

Col. Randal was limping on the leg he had initially injured jumping off the roof of the house across the street from where the Brandenburger had slaughtered the Hasapis woman.

MAJOR GENERAL SAM HOUSTON BLACKWELL PUT THE Hudson back down on the deck and slammed the throttle to the firewall. The stacked-up drums at the open-air fuel storage area flashed below as the plane crossed the beach and headed out to sea. No other sign of enemy activity was visible. The submarine pens were dug into the side of the shore making them impossible to spot from the air. At this late hour enemy personnel, bored out of their minds by the monotony of being stationed on an uninhabited island with no nightlife of any kind, would be drunk, racked out in their bunks, or both.

The Hudson screamed over Lieutenant Commander Randy "Hornblower" Seaborn's PT 10 on station outside the mouth of Alimia's harbor. Brigadier General William "Wild Bill" Donovan noted Bronc was not breaking hard right as called for in the flight plan. The idea was, or had been, to turn and head out into the Aegean to avoid flying anywhere near Rhodes during the egress aka the "getting the hell out of Dodge" phase of the air mission.

Maj. Gen. Blackwell said, "Too bad we're not able to have our annual quail hunt this year, Bill."

Brig. Gen. Donovan said, "I always look forward to the trip to your ranch—high point of my year."

Maj. Gen. Blackwell said, "Maybe we can get in a little shooting anyway."

"Oh?"

"There's a Luftwaffe airfield on the northeast tip of Rhodes. We stay on this course and it'll take us right over it in another few minutes. Air operations should be shut down for the night. The German planes will be concentrated. Either in a compact group or lined up in order to be guarded from local saboteurs or Raiding Forces conducting a Commando raid—sitting ducks for a gun run."

"What do you intend to shoot those ducks with?"

"We're packing a pretty good punch. This Hudson's weapons package has been upgraded. There's four Browning .30 cals in the nose and a pair of Browning 50s in the Boulton Paul gun turret up top. Locked and loaded."

"Don't we need aircrew to man them?"

"Negative, all the Hudson's organic weapons have been regulated to fire straight ahead like a fighter. Beverly showed me the gun switch. This baby's a regular troop-carrying gunship."

"Prior to takeoff you informed your daughter you were planning to strafe a Nazi airfield?"

"Hell no—you think I'm crazy? She just walked me through how the instrument panel's set up. Gave me strict instructions not to touch the gun button."

Brig. Gen. Donovan said, "Exploit opportunity, take calculated risks, strike hard and fast, then be away."

Maj. Gen. Blackwell said, "Military poetry . . . you come up with that, Bill?"

Brig. Gen. Donovan said, "Something Randal said addressing a class of OSS Operational Group personnel when he and Lady Jane were at my headquarters—the time she recruited Beverly. I jotted down the quote. Had it added to our guerrilla warfare curriculum."

Maj. Gen. Blackwell said, "Sounds like the Colonel was describing this golden opportunity to strafe a Nazi airfield—I'm still a fighter pilot at heart—fly, fight, win!"

Brig. Gen. Donovan said, "Likely the worst idea either of us has come up with in a very long while."

Maj. Gen. Blackwell said, "Not that long. We're generals. We have bad ideas all the time."

Brig. Gen. Donovan said, "I see your point. . . ."

LIEUTENANT COMMANDER RANDY "HORNBLOWER" Seaborn saw the Hudson come thundering across the harbor so low the props were throwing up water. The twin-engine aircraft made a terrific racket as it rocketed past. Major General Sam Houston Blackwell rocked his wings slightly to say hello and good-bye.

From details briefed in the Operations Order Lt. Cdr. Seaborn knew the saddle that Strike Team dropped on was less than a mile from the harbor. With no inhabitants on the island or formations of enemy troops inland to impede progress, Colonel John Randal would be arriving at the ORP in a few minutes. From that point on the situation was going to develop rapidly.

Lieutenant General "Geronimo" Joe McKoy said, "Get ready to shake and bake, Randy."

Lt. Cdr. Seaborn said, "General, when the balloon goes up, you and Mr. Treywick try not to hit any of my crew with those Baby BARs of yours."

Lt. Gen. McKoy said, "Don't worry about us, young Commander. This ain't our first rodeo. You just take out that sub before it takes us out."

The idea of engaging a deadly Italian submarine armed with a 102mm deck gun and at the very least a pair of 20mm antiaircraft guns head-on at point-blank range in a mahogany PT boat was losing its appeal as the seconds ticked off. One of Raiding Forces' unwritten but often quoted rules was "be careful what you wish for." When the plan of ambushing the Italian sub had first been floated, it sounded good. Now, not so much.

Waldo Treywick said, "This is beginnin' to remind me 'a huntin' bad cat with the Colonel back in the day when he was the worst lion man on the African continent."

Lt. Cdr. Seaborn, who served as the liaison between Col. Randal's Force N and Brigadier Orde Wingate's Gideon Force during the Abyssinian Campaign, said, "I always wondered what it felt like to sit up in the jungle at night waiting for a hungry maneater to appear out of the dark to eat me."

Waldo said, "Well, now you know."

Out at sea a burst of tracers was seen in the sky.

Lt. Cdr. Seaborn said, "What is that?"

It was Maj. Gen. Blackwell test-firing the Hudson's weapons in the distance preparatory to making a low-level pass on the Luftwaffe airfield on the northwest coast of Rhodes. He was checking to see where the six machine guns were regulated to converge. Bronc never left anything to chance when he could avoid it. The synchronized gun system worked fine with the guns converging approximately 100 yards in front of the plane.

The Hudson was one minute out from its target.

COLONEL JOHN RANDAL WAS STRUGGLING TO KEEP UP WITH the column. King was leading the way at a fast clip. The Merc was fully cognizant of the problem but had a timetable to keep. The rule once an operation commenced was "mission over man." The terrain was not making matters easy, it being rugged in a small way, which can be as bad as having to hump up and down actual mountains.

The three-quarter moon helped, but not much.

A sense of urgency is always felt when making a movement to contact. Adrenaline kicked in full bore following the jump but the electric feeling of exhilaration smoothed out. Senses were heightened. Strike Team personnel were very aware of the situation around them even though moving cross country almost on the double.

Tonight was the classic Commando raid. A small, determined body of men taking the fight to the enemy on a foreign shore a long way from home. It was not unknown for small raiding parties in this part of the world to simply disappear—never to be heard from again. Strike Team understood they were on their own. If anything went wrong no one was coming to rescue them.

Resolve was replacing exhilaration as the column continued to march.

Col. Randal was in a great deal of pain. However, falling out or even straggling was not an option. Another of Raiding Forces' unwritten but often quoted rules—courtesy of Lieutenant General "Geronimo" Joe McKoy—was "drive on even if your heart's shot out." The movement tonight was turning out to be one of the longest miles he had ever marched.

In fact it was only a little over three quarters of a mile.

Col. Randal whispered to King, "What's the count?"

"Fourteen-sixty-five yards."

Col. Randal turned to Lieutenant Ted Hamilton and whispered, "Send up the pace."

One of the things all Raiding Forces personnel knew was how many of their individual paces equaled one hundred yards. They practiced it during daylight, at night, over flat and hilly terrain. Everyone's was slightly different because of the length of their stride.

On patrol the pace count tells the patrol leader how far they have traveled. When asked for, it was given in one-hundred-yard increments. It is best to have two pacemen—one at the front of the column and one near the rear to compare counts.

Lt. Hamilton turned and whispered, "Pace count?"

Master Sergeant Mack Beckwith whispered, "Fourteen-fifty-three."

King and the Sergeant Major's estimate of distance traveled were within twelve yards of each other—a good count.

Col. Randal whispered to King, "Move up another one-fifty."

Even though hobbled he was serving as patrol leader, which required him to make a constant stream of tactical decisions. Col. Randal also had the added responsibility of functioning as the compass man because of his skill at that task—Rule Number 4: Right Man, Right Job. He was constantly studying the M-1938 lensatic compass he wore around his neck on a piece of parachute cord. Periodically as they traveled he whispered slight adjustments in direction to King. Teamwork between patrol leader and point man when conducting a tactical movement was essential.

Prior to moving out, Col. Randal dialed in the azimuth on the bezel ring. While traveling he kept the compass balanced on his forefinger of his left hand with his thumb hooked through the brass wire loop that doubled as a retaining band. It was important to keep the floating dial as steady as possible, but it was also a good idea to rattle the compass occasionally to make sure the disk was not stuck. The trick was to keep the floating luminous magnetic arrow pointing to the preset azimuth at all times indicating the direction of march—superior eyesight to read the tiny non-luminous numerals indicating the degrees was helpful.

An added complication to land navigation is that the M2 lensatic compass has a built-in three-degree error. There is nothing that can be done about it other than to know the error is there. And try to compensate for it, which is difficult since there is no way to know if the error is to the right or left of the arrow—it depends on the compass.

During movement Col. Randal was constantly checking and rechecking the direction of march against the azimuth. It is not easy. The best land navigators intentionally aim a degree or two to the left or right of their target—missing it on purpose—or maybe not because of the built-in error. The idea being that if the pace count indicates the patrol has arrived but they are not in the desired location, the compass man knows which side of the objective he missed on. That gives an indication of which direction he needs to search to find it.

Offset targeting is an advanced skill set beyond the ability of most land navigators.

The combination of pace count and compass work pinpointed the team's location within a reasonable certainty without having to rely on constant map reading—which is an entirely different skill. Cross-country land navigation is more art than science with a little magic needed to make it work. The best land navigators cannot always explain exactly how they do what they do.

What is important to bear in mind is that the instant the land navigator does not know exactly where the patrol is on the map . . . he is lost.

Fortunately, tonight no actual map reading was required. Trying to read a standard issue 1:25000 military topographical map under a poncho with a red-lensed flashlight so as not to destroy your night vision while trying to prevent the enemy from spotting you takes land navigation to a whole other level. Throw in inclement weather like rain, hail or incoming artillery and getting from point A to point B with a map and compass behind enemy lines is not as easy as it sounds.

King halted, "We're there, Chief."

Col. Randal whispered to Lt. Hamilton, "ORP."

The Great Teddy turned and whispered to MSgt. Beckwith, "ORP."

MSgt. Beckwith passed the word to Captain Billy Jack Jaxx who passed it on back to the Lovat Scouts.

While the team might not have been on the precise eight-digit grid coordinate down to the exact last inch Col. Randal had designated as the Objective Rally Point it was close enough. Strike Team formed a tight perimeter with everyone down on one knee facing out, weapons at the ready.

This was merely a pause.

Col. Randal whispered, "Move out, Captain."

Capt. Billy Jaxx, whispered, "Let's rock."

The two Lovat Scouts stood up, followed him out of the ORP and the team vanished like ghosts. Their task was to infiltrate the fuel storage area on the west side of the harbor, place explosives where they would do the most damage, then withdraw independently to the extraction point on the beach where Captain Penelope "Legs" Honeycutt-Parker would be waiting.

Each of them carried ten prepared demolition charges with thirty-minute fuses. The devices were simple—a quarter-pound of C-2 plastique explosive and a measured length of fuse with an M2 ring lighter. All that was necessary was to place one of the demolition charges on a stack of fuel drums and pull the ring.

Once pulled the fuse was lit and burning. After the first charge was initiated it was advisable to place the remainder of the explosives in "an expedient manner" and exfiltrate the area ASAP—or as was commonly said in Raiding Forces, "as soon as possible if not sooner."

Capt. Jaxx was hoping to find sentries to eliminate with the suppressed .45 M-1928 Thompson submachine gun he was lugging. The idea was to see how it performed in the field. From what he had seen so far, the weapon did not have much to recommend it. It was too long, too heavy, too unwieldy—particularly aboard the aircraft. All in all, it was not in the same league as the other two SMGs being tested, even though the .45 M3 Grease Gun and the 9mm Sten were made out of stamped metal parts and looked like they had been bolted together in a junior high school shop class under the supervision of a teacher who did not check his students work.

After Capt. Jack's people departed, Col. Randal's four-man element tightened up the perimeter. He redistributed the No. 69 stun grenades in his jump jacket's pockets. Five to King. Five to MSgt. Beckwith. Lt. Hamilton would be busy lighting off his M1E1 WWIII Deception Devices which meant Col. Randal could have his Brixia shoulder-fired mortar back and would not need the No.69 stun grenades. He intended to fire all forty rounds in the pack. Every single one. There would be no carrying 45mm mortar shells back to the extraction point.

Not this night.

THE HUDSON STREAKED ACROSS THE BEACH ON THE northwest tip of Rhodes at anteater level. Major General Sam Houston Blackwell, the commander of Troop Transport Command responsible for air delivery of military personnel worldwide, and Brigadier General William "Wild Bill" Donovan, the Director of the Office of Strategic Services (OSS), the first national level intelligence agency in US history, were in the process of violating every single policy covering the exposure of senior top-tier military officers to the possibility of being captured or killed in action.

Up ahead, angling slightly off to the right the two generals could see the Luftwaffe landing ground come into view. No lights were showing indicating air operations were closed down for the night. Exactly what they were counting on.

Maj. Gen. Blackwell jinked slightly to line up on the airstrip.

The Nazi base commander had elected to station his Ju-87 Stuka dive bombers along the length of the near side of the runway toward the built-up area where the tower was. It was hard to know what sized unit was stationed at the field. Luftwaffe squadrons varied wildly in size from eight to twenty-four planes. Some German squadrons consisted of as many aircraft as a normal sized wing.

There were a lot of parked airplanes, but neither Bronc nor Wild Bill was counting as the Hudson streaked in. They were both focused on the first Stuka coming up fast. Maj. Gen. Blackwell touched the firing button. The four .30 cals in the nose and the pair of .50s overhead roared to life as one. He aimed short and walked the tracers into the Ju-87.

It exploded.

The Hudson flashed through the fireball and took some hits from flying shrapnel that sounded like hail on the skin of the aircraft.

Brig. Gen. Donovan said, "That can't be good."

Apparently, the ground crew had the dive bombers topped off, armed and ready for the next days' mission. One detail needing to be taken into consideration during a low-level strafing attack was not blowing yourself out of the sky when attacking bomb-carrying aircraft parked on a runway. At this point in the gun run, there was no time to gain altitude for an extra margin of safety, so the only options were to break off or continue the mission.

Maj. Gen. Blackwell pressed on.

The Hudson's gun pip was on the second Ju-87 in the blink of an eye. Having a better idea now of where turret and nose-mounted guns were regulated to converge, Bronc gave the enemy dive bomber a short squirt. With as many planes as were lined up he was going to need to conserve ammunition.

For a former fighter pilot now reduced to being a troop transport taxi driver this was a dream target—Bronc did not intend to waste it.

Everything was happening fast. The second Stuka failed to explode but it was beginning to burn as they raced over. The third soaked up a burst as did the fourth and fifth. The sixth plane blew up and the blast rocked the Hudson again. They could hear shrapnel plinking against the skin of the fuselage—more this time.

Not a sound either general would wish on their worst enemy.

At this point in the attack, Maj. Gen. Blackwell had the end of the runway in sight. There were a half dozen Ju-87s left. He decided to dispense with short bursts of fire and just hold the gun button down and run through them.

The synchronized machine guns were stuttering like electric sewing machines. Tracer rounds were dancing on the tarmac. The AP rounds were tearing into the German dive bombers as they raced over. Planes were burning. Several cooked off behind them as the fire reached their bomb load.

From start to finish the attack was a blur of speed, tracers and explosions.

Brig. Gen. Donovan made note of the fact a single pass on an airfield by a ground strafing aircraft could do as much or more damage than a team of Commandos. Colonel John Randal had mentioned something to that effect to him previously. But he never actually believed it until now—lesson learned.

Good to know for future reference.

Strangely they were taking no return ground fire. There having never been a nighttime air raid on Rhodes previous to tonight, why would the air defense ground personnel have reason to believe there would be one tonight? The gunners might have been asleep at their duty station instead of standing their watch. Or they could have taken cover rather than standing to their guns.

As the Hudson streaked across the far end of the runway, Bronc banked hard right, headed out to sea. The new angle of flight allowed the generals to look back and see the results of their attack. Now the Germans were fighting their hearts out. As burning planes continued to blow up tracers were crisscrossing the sky behind them aimed at phantom aircraft the Nazis believed to still be attacking the airfield.

Maj. Gen. Blackwell shouted, "*Yeah.* Hook 'em Horns! What do you say, Bill? Beats bird hunting!"

Medal of Honor recipient Wild Bill Donovan said, "Never was so scared in my entire life."

COLONEL JOHN RANDAL SAID, "LET'S GO, KING."

The Merc rose from his knee and stepped off. Col. Randal, Lieutenant Ted Hamilton and Master Sergeant Mack Beckwith followed silently. This phase was somewhat tricky. They knew there was a rock building constructed by the Italians several years earlier serving as a barracks. Other than some small abandoned homes for the few previous residents, it was the only structure on Alimia besides the concrete submarine pens.

The problem was they did not know exactly where the barracks was located. Not that it really mattered. Col. Randal's assignment was to create a diversion to divert attention away from the fuel storage area where Captain Billy Jack Jaxx and the Lovat Scouts were to place the explosives.

Col. Randal did not have to be in any exact position to commence his phase of the raid. A lot of loud noise was all that was needed to draw the enemy's attention. However, he wanted to move up closer to the shore to attempt to place eyes on the garrison. The moon—only marginally helpful up to this point—was now working in their favor. In the distance they could see moonlight gleaming off the Aegean.

With contact imminent another surge of adrenaline kicked in and Col. Randal's pain went away—again.

King halted the file, turned and whispered, "Target dead ahead."

Col. Randal moved up right behind him and looked in the direction the Merc was pointing. Approximately fifty yards to their front was an off-white rectangular structure built just off the tideline. The elevation on both ends was a staggered A-frame roughly similar to the Alamo. Not having as much as a single photo or sketch to work from during mission planning, they had not known what to expect. Five large shadows were visible along the length of the building on the side they could see. Bay windows large enough to walk through, designed to catch the sea breeze, ran the length of the structure.

No lights were showing. Blackout restrictions being in force.

Col. Randal whispered, "We'll start our war from here."

Lt. Hamilton began setting up his fireworks. MSgt. Beckwith and King laid out their No. 69 concussion grenades. Col. Randal picked up the pack of 45mm mortar rounds King had dropped for him and dumped them all out on the ground. The idea was to have rapid access to them. He would be firing from the kneeling position for quicker reloads—grab, load, shoulder fire, repeat.

After a quick glance at his Rolex, Col. Randal whispered, "We'll give Captain Jaxx five more minutes."

CAPTAIN BILLY JACK JAXX AND THE LOVAT SCOUTS patrolled silently around the left flank of the harbor. The gently sloping terrain to the water's edge was characterized by tiny bushes and rocks the size of softballs. They had not traveled far before stumbling across the fuel dump. The 55-gallon cans were clustered in tight groups but not stacked up more than two high under camouflage netting supported by tent poles. The layout was not ideal for one big Pyro Percy end-of-the-world type demolition.

To Capt. Jaxx's regret, no sentries were in sight.

Without warning a major battle broke out on the other side of the harbor. The night lit up with the white flash of explosions. The Great Teddy was not overstating their effect when he named his deception device WWIII. There were aerial booms, ground booms and a swarm of what looked like large caliber tracer rounds lacing the sky and they kept coming. Grenades were banging. Mortar rounds were making their distinctive *CRUUUUUMP! CRUUUUUMP! CRUUUUUMP!*

And *return* small arms fire. Not part of the plan. There is an ancient military axiom, "Never hold your enemy in contempt." It might have been violated tonight in the belief they were going up against Italian sailors. Capt. Jaxx knew what he was hearing was supposed to be the diversion but to the experienced ear the sound was an intense, for-real firefight in progress.

"Split up boys. Spread out and place your charges. This is our final objective rally point. Meet back here in ten minutes."

The Lovat Scouts, professional red deer stalkers for wealthy paying customers in peacetime, simply disappeared—poof. Capt. Jaxx, a white tail deer hunter himself, wondered how they did it. He put a charge on a stack of fuel drums and pulled the ring on the M-2 fuse lighter. There was a small "crack" and the fuse was lit.

Ten minutes was not a lot of time to set his nine remaining charges. Fortunately, the sand muffled his boots because he was moving fast. Capt. Jaxx wound his way through the barrels spread out over approximately an acre dropping of quarter pound C-2 explosives at clusters of fuel drums.

On the other side of the harbor the battle raged.

Coming around one stack he spotted a mellow glow. That was strange. On closer inspection, it turned out to be the back of an improvised lean-to tent made out of a poncho pegged to the ground in back and propped up by pup tent poles in front. What he was seeing was a guard sitting inside smoking a cigarette—intent on standing his post with no intention of getting drawn into whatever was going on elsewhere.

From where Capt. Jaxx was standing all he could see was the glow through the thin poncho material. Setting the charge he was carrying on the ground, unslinging the .45 M-1928 Thompson submachine gun, and taking a knee was an automatic reflex action. This was the target he had been hoping for.

Aiming low, Capt. Jaxx loosed off a short pair of three-round bursts. The suppressed SMG stuttered—it was very manageable when fired with such tight trigger control. Though no one would have identified the sound as gunfire, the weapon seemed louder in the still of the night than he would have expected.

The glow was snuffed out instantly. Small sparks flew as the cigarette flipped onto the sand out the front of the lean-to. Sentry eliminated. Capt. Jaxx wondered why it seemed so anticlimactic.

He picked up his block of C-2 and continued on his way.

The Lovats were waiting in the Final Objective Rally Point.

"You hear any shooting around here?"

"Negative."

The .45 M-1928 Thompson submachine gun had passed the quietness test with flying colors, but it was still too clumsy for Raiding Forces'.

Capt. Jaxx took out his short-barreled M-2 International Flare Signal Company pistol and put up a red flare.

"OK, boys, let's go. We don't want to keep Legs Parker waiting."

With any luck they would make it to the extraction point before the first block of C-2 detonated. Not that it mattered; their mission was accomplished.

WHILE MANY OFFICERS BLEW A WHISTLE TO INITIATE AN ambush or attack, Colonel John Randal preferred the first sound an enemy heard to be one that inflicted casualties. Why give even a split-second warning? He fired the 45mm Brixia at the center window.

The *BLOOOOOP* of the shoulder-fired mortar when the round left the tube was Lieutenant Ted Hamilton's signal to light one of his M1E1 WWIII Deception Devices. The flash-boom of the mortar round detonating inside the barracks was accompanied by surprised and panicked screams from inside.

It sounded like there were more than the ten Regia Marina sailors they had expected to be in the billet. Unknown to anyone at RFHQ, a squad of 999th *Pionier Kompanie Rhodos* had been dispatched from the *Sturm-Division Rhodos* on Rhodes to construct slit trenches with overhead cover for the Italian sailors stationed on Alimia.

Sturm-Division Rhodos was a composite occupation unit hastily thrown together to occupy Rhodes. There were a number of sub-units from the 999th Light Division attached to it. The Pionier Kompanie was a labor outfit. It had very little military training.

The screaming coming from the barracks intensified when the first of the Great Teddy's M1E1 WWIII Deception Devices went into action. There was a great deal of uncertainty and indecision in the enemy ranks about what was taking place. The Nazis and their Italian Fascist counterparts were shooting out both sides of the building. Half were firing wildly at empty space on the far side out to sea and the others were not aiming their weapons on the near side—spray and pray.

Col. Randal's team was positioned well out of the line of fire.

Master Sergeant Mack Beckwith and King were throwing their No. 69 grenades as fast as they could. Each had fifteen, and while the concussion grenades were no actual threat, the enemy did not know that. The noise and violence of the explosions sounded like incoming artillery. Lt. Hamilton's M1E1 Deception Devices were booming like . . . World War III.

Col. Randal poured Brixia mortar rounds through the big open windows on their side of the building. He kept pounding away as fast as he could reload with no letup. The shoulder fired mortar was causing serious damage. The interior of the barracks lit up with each detonation as the shells slammed in. Instead of the usual hollow *CRUUUUUMP* the 45mm rounds were making a more impressive *WHOOOOOMPH* because the concussion when they exploded was trapped inside the confined space of the barracks. In addition to the hail of shrapnel, each incoming 45mm round caused a blizzard of razor sharp rock shards to fly off the billet's stone walls with each detonation. There was no way for those inside to escape the deadly barrage.

Gradually the gunfire from the barracks began to diminish.

The purpose of a tactical diversion is to mislead the enemy and cause them to freeze in place, focus their attention on an erroneous location or maneuver in the wrong direction. The enemy outnumbered the Raiding Forces' element more than five to one at the outset of the fight. Because of the intensity of the diversion, charging outside and closing with their attackers never occurred to the criminals of the 999th or the Regia Marina sailors trapped inside.

Now it was too late because they had taken so many casualties from the unrelenting barrage of 45mm mortar rounds. Resistance from the barracks tapered off and finally ceased altogether. For all practical purposes the fight was over.

Col. Randal kept pumping in mortar rounds anyway.

Captain Billy Jack Jaxx's red flare streaked high into the sky from the direction of the fuel storage area.

Col. Randal gave the order, "Break contact, fall back."

He was careful to make sure the command was loud enough for his operators to hear but not the enemy in the barracks. Why take a chance? Some of the bad guys might speak English.

In the reverse order of march starting with MSgt. Beckwith followed by Lt. Hamilton and King they started leapfrogging back. Col. Randal stayed behind to cover the withdrawal. As soon as there was an additional hundred yards between themselves and the barracks the team paused to allow him to catch up.

Col. Randal was still in place laying down a steady bombardment on the barracks. He was intent on firing up all the 45mm mortar rounds. King turned around and retraced his steps. There was no possibility he was going to leave his boss fighting alone.

King was halfway back when the two met up.

"You have a sudden death wish, Chief?"

"Negative. I didn't want to lug any of those mortar rounds to the boat."

"Works for me."

The Merc resumed his position on point and the team moved out for the extraction site. Coming down the slope to the beach on the far side of the island, they could see Captain Penelope "Legs" Honeycutt-Parker's MAS boat bobbing close inshore. Capt. Jaxx's people were on the beach facing inland in a defensive position.

As Col. Randal arrived, the first explosive charge at the fuel storage area went off.

The sound did not carry but a large fire blazed high in the night sky—tall enough to be seen from the far side of Altima. Other flames began leaping up as additional charges detonated. Then there must have been a sympathetic explosion because a conflagration lit up the skyline—not "Pyro" Percy quality but still impressive.

Col. Randal led the team wading out to the boat. Capt. Honeycutt-Parker helped him climb aboard. "Look who we found, John."

Private First Class Norvel "Horn Dog" Hansen.

Col. Randal said, "You're supposed to be a POW."

"Escaped, sir. One of the MI-9 caiques brought me off Leros. Then Captain Honeycutt-Parker spotted us at sea yesterday. Since I was the only Raiding Forces operator among the evaders onboard, she gave me a lift."

MSgt. Beckwith barked, "What took you so long, Hansen?"

LIEUTENANT COMMANDER RANDY "HORNBLOWER" Seaborn was standing on the bridge of his PT 10 staring hard into the night trying to penetrate the darkness inside the harbor. The submarine pens would be approximately half a mile from the mouth of the harbor. He had the boat closed up until it was almost inside the entrance.

Behind them on Rhodes in the distance a tiny light show had been going on. Tracers laced the sky. Silent fireballs started going up. Everyone on the PT boat wondered what that was about—not part of the plan.

The crackle of the firefight raging off to the left had died down and then ceased entirely. Lt. Cdr. Seaborn hoped that was a good thing. Resistance to the diversion had been considerably more spirited than he anticipated based on the enemy forces' intelligence. Even knowing the big explosions and fireworks streaking through the sky were the work of Lieutenant Ted Hamilton's M1E1 WWIII Deception Devices it sounded like a for real firefight—some of those were tracers. The constant booming of smaller muffled detonations was likely 45mm grenades, though nothing about the 45mm Brixia being part of the diversion team's armament had been mentioned in the Operations Order.

Raiding Forces Rules technically included Number 7: "Expect the unexpected." But on Colonel John Randal's orders it was no longer in effect. Developments not going according to plan was business as usual. Expectations tonight were for the ten Italian sailors to hit the dirt and stay down once the diversion commenced. From the sound of things that was not the case. And there were definitely more than ten Regia Marina sailors firing at the start of the diversion.

Lt. Cmdr. Seaborn wondered what other surprises might there be?

BOOOOOM!

PT 10 was close enough to hear the first charge from the direction of the petroleum, oil and lubricants (POL) storage area go off. It rolled across the harbor and was followed by a volcano of flames. Submarine fuel was flammable. Additional explosions were heard in ragged succession detonating in the haphazard sequence they had been placed.

Lieutenant General "Geronimo" Joe McKoy said, "Wasn't countin' on such a good light show the fuel drums bein' dispersed like they're supposed to be."

Waldo Treywick said, "If there's an Eyetalian submarine skipper hidin' in those pens the man's gotta be thinkin' he's about to get hisself overrun."

A brilliant explosion lit up the sky as the remaining fuel cans cooked off. Night turned into day. Because fuel was being detonated the flash did not immediately snuff out as other types of demolition targets did. Visibility into the harbor was dramatically improved.

The instant the flash lit off, a surfaced Argonauta-class submarine was seen gliding straight toward the entrance of the harbor. Right on top of the PT boat. Point blank range. And that was good because the sub was so close the Fascist crew could not depress the 102mm deck gun low enough to blow the PT boat out of the water. But they tried.

BOOOOOM!

The Italians got off the first shot. A 102mm gun is not the biggest cannon in the world but fired at virtual contact distance to those on the receiving end, it was a life-altering experience. The shell screamed past inches overhead taking off PT 10's radio antenna and detonated behind the boat throwing up a tall white geyser of water. As the round went by it whipped the clothes of the people on the deck.

The 102's muzzle blast at that range was like something from out of this world.

PT 10 lit up from stem to stern with automatic weapons fire as the sailors went into action. Lt. Cdr. Hornblower's Thunderbolt Mark XV mount had recently been upgraded by the addition of two more 20mm cannons to the four already affixed to its six coaxial .50 machine guns. The tightly concentrated burst of cannon and heavy machine gun fire swept the Italian gun crew away. Then the Thunderbolt gunner as well as any other sailor standing to a machine gun went after the conning tower command party and antiaircraft gunners.

The ship-to-ship gun battle was over fast, with everyone above deck on the submarine knocked out of action instantly.

A PT boat comes with berths for a crew of three officers and fourteen men. Lt. Cdr. Seaborn was the only officer on board not counting Lt. Gen. McKoy. However, he had his full complement of sailors because they were needed to man all the extra .50 M2 Browning machine guns he had bolted on every spare inch of available deck space. All personnel were expected to fight except the helmsman, signalman and the engine room crew. The concentrated volume of fire from the prototype seventy-foot Elco patrol torpedo boat was a broadside equal or superior to that of a destroyer minus the main gun. The difference being a destroyer was seldom able to bring all its guns to bear on a target at the same time.

Counting its torpedoes, pound for pound, a PT boat was the heaviest armed fighting vessel in the inventory of the U.S. or Royal Navy. Unfortunately, the engagement took place so fast and at such close range that Lt. Cdr. Seaborn could not launch his torpedoes.

The submarine kept steaming but it no longer posed any threat as the PT boat was too shallow a craft to be hit by its torpedoes at this range. Lt. Cdr. Seaborn ordered the helmsman to circle the "pig boat." He wanted his gunners to be able to fire up and down the boat's 200-foot length.

The effect of the high volume of fire put out by Hornblower's team of Jack Tars at such point-blank range was shocking even to the veteran crew who had seen it before. A hailstorm of rounds pockmarked the hull so fast and close together it seemed like one of the Great Teddy's illusions.

"Hey, Presto!"

One second no bullet holes—the next the skin of the sub looked like a cheese shredder. The 20mm AP rounds interspersed with HE were capable of piercing the guts of the underwater craft. Even the .50 caliber machine guns were able to puncture the pressure hull at this range.

As he was changing magazines on his .30 Baby BAR, Lt. Gen. McKoy said, "Can you imagine what conditions must be like inside that boat?"

Waldo said, "Another reason I'm not about to be a submarine man. They ain't gettin' me on one, General. Not now, not ever."

On the enemy sub the loss of the skipper caused consternation coupled with confusion and panic. One minute safe in a concrete submarine pen and the next in a hail of fire being shot to pieces. The Italian Executive Officer—finding himself thrust into the position of assuming command—hesitated, not immediately knowing what course of action to take. The blizzard of 20mm and .50 caliber rounds penetrating the hull finally motivated him to make a decision.

The new skipper chose the worst of all available courses of action. He gave the order to dive. Before a submarine submerges it is recommended that the depth of the water be known. The submarine dived and struck bottom.

The top of the conning tower was left sticking out of the water.

Lt. Cdr. Seaborn ordered, "Stand by depth charges."

Then he fired a parachute flare into the sky. When it cracked open, night turned into day. Everyone on PT 10 could see the enemy sub dead in the water—trapped.

The crew had no way to fight back.

Lt. Seaborn had the situation well in hand. His sailors were performing like the precision team they were—the Royal Navy at its best. But the fight was not over yet. The PT boat was armed with a pair of Lend Lease U.S. Navy Mark VI depth charges. Each contained 300 pounds of explosives and could be set for 30 to 300 feet depth.

Not waiting for orders, the sailors manning the M-6s started setting the dial on the depth charges to the minimum depth. As they worked, Lt. Cdr. Seaborn personally took the helm. When he had PT 10 idling down the sub's port side with the bow pointing in the direction of open water, he gave the command. "Depth Charges Away!"

Launching a depth charge on a PT boat consisted of two sailors rolling the ash can off the stern. As soon as both Mark VIs splashed, Lt. Cdr. Seaborn slammed the throttles to "All Ahead Full."

PT 10 surged forward.

When dropping depth charges in shallow water it is important for a PT boat's skipper to keep in mind the need to depart the area at a high rate of speed the instant they go overboard. Failure to do so will likely result in disaster. The M-6s were going to break the subs' back. The reverberation would break the PT's as well if it were still around when the ash cans went off.

As the boat raced away, the bow lifted out of the water gracefully as the Elco-built models were designed to do. When the depth charges detonated, two tall white columns of water shot up. The bow and stern of the pig boat raised out of the water—broken in two.

Lt. Commander Seaborn's crew erupted in cheers.

Scratch one submarine.

Waldo extracted a cigar from a watertight crocodile skin case carried in the inside pocket of his jacket and handed it to Lt. Cdr. Seaborn. "Congratulations, Commander."

Lt. Gen. McKoy said, "The Colonel ain't here so I'll do the honors. Randy—let's get the hell out of Dodge."

There were no objections.

9
HIDE AND SEEK

WHEN LIEUTENANT COMMANDER RANDY "HORNBLOWER" Seaborn's PT 10 arrived back at Castelrozzo it did not find a crowd assembled to greet it as was SOP for units returning from a war patrol. The reason being that ABCHQ had no way of knowing he was coming in. There had been no communications with his boat since moments before his attack on the Italian submarine.

PT 10's radio had been knocked out in the opening salvo of the battle.

Beverly and her father, Major General Sam Houston Blackwell, were the only people on the dock. They were inspecting the damaged Hudson. The blond beauty queen was reading her father the riot act in a high state of agitation commonly described in the part of South Texas where she was raised as "mad as a wet hen."

"What have you done to my aircraft, Daddy? All you were supposed to do was drop a stick of paratroopers and fly straight back home. But no—you *had* to go joy riding."

Maj. Gen. Blackwell said, "It's only a little shrapnel damage caused by all those Nazi planes blowing up."

Beverly said, "Do you have any understanding of how priceless our Hudson is to us? Raiding Forces has to beg, borrow, steal or improvise every piece of equipment we have. You can't tear in here like a tornado blowing through a trailer park and then fly off leaving a path of destruction in your wake."

"Don't worry, baby . . ."

"Don't you baby me. You're a Major General in the United States Army Air Force. Start acting like one."

Maj. Gen. Blackwell said, "I'll make it right. That's a promise. I've been working the phones since I got back. Troop Carrier Command is flying in a replacement we borrowed from Air Marshal Tedder. Be here tomorrow—brand new. The Air Marshal is arranging for a crew of RAF mechanics to travel to Castelrozzo to repair the battle damage to this one. Raiding Forces will end up with two Hudsons."

Beverly said, "There wasn't supposed to *be* any battle damage."

"Point taken."

As news spread that Lt. Cdr. Seaborn was coming in people stopped what they were doing and rushed out to line the pathway from ABCHQ to the waterfront. Unlike recent Raiding Forces teams returning from missions that had been met with a respectful silence, today everyone was cheering. There had been so much bad news lately it felt good to have something to celebrate.

A PT boat sinking an enemy submarine was a big deal—automatic award of the Distinguished Service Order for the skipper, his second post Leros.

While there had been no direct communications with PT 10, news of its sea battle preceded it. Radio intercepts from Rhodes reported a Fascist Regia Marina Argonauta-Class submarine sunk with all hands off Alimia. The loss of the sub and its full complement of forty-four highly trained underwater warfare officers and men was a serious blow to Axis naval forces in the AO.

However the radio silence from PT 10 following the battle had been a source of high anxiety at ABCHQ. The victory celebration was made all that much better due to it being tempered by a huge sense of relief. There being no victory message, all indications were that the boat had been lost. Lt. Cdr. Seaborn's return with mission accomplished and all hands safe was the best news Raiding Forces had received in a long time.

Things did not have to turn out this way.

Captain Penelope "Legs" Honeycutt-Parker's MAS boat warbled in and tied up. Parker's arrival was no surprise. She had radioed her ETA.

Colonel John Randal and his men stepped ashore to join the festivity.

Major the Lady Jane Seaborn and Happy were waiting on the pier.

MAJOR GENERAL SAM HOUSTON BLACKWELL AND Brigadier General William "Wild Bill" Donovan were scheduled to depart later that morning. Red had arrived on the Catalina to fly out with them since she worked for both generals in one capacity or another. Wild Bill and Bronc had unfinished business to take care of before they left the island. Some of it was best carried out discreetly. While Colonel John Randal was having breakfast with his men the two linked up with Lieutenant General "Geronimo" Joe McKoy in his suite on the second floor.

Brig. Gen. Donovan said, "General, we need a word with you about Colonel Randal."

Lt. Gen. McKoy said, "What's John done now?"

Maj. Gen. Blackwell said, "Jim Taylor told me radio intercepts from Rhodes indicated Randal single-handedly killed seventeen enemy combatants on Alimia. King confirms he was the only one firing on the enemy position. Everyone else was throwing concussion grenades to make noise. Injured on the jump and barely able to make it to the objective in the first place, he still stayed behind to cover his team's withdrawal when it pulled out. King had to go back to get him—we can't have him continue being a one-man-army, taking those kinds of risks."

Lt. Gen. McKoy said, "Comin' from the man who went after a Luftwaffe airfield like one 'a those Japanese kamikazes, a little firefight doesn't sound like much of 'a deal. John can play hurt. He leads by example. Always has."

Brig. Gen. Donovan said, "That's the problem, General. With your storied career, *you* of all people know there's only so many chances a man can take before the odds catch up. Time for you to consider scaling back as well. Your role in LONG NECK alone makes you an indispensable

National Security asset. Observing a near-suicidal mission from the storm deck of a PT boat . . . what were you thinking?"

Lt. Gen. McKoy said, "Well, Wild Bill, you landed on Sicily and at Salerno, too, when they were being invaded. Ain't what I'd call real responsible, you bein' the head of America's one and only foreign intelligence agency. What's this really about?"

Brig. Gen. Donovan said, "Raiding Forces' full name is *Strategic Raiding Forces*. The strategic part seems to have fallen out of favor lately—we need it back in. Orchestrating a small-scale raiding campaign in the Aegean to pin down German divisions that would be more useful for Hitler elsewhere is of vital importance to the overall European war strategy. But it can be carried out by someone else.

"Not to leave this room—there are big plans for Randal in the future that still have the word STRATEGIC stamped on them in bold capital letters right next to TOP SECRET. I have a temporary duty assignment for the Colonel in England coming up classified above TOP SECRET. Once the Second Front finally opens up there is an above TOP SECRET joint British/U.S. operation in the planning stage which Raiding Forces is slated to provide the U.S. contingent of troops for.

"We are talking about a Presidential-level mission that will have major consequences for the United States long after the war is over. Likely the most important military operation nobody will ever hear of—winning the peace."

Lt. Gen. McKoy said, "What's any 'a that got to do with John's leadership style?"

Maj. Gen. Blackwell said, "The Colonel can't make it happen if he gets killed leading a Commando raid against some island nobody can find on a map with a magnifying glass."

"Well, Bronc," Lt. Gen. McKoy said, "you ain't exactly in a position to cast any stones."

"Roger that—agreed. But it doesn't change the fact that I need Randal around to be my Parachute Advisor," Maj. Gen. Blackwell said. "The one thing I've learned from sitting on the Swing Committee is we're making up the concept of vertical envelopment as we go no matter who tells you different. When we finally do open up the Second Front, Troop

Transport Command, meaning me, is going to be buried under a landslide of input on things like phases of the moon, flight formations, drop zones, plane loads and who knows what else.

"We all understand full well the worst enemy is bad advice. TTC is going to need the Colonel to help sort it out. I need him to be my advisor."

Brig. Gen. Donovan said, "We can find someone else qualified to conduct the Continuous Pressure Concept. Colonel Stone for example. From a purely political perspective a British officer would be better suited for the command than Randal.

"As for those other OSS assignments I alluded to . . . because of certain of his social contacts and extensive background in Special Operations, the Colonel is in a unique position to head those up—there's no second place candidate."

Lt. Gen. McKoy said, "What do you want from me?"

Brig. Gen. Donovan said, "You know Randal better than anyone. He respects you. Try to convince him he has a responsibility to become a commander of Special Operations rather than a raid team leader."

"That's a tall order, gentlemen. John's not a rebel but he *is* a maverick—goes his own way."

Maj. Gen. Blackwell said, "Make it clear his nation needs him. Alive."

Lt. Gen. McKoy said, "I'll have a word with him—that's as far as it goes, boys."

Brig. Gen. Donovan said, "I personally monitor LONG NECK—as does President Roosevelt. You run your operation on a shoestring budget. Now is not the time to be a piker, General. For once in your military career if there's anything you need, all you have to do is ask. Contact me directly."

"I'll keep that in mind, Bill."

Lt. Gen. McKoy was too old a soldier not to recognize a "carrot and stick" approach when he heard one.

Walking down the hall a few minutes later Maj. Gen. Blackwell said, "What's LONG NECK?"

Brig. Donovan said, "That's classified."

ARMED WITH THE SUPPRESSED .45 M3 GREASE GUN, CAPTAIN Billy Jack Jaxx flew out within an hour of his arrival back at RFHQ. Major the Earl Lord George Jellicoe had a raid targeting airfields on Crete in the works, and he had offered to take one of Raiding Forces' officers along to observe his Special Boat Squadron in action. Since the insertion of the six-man SBS party was to be by submarine, Capt. Jaxx leapt at the opportunity.

The raid would launch from Alexandria. Capt. Jaxx arrived and was introduced to the team: Corporal Ronny Pomford, a former Golden Gloves boxer; Corporal Liam Riley, Irish Guards, and two Greeks, Castor and Basil. Major Lord Jellicoe had neglected to mention he would be going on the raid.

First thing, the Earl checked out the latest photo in Jack Cool's pistol grip.

Then Maj. Lord Jellicoe briefed the mission. There were three airfields each targeted for attack by a two-man SBS team. One party would depart that night by Motor Torpedo Boat to reconnoiter the beach where the four remaining team members would land ashore the following night by MTB.

Traveling independently, the SBS teams would make an approach march to their individual target. They would lie up under concealment in their ORPs in immediate proximity to their objectives the following day.

The next night each SBS team would infiltrate their assigned airfield. Demolitions would be placed with priority to aircraft. Once all the planes were rigged with explosives, secondary targets would be fuel storage facilities, heavy equipment and then thin-skinned vehicles. In that order.

After placing the charges, the three teams would withdraw and make their way to the extraction point where they would be picked up by a Royal Navy MTB. Capt. Jaxx thought the Operations Order seemed rather vague. A boy's adventure with a healthy dose of hopefulness thrown in. In Raiding Forces it was commonly said, "Hope is not a course of action." Nevertheless, Capt. Jaxx's was not to reason why—he was there to watch and learn.

It came as a shock to find out he and Basil were to conduct the beach reconnaissance, which meant no submarine insertion—oh well. The two boarded an MTB from the 10th Motor Gunboat Flotilla and set off. Capt. Jaxx went below and slept the whole way. Upon arrival at the debarkation point some three miles east of Heraklion, they launched their London-based Folboat Company folding caique and paddled for shore.

The run-in was uneventful.

Capt. Jaxx and Basil dragged the boat across the beach and attempted to conceal it on a sandhill about fifty yards inland under a handful of the stunted bushes peculiar to that part of Crete. It was not a good situation but there was no other cover. Thick patches of forest were not known in the Aegean. Some advance knowledge about conditions ashore before the actual reconnaissance went in might be something to consider on future ops.

Lesson learned.

Nothing eventful happened after the sun came up except for Capt. Jaxx making himself thirsty from eating too much of the dark chocolate found in the British iron rations. Then at 1200 hours a German staff car arrived on the road running parallel to the beach. Three officers stepped out and walked to the water's edge to go swimming. The place they chose was right next to the tracks in the sand left by the folboat when it had been drug ashore last night.

The Nazis never noticed.

Capt. Jaxx and Basil were quietly laughing at the stupid Germans when they heard the sound of men singing, coming toward them. They recognized the *Horst Wessel* song. It struck fear in their hearts. A company of Germans from the 22nd Air-Landing Division was motoring their direction in a convoy of trucks—fully two hundred men. The trucks stopped, the Nazi troops climbed down, formed up on the beach and began doing PT.

The 22nd Air-Landing Division was the Wehrmacht occupation unit stationed on Crete. It was a tough outfit consisting of paratroops and glidermen who had taken part in the airborne assault that captured the island. They trained hard, fought hard, and had no qualms about executing prisoners—especially Commandos. Following the calisthenics, the

Germans started playing hide and seek. The game may have been a form of tactical training. If so, it was not one Capt. Jaxx would ever have thought of but worth keeping in mind.

The Germans looked like idiots, but they were dangerous idiots.

Capt. Jaxx and Basil were not laughing now.

It seemed the Nazis hid behind or searched under every bush except the one where they were. The hide-and-seek seemed to go on forever. The Germans did not load back up on the trucks until the sun started going down at 1830 hours.

That night at the appointed time Capt. Jaxx flashed the signal out to sea to land the raiding teams ashore. After giving it thought he had come to the conclusion that he was not cut out for this kind of work. Pure reconnaissance requires certain skill sets like patience and the ability to endure hours and hours of mind-numbing boredom interspaced with the occasional period of sheer raw terror.

Jack Cool was more of a kick-in-the-door-and-shoot-everybody-inside operator.

THE LONG RANGE DESERT GROUP HAD UNDERGONE A complete reorganization following the end of its operations in the desert. After the standdown the Group received a directive from Middle East Headquarters ordering the unit to be able to operate "on foot in mountainous terrain with the object of liaison with patriot forces." There was no mention of who or where those "patriot forces" might be. To begin their training the Group took over the Cedars Hotel in Lebanon. It had been a prewar ski resort and the former home of the Middle East Ski School. The mountains were a radical departure after three years of desert patrolling operating out of a dusty oasis on the edge of the Great Sand Sea utilizing heavily modified Chevrolet trucks. Now the patrolmen had to walk.

And it was up the hill and down the hill.

The LRDG put in four months of hard mountain training. Patrol size was experimented with. Eventually, four-man building block elements were settled on. Two four-man teams composed an eight-man patrol consisting of one officer, one NCO, three signalers, one Greek language speaker and two general duty patrolmen—one of whom was a sniper issued a .303 Lee-Enfield No. 4 Mk1(T) rifle w/No. 32 Mk1 3.5 X scope. This table of organization and equipment (TO&E) gave patrols the flexibility to be broken down into two sub-patrols—each capable of maintaining communications of up to 100 miles. Man-portable U.S. Collins 18M transmitter receiver field sets were acquired because they possessed the required range and were lighter than the No. 11 sets mounted on their old Chevrolet trucks.

The LRDG was taught mountaineering, cross-country skiing, demolitions and the handling of pack mules. Three men from each patrol attended an advanced rock-climbing course at the Mountain Warfare School. With Bergen rucksacks or Everest carrier frames, patrolmen gradually worked up to becoming capable of carrying eighty-pound packs on seventy-five-mile treks through mountainous terrain. The fitness level and stamina achieved by the Group was of an exceptional standard.

More than a few of the desert veterans were not able to make the transition for one reason or another and had to be returned to their units. Those patrolmen who made the cut were trained to a razor's edge, capable of operating behind enemy lines for up to a month at a time while maintaining constant communications with their HQ. The LRDG had become an elite new model reconnaissance group of highly skilled, physically fit, mountain warfare specialists.

But they were still bitter about not having a desert to roam around in.

Following the intensive training, the Group's first deployment was to Leros as standard *line infantry*. On a long list of bad decisions made by Middle East Headquarters, in a small way this was arguably the worst. The LRDG sat in a static position being bombed and strafed for three months and except for one detached Beach Watch Team, the Group had not conducted a single reconnaissance mission by the time the island was invaded. Then it was virtually wiped out.

Only slightly over fifty LRDG patrolmen made it off after the island fell. The survivors were attached to Raiding Forces. For the former "knights of the desert" this was the final insult. The LRDG had always enjoyed independent status. Colonel John Randal evaluated the Group's training and found it did not meet his standards. There had been no boat handling instruction and the men were not parachute qualified. Both were a must if the LRDG was to be a part of Raiding Forces. New training commenced immediately. Col. Randal thought it advisable to get the patrolmen's mind off the senseless sacrifice of Leros. Jumping out of an aircraft in flight would do that.

Once the LRDG completed airborne training he dispatched two of his prized Life Boat Service Men (LBSM) to put the patrolmen through an intensive course in small boat handling. For those uninitiated to the joys of going to sea in small boats—who were used to desert, mountains and even mules—it was brutal, backbreaking, highly frustrating training. The skill level demanded by the LBSM was for the Group to be able to land a recon party ashore from a PT, MGB, caique or a submarine in all weather, day or night with the 18M transmitter-receiver field set still capable of sending and receiving when they crossed the beach. A lot more difficult in practice than it sounded.

Col. Randal said, "Admiral, I'd like you to consider placing the LRDG directly under you at Small Raids Inc., sir."

He and Vice Admiral Sir Randolph "Razor" Ransom were sitting on the patio next to the private pool outside his suite at ABCHQ smoking Waldo's cigars. Future operations were under discussion. The Alimia raid had been incredibly successful, but the war was not standing still. There was no time to waste on a mission that happened yesterday. Flanigan had been ordered not to let anyone interrupt them unless the island was being invaded.

VAdm. Ransom said, "Why would you make such a request for the LRDG, Colonel?"

Col. Randal said, "When we finish putting the final polish on their training the Group will be capable of conducting reconnaissance missions that stay in the field for extended periods of time. Their history of long range reconnaissance makes them best suited for gathering intelligence on enemy ship movements.

"Randy's dispatched one of his officers to teach ship recognition. In addition to flash cards of silhouettes, he's using toy model boats. Pretty interesting the way he's going about it. I'm going to want the rest of Raiding Forces to receive the same training, sir."

VAdm. Ransom said, "What does any of that have to do with your desire to transfer operational control of the LRDG to Small Raids Inc.?"

Col. Randal said, "When a patrol makes a sighting it needs to be able to report the intel directly to your HQ, sir."

"The LRDG can do that now under our current organizational structure and still belong to Raiding Forces," VAdm. Ransom said. "Not like you to voluntarily hand off such a valuable asset, Colonel. What is your real reason?"

Col. Randal realized Admiral Ransom had seen through his ploy. It was not easy to put something over on the Razor. So he tried the truth—which he should have gone with in the first place.

"The LRDG has been an independent command from day one, Admiral. Now it's a subordinate unit of Raiding Forces. That does not sit well with Major Owen even though he claims he's warming up to the idea."

VAdm. Ransom laughed, "Sounds like you have a classic leadership problem on your hands, Colonel."

"Yes, sir."

"I shall take pleasure in watching you resolve it—request denied."

RECENTLY PROMOTED LIEUTENANT JACKSON TAYLOR, USNR was waiting on the dock with Brigadier General William "Wild Bill" Donovan when Major the Lady Jane Seaborn and Happy arrived with a contingent of her Royal Marines. The Raiding Forces Catalina was inbound from RFHQ. Since the Hudson was not airworthy, the Director of the Office of Strategic Services and the commander of Troop Transport Command would be flying back to Cairo onboard the *Black Cat* later this morning.

The group on the dock was standing by to greet a twenty-man party—OSS Maritime Unit, Detachment 3 aka Det 3 arriving from the States. Detachment 3 was made up of a colorful band of volunteers for what OSS called Operational Swimmers. The men had undergone extensive training at the U.S. Marine base on Camp Pendleton, at the OSS black site Area WA on Catalina Island, at Fort Pierce, Florida, and later in Nassau in the Bahamas—with a few other stops along the way to learn specific skills. It was a composite outfit consisting of men drawn from the U.S. Coast Guard, the Naval Combat Demolition Unit, U.S. Marine Raiders, U.S. Navy Underwater Demolition Teams, Army Rangers and two instructors from the U.S. Navy Scout & Raider School who signed on to put into practice what they had been teaching.

The Maritime Unit Operational Swimmers had all grown up around the water. Most were champion swimmers in high school or college. Several had qualified for the Olympics in one aquatic event or another. The MUs were arguably the most extensively trained Special Operations unit in the U.S. military—maybe in history. Its members had volunteered for the service, volunteered for OSS, volunteered to be combat swimmers/divers, demolitions men and volunteered for immediate deployment overseas on hazardous duty. Highly motivated and fed up with all the endless training, the men were ready to get their war started.

The OSS called the Det 3 men Operational Swimmers. They called themselves "Frogmen" or "Frogs" for short.

Colonel John Randal arrived as the Catalina splashed down and taxied to the dock. As soon as it was moored, Det 3 personnel began filing off with their gear. There was a lot of it. The Frogs carried themselves with quite a bit of swagger—exuding the confidence bordering on arrogance often found in troops who thought of themselves as elite.

Once assembled the only officer in the group. Ensign Westly Slade, reported to Brig. Gen. Donovan.

"MU Det 3 reporting for duty, sir."

Brig. Gen. Donovan returned the salute, "Good to see you men. I want to introduce you to the legendary Colonel Randal—best Special Operations officer in the business. You Det 3 people should consider yourselves fortunate to have him as your commanding officer."

Det 3 exhibited no outward expression as they studied their new CO. A paperback copy of *Jump on Bela* had been supplied to each Frog prior to boarding the flight over from the States. They had been instructed to read it.

He did not look like so much.

Col. Randal said, "Welcome to Raiding Forces, men. Detachment 3 is going to be assigned to Major Lord Jellicoe's Small Boat Squadron for operations. Lieutenant Taylor, recently awarded the Navy Cross for blowing up an enemy destroyer with limpet mines, will be your new detachment commander."

All twenty sets of eyes shifted to take in their new boss. The Navy Cross was impressive. How it was earned, more so. Attaching a limpet mine to an enemy warship berthed in an enemy harbor and living to tell the tale—the Frogs could appreciate that.

Col. Randal said, "They're all yours, Lieutenant."

Lt. Taylor said, "As soon as Major Lady Seaborn and her Marines show you to your quarters, stow your gear. Then get your UDT shorts on. Caique familiarization will commence immediately. Look lively during the evolution because later tonight a four-man swim team will conduct OSS's first-ever beach reconnaissance on an enemy-occupied island. I'll select the four of you who impress me most for this history-making event. Live fire training in Raiding Forces means exactly what it says people—this is no drill."

Maritime Unit Detachment 3, being composed of operators highly skilled in the art of observation, noted Col. Randal was limping, the Royal Marines were smoking hot, Lt. Taylor looked more like a playboy surfer than a war hero, Lady Seaborn was drop-dead gorgeous and while Happy appeared to be friendly he could probably gnaw your kneecap off. Though not necessarily in that order.

Sure of themselves and accustomed to hitting the ground running, Det 3 was unfazed by the rapid pace of events. In fact, they welcomed it. The Frogs wanted to get going. However, it did not fail to register with them that the welcome was not typical of what occurred when they reported in at other duty stations for training. Absent was the harangue delivered by some puffed up martinet boasting in a loud verbose military manner about how tough life was going to be during their stay—no one was trying to impress or intimidate them today.

Was that a good thing or a bad thing?

COLONEL JOHN RANDAL CONDUCTED A FINAL BRIEFING FOR departing Major General Sam Houston Blackwell and Brigadier General William "Wild Bill" Donovan. They were in the second-floor suite he shared with Major the Lady Jane Seaborn. It was a 3,000-square-foot flat intended to be Benito Mussolini's private quarters when he visited Castelrozzo. Il Duce had tried to transform the Greek islands into a showcase of the Italian Colonial Empire by building massive public works on those that were populated in accordance with current Fascist architectural philosophy. The results were monumental municipal buildings of absolutely no practical value that mostly sat empty.

On Castelrozzo the dictator's sycophants had constructed a magnificent "art deco meets Nero's palace" that was now Advanced Base Castelrozzo Headquarters. Only Mussolini never stayed in it. As at Raiding Forces Headquarters outside of Cairo, the formal dining alcove in the suite had been converted into a private briefing area complete with wall maps.

Only this briefing area was a lot bigger.

Lieutenant General "Geronimo" Joe McKoy, Vice Admiral Sir Randolph "Razor" Ransom, Major General Sam Houston Blackwell, Brigadier Raymond J. Maunsell (who liked to be called R. J.), Brigadier Dudley Clarke, James "Baldie" Taylor (who was a local Major General when it suited him), Doctor Layton Winthrop, Lieutenant Colonel Sir Terry "Zorro" Stone, Commander Ian Fleming (curiously present at Brig. Gen. Donovan's request), and recently promoted Major Hawthorne Merryweather were assembled for what was promised to be a short briefing.

Major the Lady Jane Seaborn, Mandy Paige and Beverly Blackwell were observing. The women were the only ones who did not have a specific reason to be in the briefing. The three were sitting in because the girls wanted to observe and Lady Jane invited them.

Col. Randal said, "As most of the senior officers I report to are preparing to depart ABC, this seemed a good time to review for you the way I see Raiding Forces operations in the Aegean developing going forward. In this room are the key players of OPERATION FIRE EATER—war in the ATO post-Leros.

"As you are aware the Germans have defeated the British attempt to fight a campaign without the benefit of air cover. That's history.

"The good news for the Nazis is they've captured all the islands except Castelrozzo. And the bad news for the Nazis is they've captured all the islands except Castelrozzo. In Raiding Forces we like to say 'Be careful what you wish for.' The German situation—having taken all these islands—is what to do now?

"The flip side is what do *we* do? The situation is roughly this. Under Admiral Ransom's Small Raids Inc., Raiding Forces is the only remaining direct-action unit in theatre of any size capable of taking the fight to the enemy. The U.S. and Royal Navy are not going to risk any more capital ships in our AO. The RAF is still fighting with the aircraft it has left. Its Beaufighters in particular are putting in an impressive performance.

"Due to coalition politics, the USAAF has been largely absent except for a brief period of a few weeks—likely it won't be back.

"On the bright side, the Office of Strategic Services is ready and willing to support our activities. The same can be said for General Blackwell's Troop Transport Command—when it can. As for Small Raids Inc. Admiral Ransom is eyeing the Nazis' long lines of supply to maintain the islands like a hungry wolf. He informs me the Germans have a critical shortage of bottoms for transport. The Admiral intends to go after enemy shipping.

"We have all been told the purpose of OPERATION FIRE EATER is to tie down Axis troops who might be put to better use in other more important theatres. SOE and OSS are developing plans to raise, equip and advise underground resistance movements on the large Greek islands and in the Balkans to do exactly that.

"While the strategy shows promise in enemy-occupied countries on the mainland, like Greece or Yugoslavia, here in the Aegean, in my opinion, it's not a sound approach except on the largest islands like Crete. Unlike OSS Operational Groups who raise, arm, train and advise insurgent resistance armies, Raiding Forces is not a force multiplier. We kill Nazis when and where we can find them. That's a significant difference to keep in mind.

"The Germans are faced with demonstrating to the neutral Turks the inadvisability of coming into the war on the Allied side. The Axis also have to project their power over the Greek inhabitants of islands scattered throughout the 250,000 square miles of the ATO they now control. The Nazis will believe the best way to do that is by a massive show of force. What they have done in other conquered countries is bring in low grade, rear-echelon troops, establish a brutal police state and terrorize the population into submission—that's their MO.

"I believe it's exactly what the Germans are going to try to do here. The Wehrmacht will station troops drawn from divisions like the 999th, which is a penal unit, or from their 700 series of 'static' divisions on every occupied Greek island. Most detachments will be squad-sized or less— made-to-order targets for Raiding Forces—we'll make the Nazis pay for that strategy.

"Our Concept of the Operation will be to raid every island except for the large ones like Crete, Rhodes, and Leros—we'll leave those to SOE. Then we'll raid 'em again striking out of the sea under cover of darkness utilizing the element of surprise and concentration of force at the point of attack. Admiral Ransom and I call our strategy the Constant Pressure Concept—a modern day Special Operations equivalent of the Chinese "death by a thousand cuts".

"Due to the lethality of our raids the Nazis will come to realize garrisoning every island with a small contingent is having the opposite effect of the terror and intimidation desired. As word spreads about the success of our activities—that's guaranteed 100 percent with Brigadier Clarke and Major Merryweather driving the narrative, the Germans will begin to appear vulnerable to the Greeks. And more importantly, to the

Turks. General Taylor informs me keeping Turkey neutral is priority number one in Berlin. Hitler will not want to appear weak to the Turks.

"The German High Command will find itself with two options:

"First: The Wehrmacht commander can harden the outposts on all the islands and reinforce his garrisons. That will result in tying down even more of his troops on occupation duty—which means they give up any offensive capability, while increasing logistical problems already at semi-crisis level.

"Second: The Wehrmacht commander can consolidate his existing garrison units to make them larger in order to better defend themselves against our raids. The result will be having a lesser number of units at his disposal. He'll have to rotate what he has from island to island leaving some unoccupied at times. At which point Raiding Forces will have a free pass to pay a call to show the flag and take into custody any local collaborators.

"My guess is over time the German commander will have no choice but to go with the second option. Raiding Forces' countermove—other than to visit the undefended islands, is to transition to larger raids or maybe do nothing at all . . . we'll see. The majority of the Dodecanese Islands have no significant military value, so the option is entirely ours. Either way we'll be calling the shots—a small unit dictating the operational tempo to a larger one. That's the textbook definition of 'Economy of Force.'"

Lt. Gen. McKoy said, "You left out 'a third option, John."

"What might that be, General?"

"Nazis can run up 'a white flag right now and save the aggravation."

Brig. Gen. Donovan and Maj. Gen. Blackwell looked at each other and shook their heads. Any hopes Lt. Gen. McKoy would prove a calming influence on Col. Randal just went up in smoke.

What could they have been thinking?

THE FIRST THING NEWLY PROMOTED LIEUTENANT COLONEL the Earl Lord George Jellicoe did when he came ashore on Crete and linked up with Captain Billy Jack Jaxx's recon party was to reorganize the composition of the two-man teams while keeping the original leaders. The plan was to have a Greek speaker with each team. Since he spoke the language, his fluency having been polished to a high degree by his Greek refugee girlfriend, Lt. Col. Lord Jellicoe selected Capt. Billy Jaxx as his teammate.

There were three Luftwaffe airfields to be attacked. Each was to be targeted by a different team. The plan was to make their approach marches tonight. The following day they would lie up in their ORPs under concealment, then make their attacks that night.

After placing their explosive charges, Lt. Col. Lord Jellicoe and Capt. Jaxx would make a twenty-five-mile cross-country forced march to the extraction point where they would be picked up by a Royal Navy MTB. The other teams would be rendezvousing with them there. Having had a day to think about it, Jack Cool really did not like the plan.

Raiding Forces were hit-and-run specialists. In and out fast. Their raids were typically characterized by stealth, speed and violence of action. Since the explosives would be going off *before* the SBS departed the island, this raid was a hybrid.

It did not feel right.

Lt. Col. Lord Jellicoe said, "Good luck lads—we are off."

The SBS teams shouldered their packs and moved out into the darkness in different directions. Approach marches are all pretty much the same unless something bad happens. Hard humping through rugged terrain. Up the hill, down the hill, wait-a-minute vines, crossing streams and stumbling over deadfall or rocks.

The distance to be covered to reach an ORP planned in the comfort of a rear echelon base almost always turns out to be overly optimistic. That was exactly what happened to Lt. Col. Lord Jellicoe and Capt. Jaxx, who did not arrive at their ORP until well after daylight. That was not the plan and it was not tactically sound.

The good news was that the ORP being perched on the military crest of a steep hill a half mile away from the objective gave them a perfect view of the landing ground to study at their leisure. There were a dozen

Ju-87 Stukas parked along the edge of the runway. A made-to-order target.

Capt. Jaxx said, "It doesn't get any better than this, Colonel."

They lay up in the ORP observing the air base all day. Lt. Col. Lord Jellicoe said, "Since I speak German why not play at Nazis?"

Capt. Jaxx said, "I don't know what that means, sir."

Lt. Col. Lord Jellicoe said, "As night is falling, we infiltrate the airfield. Once in we boldly march up to each Stuka and if there is a guard present, I shall engage the man in conversation as if I was an inspecting officer. You eliminate him with your silenced submachine gun then we shall lay our charge and move on to the next plane. Fortune favors the brave."

Capt. Jaxx said, "Sounds like a plan."

He thought Lt. Col. Lord Jellicoe meant sneak through the wire to gain access.

That was wrong.

As it was growing darker and visibility was becoming more limited, they climbed down the hill. Without a moment's hesitation Lt. Col. Lord Jellicoe stepped out on the road leading to the main gate. He marched straight toward the checkpoint guarding the entrance.

Capt. Jaxx was almost paralyzed with fear.

Lt. Col. Lord Jellicoe barked out something in German that sounded like an order. The three Luftwaffe airfield security policemen on duty rushed out of the small guard post where they had been playing cards and assumed a rigid position of attention. The sentries had no idea who this officer was but he sounded like the archetypical Nazi, mad at everyone— particularly if he outranked them.

Capt. Jaxx was walking behind Lt. Col. Lord Jellicoe trying to remain inconspicuous because he knew less than five words of German— three of which had to do with girls. He stepped around in front and shot all three security police with his suppressed M3 Grease Gun. Holding it by the pistol grip, wire stock collapsed, with his right elbow tucked in tight against his side—he noted how quiet and controllable the weapon was. The big .45 caliber slugs knocked the guards off their feet.

The infiltration phase was beginning to appear like it might work.

As they walked along the perimeter road inside the wire toward the first Ju-87, its engine cranked up as did all the rest of the planes on the flight line. One by one the Stukas taxied out onto the runway, wheeled right and took off. One minute the dive bombers were there and the next they were gone—"Hey, presto."

Lt. Col. Lord Jellicoe and Capt. Jaxx watched stunned—what to do?

Then the airstrip landing lights came on. It was not a good feeling to be standing in the middle of an illuminated Luftwaffe airfield holding canvas bags full of demolitions with the motive, means, but no longer the opportunity to blow up any Nazi aircraft.

Definitely not the plan.

Before they could react, three Ju-87s arrived over the far end of the field in trail lined up in trail formation to land. Unknown to the Luftwaffe pilots, a Bristol Blenheim flown by a South African pilot had attached itself to the end of their formation. The Blenheim was an obsolete aircraft in the European Theatre but a front-line light bomber/night fighter in the Aegean. This evening its mission was to crater the all-weather German airstrip.

The assignment was one the light bomber was ideally suited for. Its bomb bay doors were kept closed during flight with bungee cords. When the bombs were released from their racks their weight forced the doors open. Since this made timing the bomb drop imprecise, a Blenheim's bomb pattern was usually erratic. Not a desirable outcome for bombing point-type targets or calling in close air support but perfectly fine for putting big random holes in runways.

The RAF plane had a gun package mounted under the nose of the fuselage, called a chin gun, containing four M-1919 .303 Browning machine guns. The South African pilot waited until the first Stuka touched down with the second one right behind in the formation having given up most of its airspeed coming in behind the leader. Then he pulled to within a few feet of the third Stuka and shot it down with a single burst.

The .303 is a light machine gun round and not the best choice for aerial dog fighting. However, four of them, with a cyclic rate of 1200 rounds per minute per gun, at point-blank range is death on thin-skinned enemy aircraft. The Ju-87 rolled left in a wing-over and crashed in a giant ball of fire.

Since the dive bombers were fully armed and topped off for an early morning mission with a load of one 1,100-pound bomb under the fuselage and a 110-pound bomb under each wing it was a big explosion.

With the number two plane in the line of Stukas committed to the landing—on the point of touching down, there was nothing it could do to take evasive action. The South African pilot put the pip of his gunsight on the cockpit and unleashed another short burst of tracers, incendiaries and AP rounds—also at point-blank range.

It exploded.

The lead Stuka was already on the ground taxiing when the German pilot became aware of what was taking place behind him. His tail gunner, having been hypnotized by the sight of what was taking place, had only belatedly notified him. At this point any attempt by the flyer to take evasive action would almost surely result in his plane going into a ground loop—a classification of crash that results in a high percentage of fatalities to pilots and crew.

The German pilot panicked and tried to jump out of the still moving aircraft. He got tangled up making his exit, hit the tarmac headfirst and bounced just as the South African pilot fired a burst and his navigator/bombardier pickled his entire load of 250-pound bombs—four of them. The Stuka blew up for a total of three crashed planes and twelve bombs of varying weights from 110 pounds to 1,100 pounds detonating rapid fire in a chain reaction of explosions.

Capt. Jaxx decided if anything could be worse than standing on an illuminated enemy airstrip, it would be standing on an illuminated enemy airstrip while it is being bombed. Highly motivated to be anywhere else, Lt. Col. Lord Jellicoe and Capt. Jaxx exfiltrated the landing ground at a high rate of speed.

Deafened from the massive explosions and nearly blinded by the brilliant flashes of the bomb blasts, they were glad to take advantage of the confusion created by the Stukas exploding, bombs bursting and every air defense gunner on the base blazing away at the now-long-gone Bristol Blenheim.

What looked like a million tracers crisscrossed an empty sky.

Once clear of the air base the two officers set off for the extraction point twenty-five miles away on the coast marching hard highly motivated to be long gone and far away. They were the first team to make it to the Rendezvous Point (RVP). The other four SBS operators never arrived— killed or captured. The MTB waited long past the prearranged time.

No joy.

Capt. Jaxx knew he was going to have to make a full report to Colonel John Randal on his return to Castelrozzo. He was not looking forward to it. The Colonel did not accept high casualty rates from his subordinate commanders.

He was not going to be happy.

THREE MILES OFF MIKROS ISLAND, ENSIGN WESTLY SLADE and a handpicked team of MU Operational Swimmers launched their paddleboards over the side of the Levant Schooner Flotilla (LSF) caique. The paddleboards were longer and thicker than a surfboard and had a strap mounted where the operator could tie down a submachine gun or his explosives. Unfortunately, OSS had not issued them suppressed SMGs for the simple reason the Outfit had none in inventory as of yet. As soon as Captain Roy Kidd completed his suppressed weapons evaluation, it was anticipated there would be a lot of them. Each member of the four-man team had either a .22 High Standard Military Model D or a .22 Colt Woodsman—the most popular semiautomatic .22 pistol in America, carried in a canvas chest holster.

The handguns were equipped with suppressors.

The idea of using paddleboards to infiltrate an enemy beach originated with Lieutenant Jackson Taylor—one of the original OSS Operational Swimmers—what was called a 'plank holder'. It was his belief a Frog utilizing one could bypass magnetic mines, acoustic devices and net defenses while slipping silently into an enemy harbor unnoticed. The goal was to transport a limpet mine strapped to each board, evade detection, and place them on enemy ships. There were no anti-ship mines tonight because Mikros was a tiny island with no harbor where ships could dock.

It boasted a prewar population of twenty-eight.

The Operational Swimmers had been briefed to make a beach reconnaissance and to locate the wooden pier where they would be met by an "agent or agents known to them" who would have further orders. It sounded like hundreds of training missions the Frogs had carried out— with one exception. Lt. Taylor informed them in the Warning Order that an element of "Criminals" from the 999th Light Division were thought to be on the island.

During the questions period upon conclusion of the Operations Order, one Frog asked, "What do you mean criminals, sir?"

Lt. Taylor explained that the 999th was a penal unit composed of convicts released from prison not expected to live out their wartime service. They were expendable. While some military units called their troops Infantry, Armor, Paratroopers, Commandos or Rangers, the official Wehrmacht designation of an individual soldier in the 999th was "Criminal." That is what they were called, how they described themselves to others and how they acted once out of sight of higher controlling authority. The Hollywood dentist also mentioned Raiding Forces almost never took Criminals prisoner.

That was an attention-getter.

The paddle to shore was routine. Lt. Taylor followed on his board observing the infiltration—he was not part of the team. While no one in Det 3 had ever been on an actual combat mission, the Operational Swimmers were overtrained for the task of making their way surreptitiously to a beach in the dark of night. The Frogs were wired tight.

This being their first mission at long, long last it actually felt good to finally be doing it for real down range. And Det 3 did it by the book . . . or thought so. The moon was getting close to full, and it was providing enough pale light to make seeing not overly difficult. The MU operators were competent at working in harmony, each man anticipating the other's moves. The landing ashore, hiding their boards and patrolling to the dock evolutions were accomplished in sync as if they were choreographed.

First missions never feel quite real and tonight was no exception.

When the team silently approached the dock, the dark shadows of the handful of tiny houses in the village could be seen close by, but no lights were showing. The natives were all in bed, there being no nightlife on Mikros. The Det 3 operators did not encounter any indication of the presence of the Criminals reported to be on the island.

There was a reason for that.

Ghosting up to the dock, weapons at the ready, Ens. Slade halted in mid-stride as if frozen. The stop was so abrupt the Frogs nearly slammed into each other. They were not supposed to do that.

Directly to the patrol's front Colonel John Randal and Beverly Blackwell were sitting on an ancient barnacle-encrusted pier dangling their legs off the end.

Beverly said, "Hi."

None of the Frogs had met Beverly before. The last thing the Det 3 Operational Swimmers had expected tonight was to find their new commanding officer and a beautiful blonde waiting on their initial objective. At this point the men had to admit their new CO was beginning to seem a little more impressive.

Col. Randal said, "Are you prepared to accept a change of mission?"

He said it exactly the way one of the Commando instructors at Achnacarry would have—not really a question.

Ens. Slade said, "Yes, sir."

"There's six of the 999th in the village. Go take 'em out. Mr. King is waiting at the end of the pier with your instructions."

In a heartbeat tonight turned out not to be like a single training mission the Frogs had ever been on. Was the Colonel joking? Take them "out" meant something entirely different than take them "down." Had he just ordered them to kill six people?

Ens. Slade said, "Wilco, sir."

The Operational Swimmers advanced up the dock. Lt. Taylor followed along behind observing. The Frogs were confident in their ability. But they failed to notice the two Lovat Scouts standing off to one side as they moved past.

King whispered, "Det 3 as of now you are a kill team. There are six Criminals sleeping in four houses up the street. I will guide you to the first two houses. The Lieutenant and I will take the third. Station a man in front and in back at each location. When you hear an owl hoot that will be the signal to enter, identify the German or Germans inside, shoot them utilizing suppressed weapons, then withdraw dragging the dead Nazis out in the street. Don't shoot the Greeks! Any questions?"

Was he crazy? The Operational Swimmers had a lot of questions. No one asked any of them.

For the Frogs tonight was like a surreal out-of-body experience. They were being swept up in a series of rapidly changing events powerless to influence the course of the action except to comply with their new orders. The situation definitely seemed dreamlike as it unfolded. Up until this moment the MUs felt like the mission was going in slow motion.

Now it switched to fast forward.

As the patrol moved out the Frogs were not doing the math, and it was a serious oversight. Based on King's change of mission frag order there were still 999th Criminals unaccounted for. It is important to keep up with numbers like that in the middle of a mission.

The Lovat Scouts passed through the Operational Swimmers unnoticed—possibly being mistaken for King and Lt. Taylor. Or it might have been because the two red deer stalkers were masters in the art of stealth and seemed to have the ability to disappear and reappear at will— like one of the Great Teddy's illusions. They took up a position next to the fourth house where one of the Criminals was staying. His location was confirmed by the recon prior to the Frogs arriving on the island.

King led each two-man team of Frogs to their target. As per orders, one took up a security position in the street, one stood by the front door ready to effect entry while the other slipped around back to cover the rear. Their suppressed .22 pistols were cocked and locked held at the ready.

Ens. Slade delegated himself to be entry man at his target. He was standing by waiting for the signal to execute, keyed up to an extraordinarily high level of anticipation. From the moment King dropped off the Det 3 people at their individual objectives, time, which had been fast-forwarding, screeched to a dead stop.

The village was tiny with only a single cobblestone street. All the actions were slated to take place in close proximity to each other. Ens. Slade could see the other entry men outside their houses by turning his head.

Hoot. Hoot.

There were no owls known to be on Mikros but it being doubtful any of the 999th Criminals were ornithologists it was unlikely they would notice.

Ens. Slade crept inside the house in a dream-like state, not really believing this was actually happening after all the endless training. Immediately after making entry he turned on a hook-nosed flashlight with a red-filtered lens so he could see to move around but not destroy his night vision. The floor creaked every time he put a boot down no matter how hard he tried to move without making a sound. Every time he heard the noise he thought he was going to go into cardiac arrest. The first bedroom he came to had two children asleep in their bed. The second, a middle-aged couple. The third had a man in his thirties sleeping next to a naked twelve or thirteen-year-old girl—the daughter?

Ens. Slade froze dead still. Nothing in his training or life experience had prepared him for anything remotely like this. The Criminals were as bad as advertised—which he had personally doubted.

What to do?

During the Operations Order it had been stated that Raiding Forces' SOP for use of suppressed .22s was two to the chest with one to the head. Or even better when a clear stationary head shot was offered, two to the head one to the chest. Inching up to the side of the bed, being extremely careful to line up his shot so as not to hit the sleeping girl, Ens. Slade did exactly what the SOP called for. At contact range he held the silencer to the Criminal's left temple, *WHIIIIIICH, WHIIIIIICH* to the head then *WHIIIIIICH* to the heart.

The Nazi never knew what hit him but his eyes came open before he died so the man knew something had happened. Ens. Slade's suppressed .22 Colt Woodsman being very quiet, the Greek girl slept through it. She was in for an unpleasant surprise in the morning—or maybe not.

This was one war story he was never going to be able to tell his mother.

Dragging the dead Nazi out and dumping him in the middle of the street per orders, Ens. Slade encountered one of his men, Corporal Josh Malakaski, a U.S. Marine and the former Florida State Champion in the 100-yard breaststroke. Being the state champion breast stroker caused him to come in for a lot of good-natured ribbing from his fellow Frogs, but it was not a bad pickup line. He seemed to be in a state of shock.

Cpl. Malakaski said, "You're not going to believe what I found in there, sir. The Nazi was in bed with the Greek's wife in his own house. That's insane."

Ens. Slade whispered, "How did you know who was who?"

Cpl. Malakaski whispered, "The German had his gear piled on a chair in the big bedroom. I had to sneak into the one next to it to locate the husband before going back to take out the Criminal. Nobody taught us any of this stuff, sir."

Ens. Slade said, "I don't think our instructors knew about it."

King came strolling down the street with Lieutenant Taylor and the Lovat Scouts, clearly no longer concerned about the necessity of maintaining patrol integrity or exercising noise discipline.

Ens. Slade said, "Who are those extra two men?"

King said, "Lovat Scouts—the lads who have been shadowing you people from the moment you paddled ashore."

Ens. Slade felt slightly sick to his stomach. So much for Operational Swimmer fieldcraft. The team had been under observation from the time they hit the beach and never knew it. That was not supposed to happen.

When he arrived back on the dock, Ens. Slade reported a good count to Col. Randal.

"All right then, Ensign, let's get the hell out of Dodge."

The Frogs who had gathered around remembered that line from *Jump on Bela*.

PRIVATE FIRST CLASS NORVEL "HORN DOG" HANSEN WAS sitting at a table in the bar with no name with some of his SOG buddies in the Beaten Zone on Castelrozzo—which might or might not have been off limits. In between strippers he was telling them about his adventures on Leros.

"*Booooom*, there was this big explosion and the next thing I know I come to in a German field hospital set up in a GP tent. Word was the Italian Army had a couple of government-sanctioned whorehouses down the coast somewhere not far away. Who'd believe that? But the ward wasn't real well-guarded so I decided to check it out.

"E&E'd straight there like I had radar.

"So there I was hanging with the unemployed Italian hookers, who were brushing up on their German language skills, and letting the good times roll. Life was good, *real* good. Then one night a couple of Mrs. Paige's MI-9 caiques pulled in to pick up evaders. She came ashore and drug me out of there. What a downer."

His buddies said, "Yeah."

Pfc. Hansen said, "We should have been in the Italian Army—those guys know how to party."

The sixteen members of Det 3 who had not gone on the Mikros raid strolled in as if they owned the place. It had not taken the Operational Swimmers long to find the action.

They must have had the same built in radar as Horn Dog.

"Who the hell are those guys?"

"Frogmen."

10
LEGENDS IN YOUR OWN MINDS

THE DET 3 TEAM ASSEMBLED FOR A CLOSED DOOR DEBRIEF as soon as their LSF caique returned them to Castelrozzo. The men had reboarded the boat and sacked out not even taking time to tell each other their war stories. They would come to discover that is a typical reaction in the immediate aftermath of a high-stress operation no matter how many an operator has been on.

They slept most of the way back to base.

Any first mission where there is enemy contact is always an intense experience. Entering a dark house alone knowing an armed enemy soldier is inside and may or may not be lying in wait is about as high stress as it gets. No one blamed the Det 3 personnel for not being talkative.

Now that they were back, the Frogs were feeling good about their inaugural performance. They could now put a checkmark in the combat veterans box—a big deal. The team had performed a reconnaissance of a German-held island, received a change of mission, transitioned to a kill team, cleared their individual targets and eliminated the enemy combatants they were charged with taking out in strict accordance to orders.

There might be medals.

Lieutenant Jackson Taylor conducted the debrief. He went straight to the main point. And he did not pull any punches.

"From the time you launched from the caique till the time you reboarded for the exfil home you men made a series of tactical errors that could have resulted in the loss of all or part of your team. Consider yourselves lucky to be alive. If you intend to continue in *my* Det 3 you people will have to retool this 'legends-in-your-own-mind' attitude you've flaunted ever since you arrived on ABC and focus on performing up to Raiding Forces standards."

The Frogs had not seen this coming. They were shocked. The mission had been a complete success—right?

Colonel John Randal was sitting with King on the far-right end of the semicircle of chairs facing Lt. Taylor. He was interested in seeing how the OSS officer intended to proceed. Debriefs were serious business. Raiding Forces was a finger-pointing outfit. The practice of identifying mistakes, admitting they took place, learning from them and not repeating them was one of the primary reasons for the unit's continued success. Anyone wishing to serve in Raiding Forces who did not admit to their errors and consequently did not learn from them found themselves RTU'd.

Debriefs were designed to be a democratic evaluation of the mission from start to finish covering tactical decisions and individual actions. All participants are allowed to speak their mind free from fear of retribution— only that feedback was apparently not happening today. Lt. Taylor did not act like he was going to be interested in the Operational Swimmers' input.

The key to a mission debrief was that no one was exempt from criticism regardless of rank.

Col. Randal had come in for his share over the years.

Lt. Taylor said, "After disembarking from the caique on your paddleboards you were paddling on your knees. The instant the beach was sighted the team should have immediately gone to the prone to provide a lower profile in the event a German sentry on shore was watching. In fact, our Lovat Scouts were. They spotted you on the way in. Ensign Slade failed to issue the order and none of you alerted him to the oversight.

"Not only did the Scouts observe the team come ashore, they paced it—unseen—during your movement to the pier.

"Upon reaching the dock you encountered Colonel Randal and Beverly Blackwell—a former University of Texas beauty queen. You became so rattled you stopped, bunched up and milled around. A well-aimed burst of machine gun fire, a single grenade or an incoming mortar round could have taken out the entire team. Since virtually everything you encounter on a recon mission is unexpected—that's why you do them, to find out things—there's no excuse for having allowed a good-looking blonde in the target area influence your actions.

"After Colonel Randal instructed you to link up with Mr. King you simply strolled up the pier passing by the Lovat Scouts standing off to one side in the shadows—and again failed to detect them.

"When you reported to Mr. King, instead of setting up a defensive perimeter while Ensign Slade was receiving a change of mission, you simply stood in a cluster and listened to the conversation.

"Then, and this is harder to explain, as Mr. King guided you to your individual objectives, the Lovat Scouts—who at that point were trailing you up the street—simply walked through your positions. No one challenged them."

The Frogs were hanging their heads. This was not the "Welcome Home Heroes" they had expected. A staccato of "you, you, you" was coming at them hard and fast and not in a good way.

"Upon completion of your secondary mission, after you exited the Greek houses and security pulled in, everyone simply congregated in the street. You people stacked arms. Mission accomplished—let's go have a beer.

"On the exfil movement once again you failed to remain tactical. You strolled down the street, walked back up the beach to recover your paddleboards and loaded them on the caique in violation of every known principle of security. You men acted like you were back on Catalina Island at the end of a training exercise—not behind enemy lines having just killed six Nazis.

"Just because someone else walks down the middle of a street on an operation does not mean you can. If Colonel Randal wants to bring a date on a raid, that's his prerogative. Throughout training you have been taught to adhere to your tactical SOPs. So what do you do on your first combat op? You forgot or ignored everything you have been taught—and that's unacceptable.

"Det 3 was selected for OSS MU's initial overseas deployment to an active combat zone—a highly coveted assignment. You men were chosen by me to carry out the first mission. OSS has a lot riding on how well you perform. People in high places have eyes on, and they're not all friendly. Admiral King at the War Department hates General Donovan and would like nothing better than to see the Maritime Unit disbanded or better yet amalgamated into the Navy's Underwater Demolition Teams. Det 3 fails and the program fails. After your performance last night I'm considering sending you four home—in Raiding Forces we call that RTU."

Lt. Taylor had not raised his voice. He had not been abusive. Not singled out any individual to criticize, though he had mentioned Ens. Slade by name. However, the contempt exhibited by his tone of voice and body language was brutal for men who thought as highly of themselves as these Frogs did. The Hollywood dentist no longer reminded anyone in the room of a surfer or a playboy.

In a way Lt. Taylor's debrief was worse than "Hell Week." They survived that on pure guts but there was no guarantee they were going make it in Raiding Forces.

"Colonel Randal, any comments, sir?"
"Negative."

CAPTAIN BILLY JACK JAXX ARRIVED BACK ON ABC. HE WAS waiting outside the closed door debrief when Colonel John Randal came out. They walked together toward the Other Ranks dining hall. It was tradition for a team returning from an operation to have its first meal together at a separate table in the OR mess. Cohesion building was a never-ending process in Raiding Forces.

Col. Randal said, "How did inserting from a submarine work out, Jack—any possibilities?"

Capt. Jaxx said, "I never saw a sub, Colonel."

"Well, that was the purpose of the exercise?"

"I'll give you a detailed report later. Right now, sir, I wanted you to hear the basics of what took place. We landed a six-man party, then broke down into two-man teams to raid three separate airfields. Colonel Jellicoe and I were the only team to make it back to the extraction point.

"While it's still unknown if the other two groups destroyed enemy aircraft before being killed or captured, the Colonel and I never had a chance to place our charges, sir."

Col. Randal said, "What stopped you?"

Capt. Jaxx said, "As we were making our approach to the flight line the German pilots scrambled and flew off with us standing there holding our demolitions. Then the RAF showed up and put in an airstrike before we could figure out our next move."

"Really?"

"Don't recommend the experience, Colonel."

"I can see why not."

Capt. Jaxx said, "Poor prior planning. Lack of coordination with higher headquarters to prevent the RAF from bombing a target an SBS team was in the process of raiding. Zero intel other than the location of the enemy landing grounds. The mission seemed to be primarily based on a map study and wishful thinking, sir."

Col. Randal said, "Sixty-six percent casualty rate . . ."

"That's why I flew straight back here to report. You always want to hear bad news immediately. I knew it would be best coming from me first, sir."

"All right. Thanks, Jack. How about you? Get any rest?"

"Roger."

"Up for a mission tonight?"

"Absolutely, sir."

Col. Randal said, "I'll get with you after breakfast with the OSS team that went out last night. Glad you're back."

"I'll be in the TOC, Colonel."

Beverly was waiting for Col. Randal outside the Other Ranks mess when he arrived. They went in and stood at the end of the buffet style food line. The Frogs were already in line but moved aside for them to go first. Accepted practice in all branches of the service is for officers to be accorded the privilege of moving to the front of lines and doing so was not considered cutting in.

Col. Randal said, "You men go ahead."

The four Det 3 operators seemed uncertain what to do. Nothing like this had happened to them before. Ensign Westly Slade was already in front of them filling his tray.

Beverly laughed, "It's OK, boys. In Raiding Forces officers eat last."

Lieutenant Jackson Taylor walked up and waited with the Colonel and Beverly—he knew the drill.

There was little or no talking among the returning Operational Swimmers sitting at the long table reserved for them. It was situated along one side of the room with the chairs all placed on the far side, backs to the wall. The team was facing the rest of the room. This was a small honor. A form of recognition. As Raiding Forces personnel arrived for breakfast, they acknowledged the Frogs with a knowing glance and moved on.

They had all sat at that table.

The OSS MU operators who had not gone on the raid strolled in hung over from the nights' adventure in the Beaten Zone. The Frogmen pulled up short when they spotted their buddies. The four raid team members seemed like changed men. They were combat veterans while the rest of Det 3 were not. A big divide.

You are either a combat veteran or you are not, which is different from being a veteran of having been in the military, trained hard in inclement weather, eaten bad food and lost sleep. The distinction is something that cannot be bought, awarded to you or inherited. The title "combat veteran" can only be earned one way. And once earned, it cannot be unearned.

A combat veteran is one for life and it shapes how others perceive you forever.

The hungover Det 3 Frogs would have been surprised to learn that their combat veteran buddies had been less affected by the mission than by Lt. Taylor's scorching debrief.

That had been brutal.

AS HE WAS GETTING UP HAVING FINISHED HIS BREAKFAST Colonel John Randal ordered, "Ensign Slade, meet me in the Tactical Operations Center when you're done here."

"Yes, sir."

Lieutenant Jackson Taylor walked Col. Randal and Beverly to the door of the Other Ranks mess.

Col. Randal said, "We've got a leadership problem in Det 3 that needs to be addressed immediately."

"Sir?"

"SOP in Raiding Forces is for officers to lead. Counting you there's only two OSS officers in Det 3. Not enough for as many teams as we'll be sending out. I need a recommendation on where we can find qualified candidates." Col. Randal had no intention of making an exception for the Maritime Unit teams.

There was a possibility Lt. Taylor could promote from within. Commissions were available to be had. Men simply had to step up and go through the process of qualifying for one. The problem was not everyone wanted to be an officer.

Which reminded him, Waldo was scheduled to speak later this morning to the group of officer candidates currently going through training at ABCHQ. This was the old ivory poacher's first teaching engagement. Col. Randal planned to sit in if he could.

Lt. Taylor said, "I'll get back to you, Colonel."

Walking toward the TOC, Beverly said, "Mandy and I have a preliminary meeting with R.J. in a few minutes to discuss plans for targeting Greek collaborators."

Col. Randal said, "Keep me informed, Beverly. I intend to be involved in a big way."

"Hoping you would say that, Johnny."

Walking down the hall Major the Lady Jane Seaborn was coming the opposite direction. They paused to talk briefly while Beverly continued on.

"You meeting with Brigadier Maunsell too?"

Lady Jane said, "I am—what is this I hear about Beverly going out with the OSS team last night?"

Col. Randal said, "She said I hadn't been . . ."

Lady Jane said, "You thought it a good idea to take her on an operation so the two of you could spend quality time together?"

"It was an impulse."

Lady Jane said, "I see."

Which was what he always said when he did not understand or did not *want* to understand the why of a thing. She knew that.

Col. Randal said, "We're not having this conversation because some of the details are not known to the Det 3 people. King and the Scouts went ashore early on prior to the MU's arrival and contacted a local to point out the houses where the 999th troops were staying. That's the Criminals' MO—sleeping in Greek houses, no defensive positions. I had a ten-man SOG team under Lt. Starrett on Parker's MAS boat standing by to come in at the first sign of trouble. Beverly was along to be a distractor when the Frogs reached their initial objective.

"It was a nice night. We sat on the dock, watched the stars and waited for the cavalry to arrive."

Lady Jane laughed, "Beverly said it was one of the best dates she has ever been on."

Col. Randal said, "Yeah well, she's almost as easy to entertain as you are. Along that line, anything you'd like to do in Haifa later today?"

"Why are you asking?"

"I'm flying out to see Jellicoe, then coming straight back. Pam's on the rotation to be the duty pilot. Bring Mandy and Beverly along if you like. You four can get in a shopping safari while I meet with the Earl."

"Love to."

The smile Lady Jane rewarded him with was best grade heart attack quality.

She really *was* easy to please.

Ensign Westly Slade was waiting at the door of the TOC. Col. Randal said, "Follow me."

As they walked in Col. Randal said, "Lieutenant Taylor's a tough grader."

Ens. Slade said, "Thought I would perform at a higher level, sir."

Col. Randal said, "On my first mission off the coast of France I nearly raided the wrong island. First missions aren't always pretty. You learn from 'em then move on. Do better next time. Appears to me you've had exhaustive training in how to be a combat swimmer, underwater diver, naval demolitions expert, beach surveyor, etc., but your training seems to have stopped at the water's edge. That the case?"

Ens. Slade said, "I would have never believed it so, sir. But you're right—not much emphasis was placed on troop leading steps or basic infantry patrolling tactics. OSS must have assumed officers already knew that stuff. I'm Navy, not Marines."

Col. Randal said, "I'm going to have you understudy our SOG commander Captain Jaxx. He's the best small unit leader I've ever served with . . . just don't tell him I said that. Observe what he does, do it and we'll have you leading independent operations on your own before you know. Time to take it to the next level, Ensign."

"I'll do my best, sir."

"All right then."

Inside the TOC, Capt. Jaxx was talking to Capt. Pamala Plum-Martin. The pilot with hair the color of snow was wearing one of her black tailor-made flight suits. As usual the Royal Marine looked like she had stepped out of the pages of a glossy high fashion magazine.

Ens. Slade tried hard not to gawk.

"We still on for Haifa today, John?"

"As soon as Lady Jane and the girls wrap up their preliminary meeting with R. J. I need to get Jack briefed on a mission and talk to a couple of people. Then we'll be good to go."

"Perfect."

Capt. Jaxx glanced at Col. Randal wondering about Haifa but did not say anything—SBS HQ was located at Athlete, twelve miles outside the city.

Capt. Plum-Martin said, "See you on the plane, love."

After she departed to perform her preflight check, Col. Randal, Capt. Jaxx and Ens. Slade moved off to one side of the room. As usual the TOC was a busy place. For a unit as small as Raiding Forces it had operations going in a wide range of faraway places.

Everything had to be coordinated. Each subordinate unit commander's problems had to be resolved. Distant detachments all had to be supplied with food, ammunition and clothing. Logistics were much more complex in the islands than they had been at Oasis X. Here all Class II supplies had to be delivered. At the oasis, patrols returned to base to be resupplied or had stores airdropped to them.

Col. Randal said, "Captain Jaxx, show Ensign Slade around. Introduce him to everyone. Before I leave we'll get back together to wire you two in on your mission tonight."

"Wilco."

Ens. Slade perked up. This was the first he had heard about going back out. He wanted another crack at an operation. Raiding Forces was clearly not the kind of outfit where people sat around waiting for something to happen. The *anything is possible, and probably will happen, but we will deal with it, business as usual,* atmosphere in the TOC had a strangely addictive quality about it.

As soon as Col. Randal walked off, Capt. Jaxx—who had heard the story about last night's raid—said, "Beverly 'a real clock stopper last night, Wesley?"

Ens. Slade said, "Damn straight, sir."

"Pam's not bad herself."

"Not bad—you are kidding, right, Captain?"

"Be advised—she's King's girlfriend."

Professor Layton Winthrop was in his spacious office strategically located next to those of Lieutenant Colonel Sir Terry "Zorro" Stone and Vice Admiral Sir Randolph "Razor" Ransom. Its whereabouts revealed everything that needed to be known about his status in Raiding Forces.

The Professor had initially been brought in to brief on the string of archeologists who doubled as SOE intelligence agents he ran throughout the Aegean and on the Greek mainland. In short order, Dr. Winthrop made himself an invaluable member of the unit. No one had planned it that way.

His cover story was that he worked for Special Operations Executive, but in reality he had maintained a relationship with the British Secret Intelligence Service going back before the war, years before SOE was conceived. Nowadays, in addition to the Professor's other activities, he was functioning as the Raiding Forces' Intelligence Officer. He had a handpicked, intelligence-trained FANY assigned by SOE (London) to assist—Lieutenant Beatrice Bancroft.

She had a desk outside his door. "Go right in, Colonel Randal."

There were maps, books and papers scattered all over the office giving it a cluttered, comfortable, academic feel.

Col. Randal said, "Doctor, I need a small island for Jack to run a reconnaissance patrol again tonight. Someplace with only a handful of enemy personnel stationed on it."

Dr. Winthrop and Capt. Jaxx were unlikely friends.

The Professor said, "Not the usual request. To what purpose, Colonel?"

Col. Randal said, "A tune-up raid to give Jack an opportunity to show our new MU officer Ensign Slade how one of our missions is supposed to be carried out—a quick in, take a look around and out."

Dr. Winthrop said, "Little Gavdos, not to be confused with Gavdos, would be tailor-made for such a task. Nine kilometers long by four and a half kilometers wide. Pre-war it was a Greek penal colony primarily used for holding communist dissidents. The prisoners were held in crude dungeons located inside the island's numerous caves. There are no military installations on the island. However, a small party of the 999th is reported to be stationed there. The local islanders, primarily fishermen, never numbered more than twenty-five or thirty people pre-war. Possibly less now. There may not be any.

"Reports indicate the prisoners were evacuated by the Germans once they took over from the Greeks. Likely the Nazis did not want to go to the effort of guarding and victualing them. Unconfirmed intelligence indicates the prisoners were executed at some later time and place. If you need an out-of-the way objective of no particular military value to run a training operation against, Little Gavdos fits the bill nicely."

Col. Randal said, "Exactly what I'm looking for, Doctor. Can you do an intel workup for Jack? He won't need much—this is pure reconnaissance. I just need him to have enough information for his Op Order to be by the book."

Dr. Winthrop said, "My pleasure, Colonel, anything for Jack. It should not take up more than a few minutes of my time—little is known about the place."

"Thanks."

As Col. Randal walked to the door he said, "Doctor, have you been brought up to speed on this counterintelligence operation Jane's working on?"

Prof. Winthrop said, "Had a preliminary conversation with Mandy. R. J. and I plan to visit later today to discuss the program. As I understand the parameters the intent is to target Greek collaborators—we arrest them and turn them over to Major Zargo. I should be able to develop enough actionable intelligence to keep Lady Seaborn and her merry band of femmes fatales busy.

"A worthy project in my opinion, Colonel."

Col. Randal said, "Good. I'll feel better knowing you're on top of things. I don't want any overreach or mission creep. You suspect outside agencies are starting to horn in or attempt to raise the mission profile, let me know."

Dr. Winthrop said, "I understand perfectly, Colonel."

Lt. Col. Stone was at his desk in his office. He was Col. Randal's Deputy Commander/Operations Officer. He and Captain Stephanie Fawcett-Tatum were the two hardest working people in Raiding Forces—putting in long hours seven days a week—week in and week out. The two complemented each other. They made running Raiding Forces (Aegean) appear easy. The key word being "appear."

Col. Randal said, "Captain Jaxx's going to be carrying out a recon on a place called Little Gavdos tonight. I'm taking off for Haifa to see

Jellicoe. Can you make sure Jack gets the support he needs to make it happen?"

"What's on Little Gavdos?"

"Nothing."

"Sounds like my kind of operation."

"The Professor's organizing the intel. This is basically a live fire training exercise for Ensign Slade without the live fire. Jack's going to show him how it's done. OSS taught the Maritime Unit everything they need to know except how to conduct patrols."

"Are you serious?"

"Det 3's skill level falls off a cliff once they step on dry land. They don't know what they don't know.

Lt. Col. Stone said, "Not a problem. We can address that. What do you have going in Haifa, old stick?"

Col. Randal said, "Jellicoe and Jaxx were the only two survivors out of a six-man SBS raid that sounds like it was planned by Cub Scouts playing army."

Lt. Col. Stone said, "Afraid George picked up bad habits while he was attached to the SAS. During the last of their cowboy jeep raiding days, before Stirling's lax radio security resulted in his capture, they just rolled out and made it up as they went along. I know Roger Courtney, the officer who initially raised and trained the SBS. He preached meticulous planning and forbade his men from taking unnecessary risks. Unfortunately, the SBS have been bounced around ever since they came out from the UK—all the good training wasted."

Col. Randal said, "Your friend Major Patterson of the 11th Parachute Battalion—still interested in coming to work with us?"

Lt. Col. Stone said, "He is."

"Have the Major meet me in Haifa when we land. Tell him to bring his bags. I have a job for him."

Lt. Col. Stone said, "Until Det 3's patrolling is up to par, you might consider employing them against enemy shipping, old stick. The concept conforms to the opening phase of FIRE EATER you outlined. I can work with the Admiral to develop the missions."

Col. Randal said, "I knew there was a reason I kept you around, Sir Zorro. Make it happen. I want to sit in on mission planning with you and the Admiral. Maybe learn something about Operational Swimmer tactics."

"I shall get with the Professor," Lt. Col. Stone said. "Start building intelligence dossiers of likely Kriegsmarine targets. This could prove interesting."

When Col. Randal walked out, Lady Jane was sitting on top of a desk holding a handset to her ear talking on the multichannel Army Command and Administrative Network (ACAN) radio/telephone. She hung up as he was coming over.

"What's going on, Jane?"

"Arranging for ground transportation. We require a car to chauffer us around town. You need one to drive you to the SBS camp at Athlete."

Col. Randal said, "Thanks . . . ready when you are."

"Let me go find Mandy and Beverly—fun."

Col. Randal thought again how she was easy to entertain.

As Lady Jane was leaving, Col. Randal crossed the room to have a word with Lt. Taylor. "Ensign Slade will be observing Captain Jaxx for the immediate future. You might want to check in on what they're doing from time to time."

"That's an outstanding idea, sir."

"Get with Colonel Stone. You need another Det 3 target."

"When do you want my next team to launch, Colonel?"

"Tonight would be fine."

"Yes, sir!"

"As you pointed out in your debrief, Det 3's understanding of basic patrolling fundamentals is lacking. I'll be setting up a training program to fix that. In the meantime, giving all your men a chance to see action as soon as possible is the best first step."

"I agree, sir."

"You're going to need at least one additional MU officer. Two would be better. I'm not sure where to get them . . . any ideas?"

Lt. Taylor said, "As far as I am aware OSS has not developed a pipeline of MU replacement officers, sir."

Col. Randal said, "That's going to be a problem, Lieutenant. Get back to me with a solution."

"Yes, sir."

Across the room Brigadier Dudley Clarke was talking to Major Hawthorne Merryweather. Col. Randal walked over. Political Warfare Executive (PWE) was charged with making the Nazis *think* something. A-Force (Deception) was charged with making the Nazis *do* something. He needed them to be on the same page for their work with Raiding Forces in FIRE EATER.

At the beginning of the war when he was working for Military Operations 4 (MO-4), Brig. Clarke recruited Col. Randal to serve in a raiding organization he had designed, persuaded the British Prime Minister to form, and had named Commandos after one of England's old enemies, the Boers. They went on the first Commando raid of the war together.

Maj. Merryweather was a PWE officer who had turned up and attached himself to Force N in Abyssinia. At the time Col. Randal had exactly zero use for a Propaganda Officer but being desperate, he took anyone he could get to lead his Force N guerrillas. Eventually the Major became a gun jeep patrol leader running patrols out of Oasis X. A popular scholar soldier, he was known in Raiding Forces as the "Happy Warrior."

The three of them had a long-established relationship.

Col. Randal was confident Brig. Clarke and Maj. Merryweather would come up with a workable plan for FIRE EATER. The idea was to bombard the Axis Forces with a blend of propaganda and misinformation designed to confuse and dishearten the Nazis. It is always good to have confused and disheartened enemy personnel on your objective when you arrive unannounced and unexpected out of the dark of night with evil intent.

Brig. Clarke said, "This has been a most productive couple of days, Colonel. General Donovan and I have been able to spend much-needed time together. Now Major Merryweather and I are making arrangements for setting up a joint office here at ABC to coordinate future operations. You shall want to have one of your people liaise with us as we shall require Raiding Forces to assist with our projects."

Col. Randal said, "Anyone special in mind?"

Brig. Clarke said, "Mandy would be ideal. I shall be working with her tangentially on another project—the MEDITERRANEAN DOUBLE CROSS. Even that name is classified by the way.

"Kill two birds with one stone."

Col. Randal said, "Mandy has more irons in the fire than anyone in Raiding Forces. Feel free to talk to her Brigadier. If she can fit it in to her schedule, fine."

Brig. Clarke said, "Considering R. J. is to be heavily involved as well—most likely running the show, my guess is Mandy shall leap at the opportunity."

Col. Randal said, "All right then."

He had no idea what the Brigadier was talking about. But then he seldom did.

Maj. Merryweather said, "PWE London has committed to me its willingness to provide our operations in the Aegean full support in our efforts to assist FIRE EATER. Never said anything remotely like that before, sir. Now all the Brigadier and I need to do is develop a long-range strategy."

Col. Randal said, "I'd like to sit in on a few of your planning sessions."

Brig. Clarke said, "I believe we can arrange something for you. There are some . . ."

"I understand, Brigadier."

Next Col. Randal went to see VAdm. Ransom. Like Dr. Winthrop, the Razor had his wall covered in maps of the Aegean AO. Unlike the Professor's office, VAdm. Ransom's was completely organized with papers, pens, and a Fairbairn Fighting Knife doubling as a letter opener all in their place dressed right with military precision.

The Admiral was a stickler for neatness.

Col. Randal said, "Sir, I need you to select ten locations where you would like me to begin stationing Long Range Desert Group Beach Watch parties to commence observations immediately."

VAdm. Ransom looked up from the report he was reading with a smile that would have made a Tyrannosaurus rex blanch. "Not wasting any time exerting your command authority over the LRDG—outstanding opening move, Colonel."

Col. Randal said, "Four men per Beach Watch team should take up most of the Leros survivors with enough patrolmen left over for a couple more teams to be on Standby in the event you have a breaking need to put eyes on some other location, sir."

"Good plan, but what is it you are really trying to accomplish, Colonel—other than taking charge of a broken unit?"

Col. Randal said, "I sent the LRDG to the jump school at Kabrit to keep the men occupied, sir. They'll be wrapping up soon. When they do, my idea is to put as many Beach Watch teams as we can in the field as quickly as possible so that they don't have time to sit around and dwell on all that's happened. With his troops back in business Major Owen will be free to concentrate on recruiting and not waste any more time feeling sorry about how unfairly his people have been treated."

VAdm. Ransom said, "You realize your plan puts a strain on Small Raid Inc's. naval resources."

"I suspect it will, Admiral."

"Not a problem for me," VAdm. Ramson said. "That is what we have sailors for."

CAPTAIN BILLY JACK JAXX WALKED COLONEL JOHN Randal to the dock where Major General Sam Houston Blackwell and Brigadier General William "Wild Bill" Donovan were waiting to board the Catalina. Major the Lady Jane Seaborn, Mandy Paige and Beverly Blackwell were right behind them. They were excited about their trip.

Col. Randal briefed Capt. Jaxx on the way. "Little Gavdos may have Germans stationed on it—maybe not. Your mission is to recon the built-up area of the island and the caves that housed Greek political prisoners in the past. That means sneak and peek, Jack—get in and get out. I don't want you shooting up the place."

Capt. Jaxx said, "Yes, sir."

Col. Randal said, "Your mission is to demonstrate to Ensign Slade how a patrol is supposed to be planned, organized and led. He needs to see you do it step by step. I don't care about what's on the island. You setting the example—that's the purpose of the exercise."

"I can do that, sir."

"Sneak and peek, Jack."

"No one will know we were ever there, sir."

"All right then, I want the whole nine yards—Warning Order, test fire, rehearsals, Op Order, troop inspection, everything down to the ground—clear?"

"Understood, sir. Are you worried, sir? Anything I should know about?"

"If you were me, Jack, and you were sending you off into the great unknown on an independent mission with freedom of maneuver, would you have a few misgivings?"

"I get the picture, sir—clandestine all the way."

"Everyone that goes in, comes out."

"Yes, sir."

Maj. Gen. Blackwell and Brig. Gen. Donovan were waiting to board for the flight back to Cairo.

Col. Randal said, "We've had a change of plans, gentlemen. You'll be flying out on the Walrus. Red's onboard now getting it set up for you. I'm going to require the *Black Cat*."

Maj. Gen. Blackwell said, "Need more cargo space to haul all the plunder the women are planning on coming back with, huh, Johnny?"

Lady Jane laughed. "Spoken like a man of experience, Bronc."

Maj. Gen. Blackwell said, "Beverly tells me you love to shop, Lady Jane. But she claims you seldom actually buy anything. A rare fine quality . . . most women I know are Neiman Marcus trophy hunters."

Lady Jane said, "While I did not actually purchase them, I do have parting gifts for you and General Donovan."

She handed each of the general officers a small brown leather box tied with a ribbon.

Maj. Gen. Donovan said, "Do we open these now?"

"Oh yes."

Lady Jane had been known to become so excited when giving gifts she actually unwrapped them for the recipient. Everyone on the dock gathered around to see. Inside the boxes were identical bank note engraved, presentation grade, 380 ACP Walther PPK pocket pistols sporting black Gutta Percha grips. A matched set, sequentially serial numbered—the two friends shared a pair, formerly in the collection of one of the late departed Big Five.

Maj. Gen. Blackwell said, "Never leaving home without mine—great present, Lady Jane!"

Brig. Gen. Donovan said, "I intend to keep this pistol on my desk as a show piece. It shall be in my pocket every time I walk out the door."

Lady Jane was an artist at giving presents strategically—like Col. Randal's Rolex. The generals were in a position to be of help to Raiding Forces. Now they were going to be reminded of that every time they handled their concealed carry handgun. And that could easily be several times a day, every day.

Beverly hugged her father good-bye. Captain Pamala Plum-Martin stuck her head out the PBY's cockpit window. "Contact."

She clicked on the mag switch of the port engine. The engine wheezed, turned over, backfired, then started running. The Haifa party queued up to begin loading.

Lady Jane laughed. "Pam's ready for our expedition to be off."

Capt. Jaxx handed Col. Randal one of the custom, heavy-duty, hard carrying cases provided by Westley Richards to discriminating clients who ordered their best grade bespoke sporting shotguns.

Col. Randal passed it to Maj. Gen. Blackwell. "Not as refined as the Walthers Lady Jane gave you, but there's a pair of Beretta M-38 SMGs inside for you and General Donovan. Thought you might have use for 'em, sir."

Brig. Gen. Donovan said, "You Raiding Forces people give excellent presents, Colonel—we'll be back to visit soon."

Maj. Gen. Blackwell said, "Make good coyote guns after the war, Bill."

Col. Randal said, "General Donovan . . . a word sir?"

The two walked off a short distance for a final conversation.

Col. Randal said, "About what you said to me concerning Commander Fleming's Red Indian operation. Fleming says 30 Assault Unit has not performed up to standard on the two missions assigned them so far. I've ordered Major Hoolihan—a Royal Marine—to retrain them. Since 30 AU is composed of Royal Marines he's the logical choice.

"You've been promising to send Raiding Forces an OSS Operational Group. If you can do it now, sir, I'll have them infused into 30 Assault Unit. Major Hoolihan can stay with the Red Indians after he finishes their training and we hijack the mission before Naval Intelligence Division realizes what we're doing."

Brig. Donovan said, "Major Hoolihan . . . he a reliable man?"

Col. Randal said, "Fleming requested him by name, sir. He was my enlisted wingman out of Seaborn House before I commissioned him prior to our jumping into Abyssinia. Been with me the whole way."

Brig. Donovan said, "May just be the best single idea you have ever had, Colonel. The OG will be on the first plane out after I return to the States and can get it organized. This is an extraordinarily high value assignment as you shall come to realize at the appropriate time. I need you to give 30 AU your paramount attention."

"Yes, sir—by assigning it to "Headhunter" Hoolihan I already have."

King walked out of the *Black Cat* as the passengers began boarding the Walrus tied off next to it. He spotted Capt. Jaxx. "Put me down for tonight, Jack."

"You got it."

King said, "Lovats want in too."

"Can do."

Now Capt. Jaxx only needed one more person to round out his team and he knew just the man.

The Catalina taxied out into open water, began its takeoff run and lifted off. The Walrus followed right behind. After a while they were both lost to sight.

LIEUTENANT GENERAL "GERONIMO" JOE MCKOY WAS walking along the ground-floor hallway at ABCHQ when he encountered Ensign Westly Slade coming out of Waldo Treywick's class.

"I hear you OSS boys had yourself a pretty good night."

This came as a surprise. No one had said anything remotely like that since he returned from Alimia. Ens. Slade did not quite know what to make of a lieutenant general with long silver gunfighter style hair and an ivory handled .45 Colt Peacemaker stuck in the front of his pants next to his sterling silver Ranger-style belt buckle—but then nothing about Raiding Forces had been what could be described as normal since Det 3 arrived. Was the general putting him on?

Ens. Slade said, "That would depend on who you talk to, sir."

He had never addressed a lieutenant general before. In fact, he had never even seen one in real life since he enlisted. The experience was more than a little intimidating.

Lt. Gen. McKoy said, "How was Waldo's class?"

Ens. Slade said, "Still trying to wrap my mind around the concept of 'the problem is the solution,' sir."

Lt. Gen. McKoy said, "Takes a little gettin' used to. Doesn't work every time . . . like say a plane crash . . . but it's pretty good once you get the hang."

Ens. Slade said, "Yes, sir. I'll keep thinking the progression through."

"Understand you're goin' out again tonight."

"I am sir."

"Better bring it, son, you'll be runnin' with the big dawgs."

What did that mean?

MAJOR IAN PATTERSON, THE SECOND IN COMMAND OF THE 11th Parachute Battalion, was standing by when the Catalina landed at Kabrit. Major the Lady Jane Seaborn, Captain Pamala Plum-Martin, Mandy and Beverly boarded a town car and were whisked away to face the perils of the boutiques in the town's legendary shopping district.

Colonel John Randal and Major Patterson climbed in another and headed south for the Special Boat Section Headquarters at Athlete.

The SBS and the LRDG were alike in some ways. The Long Range Desert Group was a specialist desert reconnaissance unit that had no more deserts in their future. The Special Boat Section was a secret beach reconnaissance unit that utilized two-man folboats, which stood for "folding boats," to conduct their surreptitious surveys and preinvasion demolitions of obstacles. There being no beaches that needed to be surveyed when it arrived in the Middle East and no invasions planned for the ATO, the unit was attached to the SAS where it carried out gun jeep patrols. After being hauled around in the jeeps, the folboats were battered to pieces.

The LRDG was out of deserts and the SBS was out of boats. The difference between the two was the Special Boat Section was not brooding about it—they could get more folboats. Col. Randal had his work cut out to bring the new model Raiding Forces up to speed.

Lieutenant Colonel the Earl Lord George Jellicoe was waiting when they arrived.

Col. Randal said, "Have someone show Major Patterson around while you brief me on your last operation."

It was not a request.

Lt. Col. Lord Jellicoe was taken off guard. This was clearly not a social call. When the two were alone, he began his briefing. Col. Randal listened quietly showing no expression.

He did not ask questions.

When the report concluded, Col. Randal said, "Have all of your officers assembled at the seaplane dock in Haifa at 1700 hours today. They will be flying to Castelrozzo for two weeks of retraining. Anyone not there when the Raiding Forces Catalina departs can consider himself RTU."

"Sir!"

"Sergeant Major Beckwith will arrive here tomorrow with a team to put your NCOs through the same training program. Advise your people they need to perform. The Sergeant Major will have full authority to RTU any man not achieving his level of expectations."

"Understood, sir."

"If this is not satisfactory, Major Patterson will assume command of SBS—your call, Colonel."

"Additional training sounds like a splendid idea, sir."

"In that case the Major is available to fill the vacant detachment command you have. Conduct your usual interview. But make no mistake, Patterson will be filling your vacancy."

"Have I offended you in some way, Colonel?"

"You took five of my men on a reckless, poorly planned operation and only brought one home. Damn right I'm offended."

It was not lost on Lt. Col. Lord Jellicoe that Col. Randal described the SBS as *his* men. Beverly had once mentioned the Colonel was "about as laid back as a snake." At the time the Earl had not understood what she meant.

Now he did.

11
CAVE OF THE CYCLOPS

CAPTAIN PENELOPE "LEGS" HONEYCUTT-PARKER WAS AT the helm of her MAS boat pounding across the turquoise Aegean Sea toward Little Gavdos as the sun was getting ready to plop into the water. When it did, the immediate result would be a kaleidoscope of colors. Some said Aegean sunsets were the most spectacular in the world. Possibly that was so but the one color no one wanted to see was the "wine dark" Homer described. That was an indication of imminent inclement weather—and bad weather in the Aegean, while of short duration, was bad.

No wine-dark sea this day but as night fell it was going to turn black.

Brandy Seaborn was on the bridge enjoying the ride as a supernumerary for a change. With Major General Sam Houston Blackwell's departure, it had been safe for her to return to Castelrozzo. Per Beverly's advice she was trying to postpone meeting Bronc for as long as possible while he had been pursuing an introduction since seeing her photo in a certain Raiding Forces officer's pistol grip.

According to his daughter, Maj. Gen. Blackwell had a colorful dating history.

Having not visited with her best friend, Parker, in quite a while due to the Small Raids Inc. commitment to MI-9 Escape operations, Brandy decided to ride along tonight to catch up.

Capt. Jaxx assembled his recon team on the stern of the boat. It consisted of Ensign Westly Slade, King, the two Lovat Scouts and Private

First Class Norvel "Horn Dog" Hansen. Colonel John Randal had ordered him to do things by the book so he did—with a little extra window dressing.

During Capt. Jaxx's Operation Order prior to the team's departure, Dr. Layton Winthrop had briefed them about the enemy forces that might be found on Little Gavdos. He described the dungeons where the Communists were held before the war. Vice Admiral Sir Randolph "Razor" Ransom came in to brief the various types of Kriegsmarine naval units that operated in the AO that they might encounter. And Captain Penelope Honeycutt-Parker briefed the team on what was expected of them during their time in transit to the target onboard her MAS boat.

Having this many senior officers directly involved was overkill for a recon mission conducted by veteran operators against a soft target. But none of them minded. They were more than willing to do their part to demonstrate to the newest officer assigned to Raiding Forces how he would be expected to prepare his Det 3 personnel for future operations.

Everyone wanted Ens. Slade to succeed.

As the MAS boat powered on, Capt. Jaxx said to the semicircle of operators sitting like an Indian war party on the deck, "This is a Frag Order." Then he proceeded to brief the team one more time top to bottom on the sequence of events that would be taking place once the boat arrived off Little Gavdos. The idea was to impress on Ens. Slade how he was going to be expected to proceed when he found himself in command of his own team headed into harm's way.

A future event coming at him fast.

Everyone except Pfc. Hansen, who did not possess a need to know, understood why all the repetition was occurring. After the Frag Order, everyone went below and racked out except Ens. Slade, who was revved up about his second mission in two nights.

Over the course of the day Ens. Slade had picked up on something he did not have an answer for or know how to describe but that had impressed him in a big way. Whenever Capt. Jaxx was in the presence of troops there was electricity in the air. It intensified when he briefed and went into overdrive when he led the rehearsal.

The best operators in Raiding Forces, who might have been expected to feel the walkthrough was a waste of time, put everything they had into it. The men executed each movement to perfection. Slow is smooth, smooth is fast. Ens. Slade had never seen the rehearsal's equal in all his training—not even the canned demonstrations at the schools he had attended. To his eye, the operators' movements were so fluid they seemed to be floating. He was more than a little disheartened to realize how far behind his Frogs were in their patrolling technique. Det 3 was going to need to put in extensive effort to reach an equivalent level of proficiency, if that was even possible.

There was another detail that he had observed while accompanying Capt. Jaxx on his rounds. Whenever they encountered enlisted personnel of all ranks, the men smiled like they had a shared secret, saluted, and continued on their way. Anytime the Captain interacted with troops there was mutual respect. The men seemed pleased to be having the conversation, whatever it might be. Not typical officer/enlisted relations in his experience—even in a unit as tight as Det 3. Ens. Slade wondered what it was going to take to be accorded the same treatment.

Few officers are—none he had ever served with.

He had been following Capt. Jaxx around ABC all day like one of the boys in "Jack's Pack." Being four years older, a graduate of the Naval ROTC program at Clemson, on the Tigers' swim team and a member of a fraternity, Ens. Slade had not expected to enjoy the experience.

But he had.

From the first, Capt. Jaxx impressed. He had an easy way about him—gave very few orders. The Captain carried his pistol sideways in a holster flat on his chest for a fast draw and so people could see the most recent photo in the grip. The man had style. And a red-hot reputation as a lifetaker and a heartbreaker.

Hanging out with Capt. Jaxx was—there being no other word for it—cool. At the start of the day had anyone told him he might feel this way, Ens. Slade would have thought they were oxygen deprived. Frogs don't do hero worship.

They reserve that for themselves.

Brandy said, "Raiding Forces living up to expectations so far, Westly?"

LIEUTENANT COCO LOVEJOY ANNOUNCED, "LIEUTENANT Hamilton to see you, sir."

The daughter of one of Brandy Seaborn's friends handpicked for the assignment as Vice Admiral Sir Randolph "Razor" Ransom's personal secretary, no one got past Wren Lovejoy unchecked.

VAdm. Ransom said, "Let's have him."

Lieutenant Ted Hamilton marched in ramrod straight and saluted. "Lt. Hamilton reports, sir."

VAdm. Ransom returned the salute. "Take a seat, Lieutenant."

Lt. Hamilton did as instructed, sitting on the forward six inches of one of the two chairs facing VAdm. Ransom's desk at a rigid position of attention.

"At ease, Lieutenant. I asked you here for your counsel on a matter of great importance. You are my go-to advisor in situations of the nature I am facing now—'Right Man, Right Job.'"

"Sir!"

"As you are aware, since you named them, Small Raids Inc. has two H-Class submarines that I plan to employ in the Aegean in support of Raiding Forces. The units have completed their sea trials and are ready to commence active operations."

Lt. Hamilton knew about the subs. He named them No. 1 and No. 12 for a reason. The idea being when the Nazi intelligence apparatus eventually discovered their presence in the Aegean, as it inevitably would, the Kriegsmarine might believe there were ten other boats in the squadron. He and VAdm. Ransom had agreed the idea was a long shot but worth a try.

Sometimes simple illusions, or in this case deceptions, work.

VAdm. Ransom said, "Here is the problem. The Aegean waters are crystal clear. Enough so that an aircraft at altitude is able to spot a submerged submarine from a distance. The two subs we have are all we shall lay our hands on—ever. We cannot afford to lose either of them. No. 1 and No. 12 are critical for our island-raiding and beach-watching activities."

Lt. Hamilton said, "What is it you would like from me, sir?"

VAdm. Ransom said, "I need you to make our subs disappear while underway during the day."

Lt. Hamilton said, "Sir, I shall need a better understanding of what is involved before I can provide a recommendation."

"I have a Walrus standing by. No. 1 is at sea. You and I are going to fly over it and see what we can see. Hopefully that shall provide you enough to work with."

The Admiral flinched the instant he heard himself say *hopefully*. Hope was a semi-banned word in Raiding Forces when it came to tactics. Like how to make a submarine disappear.

Thirty minutes later VAdm. Ransom and Lt. Hamilton were standing in the observer's open-topped cupola on the nose of the airborne Walrus, having crawled through the tunnel from the co-pilot's side of the cockpit. Even though it was late in the day, before either of them had lifted the Barr & Stroud 10x Admiralty binoculars they both wore around their necks, they could see the dark silhouette of a submarine below in the distance. VAdm. Ransom had given the Special Duties pilot the coordinates, but No. 1 was easy to spot from the air long before they arrived over the target—ridiculously easy.

Lt. Hamilton said, "Can the sub submerge to a lower depth, sir?"

VAdm. Ransom said, "Negative, it's at max depth. What you see is what we get."

"Not good, Admiral."

"The worst of it is the crew have no idea we are up here stalking them. Survivability of submarines in these waters is problematic at best. Both sides have suffered high losses. We may not be able to utilize our subs the way I originally intended."

Lt. Hamilton said, "How are you planning to use them, sir?"

"Run the boats submerged on a circuit around the Aegean," VAdm. Ransom said. "Typically submarines remain submerged eighteen hours a day. The idea is to surface at night to recharge batteries, and to send, receive and relay messages. Primarily, they shall be long-range signals platforms—sea-going radio relay stations."

Lt. Hamilton said, "So in that case, sir, it does not actually matter where the boats are at any given moment as long as it's in a general geographic area at a specific time prepared to send and receive traffic?"

"Affirmative."

Lt. Hamilton said, "In my opinion, Admiral, in these waters there is no way to effectively hide a submerged sub from aerial observation during daylight hours—it's impossible, sir. But why not consider this? Have your H-Class boats run on the surface at night. That way they are able to travel at maximum speed should they so choose, they can send and receive messages while underway and not be seen from the air except in a highly unlikely chance encounter. Even then if brought under attack, the sub would have the ability to crash dive to escape — no way to see them submerged in the dark."

VAdm. Ransom said, "We can do that."

"Instruct the crews to tie off at some unpopulated islet before dawn and go under camouflage netting, sir," Lt. Hamilton said. "That will allow the sub to remain surfaced to recharge its batteries while continuing to send and receive. You double your communications performance.

"Like Mr. Treywick says, sir, 'Occam's razor.'"

"Outstanding, Lieutenant."

VAdm. Ransom did not mention he had arrived at the same conclusion after making his own estimation of the situation. Today's exercise was merely to elicit a second opinion. After all, he *was* consulting with the Great Teddy—one never knew. The teenager was a magician. He might have known a way to make No. 1 and No. 12 disappear.

Hey, Presto!

Military decisions fall into one of three categories. Strategic: reserved for the highest level of commanders in Washington or London. Operational: reserved for Theatre Commands, which VAdm. Ransom held in the ATO for Special Operations. Tactical: For unit commanders like Colonel John Randal to implement.

While studying the submarine vulnerability to aerial observation problem, VAdm. Ransom had not been able to keep himself from reflecting on Mr. Treywick's standard-issue, knee-jerk response to any difficulty.

"The problem is the solution."

Which always made the Razor cringe. But what did he have to lose? No one would ever know so he secretly gave it a try in the privacy of his own office.

The Problem: Our submarines underway by day are vulnerable to enemy air.

The Solution. Do not have our submarines underway during the day.

Simple enough and he could make that happen. Maybe the old ivory poacher was on to something.

As was frequently pointed out in Raiding Forces, "Hope is not a course of action." In this case hoping the Small Raids Inc.'s Holland 602-type submarines would not be spotted by the Luftwaffe who now enjoyed air superiority in the Aegean. Thinking a situation through to the end and then going forward with the best available option—which is not always a great option—that's the art of military decision-making at the Operational and Tactical level.

Being able to select the best choice from a list of bad options when exigent circumstances force the issue is what separates the brilliant commander from the merely highly talented.

Improvise, adapt, overcome *and* outsmart.

COLONEL JOHN RANDAL WAS IN HIS OFFICE MEETING WITH Captain Roy "Mad Dog" Reupart just in from Camp Mackall, North Carolina. Captain Roy Kidd and Master Sergeant Mack Beckwith were also in the room. He had plans for them to run a refresher course on small unit tactics for Raiding Forces personnel when they rotated off operations. However, the need to get the SBS officers and NCOs up to speed as small unit leaders was of more immediate concern and temporarily overrode his original idea of continuing training for all Raiding Forces personnel.

Col. Randal said, "I've been reviewing SBS after-action reports. They're not good. Prior to Leros, Jellicoe's people tended to sail to some remote island in broad daylight, land, and see what happened next.

"I believe the 'roll in and shoot up the place' habits picked up from the SAS and the fact that up until now the SBS has primarily operated against substandard Italian garrison troops has caused them to develop a tendency to hold the enemy in contempt. We know that's a recipe for disaster.

"Captain Reupart . . ."

"Yes, sir,"

"I'm reinstating you as Raiding Forces Senior Training Officer. Captain Kidd and Captain Jaxx will assist, time permitting. As will any other officer or NCO you request who is currently stationed on or passing through ABC."

"Yes, sir."

"Start with the SBS officers. Teach them how we plan, organize and execute small-scale operations. Heavy emphasis on personal leadership. RTU any officer who does not meet your standards. Get back to me with the names of the Raiding Forces personnel you need as your instructors."

Capt. Reupart said, "I shall be requesting General McKoy on an as-available basis if that meets your approval, sir."

"Fine. Talk to him. I'm sure he'll be glad to be involved."

"And I would like to have you in for certain topics as well, Colonel."

"If I'm on the island, I'll teach classes," Col. Randal said. "This is a top priority. I won't have my troops led by mediocre officers—we'll RTU any not up to our standards."

Capt. Reupart said, "Understood, sir."

Col. Randal said, "Captain Kidd, hand off the curriculum you and Captain Jaxx have been working on. I need you back on troop duty. You two can rotate as leadership and small unit tactics instructors when you're back on ABC—you'll want to personally handle firearms training."

"Yes, sir."

Col. Randal said, "Sergeant Major, you're flying out to the SBS HQ this afternoon. Set up an NCO Academy. Conduct the same type of training. You're authorized to RTU anyone not Raiding Forces' material. Be ruthless in your assessments. We'll promote from within to replace those noncoms you send back to their units—I need you to be a talent spotter."

MSgt. Beckwith said, "Can do, Colonel."

"We only want the best."

"I hear you, sir—loud and clear."

"Select three of our people to take with you as instructors—show me the list of their names."

"Wilco."

Col. Randal said, "Questions? OK, then let's do this. Captain Kidd, stand fast. General McKoy is coming in when we conclude here. I want a briefing on the status of the suppressed submachine gun test."

"Yes, sir."

As soon as the room cleared Lieutenant General "Geronimo" Joe McKoy walked in with King.

Col. Randal said, "Give me a report."

"All three SMGs have now been taken on raids," Lt. Gen. McKoy said. "We've test-fired all of 'em fairly extensively. And we're in unanimous agreement on the results, John."

"Let's hear it."

Lt. Gen. McKoy said, "The Thompson's heavy to start with. Stick a suppressor on the end of the barrel and it's about as long as a BAR and as badly balanced as any weapon I've ever handled.

"The Sten is the quietest of the three—possibly because it's 9mm. I don't like it, though, because of the side-mounted magazine. Feels like it's goin' to roll over when the weapon comes to my shoulder—might be me . . . I'm just sayin'.

"The M3 gets the best all-around rating. Everybody likes it. We can use all the Grease Guns we can get our hands on, John."

Capt. Kidd said, "I'm in agreement with the General, sir."

King said, "The Sten definitely feels unwieldy if you have never spent much time with a side mounted magazine submachine gun. Training can overcome that. In the event we are unable to obtain M3s in the numbers we require the Sten should make a satisfactory substitute standard, Chief."

Lt. Gen. McKoy said, "Accordin' to Wild Bill, Guide Lamp—the division of General Motors who manufactures the .45 M3 Grease Gun, has a conversion kit that lets you modify the gun to 9mm. Make that happen, slap on a suppressor and you've got yourself a very quiet, very handy little weapon.

"My guess with the suppressor and 9mm unit installed the M3 will be so controllable on full auto you'll be able to write your name on a wall in bullet holes."

Capt. Kidd said, "Roger that sir, it should be a winner."

King said, "Affirmative, Chief—my opinion as well."

"Good report," Col. Randal said. "All right then, General, you're in charge of coordinating with OSS. I want suppressed SMGs. Make it happen and right now."

"How many do I indent for, John?"

"One per man—probably never use that many but having 'em in inventory would be good. Future raiding parties will be small. They need to be lethal. And they're going to be stealthy."

Lt. Gen. McKoy said, "Consider it done, John. I'll put in a request for M3s with the 9mm conversion kit for every man and stay on top of it."

Another unwritten rule in Raiding Forces was, "Better to have and not need than to need and not have." Or, as Lt. Gen. McKoy liked to say, "Too much ain't enough."

That especially applied to firepower.

"General, will you or Roy touch base with Sergeant Volkmann to see how he's coming with a suppressor for my Beretta M-38?"

"With pleasure."

In an outfit like Raiding Forces details were important.

CAPTAIN PENELOPE "LEGS" HONEYCUTT-PARKER NOSED IN to Little Gavdos with the motor idling. The time was 2335 hours. One of her Jack Tars was on the bow casting the lead to take soundings to ensure the MAS boat did not run aground. There may have been a dock of sorts in the small built-up area of fifteen or twenty houses, but Captain Billy Jack Jaxx had vetoed the idea of landing there because he had no current intelligence about what to expect.

Under normal circumstances Capt. Jaxx might have sailed right in and offloaded on the pier but tonight was a live fire training mission. He was not supposed to set a bad example for Ensign Westly Slade. The idea was to slip in, gather intelligence about the island and slip back out with no one knowing they were ever there.

This was a different type of reconnaissance than static observation of an enemy position. Those were conducted over a period of time ranging from a few hours to a month or so—which Capt. Jaxx did not care for— it not being his style to hide and watch. Tonight would be a recon *patrol.* The difference was it would involve movement—*that* he did like.

The team was assembled on the bow of the MAS boat. Brandy Seaborn was up there as well to see them off. She and Capt. Jaxx had been great friends ever since he asked her to pose for a photo to put in the grip of his Colt 1911 .38 Super. She loved the stories about his romantic escapades—Mandy and Beverly's versions of those stories, anyway…that they got from the girls.

Capt. Jaxx was never one to kiss and tell.

The boat nosed up to a large rock that was almost even with the MAS boat's flush deck.

Brandy said, "Good luck, Jack."

Capt. Jaxx said, "Luck is for the unprepared."

He might have been carrying the "setting the example" business a little too far.

"Let's rock."

King, armed with the suppressed 9mm Sten submachine gun, stepped off the boat first. Capt. Jaxx was next, carrying the suppressed .45 M3 Grease Gun, followed by Ensign Westly Slade, the two Lovat Scouts and Private First Class Norvel "Horn Dog" Hansen pulling rear security. The last four were armed with .30 M1 carbines. Every man in the patrol had a suppressed .22 pistol, either a High Standard Military Model D or Colt Woodsman.

The purpose of the exercise tonight was to covertly gather intelligence, a clandestine op. However, in the event of a chance encounter with a Nazi who needed to be eliminated, every attempt to use silenced weapons was to be made. There was only one guarantee a small patrol a long way from base on a faraway island well behind enemy lines could always count on, and that was there were no guarantees. Anything could happen.

One of Raiding Forces Rules was, "Expect the Unexpected." But it had been deactivated because the directive was impossible. What the recon team could do was "Stay Silent, Ready to be Violent." Not as catchy a phrase but it got the idea across.

The Mission Statement called for Capt. Jaxx's patrol to be on Little Gavdos for no more than an hour. Get in, take a look around and come back out. It was a good plan and simple.

Everyone was in dyed-black battle dress for the night's work. Faces were painted with camo in a wild assortment of patterns. Headgear was individual choice. King was wearing a German Army M-1943 billed cap of the type favored by Alpine ski-troops; Ens. Slade and the Lovat Scouts were wearing black Commando watch caps; Pfc. Hansen had on a New York Yankees baseball cap with the white NY initials blacked out; and Capt. Jaxx was sporting a headband made out of one of Beverly's cotton scarfs.

Capt. Jaxx and King both had on batting gloves with the trigger finger cut off for a better grip on their individual weapons.

It was a nice night.

The moon, just a sliver shy of full, was directly overhead. It provided enough light to help or at least give the illusion of helping. The island was perfectly silent except for the sound of waves lapping against the rocks. Temperatures in that part of the Aegean ranged from the low sixties at night to around eighty during the day. Conditions for patrolling were perfect.

Capt. Jaxx was enjoying the mission. Surreptitiously creeping around unseen in the dark of night looking for who knew what with no one the wiser was his kind of mission. Except he was not supposed to shoot anyone due to having to set a good example—which put a damper on possibilities.

King paused, held up his fist and whispered over his shoulder, "Buildings, two o'clock."

Capt. Jaxx moved up next to him. During Officer Candidate School at Ft. Benning, he was taught not to look directly at a fixed object at night. The recommended school solution was called "offset viewing." This technique utilizes your peripheral vision by looking to one side or the other of the object you are trying to observe so you can see it better in the dark. He could not remember why doing so was supposed to enhance night vision. There was a chance he might have dozed off during that part of the class. In actual practice offset viewing never worked for him.

Capt. Jaxx looked straight at where King pointed and noted a number of darker shadows. Likely they were houses in the small residential area known to be on the island though it was difficult to discern with absolute certainty at this distance. Intelligence believed most of the houses had been abandoned when the prisoners were removed from the island. But they did not know that for sure.

It was one of the things the recon patrol was there to find out.

Capt. Jaxx whispered, "You ever utilize offset viewing, King?"

"Negative."

MAJOR THE LADY JANE SEABORN WAS HOSTING A DINNER party in the suite she shared with Colonel John Randal on the second floor of ABCHQ. Flanigan was on the door. No visitors other than her invited guests were to be allowed in. Present were Brigadier Raymond J. Maunsell (who liked to be called R. J.), Brigadier Dudley Clarke, Major General James "Baldie" Taylor (who was just plain Jim tonight and not in uniform), Doctor Layton Winthrop, Commander Ian Fleming (included at Col. Randal's request for some reason), Major Hawthorne Merryweather, Major Zargo, Captain Pamala Plum-Martin, Mandy Paige and Beverly Blackwell.

Col. Randal was not there at the moment. He was downstairs having a meeting in his office. Lady Jane had made him promise to keep it brief.

The event was not a social occasion. It was a working dinner disguised as a social occasion. The purpose of the exercise was to discuss implementing the counterintelligence operation targeting Greek collaborators Lady Jane would be heading up. There was a surprising amount of interest in the program from all those in the room. For multiple reasons. Targeting collaborators demonstrated the perils of working with the Nazis—retribution being swift and highly visible. Under interrogation the turncoats would likely provide a gold mine of intelligence. They could be turned and become double agents working against the Germans—it was possible.

Mandy began the conversation.

"There are six island groups in the ATO. Raiding Forces will be responsible for eliminating Greek collaborators in three of them—the Dodecanese, Cyclades and North Aegean. Due to their proximity to the Greek mainland the Greek Sacred Squadron will be responsible for the Sporades, Ionian and Saronic groups..."

DOWNSTAIRS IN HIS OFFICE COLONEL JOHN RANDAL WAS meeting with Lieutenant Dan Bonham, Lieutenant Chase Starrett and Lieutenant Ricky Mascuch. The lieutenants were talented young officers of varying degrees of experience in Raiding Forces. They were slated to play important leadership roles in OPERATION FIRE EATER.

Col. Randal said, "OSS Maritime Unit has arrived assigned to Raiding Forces. They're combat swimmers, small boat operators, amphibious landing beach surveyors and naval demolitions experts. The MU may be the most highly trained outfit in the U.S. Armed Forces. But their training failed to encompass much in the way of across-the-beach patrolling tactics.

"I need them to be able to perform small unit tactics at our level of competence. You three officers have been tapped to demonstrate to the MU personnel how we do it. Captain Jaxx is out tonight on a recon of

Little Gavdos Island doing exactly that. Lieutenant Taylor is on his way to Irakleia Island with a team to give them their first taste of an actual mission. We don't have time for the traditional "crawl, walk, run" method of military indoctrination. This is going to be full-speed, on-the-job training—live fire.

"Report to Colonel Stone immediately upon conclusion of this meeting. He'll provide a list of four MUs for each of you to work with. They call themselves Operational Swimmers, Detachment Three—Det 3 for short, but prefer Frogmen or Frogs.

"Sir Terry will also provide each of you with a target. Pick one of your Raiding Forces people to be your assistant team leader. I want you at sea by tomorrow night. Conduct a small-scale raid on the target Colonel Stone assigns to you—hit and run. Questions?"

For Lt. Bonham and Lt. Starrett having a mission sprung on them with a decidedly short fuse was business as usual. Lt. Mascuch was getting used to operations coming hard and fast out of nowhere, as a former 551 Parachute Infantry Battalion GOYA, surprises were nothing new. From the jungles of Panama to a picturesque island in the Aegean his entire army experience had been a surprise.

There were no questions.

Col. Randal said, "Dismissed—Lieutenant Starrett stand fast."

When the room cleared Col. Randal said, "Haven't had the opportunity to personally debrief you on your Benevento jump. Nice job, stud. I've recommended you for the Silver Star."

"Sir, I was only doing . . .

"As were we all. You just did it a little bit better."

SOMEWHERE OFF THE COAST OF TURKEY.

LIEUTENANT JACKSON TAYLOR AND FIVE OSS OPERATIONAL Swimmers from his Detachment Three were underway aboard one of the Levant Schooner Flotilla caiques. Destination Irakleia Island—prewar population 150—approximately. There were likely a lot fewer people living there now.

Time to target and return was five days.

The LSF caique would run along Turkey's coastline. Then once off the coastal town of Bodrum it would lie up in Turkish waters and remain in an overnight position (RON) in a remote cove until time to make a dash straight to the island the following night.

Intelligence on the target was bare bones. Irakleia was 6.9 square miles in size. There were two settlements. Panagia, described as the "capital," was located in the center of the island. And the port town of Agios Georgios.

No one knew if German Forces were present.

According to Doctor Layton Winthrop, there were mysterious rock paintings called Bousoulas to be found on the island and the ruins of an ancient fortress. There was one other terrain feature of note—Agios Ioannis the largest cavern in the Cyclades.

Homer's legendary "Cave of the Cyclops."

Lt. Taylor's mission was to perform a clandestine reconnaissance of the port town to determine if enemy troops were stationed there.

He was hoping not to encounter a Cyclops.

CAPTAIN BILLY JACK JAXX CALLED A HALT TO REORGANIZE. He switched places with Ensign Westly Slade who had been paired off with Private First Class Norvel "Horn Dog" Hansen. The idea was for the Navy officer to work with King when he moved forward to reconnoiter the built-up area.

No one in Raiding Forces was the Merc's equal when it came to taking point on patrols or sneaking and peeking. Since tonight was on-the-job-training (OJT), Capt. Jaxx wanted the Ensign to learn from the best. Now the order of march was King, Ens. Slade, Capt. Jaxx, Pfc. Hansen, followed by the Lovat Scouts.

Before taking up his position in the file, Capt. Jaxx whispered to King, "Move our two elements by leaps and bounds."

He wanted Ens. Slade to observe how Raiding Forces operators were able to seamlessly hand off responsibilities on the march. This was standard military "monkey see, monkey do" OJT. Not every unit can pull it off in a training environment much less during the course of an actual mission. Tonight was not a canned operation with a predetermined outcome. There were likely enemy soldiers present on the island—somewhere.

Moving by leaps and bounds is more complicated than it sounds—though it is a lot like the children's game Leap Frog. The lead element, King and Ens. Slade, the Merc being the element leader, would move up to the building to be checked out—a "bound" forward. Once investigated they would freeze in place and provide overwatch for Capt. Jaxx and Pfc. Hansen to advance past them—a "leap," and close up on the next structure to be investigated. One element advancing only to be replaced by the other taking the lead would continue over and over, like Leap Frog, as the patrol worked its way through the entire built-up area until the village had been thoroughly reconned.

The Lovats would remain last in the order of march throughout the process providing rear security and ready to provide fire support or maneuver on the enemy in the event of contact.

None of this was lost on Ens. Slade. He was watching and learning—dialed in. If anything, Capt. Jaxx's patrol was more cohesive tonight than during the highly impressive rehearsal back at ABC. Nothing was said, the men simply took it to another level.

While his heart was in his throat—he could not shake the feeling he was being watched or that he was going to die at any second, Ens. Slade was beginning to get into the rhythm of the patrol. He liked the feeling of being a heavily armed nocturnal predator. What Colonel John Randal had failed to grasp about the Maritime Unit was most of the tasks they trained for—except for folboat limpet raids against enemy shipping and those were not ashore—had to be carried out during broad daylight.

This nighttime patrolling was all new.

Ens. Slade was planning to recommend to Lieutenant Jackson Taylor all future Det 3 training be conducted during the hours of darkness. There did not appear to be any immediate need for preinvasion beach surveys or clearing obstacles and/or mines for an amphibious assault—daylight missions.

Following King he moved forward performing a "bound" and flattened himself against the exterior wall of a small frame house. The two did a careful slow-motion walk around the structure, peeking in the windows. It was completely blacked out. There was no sign of life inside. Nevertheless, Ens. Slade was doing it for real on an enemy island about which next to nothing was known.

The experience was exhilarating in a quiet way.

ON THE WAY UPSTAIRS TO MAJOR THE LADY JANE Seaborn's dinner party, Colonel John Randal stopped by Vice Admiral Sir Randolph Razor Ransom's office. Lieutenant Coco Lovejoy was still on duty at her desk. The Razor put in long hours.

"You're working late, Coco."

While their motto was "Never at Sea," to date nearly one hundred members of the Women's Royal Navy Service—commonly called Wrens—had been killed in action with an equivalent number dying of wounds. Lieutenant Lovejoy's wealthy upper-class parents—her father was a viscount who had served under VAdm. Ransom in the last war—were thrilled to have their daughter stationed on what they pictured as an idyllic Aegean Island. In her letters home she had not felt any need to dissuade them of that illusion by mentioning air raids, Brandenburger Sea Raider Commandos or telling them about helping Major the Lady Jane Seaborn clean up the bloodstains from one of her Royal Marines on the floor of the TOC or serving on a firing squad.

"You shall be in trouble if you miss Lady Jane's dinner, Colonel."

"Need to see the Admiral for a minute."

"Go right in, sir."

VAdm. Ransom said, "Better get yourself upstairs with all due speed, Colonel, you are already late by my watch."

Col. Randal said, "Det Three needs another officer, sir. OSS does not have one to send. Can you pull in a lieutenant from the Royal Marine Boom Patrol for the assignment?"

"The most secretive direct-action unit in the Royal Navy, specializing in irregular warfare and who knows what else—they do not patrol booms. A big ask," VAdm. Ransom said. "Any reservations about putting a British officer in charge of OSS Operational Swimmers?"

Col. Randal said, "No problem on the British officer, sir. What I need is someone with equivalent training to the Frog's. It's a rarified field."

"I shall look into the possibility. The RMBP is only platoon strength. Nicking one of their officers is not a given. When would you like to have your lieutenant here?"

"Any time before breakfast will be fine, sir."

VAdm. Ransom laughed. "Always a pleasure, Colonel. Now report to your dinner party forthwith—that is an order. It is not in either of our best interests for my niece to blame me for detaining you."

Col. Randal said, "Thanks Admiral."

VAdm Ransom said, "We shall get Raiding Forces reconfigured to our liking. Building a fighting command is a team effort. As I have said before, if you require something bring it to me straightaway—no holding back, Colonel."

The Razor's motive was more than simply a desire to be cooperative. He wanted to know what Col. Randal believed were problems or might develop into problems. Even if he was in the process of resolving them.

Col. Randal said, "Wilco."

OVER COCKTAILS, BRIGADIER RAYMOND J. MAUNSELL WAS explaining that a number of intelligence operations could be run in conjunction with the anti-collaborator campaign. His title was Chief of Security—whatever that meant. R. J. was involved in a lot of different activities.

"For example, Professor Winthrop or General Taylor could insert a stay-behind agent while Lady Jane's people are extracting a collaborator—a sleight-of-hand trick like something the Great Teddy might perform. Brigadier Clarke might want you to "accidentally" leave behind some piece of misleading information while a team is snatching up their target. Major Merryweather can have your team disseminate propaganda targeting the enemy's hearts and minds. The possibilities are only limited by one's imagination . . ."

Colonel John Randal pulled Commander Ian Fleming aside. "Captain Hoolihan tells me you two have come to an agreement on his training your 30 Assault Unit Red Indians."

Cdr. Fleming said, "Quite right, Colonel, very generous of you to allow me to have the Headhunter even if it is only of short duration. 30 AU's Royal Marine 33 Troop's quality is sadly not up to prewar standards. Quite a shock, actually."

"Butch wants to train them here on Castelrozzo," Col. Randal said. "He'll be able to integrate your people into some of the exercises we'll be conducting for Det Three and the SBS. And I might be able to work your Red Indians into a raid or two to give them experience. Any problem with that, Commander?"

Cdr. Fleming said, "NID requires a crack team of Commandos to go ashore in the first wave of our invasion forces to obtain highly important enemy codebooks, documents, cipher machines and the like before they can be spirited away or destroyed by the Germans. Deliver to me a team capable of accomplishing that mission and you can train them wherever and however you will, sir."

Having the Red Indians on Castelrozzo would also provide an excuse to visit the island from time to time and possibly improve his chances with Beverly Blackwell. Cdr. Fleming, a Naval Intelligence Division officer known for developing ideas others had to go carry out, said, "Do you require my assistance arranging 30 AU's transportation?"

Col. Randal said, "General Blackwell has agreed to fly them to RFHQ for transport to ABC." He did not mention the request for air transport came from Brigadier General William "Wild Bill" Donovan.

"Capital!"

Cdr. Fleming had no idea he had just ceded 30 Assault Unit to Raiding Forces—game, set, match.

Col. Randal left the party and walked two doors down the hall to Captain Stephanie Fawcett-Tatum's room and knocked. The tall brunette came to the door in a robe. Her hair was tousled, and she looked drowsy. Which was understandable. Being arguably the hardest-working member of Raiding Forces, she was always putting in long hours.

"Yes, John?"

"I need you to send a TWX to General Donovan over my signature. 'REQUIRE OG ASAP STOP COWBOYS AND INDIANS STOP GAME ON STOP.'"

"Wild Bill shall understand?"

"He should."

BRIGADIER RAYMOND J. MAUNSELL, COLONEL JOHN Randal and Mandy Paige huddled in a corner of the suite's living area. The Chief of Security was Mandy's mentor. The two were close, which often worked to Raiding Forces' advantage.

Mandy said, "R. J. believes finding our mole shall prove difficult."

Brig. Maunsell said, "I could bring in a more experienced MI-5 operative but that might alert the perpetrator. Best to let Mandy continue. She has all the skills to bring this to a conclusion. Bear in mind—at this stage there is no way to be positive you only have a single mole, provided there actually is one.

"It is not unknown for counterespionage to turn out to be a wild goose chase due to an overactive imagination, paranoia or a simple misinterpretation of the events that gave cause for the concern in the first place. None of those are a bad thing. In a unit like Raiding Forces constant vigilance is of utmost importance to your security. The problem is there is no way to be absolutely one hundred percent certain you actually have a mole until you catch him or her red-handed.

"Even then you might have accidentally stumbled upon a second operative and not the one you were originally looking for, leaving the mole in place at the very time you are celebrating your victory. Counterespionage is a sophisticated game. It requires a high level of intellect to play. Rooting out an enemy agent embedded in a tight-knit unit like Raiding Forces is extraordinarily interesting and may be the most challenging of all intelligence assignments—but it is not easy and not fast."

Col. Randal said, "I see."

He was thinking a long-term internal investigation could also be bad for unit morale if word got out one was underway.

Mandy said, "R. J. says our mole shall turn out to be the last person we would ever suspect."

Col. Randal said, "Well, that would be you, Mandy—case solved."

FLANIGAN TAPPED ON THE DOOR THEN STUCK HIS HEAD inside. "Brigadier, your people are here, sir."

Brigadier Dudley Clarke excused himself saying, "I shall return momentarily."

The A-Force commander went out in the hall where two men in civilian clothes were waiting. "Ready to proceed, Brigadier?"

"Affirmative."

The three walked to the stairs and climbed to the third floor to a room where another man in a dark suit was standing guard outside the door. Rikke "Rocky" Runborg was inside with a fourth man who was also in mufti. There was a brand-new U.S.-manufactured SCR-299 long-range radio set up on a table.

Brig. Clarke handed Rocky a flimsy. "This is your message, Miss Runborg."

The stunning Norwegian with the dark tan and hair the color of ice took a seat at the table. She glanced at the piece of paper and began tapping the key. Rocky had been a spy for the Norwegians, the Russians, the Germans, and the British and was in negotiations with OSS about working for the Americans to gain U.S. citizenship. She was the exception to Colonel John Randal's often-quoted, "Hope is not a course of action."

A-Force was keeping Rocky under tight control. She was a pawn in a much bigger chess game. There would be no relocating her to the U.S. anytime soon.

The message to be transmitted tonight was being sent out over a radio setup that required a substantial amount of effort to put in place. No one other than those in the room was to know this event had taken place. To ensure maximum privacy, MI-6 signals technicians ran remote cabling to the room so Rocky did not have to be in the TOC when she sent out her message. Brig. Clarke was obsessive about secrecy, and he did not want anyone to observe what was taking place. First the techs had to measure the distance the cable needed to be run to include the height from ground level to the third-story window of the improvised radio room. Then they ran the cable from the base of ABCHQ's antenna, taking care to leave enough excess to reach the antenna's freecone. Finally, the cable was pulled through a purpose-dug twelve-inch trench to ensure it was not disturbed by normal ground-level noise.

Rocky was transmitting on a frequency used by Army Group E in Athens, Greece. Field Marshal Erwin Rommel was the addressee. She had misled the Desert Fox on two previous occasions in the past—causing him to be away from his command when the British launched attacks. However, Brig. Clarke had been attempting to repair the damage to her reputation caused by the intentionally bad intelligence. The idea was to rehabilitate her as a reliable source in the Field Marshal's eyes by feeding him snippets of accurate information at a time when it was too late for the Germans to react to it.

Tonight Brig. Clarke was rolling the dice. The entire Allied intelligence apparatus was trying to convince the Nazis that the Allies were making preparations to invade Greece. Now he had Rocky tapping out a message that said essentially, "not true—Greece is a deception."

Which it was.

The intention being that when the invasion of Greece never came, Rommel would see Rocky had been right and believe her bad information in the past—which had intentionally been only off by a day or two, was merely due to the fog of war. No agent gets it right 100 percent of the time.

By having Rocky reveal the truth about Greece this night, Brig. Clarke was attempting to put her back in position to be able to deceive Field Marshal Rommel one more time when the need arose in the future. Why the Desert Fox? Because an *ULTRA SECRET* Enigma intercept revealed orders for the Field Marshal to take command of building the Atlantic wall in France after the first of the year—where the Normandy Invasion was scheduled to take place. Intelligence was called the Great Game for good reason. Misleading the enemy by revealing actual state secrets was high risk, high reward and highly dangerous.

Brig. Clarke was taking the play to a new level.

KING AND ENSIGN WESTLY SLADE WERE LEAPED BY Captain Billy Jack Jaxx and Private First Class Norvel "Horndog" Hansen as the two teams worked their way through the village. They encountered no occupied civilian houses—every single one was empty.

Like walking through a ghost town at midnight.

Finally in the distance they saw a dim light. After advancing by inches, carefully placing each foot on the ground before trusting to full weight, it could be determined the glow was coming from inside a small one-story structure sitting off to the side of the rest of the built-up area. In the lead King and Ens. Slade went on high, contact imminent alert.

King signaled a pause to evaluate the situation. Capt. Jaxx and PFC Hansen closed up to confer. All four men went down on one knee. The light was the only sign of life they had encountered since arriving on the island. They had not come across a single person or animal since landing—not even a seagull. It was spooky.

With no one having any idea why there was a light in a building in a seemingly abandoned town, Capt. Jaxx whispered, "Move out, point."

King, followed so closely by Ens. Slade they were touching, advanced on the building—very, very cautiously.

The night was perfectly still. Not even crickets were chirping. Capt. Jaxx and PFC Hansen provided overwatch, weapons at the ready. The Lovat Scouts were tucked in tight providing rear security—ready to respond instantly if needed. As soon as the point element reached the side of the building they closed on it. The Merc and Ens. Slade took up position standing, backs flattened to the wall, on either side of a window.

It was emitting a pale yellow glow.

Capt. Jaxx advanced until he was next to King. A quick head check revealed four German soldiers playing cards around a table with a grey Wehrmacht blanket spread over it. A lantern was the only source of light in the room.

This was the perfect setup. The window was raised to catch the breeze coming in from the sea. All he had to do was toss in a frag grenade. Only Capt. Jaxx could not do that. In and out with no one ever knowing they had been there. Those were his orders.

And that was why he was not a reconnaissance specialist.

Nothing more to be done here. They needed to move on. The team was tasked with checking out the caves where the Greek political prisoners had been held and time was short.

Reluctantly, not feeling any better in the knowledge he had demonstrated to Ens. Slade on how to react when in the immediate proximity to an enemy he was ordered not to engage, Capt. Jaxx took over the lead. The patrol advanced inland traveling a little under two hundred yards before coming to a long series of sheer cliff walls. They were jutting straight up as was typical on a lot of the islands in the ATO.

Now the question. Go right or go left? With no way of knowing, King and Ens. Slade leapt past, edging along the base of the cliff to the right. Capt. Jaxx and PFC Hansen closed up. And the Lovat Scouts inched in.

Capt. Jaxx checked the black-faced Rolex with the lime green luminous hands King had brought back for him from his most recent watch-buying trip to Switzerland for the Royal Air Force. It was the same model Major the Lady Jane Seaborn gifted Colonel John Randal years earlier. She provided the Merc with the specs, knowing how much the captain wanted one like it—the watch was a special order pre-war Royal Navy divers issue.

It was time to go.

Then the smell. One minute nothing and the next the patrol was choking. Everyone instantly knew what it was—except Ens. Slade, who had never been forced to contend with anything like what he was now experiencing.

Death.

It is hard to describe what a dead person smells like. Lt. Gen. 'Geronimo' Joe McKoy said it was like "a giant prehistoric rhinoceros sized road kill armadillo". Once experienced, never forgotten, ever. The odor is a full-body overpowering attack on the senses so strong you can physically feel it.

King froze. The entrance to a cave was a few feet ahead. Capt. Jaxx and PFC Hansen retook the lead and broke out their red-filtered flashlights. Moving as cautiously as possible they made entry.

What they found was something straight out of a Saturday matinee horror show, only worse—you can't smell a movie. Chains were bolted on the cavern's walls. Decomposing bodies still in their manacles lined both sides as they crept in. The odor was so bad a gas mask would have been needed to remain inside or explore deeper into the interior of the cave. There was no time to make a body count. Capt. Jaxx and PFC Hansen stumbled back out, gasping for air on the point of blacking out.

The Lovats moved into the lead now and worked their way along the base of the cliff independently. They found another cave. King and Ens. Slade followed up, moved past them and came to another. It was the same story in all three.

Since it was now past their deadline to withdraw, the patrol reassembled and moved out for the extraction site. As they traveled to a different pickup point—it always being a good idea not to exfil from the same location you landed at, King handed Capt. Jaxx a filthy piece of khaki cloth with a pair of RAF wings stitched on it.

"I was unable to locate the man's identification disc."

"What do you think happened back there, King?"

"My guess would be when the Italians on the island found out about the armistice they flagged down the first passing caique, commandeered it, and made for neutral Turkey. Abandoned the prisoners—Germans arrived and they either did not have enough provisions or chose not to feed them.

"Might have merely been too lazy."

Capt. Jaxx said, "Starved a British pilot to death while they played cards?"

"Seems like, Jack."

"We need to do something about that."

"Affirmative."

It was shortly before sunrise when the MAS boat arrived back at Castelrozzo. Col. Randal, Lady Jane and Happy were waiting on the dock when it pulled in. Up at ABCHQ people started spilling outside to welcome the team back home.

Capt. Jaxx reported to Col. Randal and handed him the tattered RAF wings.

Col. Randal said, "What's the plan, Captain?"

It was not really a question.

Capt. Jaxx said, "Ensign Slade, are you prepared to accept a Warning Order?"

Another non-question question—there being only one answer.

"Yes, sir."

"I have a mission for you. Repair to Little Gavdos Island under cover of darkness tonight in concert with Captain Honeycutt-Parker. Conduct a prisoner snatch. Select five Det Three operators in addition to yourself. Hit the island at zero dark thirty going in hot—cocked and locked. Bring me back one of the Nazis in satisfactory enough condition to interrogate."

Ens. Slade said, "What about the other three, sir?"

"Don't bring them."

Jack Cool.

12
GOD BLESS AMERICA

VICE ADMIRAL SIR RANDOLPH "RAZOR" RANSOM LOOKED up when Lieutenant Coco Lovejoy stuck her head in the door. "Ensign Slade to see you, sir."

VAdm. Ransom said, "Let's have him."

Ensign Westly Slade marched in and saluted. "Ensign Slade reports, sir."

VAdm. Ransom returned the salute in a crisp military manner. He did not say "As you were" or "stand at ease."

Not a good sign.

"Since you are Navy, I ordered you here to inform you I have higher expectations for sailors than officers from other branches of service arriving to serve in Small Raids Inc. So far Det Three has proven a grave disappointment. Blame for that begins and ends with its officers. Lieutenant Taylor inherited the Maritime Unit in a half-trained condition not of his making. He bears no responsibility for the state of the unit at this point. That is on you, Ensign.

"Macho unit names do not cut it in Raiding Forces. Call yourself Frogmen—you people strike me more as tadpoles with inflated egos. Tighten up, Slade, and make it fast, or I shall have you relieved of your current duties and reassigned to every menial task in the Aegean Theatre of Operations, keel hauling being against King's Regulations. I believe you Yanks describe the duty I have in mind as mess kit repair officer. Do I make myself clear?"

It was dawning on Ens. Slade that Small Raids Inc. and Raiding Forces senior officers tended toward questions that were not really questions.

"Yes, sir!"

"Dismissed."

Dazed by the verbal assault, Ens. Slade stepped onto the floor of the TOC where he encountered Lieutenant General "Geronimo" Joe McKoy who took notice he was exiting the Admiral's office.

"So, what's your take on the Razor, Westly?"

"I've only had about five minutes to form an impression, sir."

"That's all you need, son."

COLONEL JOHN RANDAL WAS SITTING ON THE COUCH IN THE suite he shared with Major the Lady Jane Seaborn. He was studying an internal Office of Strategic Services memorandum that was intended to be the basis for development of Strategic Services Field Manuel No 6: Operational Groups—that's what it said on the cover leaf. He needed to learn more about OGs, not currently having much more than a general overview. His thinking was to infuse the Group Brigadier General William "Wild Bill" Donovan was sending him into Commander Ian Fleming's 30 AU. It might or might not work.

The OSS document was stamped SECRET.

"The primary mission of Operational Groups is to organize, train and equip local resistance organizations..."

That mission statement would have been useful for Force N in Abyssinia. Unfortunately, Raiding Forces was not working with any resistance units at the present time. Col. Randal did not anticipate the possibility to do so in the foreseeable future, though anything was possible at a later date.

". . . and to conduct raids against enemy controlled roads, railways, and strong points or to prevent their destruction by retreating enemy forces."

OK, that sounded better. At least two out of the three stated targets did. Being lightly armed raiders specializing in surprise, speed, and violence of action with a preplanned withdrawal, Raiding Forces shied away from attacking "strong points." Hard targets were for line infantry backed up by supporting combat arms and air or the U.S. Marines.

That did not mean Raiding Forces would not take on a hard target. However, it would require substantial prior planning, task reorganization, specific mission-oriented training and an adjustment of the hit-and-run mental attitude Col. Randal had worked so hard to instill in his troops.

"Operational Groups always operate in uniform."

Col. Randal was of the opinion that whoever wrote the paper had never actually participated in a special operation. Wild Bill, being an attorney, tended to favor hiring lawyers for his headquarters staff and this was reading like a legal treatise—especially the catalog of definitions. Raiding Forces operated in uniform or maybe not, depending on what was called for in the mission profile. "Always" was one of those semi-banned words like "assume" and "hope."

In war there is no such thing as "always."

As for military attire, Captain Billy Jack Jaxx recently requested uniform standards for raiding parties be relaxed. He wanted to wear his blue jeans on ops. Col. Randal was planning to approve the request. He did not care what his people wore around ABC, RFHQ or down range on missions—within reason.

Not so Master Sergeant Mack Beckwith. He nearly had a seizure when Col. Randal asked him for his thoughts. The Sergeant Major was a firm believer in dress and grooming uniformity. He expected strict adherence to conventional military standards.

In making his pitch, Capt. Jaxx had fallen back on the Montreux Convention of 1936 governing passage of the Turkish Straits—*"military personnel onboard belligerent ships are required to assume civilian garb."*

How he knew that was one of life's great mysteries.

"Well-played, Jack."

"Operational Groups are trained in infantry tactics, guerrilla warfare, foreign weapons and demolitions. The TO&E of a country specific OG is four officers—1 each major, 1 each captain, 2 each lieutenants and thirty enlisted men."

Col. Randal was reasonably sure that was going to turn out to be a fantasy. He was going to be well-satisfied if half that number of OGs actually showed up. OSS did not have the trained officers or enlisted personnel to meet its worldwide commitments. He doubted the Outfit ever would based on reports from his Raiding Forces operators attached to it in the U.S. and Canada. His wounded or otherwise light duty people rotated in and out of OSS on temporary duty (TDY) as trainers.

The instructors on loan to OSS provided a good source of information about OGs preparing for deployment. What his people reported was an organization struggling to get up and running. Nothing unusual about that—you cannot create a national foreign intelligence/guerrilla warfare organization from scratch overnight. Especially considering the United States had never attempted anything like it before.

Col. Randal knew that 30 Assault Unit, at least the element Major Butch "Headhunter" Hoolihan was tasked to retrain, consisted of thirty Royal Marines from 33 Troop. The men were line infantry Marines who had not volunteered for Special Service, which likely had something to do with their less-than-stellar performance in the North Africa, Sicily and Salerno invasions.

Col. Randal was of the opinion that after Maj. Hoolihan finished running Commander Ian Fleming's Red Indians through his training program the troop would be whittled down to around fifteen men. His intention was to infuse the OSS Operational Group into 30 Assault Unit's Royal Marine troop as soon as it arrived. Some of the OG's would fail to make the cut and be returned to OSS—that was inevitable. In his opinion a final AU/OG of four officers and thirty men approximately half U.K. and half U.S. would be ideal—maybe a few more officers to lead teams. He was hoping to use the combined formation for island raiding while standing by for NID missions. Why Brigadier General William "Wild

Bill" Donovan was so interested in the Red Indian project remained a mystery.

Major the Lady Jane Seaborn padded in from the bedroom like a panther in her black French-cut swimsuit. She stretched out on the couch with one tawny leg cocked up. Swimming did not seem to be her immediate priority.

And that put an end to his reading.

WHEN HE CAME DOWNSTAIRS TO THE TOC COLONEL JOHN Randal saw Captain Billy Jack Jaxx talking to Captain Stephanie Fawcett-Tatum. He made eye contact. Then Mandy walked in. He needed a word with her as well so the two moved to a corner for a private conversation.

Col. Randal said, "Stand down the search for our mole."

"Seriously?"

"It's occurred to me we'd have to vet all our Raiding Forces personnel who have ever been OSS trainers at the Farm in Virginia or Camp X in Ontario."

"Virtually impossible."

"Why do we care? There's nothing for us to hide. OSS is on our side."

"Love it. I hated the idea of investigating my friends. You really do not want to know, do you, John?"

"No, I don't."

James "Baldie" Taylor spotted them, came over.

"I have a report for the Admiral you want to hear, Colonel."

Capt. Jaxx arrived, having ended his conversation with Capt. Fawcett-Tatum. "Sir?"

Col. Randal said, "OK if Jack sits in, General?"

"Absolutely."

As they were walking toward Vice Admiral Sir Randolph "Razor" Ransom's office, Col. Randal said, "Let's conduct an inspection tour as soon as General Taylor wraps up his briefing, Jack."

Capt. Jaxx said, "Yes, sir." He wondered what the Colonel wanted to inspect.

Lieutenant Coco Lovejoy said, "The Admiral is expecting you."

As Jack Cool went past, he glanced down at the pretty black-haired Wren. Coco was a lock for a photo shoot. Next in line to appear on his pistol grip.

Lt. Lovejoy acted as if she had never seen him before in her life. Which was not true. Night before last they had a late date which, on a scale of one to ten, had been at least a twelve.

VAdm. Ransom said, "Take seats, gentlemen."

Jim said, "We are not having this conversation."

Everyone perked up. They all liked conversations they were not having.

The MI-6 officer reached into his pocket and withdrew a folded paper.

"As you are aware there are presently over forty Raiding Forces anchorages scattered along the Turkish coast from Castelrozzo in the south to the tip of Samos. Our squadrons are stationed on schooners under camouflage and rotate locations from time to time. The Nazis are aware the boats are there and know we are using them as a platform to launch raids.

"The Germans are not amused in part because OKW in Berlin tends to overreact to small Commando hit-and-run raids. Always have, ever since Combined Operations was first raised for cross-Channel raiding against coastal targets in France. Signals intelligence has indications the Nazis were so enraged by Raiding Forces anchoring in Turkish waters they gave serious consideration to attacking our floating bases. However, Hitler vetoed the idea, not wanting to risk a provocation that might result in Turkey coming into the war on the Allied side.

"Nevertheless, incensed by such a blatant breach of neutrality the Luftwaffe dispatched a reconnaissance aircraft to overfly the Turkish coast to take aerial photos. The German Ambassador in Ankara sent copies to the Turkish Foreign Office and filed a formal protest about the British presence.

"The following is a transcript of the conversation . . . do not ask how I obtained it."

Jim read, "German Ambassador: *These photos are indisputable evidence of British shipping in your coastal waters. They were taken by a Luftwaffe reconnaissance aircraft over Yedi Atala Bay. The ship shown is certainly a Royal Navy ML.*"

"Turkish Minister of Foreign Affairs: *"My dear Ambassador, as you know the British sold us some of their MLs several years ago and this may well be one of our own ships. Incidentally, if I may ask, what was this German airplane you mention doing over our territory?"*

Capt. Jaxx said, "Hate it when that happens."

VAdm. Ransom said, "Appears the Turks are choosing to turn a Nelsonian blind eye to our sloops. International law permits combatants the temporary use of neutral waters for repairs. Most ships need repairs most of the time. Whoever negotiated the arrangement for us to dock semi-permanently along their coastline with Ankara deserves to be knighted."

Col. Randal said, "Those floating bases dramatically reduce the distance our teams have to travel to reach their objectives. Caiques being our primary mode of transportation, if we were restricted to launching raids from ABC it would take a week or more at sea to reach some targets."

VAdm. Ransom said, "Affirmative, we would never be able to carry out the Constant Pressure Concept from Castelrozzo alone."

The Admiral did not bother to point out that stationing Raiding Forces aboard the schooners was his idea or that the Constant Pressure Concept was Col. Randal's— both officers improvising and adapting to local conditions and military material available.

Jim said, "MI-6 believes the exchange I read you to be a significant indication of the Turks' position on who they believe ultimately prevails in the war. The Turks recently sent an observation team to Russia. It reported back that the German Army was in serious trouble."

Col. Randal said, "Who do those MLs belong to?"

VAdm. Ransom said, "Small Raids Inc. recently had the 42nd Motor Launch Flotilla assigned—half-dozen boats. We have been using

them as water taxis to shuffle troops and provisions to Raiding Forces'
distant squadrons. My guess would be the boat in the photo is one of ours."

Capt. Jaxx said, "Since we're all such good friends now, is it OK
for me to fly the Turkish flag if I'm ever still at sea during the day,
Admiral?"

"Not if you get caught."

LIEUTENANT COCO LOVEJOY HANDED COLONEL JOHN Randal
a flimsy when he came out of Vice Admiral Sir Randolph "Razor"
Ransom's office.

"Captain Fawcett-Tatum dropped this off for you, Colonel."

He glanced at it and passed the message to Captain Billy Jack Jaxx.

```
OG(-)TO ARRIVE NEXT TWENTY-FOUR STOP
SIGNED DONOVAN STOP
```

Capt. Jaxx said, "What's an OG minus, sir?"

Col. Randal said, "What's left of good intentions after they hit
reality."

Lt. Lovejoy said, "The Captain also asked me to inform you that
two female OSS officers are flying in within the hour to assist with Lady
Jane's counterintelligence work."

As they were walking out of the TOC, Col. Randal said, "Mascuch,
Bonham and Starrett are taking out patrols tonight made up of Det Three
people to give them a taste of actual operations. Let's go see how they're
doing."

Capt. Jaxx said, "Something bothering you about these missions as
well, sir?"

Col. Randal said, "Dispatching teams to raid islands is no different
than sending out gun jeep patrols from Oasis X, but it doesn't feel the
same, Jack."

"Well, we had some idea what we were getting into in the desert,
sir. Here anything can happen at any time," Capt. Jaxx said. "You never

know what to expect. It was some shock finding those caves full of dead men shackled to the walls last night."

Col. Randal said, "I can see how it would be."

"The war out here in the islands is a different proposition, sir."

All the teams going out tonight were engaged in various stages of mission prep. They would be departing at different times based on the distance to their objective and the type of craft transporting them. The men were drawing ammunition, grenades and explosives, conducting radio checks, preparing to test-fire weapons, checking and rechecking…everything. The Frogs were obsessively adjusting their personal gear until they had it exactly right.

Then they rechecked and adjusted it again.

The OSS Operational Swimmers had done this before many, many times in training. They were hard men and capable, but tonight was going to be their first actual mission down range. Every Frog wanted to perform well once he got into action.

It was what they had been working toward for the past year.

The tension attendant to any first mission was increased by the Det 3 teams being led by officers they did not know, were not part of MU and had only just met. Not an optimal situation. However, being OSS the Frogs were well-schooled in the concept of "You fight with what you have not what you want."

If not the Office of Strategic Services official motto, it should be.

Col. Randal and Capt. Jaxx moved from team to team observing without comment. The Operational Swimmers were focused on working with their gear. They paid little or no attention to the visitors. The men knew the Colonel was there making sure. And they liked it.

LIEUTENANT COLONEL SIR TERRY "ZORRO" STONE AND Captain Billy Jack Jaxx were sitting in his office in the TOC with a couple of Waldo's cigars stuck in their teeth. They were discussing the current situation and possibilities for future operations. Raiding Forces had gone from a standing start to having five raiding parties departing Castelrozzo, if Lieutenant Jackson Taylor's team was counted—it was already at sea. On the map out in the TOC six other operations currently in progress were marked in blue grease pencil indicating they were Raiding Forces—red indicated enemy locations. Each was in one stage or another of a mission launched from schooners afloat in Turkish waters.

These did not include the ten LRDG Beach Watch parties in the process of being transported via caique to the uninhabited islets Vice Admiral Sir Randolph "Razor" Ransom had selected to set up a chain of naval observation posts.

Even with all that going on, Lt. Col. Stone and Capt. Jaxx were kicking around ideas—strategizing. Unlike Middle East Headquarters, which was reported to be paralyzed after the Leros debacle, no one in Raiding Forces was sitting around wringing his hands. Colonel John Randal's Constant Pressure Concept was off to an aggressive start. Still, having only a handful of troops, Raiding Forces was reduced to conducting only tiny, small-scale, pinprick raids.

While the raids might be driving the Nazis crazy, and indications were that was the case, the truth was that not much material damage was being inflicted. Except for Lieutenant Commander Randy "Hornblower" Seaborn. He had recorded an amazing string of successes.

Two women in U.S. Army khaki summer dress walked into the TOC and reported to Captain Stephanie Fawcett-Tatum. Lt. Col. Stone spotted them through the plate glass window in his office.

"What have we here, old stick?"

Turning toward the window, Capt. Jaxx noted the strangers were pistol-grip quality. "Must be OSS out of Washington to assist with the anti-collaborator campaign, sir. If Wild Bill's intent was for his agents to make a good first impression, he accomplished his mission."

Sir Terry said, "God Bless America."

COLONEL JOHN RANDAL AND CAPTAIN BILLY JACK JAXX wrapped up their final inspection later that afternoon by visiting Ensign Westly Slade's assembly area. Except for the Ensign, none of the five

Operational Swimmers on his team had been on an actual mission. And since this one was against a target he had previously reconned, it was known to him that German soldiers were present on the island. As this was a snatch mission to collect a prisoner, contact was a given.

The Frogs had every reason to be wired tight. Prisoner snatches are arguably the most difficult of all missions. The target almost never just rolls over and lets you capture him, even during training exercises. While none of the men had been out before, they had worked with Ens. Slade on countless stateside maneuvers and had faith in his ability as a leader. He would have been surprised to learn the Frogs now viewed him as a seasoned combat veteran.

Tonight would be his third op in the last seventy-two hours. While anxious to do well with his first battle command, he was still anxious. Ens. Slade was going to be on his own, a long way from base with no one to call for backup, or to ask what to do next if things went sideways. Success or failure rested entirely on his shoulders—100 percent.

He was justified in having concerns—good leaders always do.

Col. Randal pulled Ens. Slade aside. "Have everything you need, Ensign?"

Another non-question question.

"Yes, sir."

"Tonight you're commanding your first operation. There is only one first. Make it count."

"I'll do my best, sir." That did not come out sounding quite as positive as he would have liked.

Col. Randal said, "If I didn't have confidence in you Ensign Slade I'd send someone else."

"I won't let you down, sir."

"See to it you don't."

As they were departing the area Capt. Jaxx said, "You had the same talk with me before my first gun jeep patrol, Colonel."

"Yeah, how'd I do?"

"Nailed it, sir."

MAJOR THE LADY JANE SEABORN WAS WAITING WHEN Colonel John Randal and Captain Billy Jack Jaxx returned to the TOC.

"We need to talk, John."

The two walked into his office and she shut the door. Col. Randal clicked on. Nothing good could possibly be coming next.

Lady Jane said, "We have a situation."

"What might that be?"

"The two girls Donovan sent us worked in his office when Beverly was an intern—daughters of his law firm's wealthy clients. Both attended an exclusive Seven Sisters school, Bryn Mawr, I believe. They say only rednecks go to the University of Texas."

Col. Randal said, "Beverly told me the same thing at OSS Headquarters right after you recruited her. Claimed they took ten points off her IQ when they heard her Texas accent. Has she ever complained about anything since she's been with us?"

Lady Jane said, "Never—unless you count your misguided attempt to ground her."

Col. Randal said, "All right then. I want Mandy and Beverly accorded all rights and privileges of captains effective immediately. That needs to be known. Assign one of the OSS girls to assist Mandy and the other to Pam and fill them in about the possibility of a problem. Pick one of your Royal Marines, a FANY or recruit someone to work with Beverly.

"Make it clear to the OSS women they're on probationary status subject to being RTU'd. Either of 'em make fun of, run down or criticize Beverly, they're out of here same day. You don't need to say so. But that's the deal—make it happen."

Lady Jane said, "I knew you would have a solution."

She did not mention having already informed her uncle, Vice Admiral Sir Randolph "Razor" Ransom, he needed another Wren. Lieutenant Coco Lovejoy was in the process of an interservice transfer to her Royal Marines. Beverly and Coco were going to make the perfect team.

Col. Randal said, "Wasn't so hard."

The door being shut, Lady Jane put her arms around his neck and kissed him, forgetting the plate-glass window. "I can always count on you in a crisis, babe."

So why, Col. Randal wondered, did he have the feeling he had been played?

Lady Jane said, "What is a redneck?"

MAJOR BUTCH HOOLIHAN ARRIVED WITH 30 AU. CAPTAIN Stephanie Fawcett-Tatum was waiting to escort the Marine officers to the transient officer's quarters on the third floor. The troops were to be shown to an improvised barracks to stow their gear. Since Commander Ian Fleming's Red Indians were not being assigned to Raiding Forces—at least not yet—they did not receive the same white glove treatment the LRDG and the SBS had on their arrival. Colonel John Randal was not there to welcome them nor were Major the Lady Jane Seaborn or Happy.

Captain Mike "Mad Dog" Reupart was.

By coincidence Cdr. Fleming was also at the pier with his bags, waiting to depart the island. He observed 30 Assault Unit's arrival. He was pleased to have been able to negotiate turning over the training of his problem Red Indians to Col. Randal. Cdr. Fleming was an idea man/delegator—not a troop commander. It was time for him to move on to other projects.

Cdr. Fleming, being on TOP SECRET ULTRA access—a list consisting of a mere twenty-five people worldwide with the Need To Know, only four of whom had full knowledge of the program and two of those were the U.S. and U.K. heads of state—was prohibited from participating in active operations. At times he traveled with a Royal Marine officer whose standing orders were to shoot him in the event his falling into enemy hands became a possibility. Cdr. Fleming was a much bigger player in the world of intelligence than he let on.

That was classified.

Cdr. Fleming had no intention of completely letting go of 30 AU even if he could not accompany it on missions. The Red Indians' real work was at least six months or more in the future when the Allies opened the Second Front. Then it would continue nonstop to the end of the war and *after*. He planned to check in on them from time to time and would function as the senior NID intelligence liaison when there was a 30 Assault Unit mission in the offing. He would also plan certain assignments.

Capt. Reupart was waiting as the Red Indians disembarked from a 42nd Flotilla Motor Launch, which would in turn be used later that night to insert one of the OSS Maritime Unit teams.

"You will be escorted to your barracks to stow your gear. Then immediately fall out for a formation. Your first class is starting in three zero. During your stay on ABC you have two options—perform to standards or be returned to your unit. Am I going too fast for anyone?"

Mad Dog believed in hitting the ground running. He and the Headhunter had plans for 30 AU. There was much work to be done. When the two finished, the Red Indians would be the finest Special Forces outfit in the Royal Marines.

The few who remained.

AT 1300 HOURS OR THEREABOUTS, THE TEAM LEADERS FOR the night's missions began issuing their individual Operations Orders. All parties would be going in by PT boat, MAS boat or Motor Launch. The skippers were on hand to brief the team they would be transporting on procedure aboard their boats.

In turn the boat captains needed to be read into the Concept of the Operation and the Command and Signals paras of the order. It was vital for them to know the details of their team's mission in the event they had to adapt to a changing situation that could not be foreseen at this stage.

Everyone had to be on the same page from the start.

First to brief his troops was Lieutenant Ricky Mascuch. He was taking a team to raid five-square-mile Agistri Island. A small contingent of the 999th was believed to be stationed on it. The island had zero military value. There was little chance it would contain any military equipment of intelligence value. Lt. Mascuch was not tasked to gather intelligence. His orders were simple: land, eliminate the enemy presence and return to the boat—in and out fast.

A kill mission.

Lieutenant Commander Randy "Hornblower" Seaborn would be inserting the team. They would depart Castelrozzo immediately following the order. It was a long passage to Agistri. Lt. Mascuch would have to get ashore, locate the Germans believed to be in the town of Skala, engage them, and return to the PT boat in ninety minutes or less in order to make it to Turkey without being exposed to enemy air after sunrise. The boat would have to lay up all day in a remote location and wait for nightfall to return to Castelrozzo.

An NCO from the Greek Sacred Squadron was attached to serve as Lt. Mascuch's interpreter.

While this was the 551st GOYA's first independent operation, he had seen action since he joined Raiding Forces. Nevertheless, Colonel John Randal was on hand to observe the Lieutenant's Operations Order.

He had a dangerous mission.

TECHNICAL SERGEANT LUKE VOLKMANN WAS STANDING in front of one of the large rooms on the ground floor of the TOC. Present were the officers of the Small Boat Section to include Lieutenant Colonel the Earl Lord George Jellicoe sitting with famous American author John Steinbeck, who had attached himself to and been actively participating in operations with the SBS for some time. (Steinbeck had also invaded Ventotene Island to capture a radar station with Lieutenant Jake Novak's old outfit—the Scout Company of the 509th Parachute Infantry Battalion—attached to the actor Lieutenant Douglas Fairbanks Jr.'s OSS Beach Jumpers for the operation.). Additionally, the entire 30 Assault Unit and a handful of Raiding Forces officer candidates were present. Also in the audience were Lieutenant General "Geronimo" Joe McKoy, Captain Roy Kidd, Waldo Treywick and last but not least, Major Butch "Headhunter" Hoolihan with Captain Mike "Mad Dog" Reupart.

The Maritime Unit Operational Swimmers were not present because all of them were preparing for missions. The Frogs would receive the block of instruction at a later time. It was mandatory.

Prior to the start of class, Lt. Gen. McKoy entertained the students by twirling his Colt .45 Single Action Army revolvers and juggling knives. Everyone was clapping, enjoying the show, having a good time. The fun stopped the instant TSgt. Volkmann came in and took up his position front and center.

TSgt. Volkmann was not there to entertain.

"Demonstrator POST!"

Private First Class Norvel "Horn Dog" Hansen marched in and assumed a rigid position of parade rest to the right of TSgt Volkmann with a rifle at sling arms. He would be serving as the Sergeant's demonstrator. PFC Hansen could soldier when he wanted to.

Sounding not unlike a robot in a loud, semi-monotone voice, having memorized his lecture word for word, TSgt. Volkmann said, "During this block of instruction we will cover the United States Rifle caliber .30, hereafter referred to as the 1903 Springfield or .30 M-1903 and some of its variations—hereafter referred to as the M-1903 or 03."

PFC Hansen snapped to attention, unslung the .30 M-1903 from over his shoulder and brought it to the position of Port Arms.

"Approval for adoption of the M-1903 rifle was on 19 June 03 thus the name 1903 or 03. Production began immediately at the Springfield Armory. The name Springfield is used for all subsequent variations regardless of where the weapons are manufactured, Rock Island Armory, Remington Arms or Smith Corona. The original caliber was 30–03. However, in 1906 when a spire point bullet was adopted to obtain flatter trajectory it was changed to 30–06. Meaning .30 caliber of 1906—the standard battle rifle caliber in the U.S. Army today.

"The M-1903 came with an 'S' type straight stock not unlike that found on a saddle carbine. The rifle fought WWI in that configuration. However, in 1929 a 'C' type stock with a pistol grip was approved for National Match rifles. It was so favorably received the 'C' type stock was adopted for all new M-1903 rifles once the supplies of 'S' type were depleted for rifles being armory rebuilt. There were no other changes or modifications. This 'C' stock rifle—the weapon my demonstrator is presenting, is officially designated the M-1903 A-1 no matter what the actual year of manufacture . . ."

JAMES "BALDIE" TAYLOR SAID, "COLONEL, YOU AND I NEED to have a conversation in private—the two of us—no one else."

Colonel John Randal clicked on. Something he had been doing a lot lately because a high percentage of his conversations in the past two days had started with some version of, "We are not having . . ." Jim's tone did not indicate he wanted to discuss minor details or deliver good news. The two had worked together under difficult conditions since the long ago raid on Rio Bonita. They knew each other's tendencies.

"My office?"

"That would be best."

They walked across the TOC, went into his office and shut the door.

Jim said, "I realize this is bad timing, Colonel. You have a lot going on. But what I have to report . . . there is never going to be a good time."

Col. Randal said, "Lovely."

Jim said, "I have been in possession of certain intelligence for a number of days now, trying to decide whether to disseminate it or not or to whom or when. The fact is I have no idea how to proceed. So I am taking the coward's way out. Deferring the decision to you, Colonel."

"What's going on, Jim?"

"It's Lady Jane's husband, Mallory. MI-6 has confirmation Commander Seaborn survived the sinking of the ship he was sailing aboard en route to his new posting in the CBI. He and a few others were picked up by a Japanese submarine and taken to the nearest port.

"Eventually the Commander ended up in a slave labor cantonment, the identity of which I am not at liberty to divulge. The POWs work dawn to dark at hard labor building a railroad through dense jungle terrain. The Japs provide only one bowl of rice per day per man. Prisoners are worked until they die, then thrown in a pile and burned. It's a death camp."

Col. Randal said, "I can see why you wouldn't want to tell Lady Jane."

Jim said, "I have not gotten to the bad part yet, Colonel."

"Really?"

Jim said, "Mallory was caught stealing food. The single worst crime a man in a prison camp can commit. The other POW's held a mock trial, found the bloody fool guilty, then boreholed him."

Col. Randal said, "What does that mean?"

"The prisoners held Mallory upside down by his ankles, lowered him into a latrine headfirst and drowned him in the excrement."

"Damn!"

"My sentiments exactly, Colonel."

"And you know this for a fact?"

Jim said, "Have it on reliable authority. I am not able to disclose sources, methods or means but you can consider it a firsthand eyewitness account. Mallory Seaborn is dead. However, the navy will not list him as such until his death can be confirmed by more than a single source."

Col. Randal said, "That could be a problem."

Jim said, "While I do not want to be responsible for upsetting Lady Jane, I am uncomfortable withholding the death of her husband—at least from you. She is a widow but that is not confirmed and it may take years before her husband's death becomes official. The POWs involved are never going to divulge Mallory's execution even after the war afraid they might be charged with murder. You hear about win-win situations, this is lose-lose with another lose or two in the mix."

Col. Randal said, "Roger that."

"Boreholing is too gruesome to explain to Lady Jane unless you want to do it."

Col. Randal said, "Are you crazy?"

"Not any more than usual. What is our next move?"

Col. Randal said, "Any chance this news comes out if we don't say anything to Jane?"

"Negative—I should not even be telling you."

"In that case we never had this conversation and if we did, we're not going to admit it," Col. Randal said. "Boreholing is never to be mentioned again—ever. When his death's confirmed Mallory's simply KIA."

"One of your best calls."

COLONEL JOHN RANDAL STEPPED THROUGH THE REAR DOOR of an adjoining room into the class Technical Sergeant Luke Volkmann was teaching. He remained standing behind the back row of chairs. He wanted to see how the mix of Raiding Forces officer candidates, Special Boat Squadron and 30 Assault Unit personnel were settling in. Major Butch "Headhunter" Hoolihan and Captain Mike "Mad Dog" Reupart had decided to start with the basics. There is nothing magic about Special Forces units. The tactics used by the best of the best are nothing more than standard infantry tactics executed to perfection.

To have a true grasp of infantry tactics it is essential for every man to understand not only his own weapon but to be familiar with the capabilities of those used by every other soldier in his unit.

Today they were starting at the beginning, "This is my rifle . . ."

Captain Billy Jack Jaxx came in and stood beside him.

In a crisp military manner TSgt. Volkmann said, "The M-1903 and all subsequent variations is a five-round stripper clip-fed magazine..."

Private First Class Norvel "Horn Dog" Hansen produced a clip from a pouch on the load-bearing web gear he was wearing and held it up for the class.

" . . . loaded . . ."

PFC Hansen pantomimed inserting the stripper clip into the magazine.

" . . . manually operated bolt action repeater."

After placing the stripper clip back in its canvas pouch for safekeeping, PFC Hansen racked the bolt.

"The M-1903 has a battle sight zero set at 547 yards. The sight can be adjusted out to a maximum range of 2,800 yards.

"The M-1903 A3 is simply the M-1903 with a 'S' type' stock and a simpler, cheaper more effective aperture battlesight . . ."

Captain Fontain Blondell-Pericrinkle, the Royal Marine commanding officer of 30 AU, stood up, interrupting the presentation. "Why in the blue blazes are you wasting our valuable time teaching a highly technical class on a rifle, some of which are manufactured by a bloody typewriter company, that is the substitute standard in the U.S. Army for the .30 M1 Garand? Not a weapon my 30 AU Marines or anyone else in this room shall ever be issued."

Maj. Hoolihan turned in his seat on the front row. The Captain was so angry he was glowering. Most likely frustrated by his unit having been abruptly shipped to Castelrozzo for retraining with no prior consultation. And he had been on an airplane for over thirty hours which could make anyone bad-tempered.

The Headhunter spotted Col. Randal standing in the back of the room and made eye contact but received zero response.

"Captain, step outside with me," Maj. Hoolihan said.

Unfazed by the outburst, TSgt. Volkmann ordered, "Demonstrator recover. Class, take a short break in place. Smoke 'em if you've got 'em."

Moments later Maj. Hoolihan returned to the room alone. Capt. Blondell-Pericrinkle was on his way to the TOC to arrange transportation off the island. RTU'd before he even unpacked.

It became very quiet in the room.

"Please continue, Sergeant."

TSgt. Volkmann said, "Before our break the class was at the point where I was about to invite General McKoy to come up and explain why it is of paramount importance for you to be familiar with the M-1903 Springfield Rifle—a U.S. Army substitute standard weapon as has been pointed out.

"General, if you will, sir."

Lieutenant General "Geronimo" Joe McKoy stepped up to the front of the room. "Go ahead and finish your cigarettes, boys. This won't take long. Outstandin' presentation, Sergeant, that's the way it's supposed to be done.

"We'll be conductin' a live fire exercise immediately following this class so I'll keep my talk short and simple which is one 'a Raidin' Forces' Rules you'll all be expected to memorize word for word—there'll be a test later. The purpose of you sittin' in this class is the Projection Adapter, M1, consistin' of an add-on 22mm tube for the M-1903 Springfield Rifle.

"It's a device more commonly and hereafter to be referred to, at least by me, as a 'grenade launcher—'Projection Adapter' bein' some kinda sissy armchair commando nomenclature, not doin' real justice to the piece 'a equipment bein' so described."

PFC Hansen moved into the position of Parade Rest with his rifle's butt on the ground next to his right boot — right arm extended holding the M-1903 Springfield by the forearm of the stock. He extracted the M1 Projection Adapter aka grenade launcher from another pouch on his web belt and affixed it to the barrel of the rifle.

"The M1 device is designed to launch the standard issue U.S. Mark 2 fragmentation grenade frequently called the 'Pineapple' or 'Frag Grenade.' It fits in the cup . . ."

PFC Hansen produced a frag grenade and placed it in the cup on the adapter.

" . . . and the pin is then pulled."

PFC Hansen pantomimed pulling the pin not having an inert training grenade to work with.

"At that time the rifle grenade is up, good to go. There are all manner 'a ways to launch it—from under your arm, butt on the ground, aimed high, barrel at an angle, etc. There's a chart you can memorize giving ranges, angles and stuff. However, for the kinda work Raiding Forces does in the dark 'a night up close and personal, firin' from the shoulder is the method 'a choice utilized by our experienced operators. This technique is ideal for ranges out to about seventy-five yards. You'll mostly be engagin' at twenty-five or less the purpose of the exercise bein' to put the grenade through a window or door of a building to announce yourself to the bad guys inside in a loud vagarous manner prior to goin in and lightin' the survivors up . . . close and personal.

"From now on every team that goes out will have a man carryin' an M-1903 Springfield with M1 grenade adapter affixed as a secondary weapon. You boys have blowin' up enemy personnel inside houses and small buildins in your immediate future—count on it.

"We'll modify your Springfields so the rear slings are on the left side of the stock M1 Carbine style in order for the weapon to lay flat across the back for easier carryin' or you can hang it around across your front for quick access—DO NOT HAVE YOUR GRENADE INSERTED IN THE MUZZLE DOWN FRONT-CARRY POSITION."

PFC Hansen brought the rifle up to his shoulder, then flipped it over and slung it muzzle down flat across his back, then whipped it off and over his head to show the front-carry method.

Lt. Gen. McKoy ordered, "Demonstrator recover."

PFC Hansen unslung his weapon and returned to the position of parade rest, his part in the class concluded.

Lt. Gen. McKoy said, "Once you pull the pin on the frag grenade, the cup holds the handle down. At that point the recommended carry method is 'keep the muzzle up.' The grenade's not goin' to fall off but why take a chance—something else we say a lot in Raidin' Forces. If it does you've got yourself four seconds to get the hell out of Dodge.

"Now the book says the killin' radius of the Mark 2 Fragmentation Grenade is five yards with a woundin' radius of fifteen yards. But I know for a fact the Aberdeen Proving Ground determined some fragments from a Pineapple Grenade can reach out to 250 yards. Anyone here believe they can run 250 yards in four seconds?

"The thing to keep in mind at all times is you have to use a *blank* round when you fire the rifle grenade. Forget that little detail, touch off a live one and you detonate yourself—*BOOM*!

"What are your questions?"

UP ON THE PLATEAU BEHIND THE ORDER OF THE KNIGHTS OF St. John's castle, explosions could be heard coming from where the class on the .30 M-1903 Springfield Rifle w/Projection Adapter, M1 affixed was conducting a live fire demonstration. Every student was being allowed to fire a rifle-launched grenade. The act of placing a Mk 2 Fragmentation Grenade in the cup and pulling the pin sounded easy enough. Doing it was proving more challenging. How do you place your hands on the cup, hold the grenade and the rifle and then pull the pin when you only have two hands?

That is why the practice.

Raiding Forces did not have any inert grenades to train with. This was live fire all the way. The students found out certain aspects of handling the M1 grenade launcher required nerves of steel.

At least at first.

THE SUN WAS GOING DOWN. NOW IT WAS TIME FOR THE patrols to begin departing on their missions. In the movies there would have been martial music playing or drums beating. This was not a movie—though to the Frogmen of the OSS Maritime Unit who were headed out on their first mission, strangely enough it felt like they were living one. Were they really going to do this? In the TOC, and everywhere else around the island, it was business as usual. The casualness of it all made an impression on the green Operational Swimmers.

Det 3 was departing on a series of raids deep in enemy controlled waters and no one at ABCHQ seemed particularly impressed… they kept on with whatever they were doing business as usual.

Colonel John Randal, Major the Lady Jane Seaborn, Happy and Captain Billy Jack Jaxx walked down to the dock. Capt. Jaxx had taken an interest in helping work with the Frogs. Coming from an intensive stateside training environment under instructors who had never been to war themselves and being thrown into a high-tempo special operations unit like Raiding Forces full of highly decorated combat veterans was not an easy transition, and Capt. Jaxx knew that.

Det. 3 consisted of a mere twenty men, but to Raiding Forces they represented more than the numbers implied. The Operational Swimmers brought valuable specialist skills to the unit that would provide a unique strike capability if properly utilized. It was important their assimilation be handled with care. As it was.

This concept was what the British called "man management." Not that Col. Randal liked the word *management* being used in relation to

Raiding Forces. His officers and NCOs commanded or led—period. Managers work behind desks in offices.

Lieutenant Dan Bonham was first to depart this afternoon. His objective was Pavlos Island—translated it meant "small." It was tiny, less than a mile square and did not even show up on some maps. Lt. Bonham was an experienced Raiding Forces SOG officer, a take-charge type whose professional military manner projected confidence. It was clear to the Frogs from the start that their team leader knew his business. Pavlos was almost uninhabited—an estimated fourteen Greeks lived there before the war. The civilians may have all been evacuated. A German Telephone Cable Signals Station manned by a half dozen or so 999th Criminals was known to be on the island.

Mission: Destroy the Signals Station—kill the Nazis.

The second team out—target seven-square mile Irakleia Island, was led by a rising star in Raiding Forces, Lieutenant Chase Starrett. It took a lot to impress Col. Randal and his veteran special warfare operators. Lt. Starrett had done so in a big way with his performance following a record bad miss of over 100 miles on the Benevento jump. Unfazed, Lt. Starrett assembled his stick and conducted a fighting withdrawal to friendly lines without losing a man. Which did not seem possible—not to anyone who had made the drop.

The five Operational Swimmers on the team had heard the story. They would never acknowledge it, but the MUs were impressed. No leadership concerns on Lt. Starrett's team. If he said "frog" the Frogs jumped.

Beverly and Mandy escorted Lt. Starrett and his team down to the dock. He was a great favorite with the female contingent of Raiding Forces/Small Raids Inc. Col. Randal, Lady Jane, Capt. Jaxx and Happy were standing by to see them off.

The Frogmen noticed the attention.

Conspicuously absent was Vice Admiral Sir Randolph "Razor" Ransom even though his daughter Brandy would be the skipper transporting Lt. Starrett's team. It was no oversight. The Admiral would have loved to be on the dock. But he did not wish to detract from Col.

Randal being in charge. The Razor knew quite a bit about the art of leadership himself.

VAdm. Ransom watched from the third-floor balcony of ABCHQ. No matter how many times he had seen men put to sea on a hazardous mission it was always a stirring sight. To his mind these Commandos were the modern-day equivalent of Morgan and Tarleton, Drake and Laurence… "threw down a last double whiskey in their messes and went out once again to deal with the King's enemies."

Lieutenant Ricky Mascuch was out next to last. His objective was five-square-mile Agistri Island. Col. Randal had carefully selected his objective—a Wehrmacht Beach Watch team of one NCO and three men with a man portable long-range radio. The perfect target for a first raid.

Mission: Capture the radio equipment—kill the Nazis.

The OSS Operational Swimmers had no idea tonight was Lt. Mascuch's first independent command. This was a case when Need to Know actually had merit. While Lt. Mascuch was an experienced officer having previously served in several challenging capacities in the 551st PIB, he had not engaged in combat until recently when Colonel John Randal recruited him to come to Raiding Forces.

However, since arriving from Camp Mackall he had seen his share of action. As for the OSS Operational Swimmers making up his team, the nature of their assignment—a kill team—tended to narrow their focus on following his lead. The Frogs were counting on the GOYA to lead them in and bring them home.

Last out was Ensign Westly Slade. His assignment was a return to Little Gavdos. He was the least experienced officer in all of Raiding Forces but enjoyed the dual advantage of having personally laid eyes on his target and being well-known to the Frogs on his team. The OSS officer had been handed a difficult task.

Mission: Capture a prisoner.

Left unsaid but implied . . . kill the rest.

There were no softball missions tonight.

Capt. Jaxx pulled Ens. Slade aside as his men were boarding. "Bad advice is worse than anything the Nazis can throw at you, Westly. Det 3 hasn't been given any—not by us. You've got this.

"Go get 'em, Frogman."

13
KILL BAD GUYS, BLOW STUFF UP, COME HOME

WHILE IT PROBABLY SHOULD NOT HAVE, ADVANCED BASE Castelrozzo Headquarters seemed deserted with all the Maritime Unit teams having departed on their missions. In fact, the entire island felt like a ghost town. One-third of the 575th Ranger Task Force who had jumped on Benevento were still MIA. Most of those who had returned were on leave in Cairo. The LRDG had ten recon teams at sea en route to their assigned Beach Watch stations. Captain Roy "Mad Dog" Reupart was with the SBS officers undergoing caique familiarization in Cyprus. Major Butch "Headhunter" Hoolihan had the 30 Assault Red Indians in Kabrit at No. 4 Middle East Training School (Parachute). And most of the rest of Raiding Forces were stationed on schooners along the coastline of Turkey conducting independent operations.

Colonel John Randal was sitting all alone in the suite he shared with Major the Lady Jane Seaborn. Nearly all the VIPs had departed the island. Lady Jane was in a meeting somewhere downstairs with Brigadier Raymond J. Maunsell, Captain Pamala Plum-Martin, Beverly Blackwell and Mandy Paige. Lieutenant General "Geronimo" Joe McKoy was playing penny ante poker in his suite with Vice Admiral Sir Randolph "Razor" Ransom, Chief Warrant Officer Hank Rawlston and Waldo Treywick. Lieutenant Colonel Sir Terry "Zorro" Stone had flown to RFHQ in Cairo on "business" and was likely at the Kit-Kat Club right this minute. And Captain Billy Jack Jaxx was in the building somewhere shacked up with the flavor of the day—that was not confirmed and may have been harsh.

Col. Randal decided to clean his pistols. Usually something he took pleasure in. Not tonight. He did not feel so great about lounging in the lap of luxury in an opulent palace designed for an emperor while his troops were in danger's path from Italy to the Congo. Not even any Brandenburger Sea Raiders were left for him to hunt down.

There was nothing to do but wait for reports to come in. Time had ground to a halt. At least for him.

LIEUTENANT DAN BONHAM LED HIS TEAM ASHORE IN water up to their knees. Pavlos was as flat as a pancake, which is what it looked like on his map. There were no terrain features. An island less than a mile square is tiny but still large enough to make locating a single building at night difficult. The mission was complicated by the fact that he could not count on there being a local Greek to guide them to their objective—the Telephone Cable Signals Station.

Lt. Bonham selected Sergeant Jerry Schmidt as his assistant team leader. Sgt. Schmidt was a tough 10th Ranger Battalion NCO he had encountered following the chaotic drop on Benevento. The two had rounded up an assortment of stray jumpers and operated for five days behind the lines. Aware there were estimated to be at least as many 999th Criminals on Pavlos as in the Raiding Forces team, Sgt. Schmidt recommended they take along a pair of Stingers to increase their firepower. The chopped and modified man-portable, belt-fed, .30 Browning AN/M2 light machine gun was popular with U.S. Marines in the Pacific because of the volume of suppressive fire the weapons could put out. Because the Frogs had never heard of a Stinger, much less seen one, the Ranger Sergeant put two MU volunteer light machine gunners through a familiarization course on the trip out.

Since Stingers were essentially custom local armory, hand-built, no two were exactly alike. Barrels ran the gamut from full-length to cut off at the receiver. Raiding Forces preferred the shortest barrel possible for ease of handling aboard aircraft and boats. The chopped barrels dramatically increased muzzle flash so Vickers Flash Hiders designed for tripod-mounted machine guns were installed—the idea being to hide the flash from the *shooter,* not the enemy. The cone-shaped devices gave the weapon a deadly Buck Rogers look.

Order of march was Lt. Bonham, the GSS interpreter—one could always hope—and the four OSS operators, with Sgt. Schmidt bringing up the rear in the traditional position occupied by an assistant patrol leader. He would move forward to confer during halts. Visibility was limited. Although the moon was full, it was not providing much help. Nothing was moving on Pavlos.

Lt. Bonham had no idea where he was going. There was no intel on where to locate the Telephone Cable Signals Station. And while flat, Pavlos was covered in a dense carpet of thick scrub brush about a foot tall that made tromping through it difficult. He made a command decision. The patrol would fall back and move along the shoreline to stay out of the vegetation until they came across some sign of structures even if they had to circle the entire island. Not a good plan, but it was the only one he had.

The going was a lot easier along the shore. The patrol began making good time. Only they were not finding anything.

Lt. Bonham was on point carrying a 9mm Beretta M-38 submachine gun. The GSS interpreter was pulling slack, meaning he was number two in the column covering the point with a .30 M1 Carbine. The two MUs carrying the Stingers were numbers three and four—on contact Lt. Bonham intended to employ the LMGs in pairs. Numbers four and five in the file were follow-on Frogs armed with .30 M1 Carbines, and Sgt. Schmidt was pulling rear security armed with an M-1928 .45 Thompson submachine gun. For a small team, the patrol packed almost as much punch as a U.S. Army rifle platoon. No one was expecting a fight—the idea tonight being to utilize stealth and the element of surprise to take down the 999th Criminals without giving them a chance to offer much resistance. But it was best to be ready in the event one developed.

The team patrolled along the shore until eventually stumbling across a rotting single board pier so ancient it looked like it might have seen service in the Trojan War. Lt. Bonham felt a surge of relief. He was running out of time before having to withdraw in order to make it back to ABC before sunrise. Returning with nothing to show for the night's effort was not part of the plan. The dock was like the orienting arrow on a lensatic compass pointing straight toward the half-dozen houses on Pavlos. The team traveled inland about 100 yards and there they were.

Moving by leaps and bounds, each structure was thoroughly checked out. All of them were abandoned. There was no sign of any of the 999th Criminals. And they could not find their primary objective—the Telephone Cable Signals Station. Lt. Bonham consulted with Sgt. Schmidt. They had no idea what to do next. Time was short.

Sgt. Schmidt said, "We could put up illumination LT."

Lt. Bonham said, "Sounds like a plan."

"Sir, I was just . . ."

WHOOOOOSH!

CRAAACK!"

A small parachute popped open and the white phosphorus flare dangling down started burning, casting an eerie stark white light with strange dark shadows around the edges as it swung back and forth drifting down. The Frogs watched in awe. It took a bold man to stand up on an enemy-held island in the dark of night and fire off a parachute flare—or a desperate one. Lt. Bonham had not impressed them as being wild and crazy . . . but maybe he was.

The GSS interpreter pointed excitedly. There in the distance fifty yards off to the side of the sparse residential area was a small concrete structure—the Telephone Cable Signals Station. Why it was built where it was had to have some reason but its location made no sense to them. Without the illumination the patrol would have likely never found it.

Lt. Bonham led the team straight there. The parachute flare drifted down and fizzled out as they traveled. The Relay Station was built like a bunker without the firing slits. It was designed to hold equipment, protect it from the elements and keep people out. There was only one heavy wooden door with a giant padlock.

The patrol knelt down in a tight perimeter, all the men facing out with weapons at the ready. Lt. Bonham moved into the center, "OK,

Frogmen, time to do your stuff. Knock down that door. Blow everything inside and let's go home."

The OSS operators went into action like a well-oiled machine. Corporal Randy Henderson, the senior Operational Swimmer, sent one man to place a small charge of C3 on the door. The Frog shouted, "FIRE IN THE HOLE!" and pulled the ring on the fuse lighter. Then he moved around to the side of the building to be shielded from the blast.

BOOOOOM!

The charge may have been small but it sounded like a 500-pound bomb in the quiet of the deserted island. The door was reduced to kindling. All three of the remaining Frogs jumped up and ran to the building while the other came around from his position on the side to make entry. Each man placed a one-pound charge against the side of a wall to force the blast back toward the center of the room for maximum destruction. The MUs had not taken the time to construct a ring main system. All the charges had a one-minute fuse.

Less experienced demolition men might have opted for a delayed fuse that would go off after the patrol moved out and departed the area. However, doing so might have allowed the 999th to emerge from hiding, find the explosive device and dismantle it. Why take a chance?

All the Frogs had their red lensed flashlights on. Cpl. Henderson said, "On three—one, two, three—EXECUTE, EXECUTE, EXECUTE!"

The MUs pulled the ring lighters on their charge of C3 in unison on the third "EXECUTE" and then, walking slowly, made their exit from the building. Experienced demolitions men never run from their explosives. If they tripped the fall might injure them enough to prevent being able to escape from the blast. The OSS operators moved away at a forty-five-degree angle to the door to be out of the line of blowback from the explosion. Lt. Bonham was pleased with their professionalism—the Frogs knew what they were doing.

The detonation, when it came, was a solid *WHUUUUUUMP!* The sound was not as sharp as the charge on the door, even though there were a lot more explosives involved, because it was contained inside the thick concrete walls. Dust and smoke billowed out the open door. Lt. Bonham and Sgt. Schmidt moved up and shined their flashlights inside. The room was a shambles. The force of the blast contained in such a restricted space by the thick concrete walls had smashed the equipment beyond repair. The Telephone Cable Signals Station would have to be completely replaced.

Mission accomplished. At least most of it. The 999th Criminals must have detected the patrol coming and run away to hide in the interior of the island or found a way to desert to Turkey. The two Frogs armed with the Stingers were disappointed. They wanted to light somebody up.

Another saying in Raiding Forces: "Better to have and not need than to need and not have."

LIEUTENANT CHASE STARRETT WAS STANDING NEXT TO Brandy Seaborn at the helm of her Series 500 MAS boat. The graceful craft was blazing across the waves performing like the high-performance speedboat it was designed to be. The MAS boats might not be as seaworthy as a PT boat or Motor Gun Boat (MGB) in weather but it could make forty-five knots—fifty-one miles per hour. They were en route to Irakleia Island.

Before the war the island had a population of eighty-nine. Since the fighting started, military-age Greek men had departed to join the armed forces. Dr. Layton Winthrop was in possession of information that there were not more than forty residents still in residence. The Professor did not mention that he had a clandestine radio operator on the island… intel was current and accurate. He also provided the important detail that there was a small contingent of 999th Light Division Criminals consisting of half dozen Germans guarding a Telephone Cable Signals Station.

Lt. Starrett's mission was to eliminate the Criminals and destroy the Telephone Cable Signals Station located in the tiny port village of Agios Georgios. He had five OSS Operational Swimmers to make it happen. Since he would be interacting with civilians, a Greek Sacred Squadron interpreter was attached to his team. If the 999th was running true to form they would have a guard or two at the signal station and the remainder of the Nazis would be sleeping in civilian houses or hanging out together in a local bar. The Criminals did take their creature comforts seriously.

Lt. Starrett was the newest member of Captain Billy Jack Jaxx's Small Operations Group. Capt. Jaxx had hand-picked him for the slot and spent a great deal of time grooming him for the job. The attention paid dividends. Now, despite his young age he was an experienced Special Operations Officer and an up-and-comer in Raiding Forces. Tonight's mission demanded one. For such a tiny operation there were a lot of moving parts.

And not much time in which to accomplish the assigned tasks.

Brandy cut back on the throttle. "My navigation officer informs me we are a mile out, Chase. Are we conforming to the Operations Order on where to land? If you have second thoughts there is still time to make a change."

Lt. Starrett had crafted a bold plan. The MAS boat was going to enter the harbor and tie off at the dock. The team would disembark and move along the jetty to the village where the GSS interpreter would make contact with the first local Greek islander he could find. It was a scheme of maneuver that would make Capt. Jaxx proud. And it had. The SOG commander had discreetly listened in as Lt. Starrett was issuing his order.

Jack Cool would have really liked to come along on this raid—kill bad guys, blow stuff up, come home—it did not get any better than that.

Lt. Starrett said, "Continue the mission."

The MAS boat had been traveling at top speed—fifty-one mph. While Brandy had made better time than expected, the team needed to get ashore, carry out their assignments and return to the boat in short order for the run back to Castelrozzo. Time was of the essence.

Being caught at sea once the sun came up was not a good idea.

Lt. Starrett ordered the team on deck. His Frogs were a colorful crew. There was the GSS interpreter—a former Greek Army officer serving in the ranks like the majority of Major Zargo's men—a Navy UDT swimmer, a U.S. Marine—making him a Devil Dog Frog—a 2nd Ranger Battalion OSS volunteer and two varsity swimmers from USC and Florida State specifically recruited by OSS for the Maritime Unit.

Everyone on the team was older than Lt. Starrett, who was not old enough to vote, though that fact was not advertised.

The men gathered on the stern as he took the slow-speed run-in to the dock for one last opportunity to go over the details of the raid. The plan was as simple as Lt. Starrett could make it. First they would take out the Criminals in the village. Next they would go after the Telephone Cable Signals Station.

Then return to the boat for a high-speed run back to Castelrozzo.

Anticipation was building as the MAS boat continued reducing speed to make the approach as silently as possible. The Frogs were eager to get started. After all the hard training, the cold and the wet, tonight was what it had come down to—it was really happening. Not what they had expected once they deployed but no one was complaining. This was as good as it gets for men who signed on with OSS to travel to distant lands, meet exotic people and kill them. At least that's what the Frogs liked to say back in the States while drinking beer after the end of the training day.

Lt. Starrett had the team move to midships on the port side of the MAS boat as Brandy cut the engine and coasted to the pier. She was a highly skilled skipper. The boat glided up alongside the jetty without a sound. Lt. Starrett and the Operational Swimmers stepped off.

"Stay frosty, boys."

The Frogs had no idea what that meant.

The GSS interpreter, who went by the pseudonym "Angelos" to protect his family living in enemy-occupied Greece from Nazi reprisals, took point. Lt. Starrett had been briefed there were known to be six Germans on the island—all in the port village, two of whom were usually on guard duty at the Telephone Cable Station at night. Dr. Winthrop had information there was one tavern still in business but only during daylight hours because of the German-imposed curfew on the islanders.

From past experience it was known the 999th liked to commandeer a bar for their own personal use since they were reluctant to move around at night for fear of curfew violators who would kill them under cover of darkness if they could. The Criminals were also well-known for forcing local Greek women to put on live sex shows in their clubs—which did nothing to endear them to the islanders.

In Lt. Starrett's opinion his mission would be much easier if all four Nazis off duty tonight were in a single bar blind drunk with naked women dancing on tables creating a diversion for him to arrive unannounced and unexpected and shoot them. Unfortunately, there was no intel to indicate that would be the case.

Angelos halted. Lt. Starrett moved up beside him to confer. Up ahead were two men fishing off the pier in clear violation of the island's curfew. The fishermen saw them but they did not appear alarmed.

Lt. Starrett whispered, "Go see what you can find out."

Angelos walked up to the two men and introduced himself. When the fishermen realized he was a member of the Greek Sacred Squadron there was much effusive hugging and kissing on the cheeks.

Lt. Starrett walked up and received the same welcome.

Angelos said, "These men want us to come kill the Nazis right now, Lieutenant."

Lt. Starrett said, "Do they know where they are?"

Angelos said, "Four of the Germans are sleeping with Greek women in their homes. Two are at the Telephone Cable Signals Station. The cowards never go outside after dark in fear of their life. This is a fishing village and fishermen are capable with their knives."

Lt. Starrett said, "We need 'em to guide us to the houses."

"This they will do."

The Det 3 team was down on one knee waiting to see what was going to happen next. The night had a surreal quality to it. Anything seemed possible. Lt. Starrett had them pull in tight. "We have two locals willing to lead us to where the Germans are staying. We'll go smoke them first—one at a time. Then we'll blow the Telephone Cable Station. Sling your weapons, boys. From this point on it's silenced pistols out and ready.

"Do not under any circumstances fire off an unsuppressed round—is that clear?"

The Frogs whispered, "Clear, sir."

This was beginning to get real.

The two local Greeks led the way up the street with their fishing poles over their shoulders. They were followed by Angelos and Lt. Starrett. The Frogs were moving in a column formation staggered heavy right—meaning three men on the right side of the road and two on the left.

The one detail that had come out of the first Det 3 raiding debut was never EVER walk down the center of a street no matter what other people are doing. Their buddies had been adamant about that. Apparently, Lt. Starrett had not gotten the memo.

This was noted by the Frogs.

The moon was full and so bright it looked like it had a light bulb in it. Not desirable for sneaking through an enemy-occupied hamlet. But then the patrol was not exactly sneaking.

It was advancing to contact.

The locals seemed to be sure there would be no Germans out and about. And at this late hour they should be asleep. Time was short so Lt. Starrett made the decision to follow their lead—a judgment call.

A big burly German came staggering down the street. He was shirtless, carrying a large green bottle of ouzo. And firing his 9mm P-08 Luger in the air. *BLAAAAAM! BLAAAAAM!*

The pistol shots seemed extraordinarily loud.

BLAAAAAM!

The fishermen guides dived off to the side of the street. The Frogs went to ground. Moments like this were why Colonel John Randal had canceled Rule Number 7—Expect the Unexpected.

It was impossible—no one saw this coming.

As the Nazi lumbered past, Lt. Starrett stepped out of the shadows and shot him in the back of the head with his suppressed .22 High Standard Military Model D.

WHIIIIIICH!

The German went down.

WHIIIIIICH! WHIIIIIICH!

Two more rounds to the head after he was on the ground.

The Operational Swimmers were not exactly stunned by developments, but they were interested. It did not pass unnoticed that the Lieutenant had not followed Raiding Forces protocol of "one round to the head two to the body" as briefed—maybe his action had fallen under "improvising and adapting" or maybe he had just wanted to shoot the Nazi in the head. The Det 3 operators all came to the same conclusion. Lt. Starrett was one cool dude.

The GSS interpreter secured the Luger and the patrol continued up the street as if nothing out of the ordinary had happened. After a short distance the guides stopped and pointed to a house. The Frogs transitioned into a tight perimeter in the yard.

Lt. Starrett whispered, "There's a Nazi directly to our front. Terhune, you and Franklin set up rear security. Cover the exit and if anyone comes out without first giving the password 'Hotdog'—light 'em up.

"Carlton, you and I will make entry followed by Angelos in case we need a Greek speaker. The rest of you men secure the front. We're going to pause here for five minutes so rear security can get in place and to give things time to settle down after all the excitement."

The Frogs glanced at their synchronized USN issue UDT BUSHIPS dive watches.

Lt. Starrett said, "Our guides say no cause for alarm. Drunk Germans firing off their pistols at night is fairly common, though walking around outside doing it is rare. Lesson learned, boys—you can't always depend on the locals to get it right.

"Rear security, move out. Don't forget—no 'Hotdog,' shoot 'em."

Under the circumstances five minutes seemed like five hours.

Finally, Lt. Starrett said, "Entry team, follow me."

As soon as they moved toward the front door of the house the remaining three Frogs closed up the perimeter even tighter. Two men trained their .30 M1 carbines on the house while one covered the street. The fishermen stood in the yard and watched.

The Aegean had rich islands and poor islands. Irakleia was on the lower end of the economic scale. No one locked their doors. Possibly because most of the locks were rusted from the salt air and no longer worked. Besides no one had anything worth stealing.

Whatever the reason the door opened when Lt. Starrett turned the knob. He carefully led the way inside with his suppressed .22 High Standard Military Model D resting supported on the wrist of his left hand which was holding a red lensed hook-nosed flashlight.

Red light has the least effect on night vision and it does not usually wake sleeping people.

Corporal Ray Carlton, formerly of the 2nd Ranger Battalion, was closed up so tight behind he was physically touching Lt. Starrett and aiming his suppressed .22 Colt Woodsman and flashlight over the Lieutenant's left shoulder. Angelos did not have a suppressed handgun and trailed farther back. He was only there to intervene in case the need arose to mollify a startled Greek.

Stepping through the front door they entered a living room. It was an old house and it had an old house smell—musty. Lt. Starrett started edging down the hallway. The floor creaked no matter how carefully he stepped. Not a problem . . . the house creaked even when no one was moving around. The first door on the left was a bedroom. People were in bed, so they crept in. A man in his mid-thirties with a large swastika tattooed on his chest was asleep next to a naked woman.

Lt. Starrett was tempted to put a round in the Nazi's ear—the aiming point of choice for contact range wet work. However, the purpose of the exercise tonight was to give the Frogs experience. He reached back, grabbed a handful of Cpl. Carlton's blouse and pulled him forward to have a clear shot.

WHIIIIIICH! WHIIIIIICH! WHIIIIIICH!

Lt. Starrett noted the former Ranger was an excellent marksman. Even at only six inches range, the shooting was impressive. It would have been possible to cover all three .22 caliber bullet holes with a quarter. His three rounds were in a triangle pattern under the Nazi's left cheekbone.

The Criminal never knew what happened. Lt Starrett felt a slight pang of remorse. He might have set a bad example out in the street when he put three rounds in the back of the drunk pistol-shooting Criminal's head.

Cpl. Carlton had not followed SOP any more than he had.

The entry team cleared the rest of the house but there was no one else inside. Lt. Starrett went to the back door, opened it a crack and said in a low voice that did not carry far, "Hotdog, Hotdog, Hotdog—rear security recover."

Going back through the house, Lt. Starrett secured the German's 9mm Walther P-38 laying on the night stand next to the bed. He handed it to Cpl. Carlton. The Ranger Frog stuck it in his belt.

Outside, the patrol continued up the street. The setup at the next house was a repeat of the first. Private First Class Marion Terhune and Private First Class Ralph Franklin went around back again. This time Private First Class Tom Gergretti was tapped to make entry with Lt. Starrett and Angelos. The door was locked.

A surprise.

Lt. Starrett led the entry team off the porch to one of the two large front windows which were up to catch the breeze coming in off the sea. They climbed in. The thing about security is for it to have any value, it has to be thought all the way through. The locked door might not have been much protection from armed intruders but could be an indication there was a light sleeping Criminal inside who worried about Greeks with sharp knives, which was worth knowing.

Creeping down the hall the floor creaked badly. A woman screamed. There was the pounding of someone heavy running down the hall toward the back—the rear door crashed open.

Then nothing.

Lt. Starrett ordered, "Gergretti, you and Angelos secure the woman."

Then he went to the back door. It was standing wide open. "Hotdog, Hotdog, Hotdog—give me a report."

"We got him, sir."

The suppressed .22s were truly quiet—he never heard a sound.

"Good job men, recover."

Back inside Angelos was talking to an overwrought thirty-something Greek woman clutching a robe who was terrified she would be considered a collaborator for sleeping with the Nazi. Lt. Starrett had no way of knowing the true story and did not really care. He had no intention of allowing the team to being drawn into a Civil Affairs issue. The locals could sort it out after his team left the island.

He was staying on mission.

At the last house that needed to be cleared the sound of music was heard and the dim glow of candles burning in the windows of the front room could be seen. PFCs Franklin and Terhune moved to the rear and took up their position. Corporal Andy Trueman was selected to be on the entry team this time.

With security in place Lt. Starrett led the way to the door. It was not locked. He entered and took one step to his right to allow Cpl. Trueman to come in and have a clear field of fire. A naked couple was dancing in the candlelight. It did not look like rape or even coercion.

Lt. Starrett shot the startled Criminal in the face, *WHIIIIIICH!*

Cpl. Trueman fired twice, *WHIIIIIICH! WHIIIIIICH!*

The Nazi went down.

Angelos wrestled the .22 Colt Woodsman out of Cpl. Trueman's hand and shot the woman as fast as he could work the trigger—emptied the clip. The Greek Sacred Squadron had strong feelings about their citizens who provided substance and comfort to the enemy.

After clearing the rest of the house and ordering rear security in, Lt. Starrett went out front. "Angelos, tell our guides to take us to the Telephone Cable Station."

Before the patrol moved out, Angelos explained the details of what had taken place inside to the two fishermen. They seemed untroubled by the news. The penalty for collaboration was well-known and the Greeks did not like the idea of their women sleeping with the enemy.

The Frogs were beginning to get into the rhythm of the operation. Professionalism comes from training coupled with experience and the desire to execute. While Det 3's training had some gaps in the syllabus as it pertained to Raiding Forces-type operations, the team was gaining experience, and the men were performing well. Missions down range conducted with green troops did not have to go like this.

Lt. Starrett was more pleased with the OSS operators than he expected to be.

Now the moon was so low in the sky it was more like a decoration and not casting appreciable light. The lack was not creating any problem for the guides. Moving through the dead-silent village was a little spooky, but then it always was. The feeling you were being watched, which may or may not have been the case, made the hairs on the back of your neck stand up. They came to a small frame building approximately 500 square feet in size. The patrol halted.

The Frogs went to ground setting up a tight perimeter providing all-around security.

Angelos whispered, "This is the telephone exchange. There are two Nazis inside. What is your plan, Lieutenant?"

Lt. Starrett whispered, "These men are demolitions experts. We're going to let them do what they do best. Watch and learn, Angelos."

"Very good, sir."

Lt. Starrett moved to the center of the perimeter so everyone could hear his instructions, "There's the target, boys. Imagine it's an obstacle to an amphibious beach landing. Make it disappear and let's go home."

These orders caught the OSS Operational Swimmers off guard. During their rehearsal they had practiced making entry to the Telephone Cable Signals Station and shooting the 999th Criminals inside. Lt. Starrett was giving them a change of mission with no advance warning and no guidelines on how to carry it out.

Cpl. Trueman was the senior Frog on the team. He did not hesitate.

"Listen up, gents, we're going to turn this building into sawdust. Break out the det cord and C-3. Build a ring main system with a one-pound block of plastique to be put in place against each wall. Johansen and I will run the loop around the building—we'll initiate from here."

When set off by their 10-cap Blasting Machine all four charges would detonate simultaneously. Cpl. Trueman intended to take the blasting machine with him to prevent any unintended consequences. When demolitions were in play he was a firm subscriber to the often-quoted Raiding Forces concept, "Why take a chance?"

The Frogs went to work with a will, splicing the det cord with their Weske UDT knives. At last the Operational Swimmers were finally getting to do something that, in their opinion, they were the best in the business at—blowing stuff up. It did not take long for Cpl. Trueman and Seaman 2nd Class Bobby Johansen to be sneaking up on the Telephone Cable Station stringing out det cord as they went from the spool every Operational Swimmer team always carried regardless of mission profile.

Frogmen never leave home without their demo.

Cpl. Trueman strung the cord and S2c Johansen emplaced the blocks of C-3 as they stealthily circled the small structure mindful there were two Nazis inside. For the size and simple wooden construction of the building the amount of explosives was way overkill. Business as usual for Det 3. Frogs like big bangs.

Cpl. Trueman said, "Lieutenant?"

Lt. Starrett said, "Negative, you do the honors, Corporal."

"Fire in the hole!"

KABOOOOOOM!

Mission accomplished.

LIEUTENANT COMMANDER RANDY "HORNBLOWER" Seaborn's PT boat reached Lieutenant Ricky Mascuch's target, Agistri Island, after a long moonlight voyage at speed. The GOYA's team would have to go ashore, locate the Wehrmacht five-man Beach Watch Party stationed on the island, kill them and return to the boat in time to make a dash to Turkey before sunrise. They would remain in the Turks' territorial water the following day "making repairs" until they could sail for Castelrozzo under cover of darkness the following evening.

Dr. Layton Winthrop had provided information that the Germans would be found in the tiny coastal community of Skala. The enemy were Criminals from the 999th Light Division—a penal formation. Not much else was known about the island other than there was no electricity.

Lt. Mascuch had spent a year with the 551st Parachute Infantry Battalion in the Canal Zone training for a drop on St. Martinique which never came off. He had made parachute jumps into a triple canopy jungle to experiment with landing in the tops of sixty-foot tall trees, then rappelling down. And he had jumped (been blown) out of a CG-4A Waco glider backwards when making the first glider parachute drop in history with Colonel John Randal at Camp Mackall.

From the sound of it some might have thought his time in service was a hard-luck tour of duty. Not Lt. Mascuch. He believed his military background had perfectly prepared him for what he was doing right now this minute—leading a team of men on a desperate mission far behind enemy lines.

The idea being it was going to be desperate for the bad guys, not his people.

Lt. Mascuch was on his first independent operation in command. The enormity of his assignment would have given most officers pause—not Ricky. He was thinking he had done worse things than this.

The OSS operators on his team were a colorful crew. One had been a bit actor in Hollywood, two were college football players at USC and Miami, another was an instructor from the Scouts & Raiders School, and an Olympic swimmer rounded out the group. They had heard the story about him exiting a glider backwards. Not being jump qualified—parachute training was still in their future, the Operational Swimmers were not able to judge if that was a good thing or a bad thing.

What they did know was their mission commander struck them as a highly competent professional who exuded confidence and gave the impression of knowing exactly what he was doing at all times. Lt. Mascuch was a natural leader, in charge without ever actually saying he was. The laid-back self-assured way he had organized the team for the mission had been impressive.

The Frogs loved the acronym GOYA—which he was never going to live down.

Not knowing what to expect from the 999th Beach Watch Team—were they sleeping in houses, in a bar partying or staying in a barracks for security?—Lt. Mascuch had his Frogs put ashore east of Skala so they could patrol cautiously to the village unseen. He would have preferred a more direct approach due to the lack of time the team had to spend on the ground. However, the shortage of intelligence meant he had to take what the mission gave him to work with and not try to force things.

His GSS interpreter, Xanthos, a pseudonym that meant "golden haired" because he had blond hair—the Frogs called him Blondie—led out on point. There were no lights showing in the village. Tension was thick in the air and the men were on high alert.

No one knew what to expect.

Lt. Mascuch was in his element. Patrolling is the purest form of small unit tactics. Leading one is the ultimate test of a junior officer's skills. He had done a lot of it in the Panamanian jungle searching for Nazi saboteurs on the Atlantic side of the forty-three-mile long canal. And Japanese saboteurs on the Pacific side. Not that he ever found any. The intel reports always turned out to be nothing more than rumors.

Lt. Mascuch recognized almost immediately that the Det 3 operators were not as skilled in patrolling as he would have liked. A patrol needs to move slow and easy—almost flowing as it travels. The Frogs were hyped up, overeager. They were headed to Skala under orders to shoot bad guys and they wanted to get it on.

He could not blame them for that. Still, patrolling is an art form. He intended for it to be done right.

Skala was not a town or even a village. It had been described by Dr. Winthrop as a "community." Lt. Mascuch was not sure what that meant exactly. But according to the Professor it contained the largest concentration of Greeks on Agistri. Best guess was that would be a population of around twenty or so. The island itself was only a fraction over five square miles in size with mostly flat terrain. During the day it was possible to stand in the center and see water all the way around.

The choice of such a small target was no accident. Col. Randal had carefully handpicked tiny islands for the likelihood their size would limit the number of Germans stationed on them in the event the intelligence on enemy strength turned out to be wrong. He had tried to stack the deck in favor of the inexperienced teams he was sending out as much as possible. The idea was not only for the OSS Maritime Unit Operational Swimmers to gain experience, he wanted them to come home with victories under their belts.

There was more at stake tonight than killing a few Nazis.

Blondie came to a halt. Lt. Mascuch was traveling in the slack position right behind him. He moved up. Directly ahead was the dark shadow of a house.

"Let's check it out."

The patrol slinked up to the building, weapons at the ready. It was pitch dark. Lt. Mascuch sent two men around back to cover the rear with orders not to shoot anybody unless absolutely forced to—suppressed .22 handguns only.

He needed information, not a body count.

Blondie pounded on the door. There was the sound of someone running inside. Then the rear security team came around from the back of the house bringing a struggling middle-aged man in an oversized nightshirt with them.

Cpl. Clint Loren, who because he was an actor might or might not have been the actual name he was born with, said, "Nabbed this guy trying to make a run for it, Lieutenant."

Blondie spoke to him in Greek. The local went wild with joy upon finding out it was the GSS who had come to his home and not a Nazi. A lengthy conversation ensued.

Lt. Mascuch said, "What's the story?"

Blondie said, "There are five Germans on the island as reported. All of them are living in the post office because it is the strongest building on the island and easiest to defend. The Nazis are disillusioned about being left in this remote post. The men are terrified British Commandos will come to kill them."

Lt. Mascuch said, "We're not British Commandos but we *are* here to kill them."

Blondie said, "The Germans have been trying to find a fisherman willing to take them to Turkey where they hope to sit out the war in internment.

"No one will cooperate . . . afraid of reprisals from the Nazis later."

Lt. Mascuch said, "Why don't you take 'em, Blondie?"

"How would I do so, Lieutenant?"

Lt. Mascuch said, "Pretend to be a fisherman. Lure the Germans out of their quarters with an offer to take them to Turkey. See what develops."

Blondie spoke to the local.

"He has agreed to lead us to the post office. If the Germans do not come out, what do you intend to do then. Lieutenant?"

Lt. Mascuch said, "We'll blow the building down. These Frogmen are demolitions experts. I'd like to see what they've got."

Xanthos said, "In that case, I hope the Nazis choose not to accept the offer of transport to Turkey."

The two OSS operators said, "Yeah!"

Lt. Mascuch had the patrol gather around in a tight perimeter for a quick change-of-mission briefing. The Frogs listened intently. They were flexible. Swimming to a fortified enemy shore to clear a path through beach obstacles, no two of which are exactly alike, requires a mindset open to improvising on the fly.

The plan was simple in the extreme. The guide would lead the patrol to the post office. The Frogs would prepare a ring main system and put it in place around the building. Blondie would knock on the door and make the offer of a caique to transport them to Turkey. If the 999th Criminals rejected the offer, Lt. Mascuch would give the order to blow the place in accordance to Raiding Forces Rule Number 6—It's Good to Have a Plan B.

Before the patrol moved out, Lt. Mascuch pulled Cpl. Loren aside. "Don't let our local Greek out of your sight. Stay right with him. If he makes any attempt to get away, shoot him with your suppressed handgun."

"Yes, sir."

"No second guessing."

"Understood, Lieutenant."

The patrol advanced toward the tiny built-up area consisting of fewer than a dozen houses. All of them were dark. Not even candles burning this late at night. The place looked dead and it seemed quite a few of the residences had been abandoned.

The one-story post office was the newest building in Skala. The Italians had built it. Il Duce Benito Mussolini liked to demonstrate Fascist dominance even in out-of-the-way places. On top over the front door was a carved fasces, the ancient Roman symbol of the "power of life over death," and a double-winged eagle.

The patrol halted a short distance away. The Frogs began assembling the demolitions, splicing the branch lines to the trunk line. It did not take long.

Lt. Mascuch pulled Cpl. Loren aside again. "Have one of your men get up on the roof and put a seperate charge on that Italian Eagle with a one-hour delay fuse."

Cpl. Loren said, "Can do, sir."

Lt. Mascuch said, "Let me know when you're good to go."

"We should be ready in another zero five, Lieutenant."

Lt. Mascuch noted the Det 3 operators performed magnificently once he gave them a task they were trained for. The precision with which the Combat Swimmers handled explosives was a thing of beauty. The men knew their demolitions.

In Raiding Forces it was SOP to put round pegs in round holes—Frogs like to blow stuff up.

The demolitions were ready in less than the time promised.

Lt. Mascuch said, "Do it, Corporal."

Cpl. Loren and one man advanced on the building stringing the det cord trunk line while another scaled the building with a pound of C-3 for the fasces. That much plastique explosive to blow the Italian Eagle was way excessive. Not a problem. The Frogs had the demolitions and a liking for big bangs. Unfortunately the plan was for them to be away and gone long before the charge on the roof went off.

Still, it was the thought that counted.

When the Det 3 operator was back down from the roof and Cpl. Loren returned, Lt. Mascuch said, "Don't hook it up yet—stand by."

"Awaiting your orders, Lieutenant."

Lt. Mascuch said, "OK, Blondie, show time."

The GSS interpreter stood up, walked to the big double door and pounded on it with the steel butt of his US 1911 .45 Colt Government Model automatic. No response. Nothing happened.

He repeated the process.

An angry voice called out from inside. Probably a demand to know who was there. The Criminals had no intention of opening the doors.

Not at night.

Blondie replied in German.

His response precipitated a lengthy back-and-forth conversation through the closed door. Lt. Mascuch wished he spoke German. And he really wished he had gone with Blondie so he could get an immediate idea of what was being said.

Lesson Learned.

What Lt. Mascuch did not know was that the GSS interpreter had changed the play. When the Criminals balked at his offer of transportation to Turkey, not believing he was a fisherman, Blondie gave them one minute to come out or the building was going to be blown down with them inside.

Finally the door opened and five Nazis came stumbling out with their hands in the air. One was half-heartedly waving a white undershirt. They were young. They were scared. And they did not look like supermen. Nor did they look like murderers, rapists or child molesters. But they might have been. The penal troops making up the 999th Light Division were representative of the Third Reich scraping the bottom of the barrel for manpower. These five were the bottom of the 999th's barrel.

The absolute dregs.

The Beach Watch party was expendable and the Criminals had figured that out for themselves. It is one thing to be expendable. It is another to sit around and wait to be expended.

Turkey was their best bet.

Lt. Mascuch ordered, "Recover your explosives, Corporal. Leave the charge on the eagle. Have your people search these men, then tie their hands. Probably won't be much of military value inside but check it out anyway—secure all weapons.

"I want to be moving in ten."

When the patrol arrived back at the PT boat, Lt. Cdr. Seaborn said, "What am I supposed to do with these Nazi juvenile delinquents, Ricky?"

Lt. Mascuch said, "When we reach Turkey, put 'em ashore in the most remote location you can find, Commander. Let the Turks sort it out once they eventually make their way to civilization. We'll be long gone by then."

Lt. Cdr. Seaborn said, "We can arrange that."

CAPTAIN PENELOPE "LEGS" HONEYCUTT-PARKER WAS AT the helm of her MAS boat. She was pounding through the night en route to Little Gavdos Island. This was her second trip to the place in two nights.

She had Ensign Westly Slade and his Frogs onboard. The OSS operators were all below.

This operation was intended to be a quick in-and-out. If things went according to plan Capt. Honeycutt-Parker would be back at Castelrozzo for breakfast. She loved blazing across the waves in the dark of night through enemy-controlled waters. It would not be out of line to say she and her best friend Brandy Seaborn were adrenaline junkies.

A mile off Little Gavdos, Capt. Honeycutt-Parker reduced speed. When he heard the change in the engine's pitch, Ens. Slade came up on deck. He stood beside her staring off into the distance. The moon was not up yet, making it very dark.

Tonight the plan was the same as last night. The team would be dropped off on one side of the tiny, deserted village. Then the MAS boat would relocate to the other side to stand by for the extraction. Upon completing their prisoner snatch, the Det 3 Operational Swimmers would return to the shore for pickup. In the unlikely event they could not spot the MAS boat in its new location Ens. Slade would put up a single green flare.

Upon seeing the flare Capt. Honeycutt-Parker would cruise to where the Frogs were waiting. It was a simple plan. However, clear signals between the boat and the ground element were crucial to success.

The rest of the six-man team came up on deck. The MAS boat coasted into shore with its motors idling allowing momentum and the waves to drift it in. There was no sign of life ashore but then none had been expected. The Criminals of the 999th were creatures of habit. There being no bars or women they would be in their barracks. Most likely playing cards like last night. There was nothing else to do.

The Operational Swimmers went over the side into water almost to their knees. They waded ashore. Ens. Slade had been here before but for the men on his team this was their first experience of being on enemy soil. Tension was running high, but the truth was tonight did not feel much different than all the training missions they had been on and that was something of a surprise. The Frogs were dialed in.

They were here to hurt somebody.

Since tonight was not a reconnaissance mission, Ens. Slade elected to forgo the movement to the ORP by leaps and bounds. He knew the houses in the village to be abandoned and had an idea of where the patrol would find the Germans.

He pulled point and led the way.

The patrol skirted the tiny built-up area. Within a matter of minutes, the same yellow glow seen the night previous appeared in the distance. Ens. Slade felt a sense of relief. He was not going to have to go searching for the Nazis.

To the Frogs it appeared their patrol leader was a tactical genius.

Ens. Slade signaled a halt. This was a hasty ORP. One last pause for a whispered briefing to make absolutely certain everyone understood their role during the Actions on the Objective. The team was in a tight huddle down on one knee with their shoulders touching.

"Leahy, you and Dyer fall back and take up the position of tail-end Charlies in the column. I'll lead the patrol to the door. The minute we halt you two slide around to the side window. Each of you toss in a stun grenade as soon as you're in position—no hesitation.

"When the grenades go off, Jenkins, that's your signal to kick in the door and I'll lead the team inside, grab one of the Nazis and we'll shoot the rest. As rehearsed, silenced handguns only, gunshots sound like gunshots, muffled explosions could be anything. Collect the German weapons and back outside with our package in under a minute, then head to the extraction point.

"OK, questions? No? Then Prepare to Move Out. Move Out! Let's do this!"

The Frogs crept the twenty-five yards or so to the shack the 999th Criminals were using as their barracks. The Det 3 Operational Swimmers were not very well trained in night work—needing daylight to be able to see to accomplish most of the combat tasks envisioned for them during their training back in the States. Nevertheless, they were handpicked, highly motivated individuals and in their defense, they had not deployed to Castelrozzo expecting to operate as over-the-beach Commandos against point-type targets.

The Det 3 operators were nowhere near as quiet as last night's recon team led by Captain Billy Jack Jaxx. By comparison, to Ens. Slade who had the advantage of having seen it done right, they sounded like a herd of elephants. But with the sea breeze blowing, waves lapping the shore and being inside drinking heavily, the Germans never heard them coming. Ens. Slade led the patrol to the front door. The men stacked for the entry behind Corporal David E. Mallory, a former linebacker for UCLA—the door kicker. The Frogs slung arms and took out their .22 pistols—a combination of Colt Woodsman and High Standard Military Model Ds.

A quick head check in the window showed the four Nazis were playing cards.

Corporal Gary Leahy and Private First Class Ralph Dyer ducked under the window on the front of the barracks and slipped around the corner of the building. The window was open to catch the breeze. They had been prepared to break the pane if it were closed. The noise was not an issue. Events would be moving too fast for the card players inside to react before the grenades went off.

Per the brief instructions on the operation of the No. 69 grenade—they had never seen one before earlier today—the Frogs unscrewed the caps and discarded them. Corp. Leahy nodded to Pfc. Dyer. Then, standing on opposite sides of the window both men pitched their grenade in.

The No. 69 is "idiot proof" and designed to detonate on contact no matter how it lands. These two performed exactly as advertised. The sound of the grenades exploding was muffled in the small enclosure. *WHUUUUUUP! WHUUUUUUP!*

Around front, Cpl. Mallory kicked in the door and stood aside as Ens. Slade charged past into the smoke and dust-filled room. Inside the four Criminals were crumpled on the floor stunned from the concussion, bleeding in places dinged up by tiny bits of shrapnel from the No. 69's Bakelite casings. The card table was upended. Playing cards were scattered everywhere. Everything in the room made of glass was shattered and crunched under the Frog's boots.

Ens. Slade grabbed one of the Nazis by his collar with one hand and shot another with his .22 Colt Woodsman. *WHIIIIIICH! WHIIIIIICH!*

WHIIIIICH! Then he dragged the German out the door as the entry team swarming in behind him shot the other two. The Frogs kept in mind what Lieutenant General "Geronimo" Joe McKoy advised them during a break from their rehearsal back at Castelrozzo: "If you shoot somebody, boys, make hamburger out of 'em."

They did.

COLONEL JOHN RANDAL WAS STARING AT THE CEILING OF the master bedroom. He reached over to the nightstand and picked up the Rolex Major the Lady Jane Seaborn had given him so he would think about her whenever he checked the time. Originally the watch had been intended as a gift for her husband, which gave him something else to think about now besides the drop-dead gorgeous Lady Jane. He could not shake the image of Mallory's boots sticking out of a Japanese POW camp latrine having been boreholed.

The lime green digits on the Rolex read 0505 hours. Col. Randal decided to get up. He had never actually been asleep. Easing Lady Jane's tawny thigh off his chest where she liked to keep it, he slipped off the bed being careful not to wake her.

In the living room he put on a faded pair of blue jeans, the battered yellow cowboy boots he had worn to the Gunfight at the Blue Duck a lifetime ago, and a faded green jungle jacket from his Abyssinian Campaign days. Col. Randal had relaxed uniform standards for Castelrozzo and points north.

Master Sergeant Mack Beckwith was going to have a cardiac arrest when he returned from retraining the SBS Other Ranks.

Col. Randal buckled on one of his 1911 Colt .38 Super pistols and went out into the hall. A Vulnerable Points Wing NCO was sitting at the security desk outside the door.

"Morning, sir."

"Good morning, Sergeant McPheters."

It was quiet in ABCHQ at this time of morning. Things would not get started for about another hour. Then the pace would pick up speed fast.

Col. Randal went downstairs, exited the building and walked along the path to the dock in the dark. In a few minutes Happy came trotting down the lane and sat down. Lady Jane was not far behind. She stood beside him not saying anything. They stared out at the empty sea.

Waiting.

~~~

THE MISSION CONTINUES IN

– *MILITARY DECEPTION* –

BOOK XVII IN THE RAIDING FORCES SERIES
Coming soon

~~~

The Raiding Forces series continues…all the way to VE Day.
To be on our notification list for the next book, contact
phil@philward.com.

ABBREVIATIONS
ORDERS & AWARDS

Bt	Baronet
CB	Companion of the Bath
CMG	Companion of the Order of St. Michael & St. George
DCM	Distinguished Conduct Medal—Awarded to noncommissioned officers for distinguished conduct in action in the field
DFC	Distinguished Flying Cross (Royal Air Force)
DSC	Distinguished Service Cross (Royal Navy)
DSM	Distinguished Service Medal—Awarded to ranks up to and including Chief Petty
DSO	Distinguished Service Order
GC	George Cross
GCB	Grand Cross in the Order of the Bath
GM	George Medal
KBE	Knight Commander of the Most Excellent Order of the British Empire
KCVO	Knight Commander of the Royal Victorian Order
LG	Lady Companion of the Order of the Garter
MC	Military Cross
MM	Military Medal
MVO	Member of the Royal Victorian Order
OBE	Order of the British Empire
SS	Silver Star Medal (U.S. Armed Forces)
VC	Victoria Cross

ACRONYMS

NID	Naval Intelligence Division
OG	Operational Group
OJT	On the Job Training
OR	Other Ranks (mess)
ORP	Objective Rally Point
OSS	Office of Strategic Services aka the Outfit
PAX	Passengers
PBY	Patrol Bomber, the "Y" denotes the manufacturer
PIB	Parachute Infantry
PIR	Parachute Infantry Regiment
PLF	Parachute Landing Fall
POL	Petroleum, Oil and Lubricants
PT	Patrol Torpedo (boat)
PTL	Patrol Leader
PWE	Political Warfare Executive
QRS	Quick Release System
RAF	Royal Air Force
RFHQ	Raiding Forces Headquarters
RMBP	Royal Marine Boom Patrol
RNSDD	Royal Navy Submarine Deception Devices
RON	Remain Overnight Position
RTU	Returned to Unit
RVP	Rendezvous Point.
SALUTE	Size, Action, Location, Unit, Time, and Equipment
SAS	Special Air Service
SBS	Special Boat Squadron or Special Boat Section
SITREP	Situation Report
SOE	Special Operations Executive
SOG	Small Operations Group
SOP	Standard Operating Procedure
TDY	Temporary Duty
TOC	Tactical Operations Center
TO&E	Table of Organization and Equipment
TTC	Troop Transport Command
TWX	Teletypewriter Exchange Service
UDT	Underwater Demolition Team
USAAF	United States Army Air Force
WRNS/Wrens	Women's Royal Navy Service

ACRONYMS

ABC	Advanced Base Castelrozzo
ABCHQ	Advanced Base Castelrozzo Headquarters
ACAN	Army Command and Administrative Network
AO	Area of Operation
AP	Armor Piercing
ATO	Aegean Theatre of Operation
AU	Assault Unit
AVG	American Volunteer Group
BAR	Browning Automatic Rifle
BMNT	Begin Morning Nautical Twilight
CBI	China Burma India
CBTC	Commando Basic Training Center
CI	Counterintelligence
CIC	Counterintelligence Corps
CO	Commanding Officer
CQC	Close-Quarters Combat
DZ	Drop Zone
E&E	Evasion & Escape
FANY	Field Auxiliary Nursing Yeomanry
FORP	Final Objective Rally Point
GOYA	Get Off Your Ass / Great Outstanding Young Americans
GP	General Purpose
GSS	Greek Sacred Squadron
HE	High Explosive
HMG	Heavy Machine Gun
KIA	Killed in Action
LBSM	Life Boat Service Men
LCS	London Controlling Section
LCT	Landing Craft Tank
LRDG	Long Range Desert Group
LSF	Levant Schooner Flotilla
MAS boat	*Motoscafo armato silurante*, torpedo armed motorboat (Italian)
MI	Military Intelligence
MIA	Missing in Action
ML	Motor Launch
MTB	Motor Torpedo Boat
MU	Maritime Unit (OSS)

LIST OF CHARACTERS

Alex "Cat" Gataki
Angelos
Basil
Beverly Blackwell
Brig. Raymond J. "R. J." Maunsell
Brig. Gen. William "Wild Bill" Donovan
Capt. Billy Jack Jaxx
Capt. Fontain Blondell-Pericrinkle
Capt. Hawthorne Merryweather
Capt. Lionel Chatterhorn
Capt. Pamala Plum-Martin, DSO, OBE, DFC
Capt. Penelope "Legs" Honeycutt-Parker, OBE, GM, RM
Capt. Roy Kidd
Capt. Roy "Mad Dog" Reupart
Capt. Stephanie Fawcett-Tatum, RM
Castor
Cdr. Ian Fleming, RNVR
Chloe Hasapis
Col. John Randal
Cpl. Andy Trueman
Cpl. Clint Loren
Cpl. David E. Mallory
Cpl. Gary Leahy
Cpl. Josh Malakaski
Cpl. Liam Riley
Cpl. Randy Henderson
Cpl. Ray Carlton
Cpl. Ronny Pomford
Cpl. Tom "Murph the Surf" Murphy
Dr. Layton Winthrop
Ens. Westly Slade
Flanigan
Guido "GG" Grazinni, MC

LIST OF CHARACTERS

Happy
John Steinbeck
King
Lana Turner
Lovat Scout Lionel Fenwick
Lovat Scout Munro Ferguson
Lt. "Dynamite" Dick Coogan
Lt. Alexandra (Mandy) Paige, OBE, RM
Lt. Beatrice Bancroft
Lt. Chase Starrett
Lt. Coco Lovejoy, Wren
Lt. Dan Bonham
Lt. Jackson Taylor, USNR
Lt. Ricky Mascuch
Lt. Ted "The Great Teddy" Hamilton, OBE
Lt. Col. Dudley Clarke
Lt. Col. Sir Terry "Zorro" Stone, KBE, DSO, MC
Lt. Gen. "Geronimo" Joe McKoy
Lt. Cdr. Randy "Hornblower" Seaborn, DSO, OBE, DSC, RN
Maj. Zargo
Maj. "Pyro" Percy Stirling, DSO, MC
Maj. Baltimore "Mongo" Farquhar, MC
Maj. Butch "Headhunter" Hoolihan, DSO, MC, MM, RM
Maj. Clive Adair
Maj. David Lloyd Owen
Maj. Duke Slater
Maj. Ian Patterson
Maj. Jack Dance
Maj. Peter Fleming
Maj. the Lady Jane Seaborn, LG, OBE, RM
Maj. Travis McCloud
Maj. Valentine Fabian
Maj. Gen. James "Baldie" Taylor, OBE

LIST OF CHARACTERS

Lt. Col. the Earl Lord George Jellicoe, 2nd Earl, DSO, MC
MSgt. Mack Beckwith
Officer Diakos
PFC Marion Terhune
PFC Norvel "Horn Dog" Hansen
PFC Ralph Dyer
PFC Ralph Franklin
PFC Tom Gergretti
Pvt. David Hale
Rita Hayworth
S/Lt. Warthog Finley, OBE, DSO, DSC, RNPS
S2c Bobby Johansen
Sergeant McPheters
Sgt. Mike "March or Die" Mikkalis, DSM, MM
TSgt. Luke Volkmann
VAdm. Sir Randolph "Razor" Ransom, VC, KCB, DSO, OBE,
    DSC, RN
Veronica Paige, OBE
Waldo Treywick
Wg. Cdr. Paddy Wilcox, DSO, OBE, MC, DFC
Xanthos

ABOUT THE AUTHOR

Phil Ward is a decorated combat veteran commissioned at age nineteen. A former instructor at the Army Ranger School, he has had a lifelong interest in small unit tactics and special operations. He lives in Texas on a mountain overlooking Lake Austin.

~ ~ ~

OTHER BOOKS IN THE RAIDING FORCES SERIES

Those Who Dare

Dead Eagles

Blood Wings

Roman Candle

Guerrilla Command

Necessary Force

Desert Patrol

Private Army

Africa 1941

The Sharp End

Raiding Rommel

Strategic Services

Tip of the Sword

Always So Few

The War That Never Was